CW01084491

The Buzz Building

Scott O'Neill

Published in 2014 by FeedARead.com Publishing – Arts Council funded

Copyright © Scott O'Neill.

First Edition

The author has asserted their moral right under the Copyright, Designs and Patents Act, 1988, to be identified as the author of this work.

All Rights reserved. No part of this publication may be reproduced, copied, stored in a retrieval system, or transmitted, in any form or by any means, without the prior written consent of the copyright holder, nor be otherwise circulated in any form of binding or cover other than that in which it is published and without a similar condition being imposed on the subsequent purchaser.

A CIP catalogue record for this title is available from the British Library.

For my grandparents.

1:   two grubby little troglodytes

'Shut yer face ya smelly fat basturt!'

'What did you say boy?'

'I said shut yer face ya smelly fat basturt!'

Clearly, Mister Mac was not a happy man.

'Right, you foul-mouthed wee swine! Step up to the front! *Now!*' he spluttered almost choking on his own outrage.

'If yer gonnae give me the belt sir, you'll have tae give it tae Haig as well. He told me tae say that tae ye sir,' Danny said calmly.

I was mortified. I picked at the wallpaper dust-jacket Mum had carefully wrapped around my exercise book and watched our headmaster (who was indeed fat and smelly but I certainly had *not* told Danny to tell him that) reach down to his desk and remove the thick leather strap from its own special drawer.

'Did he now?' he grumbled.

No questions offering me the chance to confirm my innocence, just - '*Did he now?*'...

Next thing I knew Danny and I were standing before an enthralled class with our sweaty palms held aloft, poised and ready to receive.

And receive they did. The maximum sentence. Six belts apiece. (I can feel my palms stinging just thinking about it). Mister Mac did not hold back. I swear he put more effort in to delivering those blows than he ever did in to educating our ravenous minds. His bulging, veiny eyes homed in on their target. With a protracted grunt he hoisted his right arm, tightly encased in its puce nylon sleeve, way back between his shoulder blades giving us and the entire class a stunning view of the sweat stain soaking his armpit. Unfortunately Danny and I were hit with the full force of the accompanying odour.

I had to be brave. I couldn't back out and make a complete tube of myself by blubbering or pulling my hand away at the last moment... The first was a mishit which nearly snapped my little finger in two. The second was a beauty. Oh yes. Number two connected with an almighty *thrack!* which echoed throughout the classroom. Through my burning eyes I'm sure I saw half the class wince in unison, including Elspeth, while the other half continued to chant out the number of swipes. Judging by the pain, I was convinced the tawse had split my skin open but I refused to cry and braced myself for the others. Numbers three and four connected with equal precision. Mister Mac was good at this, maybe too good because five and six passed me by - my hands too numb to feel anything by this point. He ordered me back to my seat barely able to hide his disappointment at having failed to make me cry. This did not bode well for Danny. Even more determination was put into his punishment. Danny's only reaction was to blink hard and adjust his rigidly defiant stance with each impact.

I watched him standing there flashing his brazen smile at me - a smile I'd first encountered two years previously when he first arrived on the island. His olive skin and green eyes had convinced me that he came from somewhere exotic so I was a little disillusioned to discover that he hailed from Castlemilk. Then again, even Glasgow seemed exotic to a boy who had lived his whole life on Bute. Danny was tall and strong for his age and a full month older (a fact he ruthlessly exploited whenever he felt he had a point to make; a trump card to be played whenever we disagreed. I assured him however, that the age gap was nothing more than a guarantee that he would die first).

I on the other hand, despite being the oldest of three siblings, always felt as a child that I looked more like the runt of the litter thanks to my pasty, tracing paper complexion, tufty blonde hair and spindly limbs, not to mention my slight heart murmur. There was a bright side. Whatever I lacked in strength I more than made up for in speed and a quickly developing flair for football. Although before Mum would allow me kick a ball around, Doctor Simmons had to employ all his powers of persuasion on her insisting that my heart condition was absolutely nothing to worry about and that the exercise could only be beneficial.

It really didn't take very long for Danny and I to become fiercely loyal, inseparable pals much to Mum and Dad's (particularly Mum's) chagrin. They disliked the way he kept getting me into trouble as they saw it. Even though the best part of a year had passed since Danny and I had been found guilty of *The Great Holy Water Scandal.* Mum was still a tad tetchy whenever the subject reared its ugly head. She had been so proud when I became an altar boy (Danny had already been in the service for several unblemished weeks before I joined the fold) only to have that pride replaced by cheek-burning shame with barely a handful of masses under my belt. The irony was that it had been *my* idea to substitute the holy water in Father Armstrong's sprinkler with vinegar. When the appropriate moment came and the priest set off down the aisle to bless his congregation we almost wet ourselves with the superhuman effort required to prevent us from howling uncontrollably as he showered his faithful flock with the stuff. A handful of the devoted had to leave the mass on an urgent mission to bathe their smarting eyes.

Our only mistake was to attempt to repeat our success. Father Armstrong caught us red-handed. We asked the furious cleric to practice what he preached and forgive us but this only served to fuel his temper. Our plea fell on deaf ears and we were defrocked. Mum skelped my backside and dragged me off to confession to collect my penance. After which she took me on an exhaustive, all-inclusive guilt trip and tried to threaten me with Dad's wrath which I knew to be an empty threat because he never raised a hand to any of us. The very worst we could expect from Dad was a raised voice.

The attack on the Catholic Church repelled, the rebellion moved on with an all out assault on the educational establishment. With the cunning use of a cold sore this campaign was, without a doubt, Danny's finest hour. He arrived in class one morning with a fine specimen of a scab cracking and splitting at the corner of his mouth. The raw, blistering infection was much worse than it should've been because Danny couldn't resist picking at it. At break time he raced around chasing girls with his lips poised and puckered until their terrified shrieks could be heard all over Rothesay. His masterstroke came during Father Armstrong's weekly Religious Instruction class.

3

On the premise that he was in dire need of a pee, Danny was excused from class and headed straight for the staffroom. Making sure the coast was clear he snuck inside and proceeded to smear his infectious mouth around the rim of every cup and mug he could find. A few days later when Danny's scab was on the wane, we gathered for assembly and were deeply impressed with the results of his mission. Nearly every teacher gathered there had an embarrassing sore crusting around their mouths. Later in the day we heard many a loud, accusatory voice coming from the staffroom but no one made the connection.

The bell rang the instant the sixth belt smacked Danny's inflamed palm. The class hurried out before Mister Mac decided to prolong the violence.

'Did it hurt?' ventured Tommy staring in awe at our swollen hands. The morning was cold and grey and the playground sang with black blazered and black duffel-coated children playing football, chuckie-stanes or crambo. Others were hunting spiders over by the railings. On our way to the grass we passed a group of first-years playing marbles, tactfully pushing their jorries and steelies over the patterned surfaces of the access and manhole covers they employed as game boards.

'Aye,' Danny replied matter-of-factly as a few other boys with a vested interest gathered round to view the smear of colour our hands provided in contrast to the drab surroundings. He pulled out his little red notebook and flicked through the dog-eared pages. Grabbing a pencil from Tommy's blazer pocket he made some adjustments to his carefully drawn chart.

'Right. So. Me and Haig both got six belts. Which means I've got a grand total of thirty-two. So *I'm* now top o' the league. Tommy you're still third. Drew you're still fourth. Archie's doon tae second.' Danny craned his neck searching the area for his rival, 'Where is Archie?'

'He's off sick'.

'Sick wi' what?' Danny was annoyed at having his chance to gloat denied.

'Mumps.'

Danny tutted, shook his indignant head and moved on, 'Anyway. Haig you've moved up tae fifth so naebody can call ye a poof anymore and if anybody does I'll batter them. Davey, you're bottom of the league. You're the poof. You huv'nae got any belts at all. Yer gonnae have tae tell Mister Mac he stinks o' pish or somethin'.'

We all focused on Davey's blushing, crestfallen face but he wasn't going to get any sympathy from me. Here I was, five days shy of my tenth birthday and it was now official. As the figures meticulously noted in Danny's league table confirmed - I was not a poof. Not that I was clear on exactly what a poof was. In our school the term seemed to encompass all Rangers fans, Protestants, the English, rich people and anyone who had not been belted by Mister Mac. In any case, with Danny as a best pal bullying would never be a problem. After the way he'd seen off Stevie Sweet, an illiterate thug who was in the year above us, he commanded the respect of the playground. Nobody was going to mess with him. As time passed, Danny's confidence began to rub off on me. Normally shy, awkward and respectful - raised to speak only when spoken to - I became increasingly willing to take risks. To break rules and have more fun.

After school we walked home together in silence. It was Friday so I knew Danny's mood would be muted. His dad would shortly be returning home for the weekend. Danny refused to tell me what his dad did for a living and I'd long since given up asking but I was all too aware of what the man did when he was home. More often than not Danny would somehow manage to be excused from school swimming sessions, though sometimes I would catch sight of the bruises when we changed for other games lessons.

It didn't seem fair and now and then I would even feel strangely guilty. My Dad was often away for weeks on end but I always looked forward to his return trips from West Germany where he was stationed with the army - even if he did consistently forget to bring home the Bayern Munich shirt I constantly nagged him for. There could be no doubt that I was a fully paid up Celtic fan but I knew I would've been the envy of all Rothesay boys if I had a shirt as rare and glamorous as a Bayern shirt.

We crossed the road from Mill Lane into Russell Street and stopped outside the tenements where Danny lived.

'I'll see you tomorrow, Danny, aye?'

Danny nodded sullenly. 'Aye. I'll knock for ye.'

I carried on homewards turning into the High Street where I caught the dizzying smell from the 'Madeira' chip shop on the corner. I swallowed a mouthful of saliva and tried to remember the last time Mum had treated us all to chips. I entered the ancient tenement block and made my way up the gloomy stairwell to the first floor. Desperate to empty my aching bladder I headed straight for the communal toilet on the landing but someone had beaten me to it.

A painful eternity of leg crossing and dancing on the spot elapsed before old Mrs Buchanan vacated the closet.

'Awright son?' she muttered shambling her way past and back up the stone steps worn smooth and concave by well over a century of footfalls. All of them quite possibly Mrs Buchanan's.

The cloying smell and smeared toilet bowl the old woman had subjected me to put me right off my dinner. I just toyed absent-mindedly with the mince and totties Mum had placed before me. Dad wasn't coming home this weekend either. I stared glumly across the fold-away chipboard table to where Auntie Elaine was shoving a spoonful of brown goo into my baby sister's mouth. Maureen seemed content enough to let the mess ooze back out and dribble down her chin where Elaine would patiently scoop it up and try again.

Joe was making a meal out of licking his plate. Even for a four-year-old my brother's manners were less than pleasant. I watched his tongue stained gravy-brown, glide across the greasy plate seeking out every last grain of salt. Ignoring Joe's antics Mum reached for her Regals and lit her tenth cigarette since I'd returned from school less than two hours before.

'When's Dad coming home?' Joe asked with a final theatrical flick of his tongue.

'Next weekend,' said Mum as she had done for the past two weeks.

Dad must be involved in a top secret army training exercise I thought. I hoped he would remember to bring home photographs of the tanks and guns he used.

Auntie Elaine threw an odd, knowing look at Mum. 'Are you sure?' she asked, a strange note to her voice.

Mum shook her head with a world-weary sigh.

'Don't Elaine, please.'

'Have you spoken to the council yet? You can't carry on like this much longer, surely?' frowned Elaine, her eyes traversing our sparse flat as she spoke, clearly disapproving of the wallpaper, carpet and curtains representing every shade of orange and brown - from tangerine to shite in big paisley swirls. 'This place is far too wee for a start. You need a place with at least three bedrooms, especially now you've got the bairn.'

Maureen puked in agreement.

Elaine used the bib to gather up the mush then continued, 'And make sure they give you a place with your own loo for God's sake.'

'Don't blaspheme,' Mum said yawning.

'Och away Susan! You know what I mean. A shared loo in this day and age? You'd think it was *eighteen*-seventy not *nineteen*-seventy. And a bathroom! You really need a bathroom. You can't keep traipsing over to Mum's every Sunday to bath the weans. And is it not about time you had a telephone as well? Next time you speak to that *husband* of yours tell him to pull his finger out and move his family out of the dark ages will ye? For God's sake.'

'Don't blaspheme in front of the weans Elaine!' Mum countered exasperated, 'I'm doing my best. We're near the top of the housing list. With a bit of luck we'll be out of here in a couple of months.'

I wasn't happy with the way my aunt talked about Dad. What was her problem? What had he ever done to her? *She wouldn't dare speak like that if he was here.* Auntie Elaine wasn't married, never had been as far as I could recall, even though she was several years older than Mum. I put it down to jealousy on her part. That was why she kept

7

putting her sister's husband down. Because she couldn't find one of her own. Plain old fashioned jealousy.

Maureen gripped the upside-down watch pinned to the bosom of my auntie's uniform in one chubby hand while Elaine jiggled the baby's equally fat legs and started to sing, '*Skinny Malinky Longlegs, big banana feet...*' Elaine's face suddenly curled up in disgust and for an unsettling second I'd thought she'd been reading my thoughts. She pulled her hand out, shiny and damp, from under Maureen.

'Och! You got a clean nappy? The wee yin's wet herself.'

Mum stretched over to the terry-draped clothes-horse hogging the heat from the coal fire and squeezed each nappy until she found one dry enough to give Elaine.

She tutted, harassed by the loud knock at the door. Instinctively knowing it was for me I hurried off to answer it. Sure enough, I opened the door to find Danny standing on the other side, his eyes rimmed red and a bruise swelling beneath his left ear.

'I'm goin' tae spend the night in the Buzz Building. You coming?' he asked in an unsteady whisper.

A thrill shot through me. Did he know what he was saying? This was risky stuff. The Buzz Building was our sacred den. We were absolutely convinced that nobody else knew of its existence. It was ours and ours alone. However, this was a first. We had spent many a long hour hiding, playing, talking and plotting in the place but always during the day, never at night and we had certainly never slept in the place.

How was I going to pull this off without Mum finding out?

Danny had all the answers.

'Tell yer mum yer stayin' at ma hoose tonight. I've already told ma mum I'm stayin' in your hoose.'

I ushered Danny into the living room knowing I would need him to back me up.

'And tell him to buy you a washing machine as well.' Auntie Elaine was still badgering Mum whilst wiping Maureen's backside, 'You can't keep washing all these clatty nappies by hand for Christ's sake.'

Mum scowled. 'Elaine. How many times? Will ye...'

'Aye I get it. *Don't blaspheme in front of the weans,*' Elaine said mimicking Mum's frown. 'How about - *For the love of Allah* - is that acceptable? Can I say that?'

'Smells like Mister Mac,' Danny grinned nodding to the baby.

Mum rolled her eyes to the heavens on seeing my dishevelled pal.

'Oh look. It's Mockit and Manky!' Elaine teased, smiling at us.

Joe tugged at Mum's sleeve. 'Can I have a piece n' jam?'

'You've just had your dinner Joseph.'

'Aye but I'm still hungry.'

'Mum is it awright if I ...'

'Can I have a piece n' jam?' Joe repeated cutting me short.

'What do you say?'

'Please. Can I? Please, please...'

'Okay. In a minute. Will you stop pulling my blouse you'll stretch it!'

'Mum...?'

'What is it Haig?' Mum snapped causing Maureen to burst out wailing.

Elaine ran through her full repertoire of comforting noises but the bairn was determined to have her say.

'Where's her dummy-tit?' asked Elaine finally accepting defeat.

Mum passed the soother which Maureen dutifully sucked in contented silence when Elaine shoved the rubber teat into her mouth. With the mood she was in this was obviously not the best time to ask Mum for anything and I was tempted to back out but this was too important. I swallowed hard.

'Is it awright if I stay at Danny's hoose tonight?' My insides were rigid. Would it work? Could I deceive my own mother? I'd done it loads of times before but they were all wee white lies and besides, she'd caught me out half the time. But this? This was a biggie. I prayed - *Please God let her say 'Yes'. I promise I won't lie at my next confession. Honest.*

'Oh Haig I don't know. And it's *house* not *hoose,*' she said shaking her head, expelling a vexed sigh. 'And why do you have to spend the night there anyway? He only lives round the corner doesn't he? Can't you just go round and play for a few hours? Away and give me peace will ye?'

This barrage of questions stunned my immature brain into a moment of confusion. Luckily, Auntie Elaine stepped in.

'Let him go Suzie. It'll give you some time to relax.'

'Relax? Chance would be a fine thing. Did Danny's mum say it was okay for you to stay?' Mum asked, turning to me with her lie-detecting stare. Danny answered for me.

'Aye Missus Dumfries. She said it'd be nae bother,'

'Oh go on then. But behave yourself. Do you hear me Haig?' Mum conceded lighting another Regal.

I promised.

'Bloody weans will be the death of me so you will.'

'You got a snottery beak hen?' Elaine grinned down at the expanding bubble on Maureen's nose before wiping it clean.

'Piece n' jam! Piece n' jam! Now please!' demanded Joe tugging at Mum's skirt.

Mum looked at Elaine with a wistful smile, her body swaying with the little boy's effort. They both started laughing.

We darted down the stairs laughing and cheering through the close and into the High Street where we sprinted on down towards Guildford Square. We were so anxious to escape before our master plan was discovered I hadn't even had time to put on my coat or gloves or do my shoelaces up.

We were still laughing when we sat down on the bus. We'd done it! The adults had been defeated. The sense of relief, achievement and victory was there but it all seemed too easy after having built myself up for a much fiercer battle. However, in the face of such overwhelming odds the enemy simply had no choice but to surrender.

Nae bother.

In less than half an hour the bus dropped us off in Kilchattan Bay. With daylight fading fast we knew we didn't have long but Danny used some time to sneak round the back of St. Blane's Hotel. I fidgeted, suddenly feeling awkward and vulnerable as I waited across the road acting as a look-out. He re-emerged just a few seconds later with a dustbin lid in his arms.

'Go! Quick! Just go!' he urged racing past me.

I looked up at the hotel and saw a concerned guest peering from the lounge bar window watching Danny make off with his booty. The man turned to face someone inside, mouthing and pointing at us. I chased after Danny. Reaching the end of the road, we clambered over the big wooden gate and on to the coastal footpath.

Crouched behind a dry stone wall, we waited a while, hiding and catching our breath fully expecting to hear loud, angry footsteps running after us. I tentatively peeked over the wall through the bushes and trees beyond and saw the hotelier standing in the middle of the road vainly looking around for us. With a shrug of his shoulders he headed back inside.

The path changed from a flattened grass trail trampled by sheep to a precarious twisting shale track never more than two foot wide, flanked on one side by a sheer wall of rock while a twenty foot drop fell away to our left. I watched the waves slapping against those glistening boulders half submerged in the sea below.

We trekked on in silence under a surprisingly mild sky. I was happy enough, taking in the views over the Firth towards the Cumbraes. Between those sibling islands, over on the mainland, a string of orange lights sparkled from the ore and coal terminal at Southannan Sands.

Danny strode on several metres ahead. I couldn't resist asking him what the dustbin lid was for. He told me to wait and see. All in good time. The jagged flakes of stone poking through the soil of the path were punishing my shoes. My good *school* shoes. I knew Mum would be less than happy with the scratches and scuffs. I really should have worn my plimsolls.

We were the only human beings to be seen along the entire journey. The only noises to be heard came from startled oyster-catchers, ducks, curlews and a host of other sea-birds. Rounding the headland we arrived at our favourite landmark. Rubh'an Eun. The unmanned lighthouse at Glencallum Bay. This meant we were close to our destination. We took the opportunity to gather up some firewood as we passed along the beach, using the bin lid as a basket. Danny assured me this was not what he had in mind when he stole it.

The distant mountains of Arran were grasping at the last shards of daylight by the time we stole over the rocks and began our decent into a deep crevice. Allowing Glencallum Bay to disappear behind us, we crept cautiously along the sandy floor of the darkening fissure. We followed the incline until we finally reached the entrance. The mouth-like aperture barely a yard high and wide, gaped black on black, like a toothless grin set at the base of the vertical mass of rock looming high over our heads. The tide was out enabling us to crawl through the hole unhindered. Once inside, in the total darkness, we had to feel our way up the side of the cave to the ledge we knew was some ten feet above us.

Danny struck a match from the box he'd pulled from his pocket. The flame burst brightly. He reached into a nook and removed a candle from our store. It took a little while for my eyes to adjust to its flickering glow.

There was room to spread out and relax on the ledge, the ceiling was another fifteen feet above us and the back of the cave stretched back ten yards from the entrance. The wall opposite our ledge faced us five yards across the divide. The overall shape of the cavern gave the impression of being inside a giant, deflated rugby ball.

Set high in the opposing side of the cave, a rough cut diamond shaped hole acted as a window and provided ventilation. Unfortunately it had proved too small to act as an exit. I had tried to squeeze through it once but panicked when my shoulders got stuck. Danny had to yank me back inside almost skinning my arms in the process. We had chipped and scraped away at the edges of the hole, trying to hammer lumps away in order expand the opening but all to no avail. The rock here was as tough as granite and we eventually had to accept that when the tide was in, we were effectively trapped, locked inside this beautiful damp-dark, shiny hide-away for the duration.

Every surface was pockmarked with countless cracks and recesses perfect for storing things like books, comics, games, sweets, anything we felt would make life in The Buzz Building more comfortable. Nature had gone as far as to kindly hollow out a bowl-like hearth in the ledge for us. It was always a pleasure to find the remnants of our previous fires still there exactly as we'd left them. A sure sign that not another soul had invaded our space in the interim. At the back of the cave there was a split in the rock running in a jagged vertical line like the shadow of a lightning bolt. At no point was it wide enough to allow even our child hands to poke through. We shone a torch into the split when we first discovered it to see if it hid any creepy-crawlies but found nothing. The blackness easily absorbed our feeble light and continued indefinitely. We decided to use the split as a place of honour for some of our more interesting finds left behind on the carpet of sand by the departing tide. Now it was stuffed with sea-urchin shells, dead starfish, intriguingly shaped pieces of wood, bones and fragments of glass smoothed and sculpted by the sea. Our most precious find was a dead seahorse no bigger than my thumb, which was given a shelf all to itself with its own candle. This was our altar.

I often wondered if we could live in The Buzz Building, self-sufficiently. The sea provided plenty of driftwood for fuel. But food? Well, there was an abundance of shellfish. Clusters of mussels and clams were scattered all over the rocks almost reaching the high tide mark. Danny quite liked eating these but I always thought they felt and tasted like cold lumps of salty phlegm sliding down the back of my throat. However, the seaweed did offer side-salad potential. Starfish were a no-no. The blood red anemones glued to the rocks beneath us looked like chewy, raspberry flavoured sweets but somehow we had managed to convince ourselves that they possessed a fatal sting and so we never dared to touch them. Our paranoia about potential food not conveniently placed before us boxed and dead, extended to the sizeable fish we occasionally spotted gliding around the deep pool that flooded The Buzz Building when the tide had risen to its fullest. We considered trying to catch these beasts but when Danny put forward the theory that if we put our hands too near the water the fish might leap out, drag us under and rip us apart piranha-like, it seemed sensible to leave them alone. This theory also put paid to any desire for a swim. We were not going to risk anything that might upset the uneasy truce we'd agreed with the fish.

Danny handed me a box of matches from one of our supply crannies and we set about lighting the dozens of stubby candles peppering the cave walls. Most of these were candles we'd pinched from home but we also had a couple of big, chunky church candles that we'd 'borrowed' from the vestry during our time as altar boys. After lining the natural hearth with handfuls of dried ferns and twigs collected from the fuel recess, we topped up the kindling with some of the smaller pieces of driftwood. It was my turn to light the fire. Such an important ritual demanded we take turns. This was an exciting act of rebellion against all the relatives, teachers and television personalities that had warned us not to play with matches. Other kids didn't know what they were missing.

With the contained flames taking root we settled back to soak up the heat and listen to the crackling, popping noises bouncing around the glossy black surfaces.

I couldn't get comfortable, shifting from cheek to cheek on the hard, lumpy surface.

'D'you need a jobby?' Danny frowned at me. I was a little put out by the suggestion.

'Naw, I don't need a jobby.'

'Is it a pish yer needin'?'

'Naw I don't need a pish.'

'If ye need a pish, just pish in the water.'

'I don't need a pish or a jobby. Anyway I wouldnae dare pish in the water.'

'Why not?'

'Cos it's dangerous.'

'How's it dangerous?' Danny's frown deepened.

'I 'member ma Dad tellin' me about this fish that lives in the Amazon. If ye go for a pish in the water it swims up yer pish, straight up yer willie, sticks its spines oot an' gets stuck up there.' I was pleased with the effect my story was having. Danny's face had twisted in horror. 'Aye. And the only way ye can get this fish oot yer willie is tae have an operation. The doctor has tae cut yer willie in half right doon the middle tae get it oot.'

'Eh?!'

'It's true! Dad learned about it in his army training. For when they're in the jungle an' that?'

'How big is this fish?'

I parted my forefinger and thumb leaving a gap of about an inch between them. 'He says it's about that big. I tried tae look it up in one o' ma animal books but I couldnae find a picture of it.'

I finally found a comfortable position lying on my side, elbow against the floor propping my head up in my hand. 'We should bring a couple of cushions or pillows next time.'

'Aye...' Danny struck a match and watched the flame devour the wood while he drifted away on a different train of thought. 'How would you... kill yerself?' he asked flicking the match into the fire before the flame touched his skin.

'What d'you mean?' I scowled, unprepared for such a peculiar question.

Danny struck another match and stared into its steady flame, 'I mean if you wanted tae kill yerself, how would ye dae it?' He paused to watch the flame shrink into a blue jewel clinging to the curved black stalk, 'I think I'd throw maself aff a boat an' get chopped up by the propellers. That'd be good and quick, naw?' A wisp of smoke drifted from the dead match.

'Aw that's disgustin'! What're you talkin' about? I don't want to

15

kill maself. What would I want to do that for?'

'I know. Keep yer heid. It's just a wee game,' insisted Danny. 'How about chuckin' yerself intae a fire?'

'No way! That'd be too sore!' I wracked my brain for a less painful alternative, my eyes drawn to the shadows flickering below the window-hole. A black hole. It was definitely night outside. 'Some people stick their heid in the oven,' I said with authority.

'Aye,' Danny nodded placing a couple of much larger logs on the fire, 'Some folk chuck themselves in front o' trains,'.

'Nae trains on Bute,' I confirmed, ruefully.

'Stickin' yer fingers in a plug hole...'

'Electric shock?'

'Aye.'

'I saw somebody dae that on the telly once. Their hair stuck oot. Their eyes went all funny, then they caught fire and burst like a balloon,' I said trying to remember what programme or film I'd seen this incident occur in.

'Drinkin' a whole bottle o' bleach!' Danny was flying.

'That wouldnae kill ye, would it?'

'Bloody right it would kill ye! Drinkin' bleach makes your blood bubble and yer eyes pop oot!'

'Pencils up the nose!' I shouted suddenly remembering.

'Eh!'

I sat up properly, 'I remember Mrs Gilchrist tellin' me off in drawing class. D'you no' remember? Were you no' there?'

He shook his head, ' What happened?'

'I took two pencils out of Elspeth's fluffy pink pencil case and stuck them up my nose. Mrs Gilchrist went mad. She told me it was dangerous tae stick pencils up yer nose because if ye tripped up and banged yer heid on the table you'd knock the pencils right up intae yer brain and kill yerself. Aye she lost the heid so she did.' I pushed a finger up each nostril, mimed the action of banging my head against a hard surface and feigned a pencil-induced brain injury.

We both laughed hysterically.

'Pencils up the nose,' Danny nodded in appreciation once he'd managed to rein in his laughter, 'That's a good one.'

We both peered into the fire tapping into our grisly imaginings.

Danny suddenly flashed his smile, 'How aboot chuckin' yerself oot an airplane wi'oot a parachute! Can ye imagine that?!' He used a hand to simulate a steep, fatal dive whilst blowing air sharply through his teeth creating a dramatic sound effect, 'Splat!' his hand slapped against the ledge, 'Can ye imagine the mess?! Urgh! You'd be spread oot like strawberry jam! Ha!'

Our mutual sense of gleefully sick humour was now fully synchronised and we soon found ourselves laughing helplessly at every morbidly comic image we shared.

'Or... or how about... How about lying in front of a steam roller and lettin' it run over ye? Imagine the noise of the bones crackin' and yer skin splittin' open. Yeuch!'

Danny was in fits. 'Aye! Imagine it rollin' over yer skull! It would go bang! Burst open and spray yer brains all over the place!'

'All over Mister Mac!'

That was it. We creased up, reduced to tears by the ridiculous image of our heads being crushed and our brains spattering over the face of our horrified headmaster.

We laughed for what must have been a record breaking length of time, rolling around the ledge gasping noisily for air, The Buzz Building singing with our merry howls. At one point I nearly rolled over the edge but this only served to prolong the hysteria. Eventually the pain forced us to stop. We sat up taking deep breaths and clutching our sides. It still took quite a while before we could look at each other without succumbing to another round of hilarity.

'Have we got any swedgers left?' I asked able to speak at last, the pain nearly gone.

Danny reached into the nearby cleft where we stored our provisions and produced a jar of sweets. I dipped my fingers inside, plucked out a cola-cube and popped it in my mouth. Danny plumped for a soor ploom.

I added some much needed wood to the anaemic fire.

Noisily sucking our boiled sweets we both watched the orange-yellow tendrils flicking like snakes' tongues over the new wood. Testing...tasting. The log slipped an inch when the fire bit. The organic, patient, fascinating process of incineration was mesmerising. The colours belonged to another world. A place where things didn't last. The pungent wood smoke had a soporific effect on me. I almost didn't notice Danny's voice.

'Before ma dad... battered me,' he began softly, gently feeling the bruise under his ear, 'Before I knocked for ye, he was tellin' me aboot all the different ways ye can kill yersel. He... he said drownin's best because... afore ye die, ye feel really, really happy and don't feel scared at all,' he told me, sucking harder on his sweet which made it hard for me to tell if his voice was wavering or not. 'Another good way,' he continued, 'is tae get one o' they...' he paused searching for the word, '... hypree.. hypredormic needles, ye ken? Like nurses use tae jab ye? Ma dad says if ye get one o' them, fill it with' air and inject the air intae yer blood, it will make yer heart explode and kill ye.' His voice was definitely wavering, he wasn't cheery like before and this all sounded less like a joke and more like a spooky ghost story with each passing word. I certainly didn't feel like laughing. He stopped to prod another stick into the fire then added, 'He said... he said he can get me a needle if I wanted tae try it. I told him tae fuck off.'

Danny only ever swore when he was talking about his dad.

On the few occasions I'd met Mr Crarae, he seemed to do nothing *but* swear. He was a big ugly man with a constantly threatening glare who wore too much aftershave under his smart outfits. His right hand was missing half of its little finger and the thought of that deformed fist punching Danny made me shiver. Danny didn't have a brother or sister to share the violence with and his mother, who appeared very nice and normal in comparison, didn't seem to offer anything in the way of protection, though Danny would never hear a word said against her as one or two of our mouthier schoolmates had discovered to their cost. I sorely wished I was even bigger than Mr Crarae so I could thump him hard if he ever dared to hit my best pal again.

'He gave me a right good doin' after that. If he does give me that needle I'm no' gonnae use it on maself, I'm tellin ye. I'll stick the fuckin' thing right in his eye!' Danny yelled, his voice increasingly angry and emotional. He spat spitefully into the fire and turned his face away from me to wipe a cuff across his eye but he was too late. I'd already caught the glint of the welling tear.

I didn't know what to say. I wanted to help somehow but instead I just sat there silently letting the last of the cola flavoured sugar swill around my mouth.

And then it started - the sound that inspired the cave's name and signalled the arrival or departure of the tide. A barely audible hiss of white noise at first which gradually, inexorably expanded to become a shifting, mutating buzz relentlessly reverberating into every detail, burrowing into our ears and drilling through our bones. I looked down over the ledge and saw the sea-water pulsing and frothing, staining the shadows on the cave floor even darker. It always surprised me how quickly the place filled with water. From nothing to something that would put our local swimming baths to shame in less than half an hour. The buzzing reached a crescendo when the water began to flow inside the split at the back of the cave.

'D'you remember the first time we were here when the tide came in and we thought we were gonnae die 'cos we didnae think the water was gonnae stop risin?' asked Danny, a smile returning to his face, once the noise had faded sufficiently to allow conversation.

I nodded remembering the event perfectly. The frantic attempt to squeeze through the window-hole as the din and the water kept rising. I nearly shat myself.

'You nearly shat yerself, 'member?' Danny was laughing now.

'So did you,' I said looking into the water, a little hurt. A tiny paranoid piece of me still worried about these invasions. At the back of my mind there was no absolute guarantee that the water would stop rising or indeed that it would ever drain away again... And as for the buzzing... Well that never failed to make my skin prickle with goosebumps and freeze my muscles as hard as the cave itself. I would not have been able to bear its sonorous tones on my own. I think we relied on our combined bravado to help laugh away our fear but there would always be a palpable sense of relief when the sea stopped swelling and the buzz died away leaving only the gentle glooping, slopping and slapping of lazy, harmless waves against the sides of the cave. We noticed that when we spoke our voices sounded different somehow. Lighter, less echoey. Even the air pressure must have been affected by the encroaching reservoir because every now and then my ears would pop.

For all its eeriness and dubious secrets or perhaps thanks to those very qualities, The Buzz Building was an exciting place. A safe haven. A whole other world away.

We sat in silence lulled by the ambient sounds of the water, lost in thought. I was drawn back to the very first time we set foot in the cave the previous summer and remembered our pact.

I opened my mouth ready to ask Danny something important but he had fallen asleep, curled up under his coat next to the fire. I watched him for a while to make sure he really was sleeping and not just pretending like I sometimes did at home when I would try to catch Mum out (my theory being that maybe, under a false sense of security, she'd let slip some vital piece of information if she thought I was zonked. She never did and would even surprise me on occasion with a gentle kiss on the forehead or by running an affectionate hand through my hair). Danny's expression remained relaxed in the lambent glow, his shoulder rising and falling with each breath. He wasn't pretending.

I turned my attention to the reflected flames dancing and flickering on the dappled pool's tar-like surface and even considered dangling my feet over the edge before remembering our truce with the fish. I was having trouble staying awake myself and decided to bed down. I think I fell asleep watching trails of smoke feeling their way across the ceiling to escape through the hole and head for the handful of stars caught in its ragged frame.

'Definitely aliens I'm tellin' ye. I reckon there's a space-ship hidden behind that crack at the back,' whispered Danny.

We were swapping yet more theories on what caused The Buzz Building's buzz.

'Naw,' I whispered back, shaking my head thoughtfully, 'It's a sea monster. There's a sea monster behind that crack. It sucks the water in, then spits it back oot again.'

We were only being half serious of course. It was our way of passing the time as we lay there, obscured behind a lichen mottled boulder, flat on our fronts on a bed of moss and heather.

A few hours earlier I had woken up to find Danny holding a mackerel's decapitated head under my nose. He may as well have been holding smelling salts. The rotten stench jolted me alert and upright in a second. I told him he was a basturt and was then amazed to learn that I had slept through the tide's noisy withdrawal. Danny on the other hand had been up since dawn scouring the cave floor for anything of interest and the fish head was the best he could come up with. He shoved the head in his pocket grinning at me and grabbed the bin lid. According to Danny, The Buzz Building's food stock was low and the time had come to hunt. And so out we ventured through the fresh daylight bleaching the entrance.

We headed inland until we came across a small, flat, grassy clearing on which to set our trap. Danny propped up the dustbin lid with a stick, placed the mackerel head underneath, tied the end of a ball of string to the base of the stick and retreated a safe distance unravelling the string as he went until he joined me behind the boulder. We had been lying there for over an hour peering over the huge sunken rock to our bird trap, whispering under an azure, late morning sky on the kind of day God uses to tease the Scottish Tourist Board.

Danny had tied the other end of the string a little too tightly around his index finger. I noticed the top part above the knuckle had turned an interesting shade of plum.

'Aliens,' he murmured without taking his eyes off the trap and only now deciding to loosen the knot on his throbbing finger.

'Sea monster.'

'Shh...!' Danny hushed tersely.

I froze. My eyes widened and refused to blink. Invisible quick-drying cement flooded my chest encasing my heart and lungs. Breathing was no longer a subconscious effort. The swish of blood pulsed loudly in my inner ears. We had been hoping to catch a seagull or maybe a crow. Even a starling would've done but up until now all we had managed to attract was a gang of bustling insects.

The sparrowhawk's wings twisted vertically, the breeze rushed across its feathers as it braked to a silent, graceful landing just a couple of feet from the trap. I had seen a lone individual patrolling the skies many times before but I'd never seen one on the ground and certainly not this close. Its stern, suspicious eyes were fixed in a permanent frown. Its head twisted, tilted and spun as it stood rooted to the spot surveying the surroundings. The raptor walked awkwardly, bouncing a few paces to the edge of the trap where it paused for another look around before cocking its head under the dustbin lid. A gut-wrenching aeon passed. *So close!* I was so tense, so rigid I thought I was going to be sick.

An earwig crawled over the moss in front of my face. I glanced at Danny. His eyes were as fixed as the hawk's. A trickle of sweat weaved over the bruise on his neck. His hand tightened ever so carefully around the string. I badly wanted to blow the earwig away worried that it would make a bee-line for my ear and bury its way into my brain. The sparrowhawk took another age to inspect the supporting stick but refused to step inside the shadow of the trap, choosing instead to traverse the perimeter as if repelled by an invisible force field. It looked in our direction. I wondered if it had heard my stomach rumble and was sure the game was up but then the bird looked back towards the fish head. It was all I could do to suppress what I knew would be, in any other situation, a really impressive fart. My bum cheeks were clenched so tight my whole body was shaking with the strain. To my immense relief the gas eased gently through my pants without a sound.

The hawk sprang at the bait in a soft brown blur, its bill stabbing into the gaping fleshy pink hole behind the torn gills but its speed was matched by Danny. With a strong, fluid flick of his arm he yanked the string. The hawk's glowering eyes jerked to the toppling stick. Before it could even spread its wings, the broad, corrugated steel disc flopped heavily to the ground encircling our bird of prey.

Flushed with the excitement of our success we scrambled to our feet and ran to the trap. The struggling bird made the lid bounce and twist slightly but not enough to allow its escape. We could hear muffled shrills of alarm coming from underneath. Danny placed a foot on the lid pressing it firmly into the ground.

'How're we gonnae kill it?' he asked breathlessly, cheeks burning red.

'I dunno. Maybe we should leave it under there 'til it suffocates.'

'No, that's cruel. It's got to be quick and painless,' he said, his eyes scanning the area in a convincing imitation of the hawk's. 'Grab that rock...! Aye, that one there.'

Things were never that straightforward. The brick-sized rock, determined to embarrass me, refused to budge. I tugged for all my scrawny arms were worth, gradually working the stone loose. In the end a few solid kicks were required to uproot the thing. A clod of soil dripped from the rock as I carried it in both hands and gave it to Danny.

'Right,' he said stepping off the trap, 'When I say so, lift up the lid and I'll batter it wi' this.' He raised the stone high above his head while I crouched by the trap taking a tentative grip on the rim of the lid. 'Now!' Danny yelled. I flung the lid back... Time seemed to judder and slip into slow-motion. I caught a glimpse of the stone thudding into the earth kicking up a spray of dirt. But the bird had taken off with a millisecond to spare, its wings and feathers blustering all over me. I quickly realised that I was blocking the hawk's frenzied escape. Clutching blindly and pulling frenetically I tried to rip the creature away. It felt huge. It was all I could do to shield myself from the furious smudged brown mass fluttering loudly around my head. My hand knocked a wing. In between the close-up squeals I heard Danny shout something. A sharp pain burned in my shoulder. The talons sunk deep. My turn to squeal. I flapped my arms trying to outdo the sparrowhawk's wings. Through the smeared light of my half closed lashes I saw its malevolent glare and hooked bill lunge towards my face. Instinct flinched my vulnerable eyes out of range and I felt it peck, pinching hard into my cheekbone. I staggered backwards and lost my balance. As I fell, I felt the raptor release its searing grip.

Hitting the ground I opened my eyes fully expecting them to be plucked out in an instant. Instead, lying there flat on my back, I saw the bird climb majestically to the blue heavens. I craned my neck following the hawk until it disappeared over the hills. Then I noticed the smell. Nestling in the grass right under my nose lay the rotting mackerel head. Its gaping mouth laced with tiny sharp teeth locked in a silent yell while one dull button eye hung loosely from its socket reflecting my bewildered face in its lifeless void.

2:   cells

Reflections, whether seen in the eye of a dead fish or here in this mirror, tell the same truth.

I study my right eye in the glass. I move closer. I see myself reflected in the eyes of my reflection. I follow the crimson capillaries branching across the white like serpentine rivers... There it is. The source of the irritation. A tiny black sliver of an eyelash glued to the moist surface near the iris. Resisting the natural inclination to blink I carefully, very carefully, tease the nail of my little finger under the cluster of white root cells at the base of the lash. The hair slides across a few millimetres closer to the pupil then gives itself up. I stare at the wet troublemaker now curled innocently on the very tip of my finger.

The same truth is that I am stuck, snared behind these weary eyes. I am trapped. At Her Majesty's Pleasure... *Her Majesty's Pleasure* - An image comes to mind of the Queen peering through the viewing flap in the cell door and laughing heartily at my misfortune - *I'm tellin' you, the sooner this country becomes an independent, neutral republic working within the European Union the better...* I remind myself that by *'this country'*, I do of course mean Scotland even if I am over four hundred miles from home in this East Sussex shit hole, cooped up with a thousand other rejects like insects in a killing jar.

I had a troubled night's sleep thanks to all those memories and dreams. Now I feel edgy. I prod and press my cheekbone where the sparrow-hawk tried to consume my face. A ragged crater-shaped scar about the size of a five pence piece is all that's left of the wound. I inspect my upper body in the mirror above the sink. All trace of the runt has long since vanished. I am no longer that spindly, skinny wee boy although I have to admit, the skin tone is still sallow beyond the pale. However, I'm quite proud of my physique; tall, broad shoulders, strong limbs and a flat belly. I haven't let myself go by any means which is all too easy to do in this place.

Apart from daydreaming, exercise and reading are the only things to keep the mind engaged in here and I do plenty of both. I don't read

25

any old shite. Classics mostly. The heavyweights; Tolstoy, Dostoyevsky via a dash of Scott, a slab of Joyce and even though school had employed him as a weapon designed to annihilate any notion that literature could be interesting; Big Charlie Dickens himself. Good thick, chunky books. Though at the moment I'm enjoying the more slimline Kafka. I have even made the effort to plough through The Bible, cover to cover for the first time in my life. The Koran swiftly followed. All good stuff. Stuff to make me think. Time passes much more quickly when I'm lost in thought. Shakespeare however, can go fuck himself. I have to draw the line somewhere. Of course another criterion for selecting this kind of reading material lies in the near certainty that they won't contain any full-on sex scenes. It's difficult enough to resist the hourly temptation to indulge in the time wasting escapism a good wank has to offer.

I splash more water on to my face, quietly, taking care not to wake my cell-mate hidden somewhere on the top bunk. He's harmless enough, though intelligent conversation and a firm grasp of personal hygiene are just beyond his reach... *Oh fuckin' wake up man! Stop feeling so cynical, so negative or whatever it is you're feeling, will ye?!...* I feel apprehensive and with good reason. Today is my birthday or to be more exact, my fortieth birthday. I'm not superstitious by nature but today being a decadal birthday, will inevitably dump something nasty on me. A catastrophic, life altering tragedy has occurred on each of my previous decadal birthdays and I have no reason whatsoever to doubt that today will be any different, even if it is difficult to see where the danger could come from... No. That's a lie. In a place crawling with assorted murdering psychopaths it's all too easy to see where the danger lies. I'll have to concentrate even harder on keeping my guard up...

I push my fingertips on to my chest over my heart to feel the pulsing rhythm. I frown unable to detect anything. Obviously I'm not dead so I slide my fingers around until I pick up a better reception... There's the proof; still alive. Steady, relaxed... *There it is...* Like a misfire - a weak, palsied beat.

I return to my bunk and stare out between the heavy steel bars. The sky is waking up. I glance at my watch. Not long now before we'll all be ordered up and out. I shake my head at the solitary, faltering star caught between the middle bars. I've noticed it occupying that position every morning at this time for days now.

Today is also my tenth anniversary behind bars. I shouldn't be here... Ten years... Ten wasted years. *I should not be in here.* Two or three years perhaps. That would have been fair I suppose. That's probably what I deserved... but I was given *life*. There has been a miscarriage of justice here. I did not do *that*. *That* was not me. I clamp my eyes tight shut. I have been falsely accused, falsely convicted.

I should not be in here.

And they all say - '*That's what they all say*'.

Today is a milestone and that's why I allow myself the briefest wave of self pity, though I realise I must be careful because if I think about it for too long there is every chance it will cause me to break down completely and I refuse to give the bastards the satisfaction. I want to go back to sleep and remember some more but I can't. And so I listen... The dawn chorus is in full swing and, pleasant though the songs are, they only serve to fill me with a longing to hear the familiar calls of the sea-birds I grew up with. I miss the sea itself. The prison is less than two miles from the Channel but I can neither see the water nor smell the salt in the air. I have no affinity with this part of the world anyway.

Nevertheless this institution has been my home for well over three thousand six hundred days. It could have been worse I suppose. At least the place is fairly modern and we don't have to slop out à la Barlinnie. If I were dishing out the Michelin stars I'd have to be harsh and award only two. For a start the door policy is far too liberal with an unhealthy bias towards a generally young and obnoxious clientele. The decor is lacklustre at best. The menu uninspired and heavily reliant on overcooked rice. The staff reasonable but prone to sporadic bursts of unnecessary violence.

...Ah here comes the jangling of keys and the heavy clumping footsteps courtesy of Doctor Marten. I wonder what line we will be treated to from Spacehopper Head's extensive repertoire this morning. So far this week on his shift we've had -

1: 'Time to get up you lazy festering twats!'

2: 'Stop smearing shit into your sheets and get up!'

3: 'Time to stop tuggin' your scabby cocks and get up.'

Perhaps today we'll all be amazed to hear - 'Open your weary eyes gentlemen, raise your sleepy heads and let us spend the day together discussing our fears, hopes and dreams in a positive, constructive, rewarding and mutually beneficial manner.'

Perhaps not.

The flap flips open. A pair of narrowing eyes set deep in a fat scowling face check us out.

'Up!' he yells.

That's a new one. Can't argue with its flawless simplicity and directness. His key rattles and twists in the lock. Spacehopper Head disappears and I lie back listening to his clumping and jangling continue along the corridor.

A protracted groan reminds me that I'm not alone. I prepare to endure Jim Flack's morning ritual. Firstly he issues a rattling series of bass-note farts, then slides his legs out and over the side, dangling his yellowing feet over my bunk. I can't help looking at the dry, flaking skin cracking across the soles. A leper's feet would probably look healthier. He yawns and stretches making the bed frame tremble around me. His left foot disappears back up. Now comes the most disgusting part. I can hear him picking away at the skin. Small flicking noises like someone trying to turn a stubborn page coupled with the odd brief tearing. Crispy, pasta coloured curls varying in size drop down to the floor. His left leg comes back over the side and the process is repeated with his right foot.

Jim steps down to the smooth tiled floor and staggers over to our lovely state of the art, stainless steel toilet (the 'stainless' claim is constantly put to the test by Jim's frightening by-products). He pisses a steaming, high pressure jet straight into the water, making sure everyone on the south coast is aware that he has survived the night. With a sticky glance in my direction to see if I'm awake, he mumbles something like, 'Morrinninaigh...,' then turns back to his epic piss with a yawn. Jim's next trick is to spend a full minute hoiking up every last particle of mucous from his nose, throat and chest before collecting it all in his mouth and parting his lips allowing the whole glutinous mass to drop inside the metal bowl with a loud, soggy slap. Before he heads to the sink I have to remind him to flush. I will no longer tolerate the sight and smell of his frankly horrific emissions.

On the whole, apart from his irritating habits and eagerness to spew forth his half-arsed philosophies and slightly-right-of-Hitler politics, the phlegmbouyant Jim Flack doesn't bother me that much and tends to leave me be. I've only had to threaten him with a swift, pain enhanced death on one occasion when he accidentally placed one of his rancid feet in my face while climbing out of bed. After I'd pinned him against the wall with a hand round his throat explaining (with the visual aid of a toothpaste tube) exactly what he could expect if it ever happened again, I spent five minutes vigorously brushing my teeth trying to get rid of the sickening taste of decaying skin. Even now I can detect the phantom flavour in my mouth. That was two months ago and fortunately (for both of us) the incident hasn't been repeated.

Jim sits down on the moulded plastic chair beneath the window and lights up the scrawny half smoked retread he left on the sill last night. To the uninitiated this former cinema projectionist comes across as a laid back, mild mannered character. Even I have to remind myself that I'm sharing a cell with a man who snapped a seventy year old woman's neck with his bare hands simply because she asked him to take his cigarette outside. Jim always insists that if she hadn't made such a big deal out of it then his mother would still be alive today. I've often wondered if there was one film in particular, one truly awful movie he screened just once too often which pushed him over the edge as a result. He's been inside more than fifteen years now. Could be released before the end of the year. I think back. Flashdance? St. Elmo's Fire? Anything starring Molly Ringwald? Plenty to choose from...

*

'What's the time Haig mate?'

Breakfast had passed by without incident. I look up at the sky. Good prison weather. Bleak, grey and not a trace of sunshine. And the few hours since the sugar-coated cardboard flakes, the rubber eggs and the salty leather, had proved to be equally sparse affairs... Another reassuringly dull Saturday. Dangerously boring. There's still plenty of life left in the day, it's not even noon. The surprise is out there. Poised. I mustn't become complacent.

'Haig. Mate. What's the time?'

I show him my watch, four minutes have elapsed since he last asked and I can't be bothered telling him for the umpteenth time. Jim squints at my wrist and draws hard on the straggly roll-up until I'm certain the glowing tip is going to singe his pursed lips.

'Right,' he says clapping his hands and spitting away the tiny butt, 'I'm off for my appointment. Catch you later.' He manages to belch out the latter sentence. One of his many enviable talents.

I watch Jim hurry across the exercise yard and into the main building passing several vigilant guards along the way. He is off for his regular Saturday consultation with his 'spiritual advisor'. From what I can gather this guy is an old 'mate' who keeps trying to persuade Jim to invest all his savings and any other collateral he can secure, into the gold mine that is Welsh whisky. I suspect these visits from his 'Spiritual Advisor' will come to an abrupt end when Jim's assets have disappeared.

Still, at least he has a visitor even if it is a shyster. My strange but wonderful meeting with Elspeth apart, I haven't had a visit for nine years. A month after my conviction Joe made the long trip south to inform me that, even if she could afford the train fare, Mum was too ashamed to visit. Ever. This hurt more than anything. Especially as it was sort of her fault I ended up in this mess. I was only trying to help her. Okay, so it was a bloody stupid way of going about things but I wasn't thinking straight at the time. I could almost understand her not believing my defence but I thought she could at least visit, even if only to give me a piece of her mind. She could even have lied and said she wasn't fit enough to visit; at least that was nearly true and one day would be.

Too ashamed!

'She should bloody well start behaving like the devout catholic she pretends to be and start trying to forgive folk once in a while!' I shouted back at Joe. It took a while but over time I became practiced at putting myself in Mum's position and began to fall in line with her point of view but I always hoped, and in darker times even prayed, that maybe one day I'd be able to prove how wrong they all were about me. I stopped being angry with Mum a long time ago.

Joe assured me he'd visit as often as possible but couldn't resist playing the martyr by asking how I could stoop so low and by telling me in great detail how I'd made the Dumfries family the most reviled in Rothesay. Problem was I could imagine all too easily the gossiping, finger pointing and all those high horses being saddled up. Joe clearly didn't want to be there opposite me and apart from proudly showing me a photograph of his new girlfriend Hannah, used most of our allotted time to attack me. Despite the promise my little brother visited on only one further occasion. This came as no great surprise and in a way I was relieved because at least I could say goodbye to all those awkward silences and spiteful accusations.

Joe did continue to write to me however, and I would receive at least two letters a year until he moved down to Milton Keynes four years ago. Since then I've haven't received so much as a Christmas card.

I tried repeatedly to prise Maureen's new address from Joe. He refused every time. He would not go back on his promise. She had made him swear not to give me any details. He would only ever tell me that she was 'surviving' and took great pains to point out that it was my fault that she had to move, unable to cope with the

31

repercussions of my actions and therefore my fault that the disruption had jeopardised her teacher training. Joe went on to remind me that the peculiar faith she had converted to forbade her to fraternise in any way with 'willful sinners'. Joe said she knew where I was should she ever decide to contact me and therefore it should be left up to her... I find it increasingly difficult to picture my wee sister's face... I have long since given up trying to contact my family.

'Dumfries? The doctor wants to see you.'

I look down from the sky to see the two guards standing officiously in front of me. A few blinks are required to help my eyes adjust from the brightness above.

'I take you have nothing better to do so if you don't mind - the doctor's a busy man so let's go,'

Ah here we go! This must be it. I'm not supposed to see the doc' until Monday morning when I get my test results. The last check up revealed some irregularities with my heart complicated by the murmur. *So this must be it. The doctor doesn't come in on Saturdays unless it's important.* I suppose I can be forgiven for being a wee bit worried.

I am escorted back inside, up a flight of stairs and along a gantry running outside the first floor D Block cells. I look down through the wire mesh stretched across the open space between the opposing lines of doors - there to prevent inmates from hurling missiles, or themselves or others down to the ground floor ten feet below - where I see a few young lads playing pool. My guides seem happy enough, wittering on about this afternoon's forthcoming football fixtures. I am asked what team I support.

'Celtic.'

The beetroot-faced, screw snorts. 'Someone has to I s'pose,' is the Tottenham fan's oh-so-sharp response.

'Aye, a damn sight more than support Spurs that's for sure,' I tell him.

'Ach,' he frowns, 'you lot wouldn't last five minutes in the Premiership. Scottish football's a fuckin' joke. I mean where the fuck is Forfar or Cowden-fucking-beath for that matter?'

Deep down I almost have to accept the argument about Scottish football being a joke but I remind him of Celtic's European Cup triumph in Sixty-Seven anyway.

'That was thirty-three years ago!' he snorts again, showing a flair for maths.

'So? That hasn't stopped you lot harpin' on about winnin' the World Cup has it? Every poxy day since Sixty-Six we've had to put up with some twat on the TV or in the newspapers reminding us of that bloody match.'

'Sounds like jealousy to me. Just 'cos Scotland can't even get passed the first fuckin' round,' he laughs indignantly.

'Let me remind you that *two* of England's goals in that final should've been disallowed. That one *never* crossed the line for a start. And the last goal should never have stood either. Why? I'll tell you why. Remember the legendary commentary – "Some people are on the pitch. They think it's all over." - Rewind right there! "*Some people are on the pitch!*" If there was a bloody pitch invasion the referee should've stopped the bloody game!'

'Bollocks,' is his final, damning reply.

The taller one who appears to have no arse to speak of under the sagging backside of his black trousers, unlocks both sets of security doors leading into the administration block. I am ushered through and hear the keys work the locks behind me. A few paces along a bright, lengthy corridor and there's a distinct change in smell. The odour of warm photocopiers and fresh A4 paper; very different to the pervasive stink of disinfectant in and around the cells and the perpetual hint of mature cheddar in my cell provided by Jim's feet. We turn sharp left brushing past an impressive yucca. I forget they have carpet in here which is why, not used to having so much grip, I stub my foot. We stop outside a door on the right with a big green cross painted on the translucent glass. Beetroot Face knocks respectfully.

'Come in!' the doctor yells. We enter.

Nothing's changed since I was last here nearly a fortnight ago. The treatment table still waits patiently on the right of the clinically bright room. The opposite side is taken up with a makeshift waiting area; a row of four plastic chairs rest against the wall facing a knee high table covered in leaflets offering information on various unpleasant conditions. The walls are adorned with Health and Safety posters that seemed to be aimed at children. Don't smoke. Don't sniff glue. Don't swallow razor blades but Do clean your teeth morning, noon and night and Eat Your Greens. That kind of thing.

A couple of antiquated cabinets containing some rudimentary medical gear and a bookshelf crowded with directories, manuals and text books flank the broad double-glazed window straight ahead of me. In contrast to the nature-free sights on show from my cell, the window here offers a view of some flourishing treetops. My eyes pull focus on the man standing between the window and his cluttered desk.

Doctor Brooks (or Mengele as he is affectionately referred to by the inmates) is reading a file. He looks at me as if only now noticing the presence of another in the room and lazily waves a hand gesturing me to take the seat in front of his desk. Beetroot Face and No-Arse park themselves in the waiting area and at least pretend to respect my privacy by flicking through pamphlets on testicular cancer and haemorrhoids. Doctor Brooks drops the file on to the big black blotter defining his area of the desk with a satisfying slap and sits down with a heavy sigh. I shuffle in the uncomfortable seat clasping my hands together trying hard not to display my unease.

The doctor twists slowly back and forth in his padded swivel chair with an irritating squeak. This only serves to heighten my annoyance at having someone who is clearly the best part of a decade younger than I am having this much of a hold over me... *At least I'm not going bald...* He doesn't look too happy himself. Judging by his unusually casual appearance and dour expression I think he resents this intrusion into his weekend... *It must be serious...* He taps into the computer staring unmoved at the information revealing itself on the screen.

'How's things?' he asks clearly not interested in how things are. He taps the 'Enter' key twice.

'You tell me.' I try to view the monitor but it's frustratingly angled just out of reach. The good doctor clears his throat, removes my records from the file in front of him and leafs through the loose papers. Chewing pensively on his upper lip his frown deepens as he reads. I clench and unclench my knotted fingers. This is ominous. He's taking an eternity. *He's building himself up to tell me the bad news - I can feel it.* This is the life changing scenario I've been expecting since I woke up this morning. I study his face hoping for a clue. Doctor Brooks has made it clear in the past that he doesn't like me but I haven't taken his bad attitude personally. I imagine he basically hates having to deal with the dregs of society. I suppose he hates being in this dump almost as much as I do. His job is to locate infected cells and here he is surrounded by cells infected with the worst kind of evil, foul smelling pus.

He is *still* dragging this out, swapping his attention between the words on screen and on paper. With a sideways glance to the screws behind me, he reaches for a large brown envelope and removes a headed, typed letter. Finally he fixes his gaze directly into mine.

'Well Mister Dumfries... Your test results have come back and I'm afraid, the news is not good...'

Not good - *Don't pause for dramatic effect now ya basturt!* ...

'And?' I say struggling to maintain my veneer of hard cool.

Doctor Brooks taps 'Enter'.

'And. Basically. Acute heart disease...'

Forty...

'I'm amazed you haven't experienced more discomfort. It's quite pronounced I'm sorry to say,' he continues with a sigh, then tuts and shakes his head, 'I must be honest and tell you that the prognosis isn't good I'm afraid.'

...Disaster struck at ten, at twenty, at thirty... Today I am forty so I really shouldn't be surprised... And I'm not... So why do I feel this tightening in my chest? Why has my breathing become shallow? I feel a spasm in my guts... Why is my mind racing?... An alarm? I'm sure I can hear an alarm. A fire? A breakout? Nobody would break *in* surely?... The doctor is studying my reaction. Still frowning. Still

35

staring at me. Into me. I look back towards Beetroot Face and No-Arse. They instantly divert their embarrassed eyes back to their reading matter... They don't seem to have heard the alarm.

'Unless you receive treatment very soon you'll becoming face to face with whatever God you believe in before very much longer.' The words pass coldly from the doctor's impassive lips.

I force a breath deep into my lungs, press my eyes shut and exhale heavily, 'When?'

'Mister Dumfries... Haig...,' his voice shifts to an even more patronising tone as he leans forward hands clasped together, resting his elbows on the desk like he's about to give a party political broadcast, 'it's very difficult to be exact in these circumstances...'

He pauses again! I want to kill this smarmy prick right here and now.

'It could be anywhere between two and six months or even a year, though I'd err on the former,' he tells me with what looks like the merest flicker of a smile. 'Are you sure you haven't been experiencing any unusual chest pains recently? Any shortness of breath? Loss of appetite? Difficulty concentrating?'

I think I felt a twinge while I was exercising this morning but nothing unusual. He doesn't mean that does he? I had some chest pains last month but I reported them at my check up and Doctor Brooks didn't seem overly concerned about them then and besides they seemed to pass away and haven't bothered me since. I don't take my eyes off him as he stands, steps over to one of the cabinets and takes out a black blood pressure band. He moves around the desk asking me to roll up my sleeve. I watch him wrap the band around my upper arm.

'The nation's biggest killer, heart disease. Did you know that? Particularly among the lower classes, people from deprived areas such as yourself. Scotland leads the world when it comes to heart disease.' He sounds almost cheerful.

What is he on about? Deprived area? I want to argue with him, shout at him, thump him but I can't quite concentrate. My train of thought has been well and truly derailed... All that silence before and now the bastard won't shut up...

'A lot of it, well most of it, is down to poor diet. The less well off tend to eat a lot of rubbish, the kids eat far too many sweets and crisps and most meals tend to be fried, full of saturated fats and smothered in salt' he states starting to inflate the band. I feel it constrict, squeezing tighter and tighter. 'Is it true that chip shops in your neck of the woods sell deep fried Mars Bars? And people actually eat them? And people wonder why there's such a huge waiting list for donor hearts,' he shakes his disdainful head.

'As if all that wasn't enough, the problem in your case has been further compounded by that murmur of yours. Over the years your heart has had to over-compensate for the irregular rhythm to the point where the muscle walls have weakened to a critical level. This is a particular problem in the left ventricle. There is also evidence of a clot building up in your thoracic aorta. Again, quite serious. Potentially you are just one bacon rasher away from a shattering aneurysm. Are you *absolutely* sure you haven't been suffering severe chest pains?'

I don't answer. His increasingly rapid, enthusiastic speech leaves the distinct impression that Doctor Brooks is enjoying this. Maybe he feels his Hippocratic oath doesn't apply to convicted murderers.

He leans in to my ear, 'Believe me Dumfries, any day now that tattered organ of yours is going to rupture big time,' he whispers menacingly. 'And when it does, you will experience pain and I'm talking about crippling, monumental pain like you can't possibly imagine until it actually occurs.' He squeezes the little hand pump even harder, 'I'm actually taking a risk by doing this you know. Just taking your blood pressure might prove too much.' I can feel the blood pulsing painfully in my arm, straining to pass through the expanding barrier formed by the band.

'But who is going to care if we lose you now?' he smiles. 'I'll have the minor inconvenience of filling out a report and with the backing of our uniformed friends over there the incident will be swept under the carpet. It's not as if the public tend to get upset over the death of a murderer now is it? Especially when most decent members of society are of the opinion that you should have been hanged for what you did.'

He stops squeezing and steps back. I'm fully aware that he is watching me, waiting for a reaction. The desire to inflict as much pain as is humanly possible on my tormentor before Tweedle-dum and Tweedle-dee can react flashes through my mind. But I won't do it. I won't let them feel justified in treating me like this. I keep focus on the bustling branches outside...

I should not be in here...

Without even bothering to read the pressure gauge Doctor Brooks tears the Velcro apart, removes the band and dumps the instrument on the desk. A warmth flows through to my hand.

'I'm afraid transplantation represents your only real hope,' he says quite loudly. A crow lands on the top of the nearest tree. The doctor leans towards me again and whispers. 'And let's be realistic. You have as much chance of getting a transplant as a duck has of finding water in its rectum. Do you really believe they will waste a precious organ on the likes of you? And you're an even bigger fool if you expect me to go crusading on your behalf. As far as I'm concerned the tax payer has wasted more than enough money on you... But look on the bright side. You're supposed to have at least another five years left on your sentence but I can guarantee you'll be out of here before Christmas... Albeit on the inside of a sturdy oblong box.' He backs away slowly then returns to his desk.

He swivels in the squeaky chair, picks up a pen and scribbles a brief note onto my records. He looks at me. I decide to match his gaze. He shakes his head, tutting with mock pity, 'It really is such a shame I didn't pick up on your condition a year ago, maybe even six months ago. If you'd received a course of the appropriate drugs back then...' he can't resist a smile. The fucker winks at me! He's *planned* this! I look back to the treetops. I desperately want to rush across and burst the fucker's smug head. I breathe deep and exhale long and hard folding my arms. The crow flies off...

Doctor Brooks returns to his monitor hitting a few keys. His face splits into a gleaming grin. He settles back into his chair, 'Happy birthday by the way! I've only just noticed! Forty! Life begins at forty eh? Oops. Sorry.'

His false apologetic grimace provokes no reaction from me. I surrender myself to the situation. However, I would like to know why these fine upstanding prison officers are not doing anything to put a stop to this mental cruelty. *Attempted* mental cruelty I should say because I will not break and let them steal what little I have left.

*

I remember leaving the doctor's surgery in a kind of daze. I don't recall Beetroot Face and No-Arse saying a single word to me. A brooding silence accompanied me back to my cell. Clearly their training hasn't extended to counselling the terminally ill.

A transplant. A new heart. Hope? Who am I kidding? Young Doctor Brooks is right. Given the choice, and there's always a choice in these circumstances, there is no way on God's earth that a piece of life's washed up jetsam (i.e. me) will receive that soft, muscley holy grail, when there is undoubtedly a far more deserving and valued member of society out there who can make use of it. And this is as it should be because, if I'm honest with myself, I really don't think I could cope with the suspense of waiting to discover what my fiftieth birthday would like to clobber me with; although I do have a certain masochistic streak that would love to find out what's in store. Just for a laugh.

Forty...

Time flies as quick as thoughts...

The old neurons have been sparking constantly since my unscheduled encounter with Doctor Death. I become aware that I am lying in bed, gazing out of the window and realise I have been following the progress of a handful of stars traversing that section of late evening sky, divided into nine perfect square segments. One pin-hole sized sun, countless light-years away, disappears behind the first vertical bar. I watch and wait... It re-emerges from the other side of the steel barrier, unharmed after a length of time I forgot to measure.

'Did you hear about The Arse Grinder?' asks Jim striding into the cell instantly shattering the peace. 'Mad bastard's been up to his old tricks again.' He stands in the middle of the room facing me waving his incredulous arms, 'Picked on one of the new lads in the showers. Took him right up the back passage, know what I'm sayin'? Poor fucker can hardly walk straight now. Pisses me off that kind of behaviour y'know? The lad's only been in here two days. Nineteen I think he is. Left home not long ago. Got his own place. D'you know what he's in here for, uh? Not paying his fuckin' TV licence. Talk about getting shafted!'

Not long after I was transferred here I had a brush with The Arse Grinder. The stocky, vertically challenged, weight lifter was showing me around. He shoved me into a store room and made it perfectly clear with the aid of a razor blade that he wanted to 'fuck some Jock arse'. But before he could even finish breathing the threat over me I crunched my forehead into his nose and rammed a knee into his bollocks. I watched him writhing on the floor whimpering like a wounded puppy, clutching his groin while blood gushed from his broken nose. I grabbed his throat, took the blade, held it close to his terrified eyes and promised to slice them in half if he so much as walked in my general direction ever again.

If the same thing had happened shortly after my conviction I don't think I would have been able to defend myself. The years have hardened me, taught me to be alert and never *ever* to appear vulnerable. Even now, I still get scared by some of the people surrounding me especially by the way some of them think. They seem to inhabit a remorseless, dead world of contradictions. Logic and basic common sense are unnatural pollutants in their incomprehensible environment and no amount of considered argument will ever make even the slightest inroads into their twisted, desolate mind-set. The Arse Grinder for example thinks nothing of parading around spouting the most ludicrous homophobic statements and plastering his walls with pictures of naked women only to brag about raping young men in an attempt to convey just how hard and super-macho he really is. There is no paradox for him to deal with.

These people cannot be reasoned with and have nothing to offer but disillusion and so I do my level best to avoid them.

'I heard you were taken to see Doctor Mengele. How did it go?'

'Fine,' I lie, 'What about your visit?'

'Oh yeah, good,' he nods his head looking quite satisfied, 'my man tells me shares in Welsh Whisky are on the rise again.'

Jim steps in front of the mirror cheerfully picking at his teeth... *The Breakfast Club* or maybe it was *Pretty In Pink?*

'Bloody rice again eh? I reckon this nick's got fuckin' shares in the stuff.' Jim suddenly spins round, his face lighting up with excitement. He clicks his fingers and points at me. The man has had a revelation, 'Maybe I should have a word with my man! See what the current rice situation is.'

'Currant rice? I've never tried that.'

'Eh?' Jim is perplexed. I don't waste any breath attempting to explain the feeble pun.

'I thought yer man was strictly a spirits expert?' I ask.

'True, but he likes to keep a finger in as many pies as he can y'know?'

'So that would be a maximum of ten pies then?' I suggest trying not to laugh at my own crap jokes. I feel relaxed. I may even be coming to terms with my lack of a future. My cell-mate's puzzled face is helping to take my mind away from bleaker thoughts.

'What are you on about?' he frowns, completely lost, 'I reckon rice could be where the action is. Might be worth investing in a few shares. Never mind Uncle Ben's – here comes Uncle Jim's! Isn't there a drink made from rice? Y'know...?' he ponders scratching the back of his neck, 'That spirit... What's it called?'

'Sake.'

'That's the one,' he smiles, 'Chinese ain't it?'

'Japanese.'

'Ach, they're all the fuckin' same,' tuts Jim, 'fuckin' short arses.

Making tellies is all they're good for. Have you ever, I mean *ever* seen a decent Japanese film?'

'Yojimbo,' I suggest.

Again he looks perplexed. 'Eh? *Yo* yourself *Haigbo* mate. Anyway, you get my point? You see? Not one... The yanks should've dropped a few more atomic bombs on 'em. Then it would be us creaming the world market in electrical goods.'

Oh here we go. I sigh, close my eyes and try to block him out.

'Chinky bastards just copied what we were already making and got in there first, floodin' the high street with affordable copies. We fuckin' invented all yer televisions, videos, radios n' stuff. Thievin' yellow tossers the lot of 'em,' he complains as I hear him climbing up to his bunk.

'Mind you I was lookin' through Porno Dave's stuff the other day right? And he showed me this 'Asian Babes' mag' yeah? Fuckin' 'ell mate! You shoulda seen these girls! I'll say this for yer fuckin' nips and chinks - their women are fffffuckin' *gorgeous!* I must've tossed myself silly fifty times with that mag' I'm tellin' ya. Great stuff.'

I shake my head in disbelief. Sweet Jesus! I knew I was sleeping under a wanker but I did not need to know just how *much* of a wanker. I hope to God he deposits his essential oils into a tissue or something. The horrible image of his fluids seeping slowly through his mattress towards me makes me feel sick.

I have got to get away from this cesspit. I can't allow myself to die here, surrounded by all this ... nothingness. My mind opens up. Purposeful. A decision has been made. I now have one final goal to fulfil.

Escape...

I've nothing to lose.

How and when...?

Think...

*   *   *

Colours. Brilliant... seething... colours. I love the brightest of the blues. I should be more loyal to the blazing greens. Hues hypnotise. My palsied senses struggle to cope with the overwhelming display. No more cold. Scared at first. Unsure. Panicked... Stricken. Shivered. Now? Ecstatic... vindicated... Gold... A lapsed Catholic, lapsing. Here am I. Collapsing... Pure, pure red. Need more eyes to take this in. Wish I was a spider... Searing white. Purple. A beautiful bruise... No more cold. Only colours... Scatological? An obscene interest? Or scattered logic... Scattered beads of crimson. Something moves and a familiar face I've never seen before...

*

On the northernmost tip of the Isle Of Bute lies the wonderfully named Buttock Point. Standing here, as almost certainly the only person to be seen for miles, and facing True North, you will see Loch Ruen shimmering back at you (weather permitting). To your right you will see the tiny uninhabited Burnt Islands.

Looking across the Sound Of Bute to your left, a few miles along the distant mainland coast you will see the village of Tighnabruaich (that's; *Tie-Na-Broo-Ach*). If you walk on in this direction braving the marshy soil and thick fern cover for five, maybe ten minutes, and keeping your eyes on the steep craggy hills veering up to your left, you will come across 'The Maids Of Bute'. This trio of bulky, free-standing boulders ranging from five to eight feet tall and perched side by side near the base of the crags, face out to sea - watching. You will notice them because of the various gaudy colours of thick paint they have been daubed with.

Legend has it that these ancient decorated stones represent the wives of three fishermen who were lost at sea. According to the story, the grieving women vowed to wait on this very spot until their loved ones returned.

Centuries later they are still waiting.

43

... Light filters through. I try to focus. Conscious once more. Just... I am inside the ambulance now. Moving. Fast. They are taking me to hospital... My vision becomes more defined... Faces. Once again I have two escorts. Not Beetroot Face and No-Arse. This pair can be summed up as Moonscape Skin and Can't Smile-Won't Smile. My left wrist is cuffed to Moonscape Skin. Can't Smile-Won't Smile is giving me quite possibly the most murderous look I have ever been subjected to. He is still mopping up the gooey mess coagulating on the shoulders and collar of his once-white shirt. I'm aware of the siren and the dizzying speed. A paramedic is fussing over me, big and green, checking this, that and the other... *It might seem a bit extreme, my life saving friend, but I had to do it. I can't afford to piss about...*

I lay awake throughout the whole of last night. After Jim had completed his diatribe on the Far East he choose Australia as the destination for his next assault focusing in particular on how he felt the Aussies were too soft on the Aborigines. He was utterly convinced that this 'gutless liberalism' was affecting the quality of Australian wine. His solution was pretty final; if the Aborigines thought that Ayre's Rock was so special and sacred then they should all be forced to live on it, fenced in concentration camp style leaving the rest of Australia free to exploit whatever land it required to produce the finest vintages. That was about the gist of it, though to be honest I wasn't paying much attention.

I let him rant on while I tracked the stars drifting slowly across the window, thinking... planning. Finally, he grew tired and ran through his pre-sleep ritual which involved descending from his bunk, heading to the toilet and firing several steaming litres of his own vintage directly into the water whilst noisily shifting the day's accumulation of phlegm from his throat and pharynx before projecting the raw egg-like substance in after his piss. He flushed on his own accord then returned to his bunk where I could hear him picking at his feet for several minutes. Even in the darkness I saw the shadows of a few large hard skin peelings sailing past my bed on their way to the floor. Then silence. Jim Flack doesn't snore. (Praise the Lord for small mercies).

I lay there, hands behind my head contemplating and dissecting the day's events, trying to decide what it all meant. I looked at my watch and felt an absurd relief that midnight had passed. Several pathetic escape plans were considered then rightly dismissed. I desperately wanted to break out there and then, but had to accept that it just wasn't possible no matter how many times I'd seen *Escape From Alcatraz*.

My plotting was constantly interrupted. Having been told I only had a few months to live the bastards obviously thought I might be feeling a wee bit glum and so kept a suicide watch on me. Every half an hour a face would peer through the door to make sure I wasn't swinging from the fixtures with a cunningly fashioned noose hewn from my own intestines round my neck. These interruptions helped to make sure I didn't fall asleep (Very useful, as it turns out, in making me look even more like I'm on death's door now).

After breakfast I headed to the storeroom to collect the mop, bucket and fluids needed to perform my cleaning duties and returned to D Block to make a start on the ground floor.

The empty bleach bottle provided the spark I'd been looking for. I filled it with dirty, bleach laced water from the bucket, mixing in just enough disinfectant and a dash of window cleaner to the cocktail to make certain it was indigestible. For added effect I lifted the Celtic cross pendant from my neck, put it in my mouth and used the sharp metal edges to cut the insides of both cheeks as much as I could bear.

The nearest prison officer was watching over the lads playing pool. Allowing a trickle of blood pooling over my tongue to dribble from the corner of my mouth, I headed towards him staggering like a manic drunk (I had only used my acting skills once before and that was in a school play where I excelled in the role of an abused turtle, so I knew this was going to be a major test and one that I could not afford to fail).

'You satisfied noo ya fuckin' bunch o' fucks!' I raved putting on my roughest Glaswegian accent. The screw's face was something to behold when he saw me taking a swig from the bleach bottle. He urgently mouthed a request into his radio while a crowd of inmates gathered to enjoy the show, laughing and goading me on. Warders appeared as if from nowhere.

'I'm fuckin' dyin' here ya basturts! So fuck you an' yer floors! I'm no' cleanin' a fuckin' thing for you or any other fuck! D'ye hear me?! I'm the one that needs cleanin'! *I* need to be cleaned! Ma *insides* need cleaned before I die! D'ye unnerstan'? Ma soul is filthy!' I hollered doing my best to look suitably deranged.

I swallowed down great gulps of the concoction and must have consumed nearly half the bottle before I was pounced on by a scrum of screws. I had no idea how many there were grabbing, pulling, twisting and punching me as I flailed wildly, bucking and kicking like an animal in a snare. They wrestled the bottle from my mouth almost taking my teeth with it. The stuff splashed across my face, stinging my eyes and fizzing up my nostrils. I heard the plastic bottle bounce and skid over the polished floor. I was pinned down, coughing and spluttering, to the same surface, my face pressed into a puddle of the noxious liquid. I'm sure my jaw was prised apart while someone tried to shove their fingers down my throat until someone else ordered them not to.

I was hauled to my feet and dragged towards the stairs in the infirmary's direction. The cleaning fluids swilling and sloshing in my guts were beginning to react badly with my own chemicals. I began to feel truly bizarre. The screws knew something was amiss when I started to spasm. I was genuinely convulsing but still coherent enough to embellish the jerks to maximum effect.

I could feel my stomach lining burn. The flavour of disinfectant and blood curdled in my mouth. We'd just reached the foot of the stairs when the convulsions started. My stomach rocketed its contents upwards. I tried my best to hold back the hot flood for just a few vital seconds so that I could draw more blood from my cheeks. I had to concede. My face split apart like a ruptured dam. Anyone standing within ten feet of me must have caught it. I saw two officers including Can't Smile-Won't Smile catch it full in the face. The torrent of vomit hissed on contact with the atmosphere. I saw it bubble and fizz on the floor - I'd had muesli for breakfast.

Wave after stinging wave spurted forth. It felt as though my internal organs were being squeezed up my throat. I couldn't draw breath. I began to feel frantic, thinking that maybe I'd gone too far and was about to die a shabby, laughable death. Then some bastard punched me viciously in the kidneys. I remember being called a stupid prick and heaved up the first few steps feeling weak, spent and sore. Despite the cold sweat tickling my forehead my feverish skin was burning. My insides were hollow and I was retching air. I gave up and fell limp. Eyes streaming, nose and mouth leaking, ears shrieking. A dead, dying weight for the guards to drag.

One of them slipped on the puke causing me to lurch backwards and then they all must have let go of me at this point because I continued to fall, landing heavily across my back and banging my skull on the shiny concrete floor. Stunned and feeling more peculiar by the moment, I noticed that my head was resting in the main pool of frothing, reddish bile. It reeked. Then someone turned out the lights...

The paramedic adjusts the drip. I'm feeling better but I won't be sharing the good news with them. I can feel some sick drying on the back of my neck. There's a lump of gunk at the back of my throat. I notice splashes of vomit on one of the prison officer's shoes. I feel queasy again...

... *Christ! Did I pass out again? I have got to stay with it! Come on...!* Off the ambulance now... Flat on my back... trolley rattling into A & E, yep... strip lights hurry past on the ceiling... a doctor's enormous head swells across my vision - *Is she trying to blind me with that fuckin' thing?!*...

A voice; not hers, '... in and out of consciousness...'

That's true.

47

Another voice, '... swallowed large quantities of bleach...'

That's debatable.

'... Internal haemorrhaging...'

That's a half-truth.

'... choked on his own vomit...'

Didn't everyone? Ha ha!

... I'm wheeled through a set of those big flappy plastic doors. I do feel better, honest. If you could just persuade Cro-Magnon man here to undo this handcuff, I would be only too happy to demonstrate...

Guard rails are dropped and I am lifted from the trolley and eased on to a treatment table. The doctor flashes another light into my eyes. Bright blotches melting from white to yellow, through to orange, red and purple, wax and wane on my retina. This seems quite normal to me; don't know what she thinks though. Her face remains set in an expression of professional tolerance... I have a headache. Not too bad though. Bearable.

An attractive nurse flits around me. Cropped dark hair with no make-up. None required to enhance large, equally dark eyes. She leans over for something, her bosom leaning near my face. I peer through the winking gaps between the buttons hoping for a glimpse of bra or even cleavage but her close-fitting blue uniform reveals nothing...

I can't afford to get turned on now! Jeez! Concentrate Haig! Think!... Now you mention it doc', my vision is a wee bit blurry and I am experiencing a kind of dry cramping sensation in my guts. Do you think there's a connection? I could do with about a gallon of ice-cold water if you please nurse... My head flops to one side. I see perfect slender calves, smoothly dark inside her tights. If I get an erection now that will *surely* give the game away. *Concentrate...*

They're shoving something down my throat! Basturts! I start to thrash like a fitting epileptic on a trampoline, my wrist tugging painfully at the handcuff. I yank my arm even harder, rocking Moonscape Skin back and forth. I can feel the steel bracelets cutting deeper into my flesh with each jolt. The whole table rattles as he slams against the side. I hear the doctor demanding the cuffs be removed.

She argues that I am in no condition to spring a surprise... Here we go

I catch sight of the doctor squirting a hypodermic needle - *Get those air bubbles out that's right*... They're all trying to restrain me. Pushing down on each squirming limb. I fall limp. I worry about my thudding heart. *Don't go bang now pal...*My wrist is released... I wait until the doctor brings the needle in close to my arm. I hope all those years of exercising have paid off...

NOW!...

With an almighty effort I snatch the needle from the doctor's hand, jab the thing into Moonscape Face's thigh and hurl myself away from those two to the other side of the table. The momentum sends me crashing to the floor taking the nurse and Can't Smile-Won't Smile with me. I collide with a trolley of some sort and tumble, helplessly pawing at the air for support. Metal receptacles clatter across the floor; clanging, bouncing and spinning like tops. The drip-feed support topples over smacking Can't Smile-Won't Smile on the side of the head. He dizzily pushes himself back on to his feet only to slip on a bedpan.

My face comes to a halt just inches from the nurse's terrified, beautiful eyes. I could kiss her. Instead I smile, shyly. Must dash... I can hear the others clambering through the clutter. Reinforcements will be arriving any second now. Got to get a move on. I hop over the nurse. Can't Smile-Won't Smile is pushing himself upright against the table. I kick him squarely between the legs. He crumples back to the floor his gaping mouth releasing a succession of staccato yelps. I sprint towards the flappy doors. The doctor is clutching a phone attached to the wall, watching me wide-eyed and pale, sending a distress message into the receiver... *Shit!...* My leg is caught. I lose balance, my palms slap painfully against the dubiously stained floor breaking my fall. With the wind knocked from my ribcage I feel a warm crushing pain on my ankle. I look down to see Moonscape Skin, rapidly succumbing to the sedative, sinking his watery teeth into my Achilles' tendon. *You fucking mental headcase!* I kick him off with my other foot. With a loud sigh he flops at the doctor's feet and falls asleep. I hear people running in the corridor outside. I haul myself vertical registering a fleeting image of the nurse trying to assist the incapacitated Can't Smile-Won't Smile.

I burst through the doors. Two security guys skid to a standstill. I tell them they'd better take a look inside. To my surprise they follow my instruction giving me a vital head start.

I sprint through A & E passing a motley array of grim-faced wounded and into the outside world. Those security guys are on the chase again. I could steal that ambulance for my getaway. I hesitate and frown at the vehicle tempted by the thought but that would be unethical even for me. Plus it would be far too easy to track. I keep running. Plenty of witnesses take note of my easy to describe features. Passing out of the hospital grounds I look back and see the two security guards bursting from the A& E entrance. A pain-in-the-arse, public spirited old bastard smoking by the automatic doors points them in my direction. I race into the busy street unsure if they saw me or not. I keep running. *Where the fuck am I?* Brighton - must be... Just keep running. I've been to this town once before but I don't recall any of this... I haven't a clue where I'm going. I know where I want to be. Only another four hundred or so miles to go. Just keep running.

I turn sharply down a side alley. Less people. My legs are getting heavy now. I slow down to a jog and then to a brisk walk trying hard not to look like an escaped convict. The cannibalistic prison officer has left me with a limp. My left ankle throbs and buckles with every step. Looking behind me there is no sign of the security guards. I turn in to an adjoining, quieter alley. I need to find somewhere to rest and hide. *Everything* aches. Mouth, stomach and all internal tubing feels dry, hollow and raw. The cuts inside my cheeks have closed at last but the bitter taste of blood is still there.

I think of black puddings...

*

Awake. Night... Images saturate my aching head. It smells so good here. The scent helps my slowly rousing brain to remember... I'm hidden behind a set of wheelie bins at the back of an Indian restaurant. Empty crates and boxes are piled over and around me. The warm air billowing from the restaurant's kitchen vent keeps the cold at bay. I listen to the low gently rattling hum of the vent and breathe in the wafts of enticing, exotic flavours. I pull myself stiffly from the ground, dust myself down and try to think...

I need money and judging by the crusty puke, pebble dashing my clothes - a thorough wash and a whole new wardrobe.

3: pools

Detective Inspector Julian Craven sneezed and wiped his leaking nose. Despite three mugs of blackcurrant Lemsip and two packs of cherry Strepsils his throat still felt as though he'd swallowed and then regurgitated a cheese-grater. He hoped this was one of those twenty-four hour colds people talked about and not the beginnings of a nasty bout of flu. He checked his watch. This had to be the longest day of his life. Eleven hours had passed since he'd left for work after a typically hurried breakfast. His wife Lorna had refused to allow him to plant the customary goodbye peck on her cheek. He suspected this could be the first of several chaste nights. Who could blame her? Would he like to have some greying, sweaty, germ ridden, overweight fifty-four year old bloke with a false front tooth that didn't quite match its real partner, sneezing, coughing and dribbling snot over him? He had to admit the idea lacked romance.

His daughter had been in one hell of a mood at the breakfast table. He'd tried speaking to her, to get to the root of the problem but she remained sulkily silent. No doubt her brother had something to do with Rachael's rancour. Simon had been the polar opposite of his sister this morning; suspiciously chipper and alert as he readied himself for school without a murmur of complaint.

People keep saying what a wonderful experience it must be to have twins. Double the joy. One of nature's great miracles. Little do they know. For the most part they simply double the complications of an already complex life. Never more so than when they are a week away from their sixteenth birthday. He loves them of course but people do tend to throttle those they love the most. Murder statistics are proof of that. And then there are those strange, spooky little moments that only twins can indulge in... Perhaps he and Lorna had started their family too late in life and now the strain was taking its toll. Perhaps he was just being miserable because he was having a bad day and wasn't feeling so good.

Escaped prisoners, especially convicted murderers, were a public relations nightmare. Fortunately the prison governor had taken the brunt of the media glare so far but Craven knew it wouldn't be long before the press pack homed in on him like so many frenzied hyenas sniffing out a diet of sound bites and clichés. He hated the scaremongering halfwits but somehow he'd managed to garner a reputation for being media savvy. Craven could handle even the most obnoxious of reporters and the stare of a television camera didn't faze him in the least. No doubt this was why he had been asked to front yet another high profile case. He certainly would not have volunteered to take on such a thankless task. Even when the bastard was safely back behind bars there would be no warm glow of public gratitude to bask in because those scavenging hacks would take every given opportunity to remind them that he should never have been allowed to roam free in the first place. And they would be absolutely right.

Haig Dumfries had been on the run for over ten hours. Craven had used the time to visit the hospital to gather witness statements from the staff. The prison officers who were supposed to have been guarding Dumfries were useless. The first could barely stay awake thanks to an unwelcome dose of anaesthetic and the other kept rubbing his testicles. Very off-putting. That pretty nurse had caught his eye though. What was her name? Katie...? Lorna used to have a figure like that before the years and the twins buggered it up. Still, to be fair, she had lost weight recently and was beginning to draw looks from other men again.

Craven dug out a tissue, blew his nose and wished he'd called in sick. A stiff, chill breeze was sweeping in from the coast as he stood in the front garden of a Victorian villa which housed the local Conservative Club. He himself voted Liberal, the lesser of the three evils, always had and always will, though he had long given up any pretence that he might live to see them take the reins of power.

Craven was only half listening to the pompous old lady, his attention drawn more towards her impressive candy floss bouffant which absolutely refused to budge despite the wind. Serial hair-spray abuse he thought, then sneezed; startling the wrinkly face beneath.

'Excuse me. I'm sorry, Mrs... Mrs... erm...?' He noticed a single wayward strand dancing wildly in front of the old biddy's eyes. The longer he looked the more he wanted to pluck that maverick, quivering hair out by the root.

'Henshaw. Pollyanna Henshaw,' she answered sniffily. Over her shoulder Craven could see a police dog pissing in the flower bed beneath the club's front windows.

'This man had vomit over his clothes you say?'

'Yes. Filthy,' her padded shoulders shivered in disgust beneath her jacket. 'Positively *the* most absolutely *disgusting* individual it has ever been my misfortune to encounter. Scotch, you will not be surprised to learn. I can still smell the brute even now.'

Craven smiled and playfully wondered if she was accusing Dumfries of wearing cheap aftershave.

'Shall we go inside?'

He took Mrs Henshaw by the arm and gently ushered her along the path making sure she couldn't see the dog now defecating by the rose bushes.

They entered, passing an old dining table which acted as a reception desk behind which another old lady scanned through the pages of *Cake Decoration Monthly*. Craven sneezed again and cleaned his nose as they entered the lounge bar. They opted to occupy a small round table by the wall next to the radiator after Craven had checked to make sure the heater was functioning. The detective helped Mrs Henshaw into her comfy seat.

'I need a stiff drink to calm my nerves. Can I get you anything Inspector?'

'A coffee would be good.'

'Derek! A large G & T and a coffee if you please dear!' she hollered towards the vacant bar.

'Yes dear!' replied a voice from the storeroom beyond.

'Derek is my husband. Forty-three years and counting.'

'Congratulations.' Craven fished out his notebook. 'Now, if you could give me a full description of the man who raided the place. Give me as much detail as you can please.'

As soon as she opened her mouth Craven's mind began to drift again. The notebook was really no more than a prop. The pages of the little blue book were crammed with doodles and little sketches of the people he'd interviewed over the last year or more, interspersed with the occasional pertinent fact or telephone number. He tended to find that less than one tenth of what people had to say proved to be of any use. There were three other police officers in the bar talking to various club members including a young man wearing nothing but a pair of Calvin Klein briefs and a pair of brown Hush Puppies. He looked a little shell-shocked beneath his thick, slick backed hair, barely able to disguise his humiliation from the WPC questioning him.

Craven studied the portraits of Conservative leaders past and present lining the walls... *Talk about a rogue's gallery. This lot wouldn't look out of place on the walls of the Black Museum.*

'...Dirty, straggly blonde hair down to here,' Mrs Henshaw indicated by tapping her hands on her shoulders with an expression of severe distaste crinkling her brightly made up face. 'Pallid face, thin lips. bloodshot eyes... *Wild, manic* eyes... Late thirties, early forties I should imagine. You think people would know better at that age but I rather suspect he's had a deeply uncultured upbringing,' she said opening her expensive but tasteless little handbag. 'Tall. Perhaps six foot.'

'Is this the man?' Craven asked showing her a prison mugshot of Dumfries.

Mrs Henshaw took the picture and studied it briefly before tapping the image with one of her long, shocking pink fingernails, 'Oh yes that's him... Thank you Derek.'

Her elderly husband deposited their drinks on the table. Craven noticed his hands were trembling slightly and hoped for the old man's sake this was a symptom of stress and not Parkinson's. Derek turned back towards the bar without a word.

Mrs Henshaw took a sip from her iceless gin and tonic leaving a red lipstick kiss on the rim of the glass. She removed a silver cigarette case from her bag.

'Oh, and his *language*!' She rolled her eyes with a tut and shook her head, horrified. 'Absolutely dreadful. If he'd been my son I would have taken a good solid bar of carbolic soap to that shameful mouth. Appalling. Raving on about things he clearly had no understanding of. A labour voter I don't doubt. The kind of typical socialist thug that is bringing this country to its knees.' Mrs Henshaw paused to look wistfully at the only female Prime Minister hanging on the wall. Her bottom lip wavered briefly. 'They ought to be ashamed of themselves.'

She looked into Craven's eyes, He thought he saw a tear forming, 'All these years under a Labour government and look where it's got us. Total disarray. They are forcing their Euro claptrap on the masses. The ordinary man on the street does not have the nous to see through the propaganda. European integration is the greatest threat our nation has ever faced. It makes you wonder why we ever went to war Inspector. England does not need Europe. They need us, of course they do.'

Lowering her voice to a conspiratorial whisper she leaned in closer to Craven.

'This Government is dragging England through the mire, you only need to look at our youngsters to see that. No morals. No family values. No concept of social responsibility or the Greater Good. Their only ambition is to avoid employment at all costs and to squeeze as much as they can from the state in order to fund their druggy way of life. That's when they're not shooting or stabbing each other of course. This simply did *not* happen in my day. I blame that unholy racket they listen to. You know the thing I mean. That filth ridden noise all those black so-called singers try to pass off as music.'

Mrs Henshaw sat back, finally took a breath and allowed her fingers, shaking with emotion, to slot a cigarette into her puckered mouth. The glossy crimson lips clamped tight around the butt.

Craven looked around the room trying not to smile. 'Back to the matter at hand. I hear he somehow managed to rob your club armed with nothing more than a corkscrew?'

Mrs Henshaw took a long, hard drag before expelling a cloud of grey smoke through her shrunken mouth like a kettle letting off steam.

'It was quite a large one,' she said. 'He snatched it from Derek.'

Craven turned to a fresh page. 'Now, Mrs Henshaw. I need to get this whole incident clear in my mind. I need you to tell me *exactly* what happened, in order, from the moment the man first set foot in here.'

'Well he just barged in through there,' she pointed her cigarette to the door. 'Everyone was simply relaxing, chatting, enjoying a nice peaceful drink. I mean that is until this, this... madman stormed in swearing...' she pressed her blue eyelids shut and shook her head again with another tut. 'It was shocking. It was the kind of foul-mouthed gutter talk best left on the football terraces,' she opened her eyes sucking in another lungful.

'I understand how distressing it must've been for you but I really do need to know exactly what he said - word for word.'

Mrs Henshaw shifted in her seat looking very perturbed, 'I really don't know if I can...'

'Please, Mrs Henshaw. It could be of vital importance to us. Please try,' Craven pleaded. Obviously it was not of vital importance to have her repeat Dumfries' words verbatim but how could he pass up this opportunity to have a little fun?

'I'll try,' she sighed with a look of resignation. Craven settled back to enjoy the show. 'He came storming in, held his arms out wide and shouted; *"Ladies and gentlemen, I have a stomach full of bleach! Please excuse me if I throw up over your nice parquet flooring!"* - I thought it was a strange practical joke at first and maybe he was going to turn out to be a stripper or something equally uncouth. Anyway he dashed over to the bar - that's when I noticed the state of his clothes; covered in... *sick*. And the smell!' She shuddered, 'Eugh... Then he leapt over the counter, pushed poor Derek out of his way, opened the till and emptied out all the money.'

'*"You lot have been robbing the poor to feed the rich for far too long so I thought I'd do my bit to redress the balance."* - The yob then had the affront to pour himself a good quality single malt. He jumped back to this side of the bar and just stood there, quite brazenly, sipping his drink as if he hadn't a care in the world. I was dumbstruck as we all were. To top it all he then had the audacity to say; - *"What the f... What the... ff... ffff,"'* she stammered.

'Please Mrs Henshaw,' Craven prompted. 'I know it's difficult but it really is essential I hear everything *exactly* as it happened. Please try.'

Mrs Henshaw braced herself, tapped the lengthening ash from her cigarette into the ashtray and went for it. *'"What the fuck are you lot looking at you bunch of fucking Tory twits."'*

'You sure that last word was twits? Not twats?'

The old lady defended herself petulantly. 'Listen Inspector, he was barely comprehensible. It was all I could do to make out *anything* he said with that coarse Glaswegian accent of his. So you will excuse me if I make the odd mistake in translation.'

'Sorry,' Craven managed to say between sneezes. Blowing his nose he noticed the CCTV camera tucked high in the far corner of the room. 'You're doing a grand job Mrs Henshaw. Please, carry on.'

'Yes. Well... It was then that dear Derek prodded him with the corkscrew. I thought he was very brave. *"Now look here..."* Derek said to him but that was as far as he got. This ruffian casually took the corkscrew from Derek's hand and started off on another rant, yelling at the top of his voice, his face red and furious; - *"As you may have gathered I am from North of the border where you Tories are about as welcome as a turd in a bath. And would you like to know why? Well I will fucking tell you why! Because you are a bunch of arrogant, self-serving, conceited, smarmy, smug, hypocritical wankers! -* "There must be no Scottish Parliament,*" you cried. -* "No devolution! It will end in disaster!" *- Then, after a general election which left you without a single MP north of Hadrian's Wall, you thanked God for the Scottish Parliament because it gave you a voice in Scotland's affairs. A voice you don't fucking deserve. In a Parliament you tried to fucking prevent! You lot must honestly believe the rest of us are as thick as pig* *shit. Democracy really does scare you people shitless doesn't it?"'*

Mrs Henshaw, her hands still fraught with nerves, stubbed out her cigarette and promptly lit another. 'That's pretty close to the drivel he was spouting. I can't claim to be one hundred percent accurate but I do pride myself on my memory. Not that anything he said was worth remembering. Angry as a swarm of bees he was though. I saw spittle fly from his mouth more than once. Quite frightening... He only paused at that point because he seemed to be in some pain. I saw him grimace and rub his ankle. It must have been very sore because he even took off his shoe and sock.'

'Can you remember what foot it was?'

'Left. Definitely his left.'

Craven jotted this down.

'I could see the bruise from where I was sitting over in the television area. It looked nasty. He ordered Derek to give him a bottle of vodka which he poured all over his ankle. That was when Tom over there, courageously rushed at him,' she said raising her glass towards the virtually naked young man nodding steadily to the WPC. Someone had loaned Tom the use of a jacket which had helped clear the blushes from his subdued face.

'Unfortunately the hooligan was too quick,' she sighed. 'He grabbed Tom by the throat and held the corkscrew to his eye. My husband tried to reach the telephone but he was seen; - *"Touch that fucking phone and I'll pluck Young Winston's eyes out by the fucking roots!"* - That's what the lunatic shouted at him. And he meant it! I think we were all absolutely petrified at this juncture. In fear for our lives. He was capable of anything. I think he was high on that cracking cocaine.'

'What happened to Tom?' asked Craven, suspecting that dear old Pollyanna was starting to enjoy playing Haig's role, especially when it came to the more colourful words and phrases.

'I couldn't believe it. Even though he was held by the throat and on the verge of losing his sight, Tom was still brave enough to try and put the yob in his place... What was it he asked him? Oh yes - *"I don't see what's so democratic about Scottish MP's being allowed to vote on English issues. Where's the fairness in that?"* - Very well put I thought. So brave. But you can't reason with someone like that. They simply don't have the intelligence to fully comprehend the argument. That was it, off he went on another mindless tirade; - *"There's always someone,"* - he shouted - *"Even in a situation like this, there is always one loudmouthed, know-it-all, smart arse who thinks they've come up with the definitive retort. Listen pal we've had to put up with English MP's fucking up Scotland for three hundred years. So why not let us fuck you up for a change? Look at you all. Look at this fucking club! Newsflash – Queen Victoria's dead! Wake up people! The empire has gone! Deal with it and move on! England is just a daft wee nation populated by xenophobic twits..."* - sorry - *"twats like yourselves!"'*

'I was getting quite irate by what he was saying I can tell you. What was it he said next? Good God that's right. He pointed to Margaret's portrait and raved; - *"And as for that fascist bitch. Don't get me fucking started!"* – Then he swallowed his whisky and ordered Derek to pour him another. Then he said, erm... what was it, ah - *"The sooner Scotland becomes an independent, neutral republic within the EU the better."* - Well that was it. I'd had quite enough. I couldn't bear any more of this hogwash. I had to make a stand. So I stood up, quite deliberately and I told him in no uncertain terms; - "You Scotch are all the same! Ignoramuses one and all! Scotland would fall flat on its face without England."'

'What did he say to that?'

'He told me to shut the fuck up.'

Craven had to chew on his lower lip to prevent himself from laughing.

'I have *never* been so, so... pissed off!' Mrs Henshaw fumed, 'I am not accustomed to being spoken to in such a manner. But what could I do? I couldn't do a thing. He had poor Tom by the neck. We were all horrified when he forced Tom to remove his clothes. For one horrible moment I thought he was going to ask for his underpants! Please God! Leave the man with some dignity, I thought to myself. He even took

Tom's socks. Can you believe that? His *socks!*' The old lady shook her head incredulous, as if this was the crime to end all crimes.

'He stuffed the clothes under his arm and... well, what he said next, that's when he went too far. I simply could not sit idly by and allow him to belittle Her Majesty.' Her eyes blazed as she turned to look at the portrait of The Queen hanging behind the bar.

'Why? What did he say?'

'The ape noticed Tom was facing her portrait and said; -"*Staring at Queenie's face give you a hard-on does it son? Well let me tell you something about our beloved head of state. She's about as much use as a third bollock.*"

'Believe me Inspector, I am not one for losing my temper but I have to admit I was positively seething at this point. "How dare you! How dare you talk about Her Majesty like that! She's the finest monarch this country has ever had! So show some respect!" I yelled at him. Not that it made the slightest difference. He just told me to relax. - "*Don't get that rusty gusset of yours in a twist sweetheart.*" - Then suddenly, he leapt from table to table, completely deranged by now, all the way to the door, where he paused and smiled. *Smiled* at us.

One of the chaps started after him but had to retreat when that lunatic pointed the corkscrew very threateningly; - "*Don't fucking try it,*" - he said. Then it was; - "*Shocking isn't it? Crime in this country is spiralling out of control. You shouldn't stand for it. I suggest you write a stern letter of complaint to your MP! Goodnight ladies and gentlemen! Many thanks for your time and consideration in this matter. You are indeed my lords and ladies, members of a club run by counts for counts.*"'

'Counts?' Craven checked, puzzled.

'Yes. Counts. Makes no sense to me either but that's what it sounded like.'

'Are you sure it wasn't – cu...?' A violent sneeze cut Craven short.

'Bless you.'

'Thank you.'

A length of ash fell from Mrs Henshaw's cigarette bursting greyly

61

on the lap of her mauve slacks. She brushed the mess from her thighs absent mindedly. 'Then the swine ran off. We all rushed to aid poor Tom and Derek and that's when we called the police.'

'Thank you very much indeed Mrs Henshaw. I realise how difficult that must've been for you,' Craven said, blowing his nose. 'One more thing. How much money did he make off with?'

'One hundred and seventy-seven pounds exactly. He took all the notes and pound coins.'

Craven wrote the figure down in his notebook beside the words; - 'left foot'. The detective smiled at the caricature of Mrs Henshaw he'd sketched on the same page.

He thanked her again and assured Mrs Henshaw that the 'cowardly psychopath' would indeed be swiftly apprehended to feel the full force of the law bearing down on him - and yes it was indeed a pity that capital punishment was no more than a fond memory - after which he said his goodbyes and left the formidable matriarch to fuss over her fellow members.

Craven stepped outside the Conservative Club in time to feel the first few drops of rain. He looked at his watch.   Time to get a move on. He wrapped himself tight in his coat against the raw wind and laughed quietly, remembering the refined old lady swearing like a trooper.

He looked forward to meeting Haig Dumfries.

4:   bruises

'Happy birthday wee man!' Dad beamed, kneeling down to my level. 'Ten years old eh? You'll be chasin' the lassies soon.'

Dad only ever called me "Haig" when he was telling me off, which wasn't often, and on those rare occasions when he did, it was always at Mum's insistence. Aside from these half-hearted rebuffs, to him I was either "wee man" or "son". Conversely Mum would usually call me "Haig"; "wee man" was saved for those infrequent displays of affection which would occur during fleeting, relaxed moods - little oases in her otherwise highly strung existence - or when she was talking to a friend in my presence and felt the need to put on a show of familial contentment. "Son" was used when she wanted me to nip downstairs to the little shop to buy her fags - a task guaranteed to piss me off as soon as she asked because for some reason the shop would suddenly seem miles away in my mind and would take hours if not days, to reach. I would set off in a huff after telling her that smoking was disgusting and would kill her (not because I was particularly concerned with the health issue but because I couldn't be bothered to go) only to return three minutes later all smiles when Mum would give me the two pence change as a reward.

Mum and I always seemed to know exactly what buttons to press to wind each other up and I often felt that she was a wee bit too free with her punishment. Quite often I would receive a slap across the back of the head or a stinging skelp on the backside, sometimes hard enough to make me weep, forcing me to let her know just how much I hated her whilst feeling the huge weight of the world's injustice crushing down on my shoulders with each snuffling sob. Then I'd find myself thinking about Danny and count myself lucky.

Hindsight tells me I deserved these clouts because I could, when the mood took me, be a right cheeky wee bastard.

On this occasion however, my face was cut in half by a grin so rigid I couldn't speak. I even let the bizarre comment about lassies pass me by. My eyes did not deviate from the football Dad was handing to me.

A moment before, while his hands were still behind his back, I had been annoyed with him. He'd forgotten to bring back those tank photographs again not to mention the Bayern Munich shirt. All that disappeared the instant my present was revealed. This was a proper football, not one of those cheap plastic jobs which wobbled like a balloon in the faintest breeze. This was leather. Glossy white leather with proper stitching. It was heavy and nearly slipped through my hands when I first held it. Why in God's name would I want to chase after lassies when I could chase after a football? *This* football.

I think the word *"thanks"* rustled somewhere near the back of my throat. Gratitude was not an easy thing to display. To show it would have meant dropping my guard and thus allowing my parents the chance to pounce on my weakness and use it to bribe me into doing more room-tidying and extra cigarette and milk runs. It had to be remembered at all times that there was an ongoing conflict between us. Parents were the devious grown-up enemy, ready to attack at any moment. To become a prisoner of war in their hands would be a catastrophe.

My Gran who lived half a mile further up the High Street had bought me a Celtic top whereas my paternal grandparents in Stirling had sent me a pair of proper football boots (the ones with screw-in studs not the inferior moulded variety) so this was turning into a great day. I wanted to rush up to the park and challenge everyone to a game but then Dad offered to take me fishing.

Even before we reached the shores of Loch Fad I knew we were up to no good. Making our way across the field sloping down to the loch, stepping over the soft, deep, ploughed furrows of earth, Dad would look furtively through the trees bordering the water's edge keeping an eye out for the gamekeeper. We were poaching and not for the first time.

My heart would always beat a little faster on these dare-devil adventures aided by my habit of pretending I was actually joining Dad on a secret army mission. According to Dad the consequences of being caught didn't bear thinking about. He told me that the last person to be captured by the gamekeeper was hung, drawn and quartered in Guildford Square in front of the whole town as a warning to anyone else who may have been tempted to poach from his patch.

I had been taught how to use the rod but could only manage to cast the spinner a frustratingly short distance. Twice, due to my lack of co-ordination, I failed to reel the line back in quick enough and snagged the spinners on the rocks where, despite Dad's best efforts to salvage them, they had to be sacrificed. With only one spinner left Dad took sole charge of the rod (his casts seemed to fly for miles before eventually plopping into the still black water towards the middle of the loch) leaving me to construct the rock pool in readiness for any fish we caught.

I was quite happy to perform this task instead of the actual fishing because; a) it was fun and - b) with my poor casting technique there was always a nagging worry at the back of my mind that the spinner's hooks might embed themselves into my eye, pluck it out and hurl it into the water to become fish bait.

The rock pool's first tenant was a small perch. Dad warned me to be careful when picking it up because the dorsal fin of a perch was capable of springing out flick-knife style, jabbing needle sharp spines into anything that had a hold of it. I sat down mesmerised, admiring its colours. Orange and silver scales glinting in the sunlight. The iridescent fish flicked around its prison, prodding at small gaps between the stones but I was confident that my handiwork was escape proof. However, this fish would not receive the death penalty, merely a short custodial sentence. Perch, no matter what size they were, didn't taste very good I was told. It was trout we were after.

Studying the perch's eye, I was reminded of the decapitated mackerel head. There seemed to be a subtle difference between a dead eye and living one. I couldn't quite decide what it was. The wounds inflicted by the sparrow-hawk five days earlier, were healing nicely - just a few scratches lining my shoulders and a meaty scab on my cheek. I looked out over the loch, through the swarms of midges dancing on the surface teasing the odd fish into a leaping attack, to the hill opposite. Halfway up the slope, flanked and backed by trees, stood a big, dull white house all on its own. The first floor windows glared brilliant reflected orange sunlight into my squinting eyes. I could barely make out any detail save for its neatly manicured lawn which trailed down from the front door to the shore half a mile across the water from me.

I wondered who lived in that huge house, in such a spacious setting with such a beautiful view and felt a pang of jealousy coupled with bitterness at having to live in a cramped, ancient flat that didn't even have its own toilet, where I had to use a bucket at night because the lights in the close weren't working. I could be pretty sure the kids that lived in that house didn't have to go to their gran's every Sunday to have a bath like I did. In fact a house like that probably had two bathrooms which meant they wouldn't even have to share. I was fed up having to share a bath with Joe especially after he jobbied in the bathwater, leaving me slipping and sliding in a panic to escape the brown mines bobbing towards me while he just sat there and laughed.

'Here we go wee man!' Dad exclaimed wrestling with the reel, 'This is a big one!'

I watched the creaking rod bend in a perfect semi-circle towards the sparkling shallows and followed the taut line to where it cut jerky, distressed patterns through the surface.

Dad heaved the struggling fish over my head and on to a patch of grass. He was right. The thing was as long as my arm. Gasping and flapping, it curled its silvery brown muscular body, trying to swim away through the air.

'Ya beauty!' Dad smiled. His eyes wide and alight, were fixed on his catch. He teased the hooks from the trout's mouth and, gripping the fish in both hands, brained its skull against a rock. His joy changed to alarm when we heard the sound of a distant motor.

Some way off across the loch the gamekeeper's dinghy was powering in our direction. Dad stuffed the fish inside a carrier bag, snatched the rod, grabbed my hand and led the way back through the trees to the field. We stopped running only when Dad felt sure we'd put enough distance between ourselves and our pursuer... Then I remembered.

I hurried back down the rutted field to the loch ignoring Dad's anxious attempts to call me back. I reached the shoreline and saw the gamekeeper heading away having given up the chase but then he spotted me and raised a furious fist. Only when he turned the prow of his boat towards me did I realise I was taking one hell of a risk. My neck felt the tightening of a phantom rope and the fine hairs beneath my belly-button prickled as I imagined the executioner's knife slicing open my stomach and my innards spilling out for all of Rothesay to see.

I kneeled beside the rock pool and removed the largest stone. The perch had a clear run to freedom but seemed reluctant to leave. The fish raised its bright orange dorsal fin displaying the defensive spines. I dipped my hand into the cold, fresh water and gently touched the matching tail. The perch took the hint and shot off through the opening. I saw it shimmer briefly before disappearing into the murk then turned and ran.

When I caught up with Dad and explained why I had gone back he just laughed, shook his head and ruffled my hair.

The brown trout weighed in at six pounds. Plenty to go round our fold-away dining table. The fish provided a tasty meal spoiled only by the number of bones I had to pluck from my mouth. Anxious to go up the park to christen my new football, I left what remained of the trout's corpse to swim in its sea of melted butter, made my excuses and sped outside.

I turned into Russell Street in the warm late afternoon sunshine. Walking quickly between the imposing sandstone tenements I spent some time trying to remove a stubborn fish bone jammed in my back teeth. At first I tried to work it out with my tongue but if anything I only managed to push the fragment into my gum. I had to stop and give the problem my full attention. I shoved a couple of fingers in my mouth but couldn't quite get a grip on the pliable, plasticky sliver.

With saliva coating most of my hand I held the irritant in place with my tongue until my thumbnail finally eased the bone free. I inspected the tiny bone glued by spit to my fingertip. I thought I could taste blood. I wiped my fingers on my trousers and craned my neck looking up to the windows of the third floor flat where Danny lived.

Stepping into the cool shade of the close I bounced the ball, testing it. It passed with flying colours, slamming loudly against the stone floor and springing, firm and true, back to my hands. Danny's bike occupied its usual spot at the foot of the stairwell. I carried on up the three floors studying the football's logo with pride.

I could hear the muffled angry shouts coming from Danny's home even before I stepped on to the third floor landing. I paused outside the door and seriously considered going home while I picked at one of the screws securing the nameplate.

- A. CRARAE - The man the name referred to was raging behind that door. A never ending stream of violent spite. I had forgotten Danny's dad had the week off work. I heard a muted slap. Panic gripped my heart. *Oh God. Not again!* Then something smashed.

'Stop greetin'! Are ye a wee lassie uh!?' The splenetic voice suddenly sounded much closer to the door.

Slap...

'Are ye a wee poofter?!'

Slap...

'Ye want me tae fuckin' kill ye, eh?!'

Thump...

Danny screamed pitifully...

I slapped the letterbox as hard as I could.

The yelling ceased abruptly. The flat fell silent... Then I heard a sob from Danny, followed by what sounded like a dull thud. The sobs stopped... Heavy footfalls softened by carpet. The speed and sheer ferocity with which the door flew open startled me. The breeze rushed through my hair as the air was sucked inside to meet Mr Crarae's massive frame. His purple face shone greasily while his jaundiced eyes stabbed daggers into mine.

'Is Danny in, please?' I gulped.

'Naw!' he gnarled and was about to slam the door in my face when Danny hurtled through, shot past me and hammered on down the stairs in a blur. The next fraction of a second saw instinct take command. It must have been the gleam of murderous wrath in Mr Crarae's eyes when he realised what was happening which made it crystal clear I could not allow Danny to be dragged back inside that flat. I was only partially aware of my right foot shooting out to connect hard and true with the man's gonads.

Long after I had actually kicked him I could still feel the sensation of the impact on my foot. It felt like a perfectly struck penalty. Eyes bulging, mouth twisted and locked in a mute scream while his hands cupped his groin, Mr Crarae crumpled to his knees.

'Ya wee shitebag!' he shrieked almost comically, reaching out a jittery hand, trying to grasp me.

I tore down those stairs like I was chasing Olympic gold. Even so, to me it was as if the concrete had been freshly laid and I was sinking ever deeper into each spongy step. My legs felt as though I'd borrowed them from an arthritic elephant. Danny was a full flight ahead of me. Convinced I could feel the very tips of Mr Crarae's fingernails tingling the back of my neck I bounded down two steps at a time. I stumbled, managed to keep to my feet but dropped the ball which caught the lip of a step and zipped down, zinging past Danny's hair missing him by inches. He must have thought his dad was throwing things at him because he found a further spurt of acceleration from somewhere and increased the gap between us.

With the whole tenement resounding to our clattering shoes Danny reached the bottom first and snatched his bike. Seconds later I skidded across the close, grabbed the football before it tried to roll out the back-yard and sprinted after my friend.

I finally caught up with Danny outside in the intense, low-slung sunlight before he could hop on his bike. His tired, hoarse voice ordered me to get on the back. His lower lip was split and bleeding, his eyes swollen and wet. The tears matted the hair to his cheeks and

69

temples. I shoved the ball up my jumper and climbed aboard. Standing upright, his sturdy legs shunted like pistons peddling us to safety.

Rothesay Bay, dotted with yachts and dinghies, calmly spread small, restless waves to all shores while we cruised along the promenade. We passed the imposing Glenburn Hotel perched high on the hillside looking out to sea, a reminder of the faded splendour of Rothesay's Victorian heyday.

We swapped places at Ascog but my weaker legs struggled to settle into a rhythm and only managed to transport us as far as Kerrycroy. Both exhausted, we walked up the steep road curling around the woods which we knew shrouded the Marquess Of Bute's Mount Stuart estate.

When the hill finally subsided, Danny took the handlebars and sent us coasting all the way down to Kilchattan Bay.

My feet were wet. Also; shoes socks and trousers.

By the time we arrived at The Buzz Building the sun had been relegated by the full moon, its milky blue light guided us towards the cave entrance. The flooding tide forced us to wade urgently through knee-high water. Danny had long since dumped the bike when the terrain had made it more of a hindrance than a help. I remained pregnant with my birthday present still hoping for a kickabout on the cave floor when the tide receded. We could hear the increasingly voluminous buzzing long before we actually entered.

Danny didn't bother to remove his sodden shoes and, unusually for him, he hadn't even bothered to gather any firewood along the way. The sorry pile I had managed to collect was drying out around the hearth where I was burning what remained of our emergency fuel supply. He even left me to light all the candles; something else he normally relished.

The buzz faded to a soothing hiss... I offered Danny a Cola Cube. He declined and continued to stare silently into the mesmerising flames.

Not a single syllable had escaped Danny's lips since we left Russell

Street. Try as I might I knew I would not be capable of finding the words to comfort him so I opted to keep my mouth shut. I watched him closely. He was of course, wearing his school uniform, which he wore whether it was a school day or not - only the tie was missing at weekends and during the holidays. The knees of the black trousers had both been repaired at some time and his navy-blue jumper was a bit on the baggy side (a condition not helped by his fondness for tugging the cuffs over his hands).

Then I examined his face. Dark bruises pooled around his cheekbones and jaw. His eyes, puffed a moist, veiny red, reflected the glow of the fire. The cut on his lower lip had scabbed up. There was a trail of dried blood painted beneath his nose. He opened his mouth, I saw more blood staining his tongue and a chipped tooth. Danny pulled at another loose tooth and winced. It came away between his fingers without putting up much of a fight. He looked at it for a moment before casually dropping the tooth into the water which had swollen to its fullest extent within the cave.

'Why... does...?' I swallowed hard, unable to finish.

Danny knew what I wanted to ask and without shifting his gaze from the fire, responded with a slow shrug of his shoulders and a heavy sigh. Then he jerked upright as if suddenly remembering something and thrust a hand deep into a pocket. He withdrew a small, crumpled, brown paper bag and handed it to me.

'Happy birthday Haig,' he said quietly and without waiting for my reaction, he curled up by the fire and fell asleep. I saw a rash peppered with a necklace of bruises ringed around his exposed neck. My hand closed tightly around the bag and its contents.

I didn't know why I woke or what prompted me to open my eyes but when I did I found everything ached. Joints, muscles, bones... *everything*. I had fallen asleep on my left arm and now I couldn't feel it. I pulled the useless limb out from under me and tried to bring it back to life by bending the elbow back and forth. The weird but acute numb agony slowly subsided. Sensation began to trickle down my arm, along the skin and through the muscles, veins and arteries as if my brain had belatedly given the order to release the valves and let the blood flow back. Then came the cramp. I sat up and breathed in sharply through my teeth trying to relieve the pain. A little positive thought at the back of my mind told me to be thankful I wasn't standing in the playground where anyone who was discovered to be suffering from cramp is promptly pounced upon by a whole army of bastards determined to squeeze the affected area, inflicting as much pain as possible while claiming to be only trying to help.

The discomfort gradually dissipated to the point where I could at last take an interest in what was happening around me. The fire had reduced to a few short, stubborn, pulsing flames eating away at the charred remnants crackling in the ashes. The few candles still burning guttered in the recesses around The Buzz Building's walls. The hole in the ceiling told me it was still dark outside. I tried to work out how long I'd been asleep. The tide was on the turn. The noise was starting.

Danny stood at the far end of the ledge peering down into the water. There were silent tears trickling down his impassive face. I felt awkward and unsure. I tried to ask if he was okay but a yawn took the question's place.

Danny jumped into the water. The splash rang out like an explosion. What was he doing? I couldn't believe he felt the need to go for a swim. It was freezing in there. What about our pact with the fish? I expected his face to pop back up instantly with that grin of his challenging me to do the same. Was this just another one of his dare-devil stunts?

... Nothing...

The concentric circles rippled out from where my friend had entered the water to touch every corner of the cave.

... Nothing...

A morbid dread shivered over my skin.

I scrambled to my feet and stumbled to where Danny had been standing. I dropped to my knees frantically scanning the unyielding surface. The water shifted softly, black and thick like crude oil. It was difficult to see where the liquid ended and the rock began. The flitting candlelight revealed nothing. I felt the crawling fear scraping at the floor of my stomach, grinding my heart and crushing my lungs in its gelid, cloying grip. I thrust my hands into the sea and wished pathetically for the water to part like curtains and allow me a better view. It felt like hours had passed since he'd vanished into the molten shadows.

The awesome noise reached a crescendo even more foreboding than usual and with no moral support, it terrified me. For the first time in all my visits to The Buzz Building I felt truly trapped, threatened and at the mercy of whatever monster had captured me in its lair. Maybe I was already inside the creature's mouth. Maybe it had been biding its time waiting for the right moment to devour us. I expected the ragged teeth protruding from the walls of that mouth to close in and grind me into a blood and bone sauce. I prayed for God to wake up in my bed with Mum telling me I'd been having a bad dream...

I ran around the ledge, frenetic, quaking with terror. *I saw him...!* Or at least I saw the pale smear of his hand drifting just below the surface. I edged as close to the water as I dared, reached in and grasped his hand. It felt like frozen rubber. His fingers did not react. I felt the weight of his body but couldn't see anything beyond his elbow. The ululating static saturated my ears like never before. Tormenting me. Trying to push me into the water... I pulled. I pulled until my muscles and tendons seared and my skin stretched so taut it felt ready to tear with the effort. Danny's hand remained stationary, moving not a millimetre closer despite everything. I jammed my knees into the jutting, flint-edged rocks to gain more leverage. The pain chiselled into my flesh as the pumice scraped at my shins.

A powerful force tugged at Danny as though something was biting huge chunks from his body. I imagined those fish tearing and stripping away his flesh but still I couldn't see anything in the pitch void beyond Danny's ghostly forearm. A shockwave of panic consumed me. Was I to be next? I pulled even harder until I thought I was going to faint with the strain.

My wrists cracked. Veins and arteries sang out in protest. My arms began to spasm. The undertow twisted and rolled my friend until, as though tired of toying with me in an uneven tug of war, a sudden surge almost dislocated my shoulder and yanked his hand clean out of mine. I screamed as the rock cut and rasped deep into my knees, stopping me from being pulled into the depths to join him. In an instant the dark completely engulfed the pallid wave of Danny's hand.

And he was gone...

I waited. Prayed. Wished. Hoped. But the sea revealed nothing more. The longer I stared into it the more it became like a mirror in some grim fairy tale. It seemed to taunt me and refused to let me face reality displaying instead all the wishful thinkings of my imagination... Danny was lost. And no amount of dreaming was going to haul him alive and well from the deep.

I stretched painfully upright. Eyes stinging with tears continued their forlorn search. Time slipped with the water level and eventually my thoughts began to drift to more practical lines. The uncomfortable realisation of what might happen next filled me with a hollow dread. It was sorely tempting to take the easy way out. To leap into the retreating tide and let it wash me away from having to face the inevitable, rending aftermath and the wrenching memory of a tragic death. I wanted to escape the repercussions, the anger, the blame, guilt... confusion. I leaned over the water and saw my reflection flicker surreally. Two tears fell and sped towards their reflected counterparts. The real and unreal tears met in the middle to obliterate my features.

The buzz faded. Past its prime. A candle surrendered leaving only two to keep up the fight. There was nothing to do but wait. Wait until the water drained away. Garlands of seaweed began to emerge, followed by clusters of mussels. I shivered with trepidation. What else would the ebb tide reveal? My mind fluttered with visions of what I might find on the cave floor. I imagined Danny's bloated body, bruised and cut with seaweed trailing from his hair but not enough to hide his crushed skull. I imagined crabs snipping at his flesh and crawling into gaping wounds in his torso where eels slithered between

74

exposed ribs. I imagined dark cavities instead of eyeballs seething with sand-hoppers while rag-worms burrowed into his mouth. All this as I stood there so rigid it was as though I had been subsumed by the vitrified lava of The Buzz Building itself.

Tense. Expectant. I watched the imperceptible subsidence of the sea until I was staring at damp sand.

The first hint of daylight seeped through the entrance accompanied by a blustering breeze. I heard the wind gust through the hole above. I waited for the gloom to retreat and then descended gingerly to the cave floor. I searched the cold, wet sand and rocks and found nothing. I nervously checked every alcove and hollow. Danny's body was nowhere to be seen. I didn't know whether to feel relieved or heartbroken.

I sat down on the sand facing the entrance. My eyes adjusted to the brightness beyond to where the last clawing trails of the sea retreated along the channel cut deep in the rock. The shrill cries of sea-birds began to filter in with the draught.

The night's events rolled over me in merciless detail and, overwhelmed with abject despair, I started to cry like I'd never cried before.

I had never felt so completely alone.

5: chances

Nick Dodds wanted to put his fist through the television screen. He could not believe what he was seeing and hearing. The '*Look South*' reporter had just informed him that Haig Dumfries, the very man who had brutally murdered his wife ten years ago almost to the very day, had escaped.

Escaped! What the fuck was going on?! What was wrong with these people?! Nick's ire intensified when the television cut to some smug bastard from the Sussex Constabulary dishing out bland assurances about solid leads and a swift recapture. This Detective Inspector Julian Craven character was clearly an inept arsehole but Nick hung on every word... It was believed that Dumfries may be heading back to Scotland... (A base instinct tried to grab his attention - an inkling; the germ of an idea...) Then with a jab straight through Nick's heart the reporter retold the story of Cathy's murder. They even displayed a picture of her. The one he had supplied to the police at the time. It was his favourite photograph of her, one he'd taken only a couple of months after they'd started going out with each other. She looked flawless. An unrestrained, loving smile straight into the lens, straight into Nick. His chest throbbed with the hurt.

They showed a mugshot of Dumfries. Expressionless and malign. Nick wasn't interested in the fucker's background or life history. He was only interested in seeing him suffer. Prison had always been too good for that sick sack of shit.

An idea took root and squeezed aside his initial fury. This was an opportunity. A blessing in disguise. If the prison service couldn't give this prick what he deserved then it was up to him to track Dumfries down and exact *proper* revenge. To mete out *proper* justice.

Yes. Perhaps God existed after all. Nick ransacked his bookcase becoming increasingly annoyed when he couldn't find what he was looking for. Then he stopped and smiled. He was being an idiot.

The road atlas was under the passenger seat of his car where it always had been of course.

Time to pack...

6: ashes

Forty years and two days after my birth I am sitting in a burger joint facing out across the concourse at Euston station. Everyone seems in such a hurry. Anxious faces scour the Departures /Arrivals boards. Unfortunately I am still several hundred miles short of my eventual destination but progress has been made. I feel so much more relaxed. Twenty pence it cost to enter the toilets. Twenty pence for a good thorough washing and cleansing session. Twenty pence very well spent.

It's a blessed relief to feel clean again. After scrubbing my skin raw and virtually boil washing my hair in one of the sinks I'm pretty sure I don't smell so bad now. Everything still aches though. I don't think I've ever had so many bruises. I feel like I've taken part in a human pinball experiment. I need more sleep. I think I managed about ten minutes before I woke up inside the freight train squealing and rattling its way through South London. The taxi driver who brought me here told me I stank like a dead skunk's arse and refused to take me anywhere at first. Forty quid persuaded the bastard otherwise. I sniff the back of my hand…

Soap...

There is a train to Glasgow leaving in forty minutes. It's a tempting offer but I think I'll make a little detour before heading home. A quick trip to Milton Keynes to surprise my wee brother. I'm tempted to buy another chicken burger for the journey as, I have to confess, the one I've just had tasted fucking divine. Even the fries went down a treat and I'm confident the coffee will cool to a safe drinking temperature before the day is through.

I feel the corkscrew in my pocket and smile. What a night! The raid on the Tory club is little more than a blur now. That's the second time the mental Jock routine has paid off. I'm starting to enjoy the role though I think I may have gone a touch overboard with my cleaning fluid induced rants. Can't recall what I said but I'm pretty sure I got a few things off my chest. And if the truth were known, if I hadn't been flying high on a cocktail capable of killing all known germs then I don't think I would have been able to threaten that carefully groomed young executive with the same conviction. He only has himself to blame of course for coming at me. Unlucky for him but luckily for me he was about my size and I desperately needed a change of clothes. His Hugo Boss suit, which still has a trace of expensive aftershave, feels good and looks good. Nice matching black shirt as well. Pity his shoes didn't fit so I'm stuck with my tatty old brogues. I briefly considered his boxer shorts until I saw the moist dot blotting the top of his bulge. Better to have left the man with some dignity anyway.

Afterwards, with the Young Tory's outfit under my arm, I ran aimlessly for a mile or more until I found myself on waste ground. Feeling sick and exhausted I took shelter inside the burnt out shell of a Volkswagen Beetle. I watched a train slowly approach the freight depot on the far side of the deserted wasteland. Then I think I must have fallen asleep. The next thing I remember was the sound of dogs barking not so very far away. I knew I was pressed for time. I had no choice.

Slipping through a gaping hole in the depot's perimeter fence I sprinted towards an ageing goods-train crawling away from the sidings. I leapt aboard and scrambled inside one of the empty containers. Once inside I was glad to swap my vomit spattered shirt and jeans for the clean clothes but not so pleased at having no roof on my classless compartment. Mercifully the rain eased and I settled back to enjoy the journey.

I watched Brighton's glittering lights melt away into the horizon where a couple of helicopters circled the skies. One of the distant specks hovered over the waste ground casting out a searchlight while the old diesel locomotive grumbled onwards several miles up the track. Finally I could relax.

I discovered the cigarettes as I bedded down. I felt the pack pressing against my side and found them in the inside pocket of the jacket along with a disposable lighter. I checked the other pockets hoping to find a wallet stuffed full of bank-notes. No such luck. Then I remembered the note. I couldn't believe I'd almost forgotten it! I rescued the precious slip of tatty damp paper from the backside pocket of my old jeans and quickly stuffed it away before the drizzle caused more damage.

Unable to resist the temptation I lit a cigarette and took to smoking like a natural. No coughing or spluttering just instant stress relief. I read the health warnings on the pack. My heart was buggered anyway so I couldn't have cared less. I lay back and puffed into the featureless sky and remembered Danny's death.

Danny's body was discovered wedged into an outcrop a short but perilous walk along the shore from The Buzz Building a few hours after I'd plucked up the courage to return to Kilchattan Bay where I reported the 'accident'. The police questioned me relentlessly but sensitively. I kept my solemn vow and did not reveal the existence of our den. I lied and told them Danny had slipped into the sea just yards from where he was found and was swept away before I could do anything about it. The bruises covering his body and his broken teeth were attributed to the sea pulverising his corpse against the rocks. A verdict of accidental death was recorded.

The whole island chattered with the news. Mum treated me like a fragile china vase and even allowed me off school for a couple of weeks. There was no-one else I could turn to. Dad had long since returned to Germany. On my return to the classroom, peculiar hushed whispers and furtive glances greeted my every turn. Even Mr Mac seemed to show a modicum of pity but I suspected this facade masked a secret joy that his classroom would never be disrupted in quite the same way ever again.

Taking the time to speak to me and check how I was feeling, Elspeth was one of the very few to display some genuine concern,. Even at that tender age I could tell she had the most beautiful face. And something inside, awkward and indistinct, was awakening within me, intent on confusing my jumbled equilibrium all the more. I liked Elspeth. I liked her cleverness and the way she laughed. We became good friends - a fact I had to conceal from the lads as in their eyes, having a girl for a best pal was proof positive of poofterdom. Such was the logic of pre-pubescent boys.

As the weeks congealed into months and an uneventful summer made way for an average Christmas; the bed-wetting stopped, the nightmares became less frequent and something approaching normality returned. Other birthdays added the years and passed by without incident, serving only to remind me of the loss of my friend. I never went back to The Buzz Building even though I'd left my ball in there. In fact I hardly ever ventured out of Rothesay. Football became my main concern in life.

I haven't been on a passenger train since the days of British Rail. I stop twisting the ticket over and over between my fingers and study the carriage. Privatisation used to rankle me. I had an argument with Jim Flack on the subject only last week. I compared the whole idea to selling your favourite LP for a fiver - even though you know it's worth twenty - just so you can go down the pub and buy a pint or two. You might come out pissed and happy but you'll wake up skint and without the music you need to cheer you up.

Analogies are a waste of time with Jim. I tried to point out how much more of a folly it all was when the tax payer is expected to fork out millions in subsidies just to keep these so called private sector companies afloat. Suffice to say he disagreed, claiming it was essential in the modern age of globalisation and free market economies to protect the 'Big Boys' and longed for the day when the Prison Service would be privatised. He had already earmarked the amount he would set aside to buy shares in incarceration - '*the* growth industry of the twenty-first century' - and reasoned that their value would skyrocket as soon as the Tories returned to power with their supposedly tougher stance on law and order...

I think age might be dulling my edge. I no longer care about this sort of stuff the way I used to. After all, the train was punctual and the carriage is smart, clean and tidy enough. Funny names along this line;

Bushey, Kings Langley, Tring, Cheddington (the station with no town attached), Leighton Buzzard...

I'm feeling almost a hundred percent again. I think I've finally got rid of the disinfectant/blood/bleach/window cleaner taste from my mouth. The burning in my guts has settled into a dull, nagging throb. It's really all down to my ticker. I hope it can withstand all this agitation and survive until I get home.

I have one hundred and eighteen quid left - *That should be enough shouldn't it?* - I must keep some back for the ferry. God knows how much that is nowadays... This must be it. We've just left Bletchley and it's the next stop I'm after, so that geometric landscape must be the New City...

*

'Can you explain to me why he couldn't have been treated in the prison?' Craven asked, losing patience with the facetious doctor. Brooks' patronising demeanour had wound the detective up the wrong way from the moment they had met. Craven hated people talking down to him, especially young, professional types.

'Because thanks to the cutbacks there is no infirmary at the prison anymore. Hospital was the only option,' Doctor Brooks explained in a bored, matter-of-fact manner. At no point did he take his eyes off the little white ball nestling in the short grass in front of him.

'Next question.'

Craven watched him wiggle his backside and shuffle his legs measuring up his approach shot to the fifth green. He was aiming at a small yellow flag partially hidden behind a raised bunker a hundred yards away. Craven dimly recalled playing crazy golf with his parents on a boyhood holiday to some miserable, dank seaside resort. Crazy or otherwise he still regarded golf as one of the dullest sports known to man.

The club lashed round and thwacked the ball. Brooks immediately looked aggrieved, 'Oh shit. Sliced it... That's heading for the rough...

No. Hang on... I think we may have got away with that one.' He slotted the club inside his trolley bag, grabbed the handle and wheeled off in search of the ball. Craven followed, trying hard to conceal his irritation.

Brooks' wife, a deeply pregnant and equally charmless woman, had told him where he would find the doctor. Craven introduced himself to the balding medic while he was preparing to tee off on the first hole. The cheeky sod had asked if Craven would like to be his playing partner. He politely declined

Coughing hard Craven rooted through his pockets searching for a pack of lozenges.

'Sounds nasty Inspector. Feeling below par eh? Ha ha! Perhaps you should go back to bed. Get your wife to make you some nice hot soup.'

'What about the bleach Dumfries swallowed? Is that likely to have any lasting effect?' Craven posed the question to satisfy a personal rather than professional curiosity.

'Yes,' he sniggered. 'You're looking for someone whose piss kills ninety-nine point nine percent of all household germs. I'm sorry Inspector, can't this wait until tomorrow? I'm trying to relax and enjoy a rare afternoon off.'

'Do you have any idea why someone who's spent ten years inside without so much as a blemish against his record should suddenly make a run for it?' asked Craven ignoring the request.

Brooks suddenly veered to the left of the fairway walking quickly along the edge of the rough.

'Perhaps it's taken him this long to realise he's left his oven on,' Brooks replied with a sardonic grin.

Craven snatched a putter from the bag and jammed the head firmly between the cocky sod's legs.

'One more smart-arse comment from you and I'll be playing crazy golf with your bollocks. Understood?' Satisfied he now had the doctor's undivided attention Craven replaced the club. 'Now, why did Dumfries see you on Saturday? What was wrong with him?'

His arrogant swagger destroyed, Brooks looked skywards with a worried sigh and stroked his flustered brow.

'They were supposed to tell him. They were supposed to tell Dumfries when they took him back to his cell,' he muttered.

'Who?'

'Geoff and erm... Mike. The prison officers who escorted him. They were supposed to tell him... Have you spoken to Geoff and Mike?'

'No. But I will. What was it they were supposed to tell Dumfries?' asked Craven.

The doctor sighed heavily and shook his head. 'I can't believe those bastards. Look,' he turned to face Craven. 'It was his birthday. His *fortieth* birthday. We just thought we'd wind him up with a little joke on his birthday that's all. For heaven's sake it was just a joke.'

Craven stared at the doctor. 'Explain this joke to me.'

Doctor Brooks ground his teeth and dropped his gaze to his shoes until he worked out how to phrase his response. 'Listen. I was called in on Saturday to see another patient. Terry Collins if I remember rightly. Epileptic. Had a fit. Dislocated his scapula. Anyway...' he paused for a long, deep breath allowing him more time to choose his words. 'When I arrived I found Dumfries's test results on my desk. I wasn't expecting them back until this morning so I thought why not kill two birds with one stone.'

'And what were these test results exactly?' Craven asked as he flipped open his notebook.

Brooks puffed out his cheeks then slowly allowed them to deflate. 'He has a heart murmur. It was a routine test to see... just, er to make sure there were no complications. Anyway I noticed his date of birth on the results and I'm afraid my sense of humour got the better of me. After I'd finished treating Collins I told Geoff and Mike about my idea for a joke. They thought it was hilarious and agreed to take part.' Brooks paused to clear his throat and scratch an itch on his forehead, 'We decided just for a laugh we'd call him in and pull his leg by exaggerating the test results.'

'So it was a spur-of-the-moment thing this.., this joke?'

'Yes. That's precisely what it was,' Brooks replied shamefaced, 'But they were supposed to tell him. The instant they returned him to his cell they were supposed to tell him it was all a joke. That's what we agreed beforehand. So don't blame me. It's their fault. Morons.'

'So what exactly did you tell Dumfries?'

The doctor hesitated and picked at the logo on his golfing glove, looking for all the world like a little boy who had been caught trying to steal from a charity collection box.

'Come on,' pressed Craven.

'I told him he had heart disease. That it was untreatable. That he needed a transplant. That he'd never qualify for a transplant and that in two to six months he would die an agonising death,' Brooks explained rattling out the confession in a rapid monotone.

'And what did the test results *actually* reveal Doctor Brooks?'

'That his heart murmur remained a minor concern! No change in his condition! He had nothing to worry about!' he whined, flapping his arms dismissively.

'That's funny. No doubt about it. Comedy at its finest,' Craven dead-panned.

'Hey! Hold on! I hope you're not feeling sympathy for that animal!' Brooks turned on Craven his eyes sparkling with a belated flash of bravado. 'Let's not forget he's a murdering shit who deserves everything he gets! If I had my way, that swine *would* be dying a slow, *excruciating* death from something nasty and incurable! *That* would be justice!' he raved, the intensity of his voice catching Craven by surprise.

'You quite finished?'

Doctor Brooks nodded.

'Good,' Craven continued, 'I'll be speaking to you again no doubt when the inquiry comes round. Enjoy the rest of your round Doctor Brooks.'

Craven walked away leaving Brooks to resume the search for his ball. The man was an undoubted idiot but he couldn't help but agree with the doctor's point of view. Perhaps justice would be better served if Dumfries and his ilk were hung, gassed, electrocuted, given a lethal injection or a bullet in the back of the head - not necessarily all at the same time of course, though some of the more downright evil fuckers out there deserved the full treatment. The risk of reoffending would be eradicated. Time and money would be saved. The method didn't matter as long as the end result remained the same; to make his job easier. Then again Craven's current hassles wouldn't even exist if only that immature dickhead had remembered to leave his inane Rag Week pranks back in medical school.

He looked at his notebook. He couldn't draw very well standing up so all he'd managed to come up with was a little stickman playing golf. The figure had a few words and symbols scrawled around it;

Dr Brooks = Dr Twat,
40th b/day = joke
Dumfries = nothing to lose.

*

The man strode across the clubhouse car park popping what looked like a sweet into his mouth.

Nick checked the photograph on page four of the *Brighton & Hove Citizen* for the umpteenth time. It was definitely Detective Inspector Craven. Definitely the same man he saw on the local television news last night.

What was he doing? He hadn't been gone long enough to play a hole let alone a round. *Surely he didn't think Dumfries had gone for a game of golf?* Nick knew the police were useless but not that useless, *surely.*

Craven opened the door of a powerful, new-looking red Lexus.

Nick yawned until his eyes watered. He'd recently finished his flask of caustic black coffee. He hadn't been able to sleep last night. Too much activity whirring through his mind which was probably just as well because it allowed his anger to ferment very nicely indeed. He needed to stay focused, to keep the pain fresh and close-up. If he had gone to sleep the bloodlust may well have deserted him by the time he awoke. Instead he spent several hours cruising along the south coast on pleasantly empty roads

At one stage it looked as though his loyal Peugeot had given up the ghost. Spluttering, jumping and eventually stalling. He was relieved to find that he had simply ran out of petrol. Nick had spent so much of the journey drawing up his plans and fantasizing about the endless (but always gory) array of potential outcomes they afforded, that he had neglected to keep an eye on the fuel gauge. But this wasn't a problem. Being a practically minded person he always kept a full jerrycan in the boot. Nick found himself in Dover when daylight began to blush over the Channel. He took the hint and headed back to Brighton.

The unexpectedly helpful woman manning the police reception desk had informed him that DI Craven was due to give a statement to the press outside the prison. She told Nick he had to hurry otherwise he'd be too late. By the time he arrived at the prison several miles beyond Hove the small gang of reporters, photographers and cameramen were already packing up. He began to panic a little (unnecessarily he thought now, as there were a host of other methods he could have employed to trace the man) and asked a guy packing a bulky TV camera into a strongbox where Craven had gone. The cameraman pointed across the car park to where a man was walking towards a big red car. Nick tailed the car back in to town ending up outside a neat little house in a neat little suburb where the detective chatted briefly to a heavily pregnant woman...

And then he ended up here. Nick had tried to take up golf a few years back but found it way too hard for his liking and gave up. He yawned again. The Lexus started up. He watched Craven drive off shaking his head for some reason.

Nick Dodds followed.

7:   sins

The taxi ride from Milton Keynes Central to Bradwell Common wasn't worth four quid. If I'd known it was that close I would have walked it. I could only hope that I'd remembered the address correctly and that Joe hadn't moved house in the intervening years since I'd received his final letter, the last contact he'd made of any kind - a brief note informing me of his move south.

There were a few anxious moments after I'd rung the doorbell. I stared at the lurid yellow door. There was no name-plate to be seen. Just a number. The number thirty-two. Joe would be thirty-five years old now. The door opened and there he was; bleary-eyed in a T-shirt and boxer-shorts. We stood on opposite sides of the threshold sizing each other up. At one point it looked as though an embrace was on the cards but we made do with a simple business-like handshake when he finally invited me to enter. He showed me into the living-room before disappearing upstairs to wash and dress. He was away for so long I thought he'd gone back to his bed.

Joe hasn't changed much. A few flecks of grey, a few more lines circling the eyes and perhaps a touch more weight swelling the jowls are all that betray the passage of time. I'm sitting in a big, puffy armchair and looking around my brother's living-room. Some fine examples of Joe's photography have been neatly arranged along the walls. My personal favourite is the precisely composed, poster-sized picture of the 'Waverley' cruising out of Rothesay Bay caught in a shard of sunlight cutting through white clouds. Looking at the sea and hills surrounding the paddle steamer, I feel a pang of homesickness.

The pictures arranged along the top of the wall unit look like a line-up of the good, the bad and the ugly. There is a photo of a youthful Mum and Dad, a recent portrait of Maureen with a passport-sized picture of her when she was a schoolgirl tucked in the bottom corner of the frame and one of a fat, pug-faced baby I don't recognise at all. Other members of the clan on display include; all four grandparents, Joe himself and Aunt Elaine. Surprisingly, the finest frame has been saved for a wedding photo from his short-lived marriage to Hannah. I never did get to see her in person. I remember his pride when he showed me her picture during his first visit to see me in jail. They divorced three years later.

I am nowhere to be seen in this gallery.

The awkward silence continues. Joe must have been following my eyeline because he's gazing at the portraits now. He sips carefully from his tea which is obviously too hot. I stare into my mug hypnotised by the small cluster of white bubbles spinning in the centre of the steaming, tannin sea. Joe is definitely not pleased to see me. A couple of monosyllabic pleasantries are all he's managed to utter in half an hour.

'How's Maureen?' I ask shattering the hush and almost making myself jump with the loudness of my voice.

'She's fine, aye,' he mutters.

The edgy stillness returns. I can hear a hidden clock ticking. I find myself watching the television even though it's not switched on. I can see us both reflected on the blank screen. *Christ, this is hard work!*

'Where is she nowadays?'

'Still in Brora.'

I get up, move across to the unit painfully conscious of the floorboards creaking under the carpet and pick up the frame containing my sister's strongly defined features. Strange. What did I expect? Of course she looks different. Ten years have passed, 'I take it this is her?' For some reason I feel the need to make absolutely sure.

'Aye.'

I compare the schoolgirl Maureen of the inset with the adult Maureen of the main picture. The younger version makes more sense. The woman has none of the freckles or the puppy fat but those sparkling, mischievous grey eyes are the same. I think back, finding it hard to believe she was only twenty last time I saw her.

'What's she up tae,' I venture, hoping to obtain further scraps of what so far appears to be highly classified information.

'Nothin' much,' he slurps.

89

I'm sure he never used to be like this.

'Still teachin'?' Fingers crossed. *C'mon Joe you can do it!* Spill the beans.

'Naw. She had tae give that up for a while, since she had the baby.'

Baby? I'm an uncle! Uncle Haig!

'A baby! Nobody told me! Is it a boy or a lassie?' *Well Joe, you got me. I wasn't expecting that.*

'A wee lassie. Shona. She must be about four months noo. Maybe five,' he tells me with a not entirely certain nod.

I pick up the photograph of the sleeping baby and study its red and fit-to-burst face. I shake my head with a smile. Even as babies go this is one is undeniably ugly. I can only hope, for the sake of my new-found niece, that she blossoms.

Pleased to meet you Shona.

'Is Maureen still married to that Bible-bashin' moron whatsisface?' I ask.

'Big Alan? Aye. Still married,' Joe breathes deeply. I think he wants to move away from this subject. He glances at me for the first time in the conversation, aware that I have always disapproved of Big Alan; AKA - The Hairy Heathen.

Aside from being responsible for changing my sister's surname from Dumfries to the frankly ludicrous Farquharson, Alan (who is indeed big in terms of height, width and beard) purports to be a Seventh Day Born Again Adventist Witness Of The Holy Tabernacle or something. Basically a door-to-door salesman stubbornly trying to flog his own peculiar take on Christianity to folk who are quite happy with their current brand thank you very much.

Maureen introduced him to the family about six months before I was jailed. The moment imprinted itself on my memory. Maureen walked into the house with a cheery grin and asked us all to say hello to her new boyfriend. Mum was struck dumb at the mere sight of the man she described as 'a hairy heathen' - a description that became his name whenever she referred to him. Joe had to leave the room to hide his mirth but I could still hear his laughter drifting through from the toilet. I honestly thought Maureen was playing an elaborate joke solely to provoke exactly that kind of reaction from us. The truth was she always had been a bizarre, scatter-brained wee thing; something I always put down to the fact that she had been born in Greenock rather than Rothesay and therefore not a true *Brandane* like the rest of us.

Unfortunately as it turned out, Maureen was not joking and to this day her attraction to the man remains a mystery. Maureen is twelve years younger than her husband and put bluntly, she is too good looking for such a grotesque lump. I know she could have done better. I feel sorry for my niece. Shona... Shona Farquharson... *Christ...*

I put the picture back where it belongs and return to my seat.

'What about yerself Joe? What are you up tae?'

'Ach, no' much,' he concedes rubbing his eyes with a yawn.

'Workin'?'

'Aye. In a warehoose. Tesco's. Night shift... S'awright.' His tone suggests otherwise.

'You never said why you left Rothesay?'

'Och I just had tae get away y'know?' he explains with a pained expression. 'There wasnae any work. Nothin' tae keep me there.'

I can't help but feel a wee bit sorry for him. I know he's lying. If he chose to confide in me I would probably learn the real reason for his move was to put distance between himself and Hannah. It was brave of my wee brother to uproot himself and make a fresh start but to have come all this way only to spend his life loading and unloading pallets of beans, nappies, bread and whatever, while trying to deal with a shitload of painful memories was, I could tell, sapping away his soul. But of all the places he could have moved to why on earth did he come here? What had drawn him to this town? A place so utterly different from home? Maybe that was the point.

'But why choose Milton Keynes, Joe? Of all places?'

With a lazy shrug of his shoulders he ponders the question for a moment. His dispassionate eyes turn to look outside, 'Ma pal Ronnie had moved here. Don't know if ye remember him. He told me it was awright... There was work. So...' he waves a dismissive hand. 'There ye go.'

I am far from convinced.

'But this place is like the furthest point in Britain from the sea and as flat as fuck. D'ye no' miss the waves? D'ye no' miss the hills?' I ask in a vain attempt to make light of things.

'Aye, sometimes,' he sighs again.

I need to get out of this funeral parlour atmosphere. I swallow my tea quickly and stand up with an exaggerated stretch, 'Is it okay if I have a bath Joe? D'ye mind?'

'Naw naw, help yerself. The water should be hot enough... So how're you by the way?' he inquires fixing me with uncomfortable eyes. 'Awright, aye?'

'No' bad. Cannae complain.' My turn to withhold information.

'You escaped then aye?' asks Joe as if it were nothing more exciting than a trip to the library.

I nod.

*   *   *

Twisting, spinning, in slow-motion circles. Can't tell if I'm floating up or down. In water immersed. In salt dissolving. So numb. I am being spun by giant, invisible fingers. Carefully. Better than any theme park ride. This one will never end... Colours. Softer now, not as dazzling. Still beautiful. Beautifully still. Soothing. Warm reds. Cold blues. Like those colour coded taps actually released colour coded water... It is all true. Reflections suspended like ethereal projections show me... things. Images. Add an 'r' and they become mirages...

*

My passing, movement, control and finishing were gelling like never before. The first was a thumping header from a decent cross. The second; a thirty yard curler which was destined for the top right postage-stamp corner the instant it left my boot. A wriggling solo drive for goal completed the hat trick; starting from just inside the halfway line, I left four or five flat-footed defenders in my wake before slotting the ball between the 'keeper's spindly legs. My fourth came after I'd picked up a loose clearance from a corner and drilled a volley from the edge of the box, low, hard and straight through a pale forest of hairy limbs. That was the final humiliation for our beleaguered opponents. Apart from scoring four I also had a hand in setting up the other four.

Final score: Brandanes - Eight, Dunoon - One.

I knew I was good and happily allowed my ego to swell with sinful pride when people would offer to buy me a post-match pint in the pub before going on to tell me that I was the best player Bute had ever produced. But today was different. The pressure was on. There was a rumour doing the rounds. All week the gossip mongers had been circulating a whisper about a Celtic scout who, having heard about my potential, was coming over to watch me play. Outwardly I put on a display of casual scepticism dismissing the story as someone's idea of a joke but secretly I knew I couldn't afford to be cynical. This could be my one and only chance to achieve the dream. I had to put on a show. I *had* to perform at my very best.

The lads treated me to a generous round of back-slapping as we trudged victoriously off the pitch. Even the Dunoon players, including the ones who'd tried to hospitalise me once they'd singled me out as the danger man, offered their congratulations. The firmest handshake of all came from their rhino-sized centre-half. I almost believed him when he apologized for a tackle that nearly chopped my legs in half and left a nasty gash below my knee.

There I was shaking like a leaf, my sock stained with the blood still trickling down from the wound when Mr McIntyre showed me his card and introduced himself. The rumour was true. Better still, the scout had been very impressed. So much so that he invited me over to Glasgow for a trial to take place the following week. He even handed me a kind of pre-contract agreement to sign in order to make sure I didn't sneak off and join another club in the interim...As if!

Barely able to conceal my joy I signed the paper over a pint in The

Black Bull (the Albert Place pub with the proud boast of being Rothesay's oldest) while we waited for Mr McIntyre's ferry. Every petty concern I'd stored up inside and used in the bleakest of moods to convince myself that life was nothing more than a God-forsaken endurance test without reward, vanished as I sat there listening to this enthusiastic man describe how he had actually watched me play on three occasions (just to make sure) before arriving at the conclusion that I was the most promising striker he had seen for years.

The praise left me grinning like a ventriloquist's dummy. So much so I felt the need to prove that I wasn't in fact made of wood by constantly nodding and grunting in response to Mr McIntyre's assurances that the trial would be nothing more than a formality.

'It's a chance for the coaching staff to assess your health and fitness as much as anything.'

From our position by the window we watched the ferry dock. Mr McIntyre downed the last mouthful of his pint, shook my hand firmly, told me how much he was looking forward to seeing me in Glasgow and with a genial smile and wave he departed. I ordered myself another pint to celebrate (knowing that from here on I would have to cut the drinking - a price well worth paying) and watched the ferry depart unable to stop smiling. If fate had chosen to play its hand, I would have died a happy man, right there and then. I couldn't wait to tell Elspeth.

Grumbling past Skeoch Woods and Ardbeg, my blue, sea-salt corroded Austin Allegro handled the road like a charging, myopic hippo. I rehearsed the many different ways I could deliver the good news in my head. I considered playing it coy, thinking Elspeth should be teased into seducing the information from me. Pretending to be depressed at first, allowing her to comfort and console me until I jumped up laughing, admitting the joke and spilling the beans, was another option.

I had performed this journey so often it was now second nature. I drove through Port Bannatyne on autopilot. A dog sat alone in the bus stop as if waiting to catch a ride out of town. It barked and wagged its tail as I passed. I indicated left, swung the old blue motor off the coastal road and headed inland...

We had been together since that terrifying school dance where I asked her if she would be my girlfriend. We were fourteen, in our third year at Rothesay Academy and had been winching for two weeks. But the occasional fraught kiss stolen in precious, all too brief moments when we found ourselves alone in the corner of the library or in an empty corridor or had arrived deliberately early in a deserted classroom - as pulsating as they were - were not enough. I needed to make it official. I needed to make sure Elspeth wasn't merely using me for target practice before moving on to the real object of her affections. My natural pessimism found it hard to accept that someone so obviously attractive would go for me without an ulterior motive.

Everything about her was easy to admire from her long black hair, the confident hazel eyes topped by wide straight brows to the small nose lightly freckled across the bridge. Her demure mouth disguised a clever, quick-witted tongue. Her body as I had surreptitiously noted many times, was filling out in all the right places. And looking the way she did I knew it wouldn't be long before some fifth or sixth form gorilla would try to lay his clammy palms all over her. That's why I had to stake my claim. My question hung in the air and I wished I could suck it back in. She looked at me with a slightly puzzled smile. I waited, fully expecting her to laugh in my face then run to the assembly hall, through the twirling dots of the multicoloured disco lights to ask everyone to join her in mocking the huge moronic waste of space otherwise known as Haig Dumfries for having the temerity to ask her out.

'What kind of a question's that?' she asked fuelling my paranoia. 'I thought I already was your girlfriend? I thought I'd made that pretty obvious?'

That wasn't one of the answers I'd been preparing for. It wasn't quite definite enough for my fragile state of mind, 'Is that a 'yes' then?'

She took my hand and without answering she led me out of the hall and together we sneaked into the girls' cloakroom, where we indulged in our most intense kissing session to date. After about ten dream-like minutes surrounded by the suspended shadows of coats and jackets, savouring every moist, warm caress of her mouth, the close up smell of her skin with the distant bass hum of the music drowned out by the faint popping sounds our lips made on each shivery contact, she finally said, 'Yes. It is definitely a yes. Okay?'

With my soul saved from gut-wrenching humiliation Elspeth led me back into the hall and onto the dance-floor in time for Bowie's *Rebel Rebel*. She had said *'yes'*! *Elspeth* had said *'yes'*! I felt like I could achieve anything. World peace?

Nae bother.

There was a catch. Elspeth lived miles away on the other side of the island. Her parents' farm overlooked Ettrick Bay. It was a stunning location. I was always slightly envious not only of the house itself but also of its solitude. I wished I could wake up to views like that every morning. However, it was a pain in the backside to get to. At least in the summer months there was a bus service to Ettrick, otherwise to visit Elspeth, I would have to catch a bus as far as the last stop in Port Bannatyne followed by a long, knackering walk. The only other alternative was to endure an arse-numbing cycle ride from home, so arse-numbing in fact that I only attempted it once (It took me hours to reach Crannog Hill Farm and several days before I could sit down in comfort again).

My old car gurned over the apex complaining with every clunking gear change. I could see the farm to the left, two miles further up the undulating straight. The otherwise flat and bare field behind the main farmhouse contained a solitary copse. These elderly trees had been spared the chainsaw and plough because they sheltered an archaic stone circle in their midst. For anthropologists these stones were a constant source of mystery. A puzzle from a long forgotten era. Who built them? How old were they? What were they for?

For myself, these stones were a testament to a far more recent event of equally historic importance. And the moment I thought back to that event I began to feel aroused all over again...

We had heard all the sordid anecdotes from various friends and acquaintances and the general consensus was that for most people, the first time inevitably turned out to be one big anti-climax - so to speak. Giggly fumblings in the back seat of a borrowed car or hushed grunts in a bedroom stricken almost impotent with the dread of an untimely visit from an unsuspecting parent offering tea. In most cases it seemed the participants didn't even have much respect for each other let alone love. The whole act being nothing more than a means to an end. A chance to brag about how they'd done 'it'. We were determined to make our first time special and not something that could be reduced to a single rueful sentence.

Elspeth having collected a clutch of excellent 'O' Grades had opted to stay on at school to do her 'A's. I on the other hand couldn't wait to leave and with the help of respectable exam results particularly in Maths and English I managed to land a traineeship at the bank. Mum had gushed with pride when I showed her the acceptance letter. She mapped out the next fifty years of my life for me; the prospects, the security, the benefits of a career spent working for a decent *respectable* company.

Not satisfied with outperforming me educationally, Elspeth went on to pass her first driving test a week after I'd failed mine. I didn't mind one iota. I was still thanking my lucky stars that she was going out with me. And now I had the big event to look forward to.

We had explored each other's bodies before but always with our clothes on; hands sliding up skirts, T-shirts and blouses or teasing down trousers, pants and knickers but time, place and other circumstances had thwarted all attempts to consummate our relationship. Until one humid August evening back in the late Seventies when the planets finally aligned in our favour.

We started planning Our Weekend the instant Elspeth's parents announced they were going to celebrate their silver wedding anniversary with a trip to Paris. Elspeth had taken a summer job in the tourist office and we would meet every lunch-time to discuss what we should do and how and where we should do it. These liaisons were really only an excuse to drive each other to distraction to the point where we would go back to work raging with desire. The blonde streak she had recently dyed in her long fringe made her look even sexier. After the final lunchtime before the main attraction I returned to the bank and stamped every book and cashed every check with a thumping hard-on. I would never be more ready to do my country proud.

We drove back to the empty farm in the brown second-hand Mini-van Elspeth's parents had bought her as a gift for her brilliant exam results. Elspeth disappeared into the bathroom. Heart thudding with anticipation I sat on the edge of her bed and waited. Her walls were plastered with posters of the Sex Pistols and numerous other leering punk bands I'd never heard of, before she blasted out their records on her Philips Disc-O-Matic. She had been tempted to adopt the safety pins, studded leather and rainbow hair look but quickly shelved the idea. She knew Bute wasn't ready to embrace those who proudly flaunted their individuality. The streak in her hair was a compromise and even that drew some odd disapproving looks. Christ knows what would have happened if she'd gone for the purple mohican.

Elspeth returned from the bathroom having changed into a pair of black jeans and a lime green T-shirt. I made a careful study of those clothes formulating a plan of attack for when the moment came to remove them.

'Well?' she asked folding her arms.

'Well what?'

'Did you buy any?'

'Buy any what?'

'Condoms you idiot.'

'I didn't get a chance,' I fibbed, cheeks flushing.

'You mean you lost your bottle.'

She was right. I lost my nerve and walked away without setting a toe inside the chemist.

'Well it's not easy, Elspeth,' I groaned pathetically.

'Looks like we'll just have to sit here and talk then doesn't it?' She leaned back against the window with a sigh. 'If you wanted me badly enough you would have got some no matter how *difficult* it was... but I understand if you're not interested.'

She looked at my crestfallen face then moved over to her bedside cabinet and opened a wooden musical jewellery box. 'Somewhere Over The Rainbow' tinkled forth. The soundtrack to my bitter frustration.

Elspeth pulled open a hidden compartment in the bottom of the box and showed me a little foil packet. She smiled slyly, pleased her teasing had worked like a charm.

'Look what I found.'

'Where did you get that?' I asked unable to conceal my joy.

'My dad's sock drawer.'

'What if he finds out?'

'Trust me – he's not gonna take me to one side and ask if I stole his rubber-johnny.'

We were now armed and ready but the bedroom was not the location we had decided on.

The setting was perfect; alfresco beneath shading trees and a clear cobalt sky. Encircled by those timeworn stones fringed orange by a setting sun sinking into the shimmering sea, we laid a blanket on the ground still warm from the day's heat. If we had cared to listen we would have heard the waves rolling up the beach behind us. We took our time. There was no hurry. No need to rush. We spent an age just looking at each other, into each other. Despite the heat I was shivering uncontrollably. Finally we lost patience. Grinning with unrestrained exhilaration we pounced on one another. We couldn't help laughing when we shared the same frustrating wrestling match with each other's jeans. I thought hers were never going to slide from her legs. T-shirts were next and overexcited kisses got in the way of underwear removal. Undoing her bra proved infuriatingly difficult. My fingers tugged, twisted, pulled, pushed and tried through sheer will power to separate those bastard hooks. When telekinesis failed, Elspeth finally intervened and set them free with one hand.

'Don't worry. You'll get the hang of it – I'll make sure of that,' she whispered warmly into my ear.

For the first time ever we were completely naked together. We spent a moment simply looking at each other. I took in every minute detail as Elspeth kneeled before me backlit by fading sunlight. The fine, minuscule hairs of her arms and shoulders raised by goose-pimples glowed like a fragile halo. Her body surpassed all my imaginings. I swallowed hard and unfurled the sheath over what must surely have been the biggest, tightest erection anywhere in the world at that time. I'd never experienced anything quite as intense before. The anticipation must have had added an extra inch to every bulging dimension. I was certain that if Elspeth so much as exhaled in its general direction my cock would explode.

We paced ourselves trying to make it last and did all we could to please each other for what seemed like hours. Several times I found myself focusing on the far off mountains of Arran, desperate to stem my own tide by concentrating hard on deeply unsexy things like chequebooks, standing orders and high interest accounts... but in the end even those hazy peaks began to resemble spectacular breasts.

After we'd finished for the second time the sun had vanished entirely. We lay silently in each other's arms looking up through the quivering leaves and branches latticing the deepening blue of the gathering night. Time slipped and lapsed unnoticed. Before dusk tightened its grip further we grabbed our clothes, ran to the beach and bathed in the sea allowing our skin to be rinsed of what we'd shared.

Watching Elspeth swim I felt a kind of lazy pride. We had achieved everything we set out to achieve. I smiled, happy and confident that the evening had etched itself firmly into my mind. A never-to-be-forgotten evening and a benchmark for all subsequent encounters. I looked back in the direction of the stone circle and wondered if it would ever be possible for us to top our debut. Maybe we had stumbled inadvertently on the truth of the stones. Maybe it had been built specifically as a private retreat for couples who wanted to lose their virginity in style - The Virgins Circle; where cherries were lost. After all there is a certain suggestiveness about the shape of a circle, especially when that shape is formed by a number of enormous, phallic rocks...

There was no point in locking the Allegro. Nobody in their right mind would want to steal it anyway and they certainly wouldn't go out of their way to visit a remote farm in order to pinch the damn thing. I looked across the field to that timeless monument. Almost three years had passed and although confident that we still loved each other I was growing concerned that things might never hit such dizzying heights again.

I planted a kiss on Elspeth's mother's cheek the instant she opened the door.

'Hello Mrs Donnelly you gorgeous creature! Is that daughter of yours around?'

She looked at me stunned but smiling and yet still managed to give off that vague sense of disapproval I felt whenever she looked at me. I had seen pictures of Margot in her prime back when she was indeed gorgeous. Even now as she stood there prissily dressed in an ankle length skirt and mumsy blouse buttoned all the way up to her throat with long greying hair tied back in a tight bun, she was facing middle age in great shape.

'Hello Haig. You seem to be in high spirits today. As you can tell by the din, Elspeth is in her room.'

I jogged up the stairs towards the source of the pulsing music, barged straight into her bedroom and caught Elspeth dancing wildly to The Beat's '*Mirror In The Bathroom*'. She shrieked when I grabbed her round the waist and swept her off her feet.

'Put me down!' she laughed.

Unable to wipe the Cheshire cat grin from my face long enough to tell the joyful news I put her down and watched her move sinuously to the music until the track came to an end.

'Haig? You look weird. Say something before I have you sectioned.'

I took a deep breath.

'I've...'

'No wait! I can't believe I almost forgot! I've got some fantastic news,' Elspeth blurted.

She stepped across slipped her arms over my shoulders and looked at me with a playful glint in her eyes.

'How much do you love me?'

'Oh God is this a trick question?'

'Would you follow me to the ends of the earth?'

'Well that depends Elspeth. Some ends are nicer than others.'

'How about London?'

'London?'

'Uh huh. The BBC have offered me a job.'

'BBC? What job?'

Elspeth reached over to her dressing table and showed me the letter.

'Trainee journalist. It's not surprising really. You've either got it or you haven't,' she beamed, folding her arms proudly.

Feeling my heart deflate I perched on the edge of her bed staring at the letter without really taking in the words.

'You can come with me. There's nothing to keep you here is there? There must be plenty of bank jobs in London. And I'm sure between us we could find...' Her words ground to a halt when she noticed the expression on my face. 'Steady now – don't get too excited.'

'Sorry. It's just...'

'I thought you'd be pleased for me?'

I was pleased for her. Of course I was. Elspeth had always set her heart on becoming a journalist. After leaving school with a raft of A Levels she'd relentlessly badgered STV until they caved in and offered her a few months work experience on *Scotland Today*. Elspeth impressed them so much they gave her a full time job as a production runner. And now it seemed all her hard work had paid off with this latest opportunity.

'I am pleased for you. I really am. It's just...'

'What?'

'London sounds great. But there *is* something to keep me here.'

In the end I decided not to give her the gushing speech about Celtic's glorious history. Nor did I submit my idea that she should become a pioneer for her sex and specialise in football journalism whereupon she could report on all my forthcoming glories at home and in Europe and the inevitable caps for Scotland which would ultimately lead to me captaining the nation to World Cup glory.

I just gave her the facts. Plain and simple.

Instantly recognising the implications Elspeth sat beside me on the bed. We should have been ecstatic. Both of our dreams were coming true. Instead we shared a sullen silence. Perhaps it was something to do with the laws of physics. Perhaps it was impossible for two pieces of positive news to collide without causing an event of equal and opposite effect to occur. But if two wrongs don't make a right then why did two rights end up making a wrong?

'We could still meet up at weekends... once in a while.'

'Long distance relationships never work,' I sighed. To me, having never ventured further than Glasgow, London seemed like a mystical far-off land. It really didn't bear thinking about.

'No harm in trying.'

'I'spose,' I replied, my voice contained even less conviction than Elspeth's.

We heard Margot calling from downstairs. Elspeth left to go and see what she wanted.

I looked around her room. The punk posters had long gone. Ska had taken its place. I was surrounded by black and white pictures of amongst others; The Specials, Madness and The Selecter. The musical jewellery box still resided on top of the bedside cabinet... It was difficult to accept that things were drawing to a close. Would I be able to let go...?

She came back to find me lying on the floor looking up at the ceiling.

'What are you thinking?' she asked placing a cup of tea beside me on the floor. I watched her sit on the end of the bed overlooking me.

I shook my head. 'Nothin'... Are you gonnae get yourself a pork-pie hat?' I asked looking at the wall behind her.

'Ach away and don't be daft,' she laughed. 'I'd look a right eejit.'

'What did your mother want?'

'Just to tell me that she's off to church with dad.'

Like myself, Elspeth had also lapsed but she had escaped lightly compared to me. Mum regularly tried to persuade me to return to the fold and every time it would result in an argument by the end of which Mum would always succeed in making me feel guilty. Elspeth and I had long since confessed to each other that the reason we stopped going to church had more to do with laziness and an inability to endure the incredibly tedious services than a lack of faith, although Elspeth would also justify her apostasy by pointing out some of the more dubious policies of the Catholic Church. (Her favourite line of attack centred on the Vatican's stance on contraception and abortion which as she saw it, served only to perpetuate disease and poverty in the Third World. I couldn't disagree).

I found myself staring at the jewellery box.

Elspeth eased down onto the floor beside me.

'You're away with the fairies again. Tell me what you're thinking or I'll spit in your belly button.'

'I'm just remembering somethin'.'

'And what exactly are you remembering?'

I continued to stare at the box. 'Our first time... Do you remember our first time? Our Weekend?'

Elspeth released a heart stopping smile. 'It's not something I'm likely to forget is it?' Her right hand worked its way down to my belt and undid the buckle, 'Now because I love you,' she whispered seductively, unzipping my fly, 'I'm going to give you your birthday present two days early okay?'

I decided I would ask her to marry me as soon as I signed fully professional terms with Celtic.

104

*   *   *

... 'Twenty! Yer an auld basturt Haig. Cannae even call yerself a teenager any more. Yer youth has gone. Ma big brother's an auld tube!' laughed Joe as he peered through the viewfinder.

He'd been gleefully ribbing me about my age since he woke me up that morning mooching for a lift down to the pier. But I didn't pay any attention. My head was too busy trying to reconcile my conflicting emotions. On the one hand I was still on a high, counting down the days and hours before it was time to leave for Glasgow. On the other hand I was on a low, counting down the days and hours before the time came for Elspeth to leave for London.

Joe made a minor adjustment to the tripod ensuring it was securely balanced in its spot perilously close to the edge of the pier. The battered old Halina once belonged to Dad but he'd given the museum piece of a camera to Joe once it became apparent that his interest in photography was more than a passing fad. Despite the antiquated nature of his equipment my little brother managed to achieve some surprisingly good results. He had an eye for composition. No doubt about it. With Joe's birthday only a couple of months away, the early plan was to chip in with Mum and Dad and buy him a new, up to date camera.

'Yer right Joe. I'm gettin' auld. Life is passing me by. I remember when I was your age I used tae play football for St Andrew's. But now...' I shook my head with mock disappointment. 'All I have to look forward to is a trial with Celtic.'

I enjoyed reminding Joe of the trial. I could tell how jealous he was. I thought I detected a hint of pride in his eyes when I first told him but he covered it with a grand show of indifference. Mum's reaction had been and remained, resolutely frosty. She just couldn't understand it. Why on earth would I want to give up such a nice, safe, respectable, reasonably well paid job with all the long-term career enhancement prospects it afforded? This was her standard argument, the mantra she

105

recited whenever I entertained the idea of moving on.

I had worked at the bank in Montague Street for almost four years and with each passing day my soul continued to leach away. I hated it. In the end I tried to reassure her that I would not quit the bank until everything had been signed and sealed but this was of no comfort to Mum.

I hadn't been able to tell Dad. He'd been away with the army for months and months.

'Ach, they'll no' take you. No' unless it's a ball boy they're after,' joked Joe trying not to laugh at his own wit. He triggered the shutter capturing a detail of the starboard paddle housing.

Boats and ships were his favourite subject. His bedroom walls were lined with a flotilla of ferries, trawlers, yachts and even a nuclear submarine interspersed with the occasional but equally well executed portrait or landscape. The 'Waverley' became the latest vessel to be caught on film. Joe released the camera from the tripod and stepped back from the pier's edge to frame a handheld shot

'Did you know that the Waverley is the last sea-going paddle-steamer in the world?' he asked clicking the shutter and winding on, ready for the next exposure.

'Is that a fact?' I said, humouring him by pretending never to have read the old ship's publicity gumph.

'Aye. Amazin' i'nt it?' He lay flat on his stomach experimenting with a different angle. 'Beautiful in't she?'

I sat down on one of the bulbous wrought-iron bollards and watched the paddles whisking the sea into an egg-white flourish. The tourists lining the open deck peered over the sides with excited smiles as the vessel pulled away from Rothesay Pier. I wondered what would remain of the body if someone fell into those immense, thrashing wheels.

'So where's my birthday present? What did ye get me?'

'I only got ye a card,' Joe muttered.

'Generous to a fault. That's you Joe.'

The thunderous, *CHOOSH, CHOOSH, CHOOSH* of the paddles

tremored through the much older timbers of the pier to agitate my bones. It was always a pleasure to see the Waverley's sleek outline appear round Bogany Point to take us back to a bygone age. She plied these waters throughout the tourist season. The very fact that she was such a regular visitor to our shores meant I had taken her for granted and never sailed in her. It wasn't that I didn't want to. It was just another minor ambition I assumed would easily be fulfilled on one of the apparently limitless opportunities the future promised.

Or so it seemed.

I remembered a long standing promise to take Elspeth for a cruise one day. We had both decided it would be fun to sail around the firth and maybe even step off at Brodick for a few hours. I made up my mind. It was time to stop being complacent. If the Waverley was in Rothesay next Saturday we would be first in the queue. I watched the steamer pick up speed, its twin red funnels purging trails of smoke into the shaft of sunlight splitting the low slung clouds. Joe steadied himself, carefully composed the viewfinder and clicked.

We dropped Joe's film into the chemist and headed back to the car. As the worn-out Austin whined noisily up Ministers Brae towards our newish home on Eden Drive (a vast improvement on the decrepit High Street flat) I wondered when the council would finally get round to offering me a place of my own. I'd been on the housing list for ages. For the sake of my sanity I had to escape the claustrophobic confines of the family home as soon as possible.

All of those worries would vanish of course if things went well at Celtic Park.

I was surprised to find the front door hanging wide open. We entered the living-room. My heart shrivelled. My skin blanched cold. I knew. No words were needed. I just knew. My eyes turned quickly to Joe hoping he hadn't seen enough to guess what was going on. Too late.

A policeman, his hat under his arm stood sullenly in front of my mother. Her hands smothered her face. On hearing us enter she took them away and looked at me, shocked, vulnerable and scared behind tear filled eyes. For the first time in my life I thought she looked old. As if following the natural order of things the policeman turned to me. I'd been nominated the man of the house. I could feel the burden, the responsibility pressing down on my shoulders. Dad was dead. Crushed...

*

'...Of all the places in the world,
This island loves you,
Our wayward father,
Of all the places in the world,
This island loves you,
So when your work is done,
Please come home.

We shall bury you deep,
Within its cherished soil,
And let your soul,
Reach its heavenly goal,
And we shall forever be,
Yours,
Truly...'

Joe stepped down from the pulpit. The large, draughty church contained barely twenty people. Dour, ashen-faced mourners grimly clutching their missals. My brother's words had stung the atmosphere with a heavy silence. This was a talent he had kept to himself until now. Perhaps wisely. An interest in poetry is not the kind of thing you declare unless you want your schoolmates to question your sexuality whilst furnishing you with a severe battering. Joe sat down next to me on the front pew, his face locked in a frown. I put a comforting arm around him and tried to draw him close. He pulled away instantly. Angrily.

Maureen sat sandwiched, sheltered and safe between Mum and Elaine. Her feet didn't quite reach the floor and I watched her nervously swinging her shiny black plastic shoes in the air and sucking her thumb - a habit we thought she'd dropped long ago. I questioned the wisdom in bringing a ten-year-old to her father's funeral. Joe was the same age when he attended Gran's funeral and the experience had all but traumatised him. (Gran's was also the first funeral I had ever been to, memorable mostly for the controversy surrounding Dad's failure to put in an appearance. The grief I felt then was different to the grief I felt for Dad). Gran's death had been expected but even so Mum had been almost inconsolable and it was her pain that I had the most trouble dealing with. Outwardly at least, she appeared to be less affected by the loss of her husband.

But poor Maureen had been left bewildered by the scale of her feelings and the reality of the event itself. She found it impossible to take her eyes away from the coffin. She understood the concept of death. Dad was gone. But how to feel? How to react? She had seen less of him in her short life than anyone but whenever Dad strolled in the door, Maureen had always been the first to greet him with arms as wide as her smile. She clearly loved him and he clearly doted on her. I felt sorry for Maureen most of all.

Elaine hugged her tight. Considering she never got on with the man, I felt my aunt had gone a wee bit over the top sitting there, face obscured behind a black veil, arms sheathed in elbow-length, black lace gloves. Her entire monochrome outfit topped with a wide rimmed black hat with a black rose pinned to the front, gave her the impression of a professional mourner. But now I knew why she disliked Dad.

Mum had cobbled together whatever black clothes she owned. Her tears having dried up long before, she fixed her stare on the crucifix suspended above the altar as if seeking to gain strength from it. I didn't know if she was paying attention to the priest's words any more than I.

Dad's death had forced her to confess like never before. Like lancing an overripe abscess the circumstances spewed the truth into the open. When I heard her attempt to explain my mind skipped, dizzied by the revelations. Everything had to be re-evaluated. Memories had to be reconstructed into new contexts. Square pegs forced into round holes. My overloaded head struggled to make sense of it all. It made me feel physically sick. Should Joe and Maureen be told?

We were invited to join together in a moment of silent prayer. I could hear the soft electric hum of a heater hidden somewhere in the shadows... I glared at my watch. I should not have been there in that freezing church. I was supposed to be in Glasgow on that hallowed turf impressing the hell out of the Celtic coaching staff... A flash of guilt parried my selfish anger. Dad may well have been a deceitful bastard but he still deserved my respect in his death. If only his timing had been better.

According to Mum we couldn't afford our own telephone so I had to use the phone box near the house to call Mr McIntyre. I told him why I couldn't make it to the trial. He understood and offered his deepest sympathies. He assured me that the offer would remain open and encouraged me to contact him as soon as I was ready. I thanked Mr McIntyre and promised I would get back to him just as soon as I had dealt with all the formalities.

We stood around the hole looking down. The buffeting wind gnawed our exposed hands and faces and made it difficult to hear the priest. The sky was a diluted uniform grey. Rain was in the offing. I picked up a fistful of earth and was reminded of Joe's poem. I let the soil fall from my grasp to thud against Dad's coffin in a series of tiny dust-brown explosions. I swallowed hard and pressed my eyes tight shut against the tears. Regardless of what the idiot had done and the mess he left behind, I would sorely miss Dad.

Elspeth slipped a comforting arm around my waist and we walked away.

No bullets were involved. No mortars. No mines. No grenades. No armed combat of any kind. His was not a life lost fighting a just cause. He did die in the line of duty that much was true but it turned out his duty was to lay bricks. Dad was a brickie. I never saw that coming. And Dad never saw the lorry driven by an inattentive half-wit and loaded with scaffolding reverse against the wall he was working on. He died instantly. An enquiry was under way into the whys and wherefores. He had laid down his life in the cause of building a petrol station in Brighton. He'd only been on the site for three days before being rubbed out against his own craftsmanship. Fatally caught between a rock and a hard place.

Mum, without consulting me, naively accepted the construction company's compensation offer. The payout barely covered the transportation and other bureaucratic costs involved in the ensuing logistical nightmare we had to negotiate to bring Dad's body back to Bute. There was little left over for the actual funeral expenses leaving Mum no choice but to demolish what little savings she had. I did what I could. Selling my car raised the princely sum of forty quid and somehow I found myself in the humiliating position of applying for a loan and having my colleagues scrutinise the paperwork.

Financially we were screwed. Mum had a part time job in the Craigmore Tearoom but there was Maureen to look after and Joe had another year left at school. Bills were flying in from all quarters. My income was the only thing preventing us from slipping under the poverty line. They depended on me now. I had become the family's provider. I didn't want this new role. It scared me to death. I tried to stave off my fate by promising myself things would soon change. My dream was still out there waiting for me. That dream would solve everything.

But nothing messed up my mind more than the secrets I uncovered about Dad. His death flung open a myriad of cupboard doors - fucking skeletons tumbled out right, left and centre, thrashing around in a scene from a mad Ray Harryhausen extravaganza! Dad died intestate. Being a superstitious soul he refused to make a will or arrange life insurance. He believed this would be tempting fate to the point where he would probably be dead before the ink dried on the documents. This same logic applied to owning an organ donor card. He refused to carry one fearing that if he did, a serious accident would inevitably follow and rather than do everything possible to save him, the surgeon would whip out his organs before the anaesthetic had time to kick in... But these were minor quirks.

Mum and Dad's marriage hit the rocks almost immediately. Only when they started living together did it become apparent that theirs was not a match made in heaven. Things settled down when I arrived but not for long. After years of embittered compromise they separated shortly after Joe's birth. The whole army thing was a lie cooked up by Mum and Dad to conveniently explain his lengthy periods away from home. Mum reckoned the truth would have devastated us. Though I suspect she lived in the forlorn hope that Dad would return permanently to the fold and with luck and a few more lies the children would never notice the join.

The rest of the family were told to tow the party line for the sake of the kids. Dad travelled the country following the work and sending back as much money as he could afford every week without fail, never shirking from his duty to support his children. He wanted a divorce. Mum refused. Already racked with guilt, her fragile conscience would not allow another admission of failure and weakness in betraying her sacred vows.

Mum knew her estranged husband enjoyed a succession of women but never demeaned herself by pressing him for details. After a brief reconciliation which resulted in Mum becoming pregnant with Maureen she finally conceded defeat. She would leave Dad alone to carry on with his life as long as he didn't push the divorce issue, continued to provide financial support and came home as often as he could to keep up appearances and prevent his children from getting hurt. This last was an unnecessary demand. He always made it obvious how much his children meant to him. He couldn't lie about that.

The last discussion Mum ever had with him focused on how they would break the whole truth to us. She ended the conversation with a promise to cooperate in divorce proceedings. He told her there was no hurry. Dad died a married man.

The conflict would rage on in my mind for years. I felt ashamed of myself for having been so gullible. Nostalgic memories of Dad became transparent and colourless. I wanted to forget them. To have them erased.

The living room was cluttered with empty glasses, bottles, cans, half consumed bowls of crisps, nuts and trays of sandwiches curling at the edges. The aftermath of the wake. Two o' clock in the morning. Only Mum and I were left.

The air was heavy with the smell of stale booze and spent smoke. Mum was pissed. The alcohol had warped her mood. She had been a model host in front of the guests even laughing once in a while but now depression seized her. Tears would flow then stop like a sudden shower. In turn she would plead with me then yell at me while spilling out her darkest fears.

'...I need, I need *you* son... Haig? You listenin' tae me? I need you son.' Mum's red-shot eyes struggled to lock on to me. 'The family allowance is no' enough son. We've got nae money. You don't want us tae be destitute dae ye? Eh?' she asked, her pained expression emphasising the worry lines. She leaned forward in the armchair and reached out a shaky hand almost knocking over the table lamp separating her from where I was sitting on the sofa. She clasped my hand.

'The bank will look after you son. Don't give it up. I'm beggin' you,' she implored. 'You're the breadwinner now. Think of yer family Haig... yer wee sister... wee Maureen dotes on you son. She loves her big brother... and Joe... and me. We need yer support son. Oor future depends on you... you don't want wee Maureen tae suffer sure ye don't...'

This was getting ridiculous. I'd had a fair measure of whisky and my drunken brain struggled to cope with such an endless volley of emotional blackmail.

'Mum yer pissed. Things are no' that bad! You wait and see. If Celtic take me on I'll have a much better wage. I'll be able tae look efter ye all much better. Pay back on, on... on the loans, buy the hoose...'

'Oh wake up Haig!' Mum sank back into her chair with a scowl. She took the last cigarette from what had been her third pack of Regals in the twelve hours since the funeral and realised just in time that she was about to light the wrong end.

'You need to stop dreaming aboot this Celtic nonsense! You're no' good enough Haig!' she bleated.

'I am! They've told me as much!' I spluttered, angry at the unwarranted put-down.

'Och! Trust you to put yer own selfish... self first!' she sniped draining the dregs of another half bottle of Smirnoff into her tumbler. 'If you quit the bank you'll end up on the dole with three million others! Would ye see us starve just so you can kick a ball aboot! I had dreams as well you know but I sacrificed *everything* to raise you lot. And this is the thanks I get!' she raged with one eye involuntarily shut and her voice growing louder with each word.

I shook my head. I refused to rise to the bait. Hurtful as her words were I knew it was the drink. Vodka always made her aggressive. The tip of her cigarette glowed amber signalling the intake of another lungful.

With the flick of some internal switch Mum became reasonable again, 'Haig. Son. What if you got injured? Have you thought about that? What if they find somebody better son? What if... I dunno - you lose yer,' she paused to suppress a belch, '..Yer... skills or something? Then where will ye be?... You need tae think of these things Haig... God's tellin' ye somethin' here son...'

Oh no here we go - I thought. I should have known the Big Fella would be putting in an appearance.

'...He's tellin' you to look out for yer family. They've always been there for you. Now it's your turn to be there for them... for us...' Another outbreak of tears seeped from her eyes. She stared into her glass, swallowed the contents and placed it on the sideboard.

Mum sat silently for a while lost in thought. She dried her eyes on the back of her hands, sniffed hard and sighed deeply. She drew on her cigarette trying to calm herself and opened her mouth but it took a few moments for the words to reveal themselves.

'Sorry son. I know I'm being daft... I'm sorry. It's me that's being selfish... You do what you like... Just,' she sniffed pushing a few strands of damp hair away from her face, '... Just don't make the same mistakes me and your Dad made. Don't get married too young son.' She sighed again. Her eyes blinked heavily, 'That was my biggest mistake - I was too young when I got married. You be careful son and, make sure you wait a few years before you marry that Elspeth of yours'.

She fell asleep. I reached over, gently pulled the cigarette from her fingers and stubbed it out. I watched her sitting there, slumped in her chair. The sheer exhaustion of the last few days had finally caught up with her. For a horrible second I thought she'd died on me as well - but then her gentle snoring kicked in.

At last. The onslaught was over. I could relax for a while and try to take stock of everything that had happened. My alcohol-addled brain whirred. Her guilt-seeking missiles had successfully connected with various targets in my heart and mind. My common sense defence systems were running low on ammunition. All those formative years of trudging reluctantly off to church every Sunday morning to endure the warblings of a monotonous priest had taken their toll. Maybe that was the point of those dreary weekly sessions. I had been brainwashed. The morals and values of that all powerful Roman institution had been ingrained into my subconscious using the tried and trusted method of dull repetition.

There was truth in what Mum had said however fuddled. The situation *was* desperate. My job *was* a life-line. Could I afford to risk chasing my ambitions at my own flesh and blood's expense? I only had to look back on the last twenty years to acknowledge that luck was not something I could rely on. Knowing me I would probably suffer a career ending injury in my very first match. The fear grew. The fear of duty and responsibility.

The delicate, middle-aged woman softly snoring in the chair next to me had sacrificed her all to raise her children. She had given *everything*. It had taken Dad's death for me to fully understand just how much she had given us and how she had scrapped like a lioness to keep a roof over our heads, food on our plates, clothes on our backs and toys in our hands. She expected little thanks and received even less. What would she be doing now if she had chased her dreams? Where would we be if she had? Why couldn't this be happening to someone else?

Looking around the room gilded by the lilac-shaded glow of the lamp, the reality hit me hard. This was my lot. The harsh realisation pierced my core like a cold blade. And I hated it. I absolutely fucking loathed it. The dingy, squalid, vulgar pointlessness of it all. Life reduced to a half-arsed pantomime. Why should I feel shame or guilt? I hadn't done anything wrong.

And therein lay the problem. I hadn't done anything at all. Life was so fucking banal and I'd wasted so much of it thinking tomorrow would be different. It was time to stop waiting and hoping and actually *do* something. Something noteworthy. Something more than merely exist. But the world appeared to be full of faceless entities employed for no other reason than to keep you trapped in your own predictable little box. It used to puzzle me why such vast numbers of people conformed. Not anymore. They weren't conforming. They were surrendering. Because like me, they had been beaten into submission.

I poured another whisky. Another measure of self-pity. The depression squeezed tighter with each burning sip. I couldn't decide whether or not I should bother to contact Mr McIntyre. What I really wanted to do was run and hide. I thought of The Buzz Building - Strong, safe and secret. A whole other world...

Two weeks later I received a letter from Celtic Football Club. The text beneath the primarily green letterhead ran as follows;

Dear Haig,

Please accept my deepest sympathies regarding your recent loss.

I realise this is a particularly painful time for you but I feel duty bound to inform you of the outcome of the recent trials.

I feel it is only fair to inform you that we were impressed by several young strikers at these games and have decided to offer three of these lads contracts.

Therefore I regret to say that we have no need to pursue further talent in this area.

I sincerely hope that you are not too disheartened by this outcome and would encourage you to approach other clubs who may be on the lookout for someone with your undoubted skills.

Meanwhile let me take this opportunity to wish you all the best for the future.

Yours sincerely,

Tommy McIntyre.

Game over.

*

I gathered Elspeth in my arms.

'You'll come down and visit me soon? Promise?' She asked wiping a tear from her cheek.

'As soon as I sort things out here. I promise.'

But we both knew that this was goodbye. Our five years together were effectively over. I ran a hand through her hair and looked deep into her magical eyes. Then we pressed our mouths together in a final embrace and kissed with all the passion of condemned lovers.

I let her go.

She picked up her bag and boarded the ferry. The Jupiter set sail and took Elspeth away from me.

*

'This has been here for nearly a thousand years.'

'D'you think oor hoose will last a thousand years Dad?' I asked.

'I doubt it wee man,' he laughed.

Dad held my hand as we approached the centre of the courtyard walking in a tight circle, taking in the ruins of Rothesay Castle. Ripples of slow moving cirrus trailed lightly across an indigo sky. Summer was ending. With the tourist season drawing to a close we were the only people visiting the castle.

We ambled over to the well and peered down its mossy throat. The sunlight penetrated a good ten feet or more but the bottom remained hidden in its black depths. Taking a firmer grip of Dad's hand, I stepped carefully on to the well's low perimeter wall. An iron mesh coated in thick black paint protected the mouth of the void, put there I surmised, to stop weans like me from falling in. I gently rested a foot on one of the struts separating me from the abyss and felt my whole body charge with the expectation of the metalwork giving way. It remained firm. I applied a little more weight, tempting fate. Dad suddenly pushed me. I jerked forward and yelped but in the same instant he grabbed me round the midriff, plonked me on the grass and couldn't stop laughing at his own little prank.

'Don't do that!' I scowled, furiously trying to pretend he hadn't scared me one jot although my pounding heart needed another moment to realise I wasn't plunging to my doom after all.

'That hole goes all the way through to Australia. Did you know that? That's what that grate's there for. To stop people leaving the country for free,' Dad said rummaging in his pocket.

I looked at his face and studied his eyes. He seemed serious enough. It must be true... Or was he trying to trick me again? I examined the well once more. Definitely couldn't see the bottom.

'Here, send a wee present to Australia,' he smiled handing me a ha'penny.

I took the shiny copper coin, gathered its cold weight on my palm, then leaned carefully over the rim. I let the coin slide from the tip of my fingers. It bounced twice flipping across the iron latticework then slipped through. I saw it glint once before it disappeared for good. I waited for a sound - a ping against stone or a plop into water. Nothing. I pondered how long it would take for the coin to reach the other side of the world.

Continuing our tour of the castle we headed inside the keep to explore the Great Hall. The broad, cool space echoed with our footfalls crossing the polished wooden floor. A slight through draught gently rippled the ornate tapestries and banners lining the walls. I approached a bronze bust of a stern-looking old man.

'Who's this s'posed to be?' I asked expecting to learn about some legendary Scottish hero.

'The Marquess.'

'What's he got to do wi' Rothesay?' I frowned, unable to disguise my disappointment.

'He likes to think he owns the place.'

'What does a Mar... Markwiss do?'

'Good question son. As soon as I find out, I'll let you know.'

Dad took my hand and led the way down the spiralling stairs until we reached the vaulted passage near the main gate. I presumed this meant we were going home but instead Dad took me across the ancient flagstones to where a rope guardrail surrounded a manhole-sized aperture. He gripped the sturdy iron ladder embedded in the hefty stones of the wall and descended into the gloom. Adrenaline tingling in full flow, I went after him. I climbed carefully down through the floor and into... the Dungeon.

A musty air filled the suitably grim and oppressive space. Dad had trouble standing up straight and even I found myself stooping against the crude, jutting ceiling in places. Apart from the thin light filtering down with the ladder, the only other illumination squeezed in through a tiny window set so far back in the thick exterior wall that my skinny little arms could barely reach it. It was easy to imagine the room in its medieval prime, cramped with dying, disease-ridden and tortured prisoners. I wondered what it would be like to spend the night in its spooky confines. I shivered. There was no way I could do it on my own. Even in the daylight, feeble as it was, the eerie chamber made my hairs stand on end.

'Is it haunted in here?' I whispered.

'Oh aye. Loads o' ghosts in here but they only appear at night,' Dad explained as he sat on the bumpy floor. He must have seen me anxiously double-checking the state of play beyond the narrow window. 'But don't worry. They're too busy fighting each other to bother wi' the likes of you.'

'How come?' I sat against the wall opposite him, primed and ready to run for the ladder at the merest hint of an apparition.

Dad picked up a handful of the grey dust which carpeted the floor.

'See this?' he asked letting the stuff drizzle away between his fingers. 'This is all that's left of the prisoners they used to keep here. All their bones ground to dust over a thousand years. Problem is, the bones of all kinds of different soldiers from all sorts of different armies are all mixed together in this dust. And believe me - they *hate* each other. They were bitter enemies when they were alive and just because they're deid doesn't mean to say they've changed their ways. Oh no...'

'What d'ye mean?'

'Well, ye see,' he leaned forward to explain. 'First the Vikings came. They raided Bute, slaughtered the Scots and took the castle. Not without a fight mind. The battle lasted three days. The Vikings lost hundreds of men - those daft helmets with the cow horns were no use against the boiling lead and tar they poured from the castle walls. Even so those Vikings kept on coming until eventually they overwhelmed the castle's defences. They rounded up the survivors, stuffed them all down here and left them to rot. Men, women and children. They didn't care. But the Vikings made a mistake. They thought the Scots would never dare to take the castle back. They didn't think the Scots would have the guts to take them on again. How wrong they were! The Scots raised an army, sailed up the Clyde and battered those cocky Norsemen good and proper until they won Rothesay back. And then it was the Vikings' turn to die in this dungeon.'

'But there was never a minute's peace on Bute in those days and the

120

Tartan Army didn't even have time to finish their fish suppers before the English invaded, stormed the castle and massacred everybody. So yet more Scottish soldiers breathed their last breath right where we're sitting now.'

'Did we manage to fight back against the English?' I had to know. Dad had me enthralled.

'You're not joking,' he smiled. 'But it wasn't easy. The good folk of Rothesay gathered together and tried to raid the castle but they didn't have any proper weapons and they were forced to retreat. Time and again they tried and time again it cost them dearly,' he sighed dramatically. 'It didn't look good. Make no mistake, the situation was dire. But they knew they couldn't surrender because if they did the English would execute every last one of them. The people of Bute had no choice. They had to run and hide. They hid in caves. They hid in the woods and in secret dens. But the English were relentless. They sent out search parties and scoured every last inch of the island hunting the rebels until eventually they cornered the last band of Scots near Barone Hill… And that's where their luck changed.'

'Ye see, a thousand years before even this battle to the death was taking place, an important person died on Bute. And this important person was buried on top of Barone Hill. And because he was important his grave was covered in a huge pile of stones as a mark of respect. That pile of rocks was still there hundreds of years later when those Scottish rebels reached the top of Barone Hill. In fact that pile of stones is there to this very day. But anyway; the Scots grabbed hundreds of those rocks and started pelting the English who were huffin' and puffin' their way up the hill. They knocked those knackered soldiers senseless, grabbed their swords and chased the rest of the English force back to the castle where most of them were chopped to pieces. The Scots showed no mercy. They even cut the English commander's heid off. Any English soldiers left standing were thrown into the dungeon.'

He leaned back and folded his arms with a smile, 'That's why you have all these different kinds of ghosts in here; English, Scottish and

Viking soldiers fighting each other every night.'

I was so mesmerised by the thought of claymores and broadswords sparking in the night I could actually hear the blades clashing.

I poked a finger into the dust.

Dad stood up taking care not to bang his head. 'Come on wee man. I better get you home before your mother sends oot her own search party.'

8: junctions

My sticky eyelids prise apart. My mind teems with echoing dreams and memories, gathering together to form an ethereal mass which fades away like the glow from a candle wick…

I can't tell if I've been sleeping or daydreaming and I don't know how long I've been lying here but this bath water is fucking freezing. Hours... It's grown dark. My eyes adjust. In keeping with the rest of my brother's house the bathroom is pristine and ordered. Joe clearly inherited all the neatness genes.

The bath was bliss. A good thorough cleansing. Warm and inviting I must have been lulled into a stupor almost immediately. I whisk some water over my face, rinsing my eyes and clearing my head. Such a relief. My scalp no longer feels as though it's playing host to a colony of fire ants. I climb out, towel myself dry and wonder if Joe has any beer in the house or maybe even a bottle of whisky. It would be nice just to sit down and relax with a decent drink. I try to imagine the flavour warming my tongue and smile. I would like to get drunk. Absolutely hammered, bladdered and smashed. Pished. I can't recall the last time I was absolutely blootered. Which is as it should be I suppose.

I feel surprisingly cheerful for a dying fugitive. Before I dress I place a hand to my heart to feel its beat… Feels strong. I can't detect anything untoward. Wait… The rhythm went a wee bit feeble there I'm sure… Again… That beat felt – *feathery?*

Having made sure to leave the bathroom in a respectable state, I tread down the soft, deep pile smothered stairs in my new (stolen) suit and a pair of Joe's socks I pinched from the bathroom radiator. Reaching the foot of the stairs I see the living-room door half open at the far end of the hall. I can see the television but the rest of the room is hidden. I scratch the itch playing havoc with my swollen ankle taking care not to tear away the scab.

The hall displays more of Joe's artwork. Seascapes and landscapes. I pause to admire a stunning picture of a half sunken boat surrendering to the waves near the shore at Balnakailly Bay. I hear a telephone handset being lifted from its cradle. Looking back inside the living-room I see the head and shoulders of a purposeful man on television. He is talking to someone off-screen. I can't hear what he is saying. The picture cuts to the presenter nodding earnestly. The man reappears looking increasingly serious. The information he continues to impart is no joke. A caption appears across his chest bearing a name I am too far away to read. I step quietly along the hall.

Attention gripped by the television my hand rests silently on the door frame. Instead of entering I remain frozen in the doorway. The pulse thuds at the side of my taut neck. They are broadcasting security footage of my raid on the Conservative Club. *There I am!* – In grainy, indistinct colour bounding across the tables on my way out. They cut to shots of the prison…

Back to the man. He witters on and mentions my name. The caption returns accompanied by a telephone number. DI Julian Craven is appealing to witnesses (not to this one he isn't). Apparently I am potentially dangerous and therefore not to be approached… This is all I'm allowed to glean because a green bar appears across the foot of the screen and a little black indicator edges to the left of that horizontal line. The volume dies away. I hear Joe's voice…

'Uh, hullo… Aye. I've got some information for ye… Yep…'

My face suddenly fills the screen. *Shit!* – A prison mugshot designed to make me look like the ugliest psychopathic mental case ever to stalk the face of the earth. *Oh magic! Even better!* – The nation is now treated to a nasty profile shot.

'I can tell you where he is right now… Eh?' My brother says in hushed tones. 'Haig Dumfries. I can tell you where he is right this second…Hold on a minute. Before I tell ye – How much is this reward…? And how long will it be before I actually have the money in ma pocket…?'

I enter the living-room without a sound while somewhere deep inside, a part of me curls up and dies. I can't believe this is happening. Joe is huddled over the phone with his back to me. I feel my throat stiffen. I swallow hard. I'm frowning as I blink rapidly to clear the water stinging my eyes. He tells them who he is, his address and his phone number.

'Joe?' I utter shakily.

He spins around to face me with a horrified expression. The phone is slammed down.

'I was just phonin'… um…' He stops. He knows he'll never come up with a convincing excuse.

I am breathing hard, pressing my eyes shut tight. I am both furious and crushed. Do I kill him? Do I beat the shit out of him? Do I stare him out and leave without a word? I don't know… I open my eyes. Joe is on his feet. He glances at the television. Then back at me. He looks nervous. Scared. I really believe he's worried that I'm going to attack him. I feel worse.

'What price did ye get for me?' I rasp, having to clear my throat.

Joe frowns unsure. He stares at me warily.

'Five grand.'

I force a wan smile.

'What d'you intend to do with the money?'

He pauses warily, like I'm asking him a trick question.

'I'm gonnae use it to help Elaine pay for Mum's care,' he says defiantly.

I can almost sympathise with the motive. I sigh and step forward slowly. Joe moves back instantly, bracing himself. I throw my despairing hands in the air.

'I'm not gonnae thump ye Joe! Unlike you I couldnae hurt my own brother.'

'What?' he scowls incredulous. 'You are one conceited bastard d'ye know that? You've got no fuckin' idea of the damage you've done have ye? You've hurt your family more than you'll ever know! You've put us through hell and you've got the fuckin' cheek tae stand there as if *you're* the victim! As if *you're* the one that's been hard done by! And you've got the fuckin' brass neck tae come tae ma hoose and ask why I left Rothesay!' He snorts in disbelief. His face is turning purple. 'Why d'ye fuckin' think! Coz I couldnae fuckin' stand any more snidey comments from wankers in the pub goin' on aboot ma murderin' scumbag brother or, or any more fuckin' dirty looks from auld grannies passin' me in the street! What is it you find so hard to understand? Why d'ye think yer family doesnae fuckin' write or visit ye? Eh? Blame yerself Haig! This is nob'dy's fault but yer own! Yer a fuckin' useless prick!'

His anger leaves me reeling. He's never sworn at me with such ferocity before. Obscenities and insults are used as punctuation marks on the inside but to have them spat at me from my wee brother... I want to retaliate. I want to say something that will bury the argument and leave him speechless the way he's left me. I wish I could pull the rabbit from the hat and produce the conclusive proof that will make him realise just how wrong he is.

I slump into the armchair he's vacated. I rub my face, bury it in my hands and try to focus on a single, clear thought...

'So don't fuckin' expect me tae feel guilty! All I'm trying tae do here is repair some of the damage you've done.' I can feel his stare burning into my head. 'As far as I'm concerned you stopped being ma brother the second you murdered that poor lassie. And if you've got any fuckin' decency left in that stinking soul of yours you'll give yerself up and let yer family take advantage of that reward money! Mum's so sick she doesnae even know what planet she's on any more! Did ye know that? She needs constant attention twenty-four fuckin' hours a day. And that kind of thing doesnae come cheap! So for once in your pointless life do somethin' tae help will ye?

He has a point. I have been too wrapped up in myself and, misguided though he is, it is nevertheless, true - I haven't given enough consideration as to how my stupidity must have affected everyone else. Everyone that is, except Elspeth. I torture myself daily thinking of her and how she must thank her lucky stars we parted when we did.

Ten years ago it was my desperate attempt to find money to help Mum that landed me in this mess. And now? All I have to do to raise a far more significant amount for her care is do nothing more than sit in this chair and wait. I find myself smiling at the irony.

Shame is creeping up on me… I shake my head. *I am not a murderer! This is not my fault!* I wish I was the only player in this nightmare game, I really do - but I can't be held responsible for dragging in a whole set of other victims… Or can I? Whichever way I look at, regardless of fate, circumstance, bad luck or whatever; it was *my* actions that led to this. I am a catalyst for misery. An unlucky charm for anyone destiny chooses to place me with.

I take my hands from my face. This futile bout of self pity is just my way of shying away from doing the right thing. Of killing time until a decision is made on my behalf. Should I stay here and wait? I look at the clock. The second hand seems to be speeding up. I have more important places to be than this puffy armchair.

I stand up wearily and turn to face Joe. He is still watching me cagily but has calmed down now having said his piece. 'I'm tempted Joe. I'm tempted to stay and help you out. But five grand? In this day and age you'll be lucky if five grand pays for one wipe of the arse and a cup o' tea in a private clinic. I'm sorry Joe but fuck it y'know?' I hold open the living-room door, 'I've got nothin' to feel guilty about either. Right from the fuckin' start I told you all I didnae kill that woman. Ten years I've been tellin' everybody that. And none of you believe me. Fine. That's fine. I've come to accept that. No doubt you'll be pleased to know that you won't have tae put up with…' I decide not to spill the beans on my life expectancy and put on an air of loud but false bonhomie.

 'Anyhow, I really must make a move if that's okay with you? Thanks again for your hospitality! For the bath and everythin'! Much appreciated. Right then! I'm away! See ye Joe!'

I step into the hall then quickly poke my head back in to Joe, 'By the way. Love the pictures! First class!'

I leave my brother for what I know will be the very last time. I stride through the hall trying to suppress confusing tears of frustration, anger and grief. I slam the front door behind me and angrily advance a few paces before I realise…

I haven't got a clue which way to go.

*

'…It's not easy for me you know. This is my own flesh and blood we're talking about here. I just want to make sure I get what I deserve.'

A smack in the mouth is what this dickhead deserves, - thought Craven, blowing his nose into a damp hanky.

Crimewatch had paid instant dividends when the fugitive's own brother rang in offering assistance. He had been surprised to get on this month's show at such short notice and his worsening cold ensured his attempts to chat up Anya, the attractive production assistant, remained a fruitless endeavour. It had been Craven's second appearance on the show. The first occurred seven years previously when he appealed for information in connection with the rape of an eighty year old woman. The culprit was never found.

As soon as he received the information, Craven had hightailed it from Shepherd's Bush to North Buckinghamshire where a couple of amiable lads from the Thames Valley force escorted him to the Milton Keynes home of Joseph Dumfries.

He had called Lorna on the way up. She'd recorded his television appearance as requested. He would review his performance when he got home. Always room for improvement. He still wasn't sure about his choice of tie. His wife had sighed, somewhat theatrically Craven thought, when he told her he might be away for a few days. She made him promise he'd be back for the twins' birthday but that was still five days away. He wouldn't be away *that* long and anyway Lorna was much better at buying presents than he was.

Craven was more than happy to escape the bosom of his family for the duration. Rachael's sulk had become a record breaker and no-one had made any progress in uncovering the cause, though the finger of blame now seemed to be pointing away from Simon and towards her dad. Craven racked his brain but for the life of him he couldn't recall having done anything to upset her.

The living-room was warm and the armchair comfy, which only served to remind him of just how tired he was. He desperately needed some sleep but the man sitting opposite was proving a touch stubborn when it came to parting with his knowledge. So far Joseph Dumfries had shown far more interest in the details surrounding the procurement of the reward. Craven, trying hard not to lose his patience looked up at the picture of an old paddle-steamer on the wall.

'If the information you give us, leads to the recapture of your brother, then yes – the reward is yours.'

'Does it have to be a cheque? Is there any chance I could have it in cash?' Joe asked.

Craven yawned. This man was a living stereotype. 'I will see what I can do. Now. Mister Dumfries...'

'Joe. Call me Joe.'

Craven leaned forward to face the tight-fisted Scotsman. He didn't look much like his brother, except perhaps around the eyes.

'Okay Joe. It's late. We're all tired and I'm sure we'd all like to get some sleep before...'

'Doesnae bother me. I work nights...'

'For Christ's sake will you just tell us what you know! Please! Before I...' Craven's raised voice crackled and croaked into a coughing fit.

'Awright. There's no need tae get arsy pal. I was only asking. Is he always this tetchy?' Joe asked the two policemen on the sofa but they were too concerned with their now choking superior to answer. 'Shite. You awright pal?' Joe asked Craven. 'D'ye want a glass o' water or somethin?' He began to rise from his chair but Craven gestured for him to remain seated. The coughing subsided and with a long, deep breath Craven regained his composure. 'Oh and by the way – I should be in work right now but I phoned in sick earlier just so as I could help you lot out. I won't be getting any sick pay so is there any chance I could get compensation for loss of earnings?'

'If you don't start being more cooperative,' Craven's voice strained, 'I will tell your boss you've been arrested for molesting schoolboys.'

Joe sank back into his chair looking hurt. 'He knocked on the door... It must've been about half one, two o' clock or somethin'. Bastard got me oot ma bed. He came in and sat doon where you're sittin'. We didnae say very much. I made him a cup o' tea, then he went for a bath. He spent bloody hours in that bath... Try tae understand big man, this is really awkward for me, awkward for the whole family. I mean there was a time when Haig would've done anything for his family. He even gave up the chance tae be a professional footballer after Dad died tae look after us but...'

'Pass me the phone. I need to call the Pope and tell him there's a saint on the loose,' Craven yawned, too tired to reel in the sarcasm.

Joe ignored the jibe and ploughed on. 'But that was a long time ago and it just goes to show ye can never tell how someone will turn oot. No' even yer own brother. Imagine how oor Mum felt after what he done. She was fuckin' devastated. She'll never forgive him. None of us will. Did ye know that she even visits a priest every week to confess on his behalf?'

'What did he do after his bath?'

'He caught me phonin' you lot. We argued. Then he was off. That was it basically.'

'So he left here about quarter to eleven. Is that right?' Craven glanced at the clock – it was approaching one.

'Aye, that sounds about right,' confirmed Joe.

'Was he in good health when he left?'

Joseph Dumfries looked puzzled. 'What d'ye mean?'

Craven sighed, 'I mean was your brother fit and well?'

'Aye. He seemed awright tae me.'

'Where do you think he'll go?' asked Craven, flicking open his notebook.

'Bute. No doubt about it.'

'What makes you so certain?'

'Because he'll want tae go home. He hasn't seen or spoken tae

Mum in over ten years. He'll want tae see her. Tae try an' convince her that he's innocent. That *he's* been hard done by. The sick basturt's never faced up tae the truth.'

'Close to his mother was he?' Craven couldn't resist a little sneer.

'No more than any normal son. But that's where he's goin' I'm tellin' ye. Home tae Rothesay tae see if Mum will listen tae him. But she'll no'. She never wants tae speak tae him again.' Joe looked up at the row of photographs lining the top of the wall unit. 'Sounds bad I know but it would be so much easier for us all if he was deid.'

Sitting behind the wheel of his car Craven stared at Joe's house lost in thought. He'd asked all he could be bothered to ask and had said his goodbyes to the lads who'd brought him here. His vision drifted back into focus. Craven looked carefully at the open notebook in his hands. The only words on the page were:

Rothesay – Bute.

He yawned again, cleared his throat and swallowed the mucous gathering at the back of his mouth. He tossed the notebook aside and picked up his oversized *Master Road Atlas*. The little overhead light would only work if the door was open. *Must get that fixed* - he thought, knowing he wouldn't. He scanned through the index pages. Where the hell was this place…?

Rothesay: 73 – D16.

Craven thumbed to the indicated page and didn't need to follow the co-ordinates because there it was big and obvious – Isle Of Bute. He wondered if the Strathclyde force would be as accommodating as Thames Valley.

Craven had been to Scotland once before. It was his and Lorna's last holiday together before the kids arrived. They spent a week in Edinburgh during the festival. He had particularly enjoyed looking around the castle and museums but the theatre, arts and stuff were really his wife's domain. She loved it – even the irritating street theatre. Craven wanted to leave Lorna to her mime artists and alternative comedians while he sloped off to climb the hills, explore the glens and indulge in a spot of salmon fishing but this was early in their relationship. The point at which couples feel obliged to do everything together. If they were to take the same trip today he knew they would both happily spend time apart to do their own thing.

The west of Scotland was virgin territory and to make matters worse, the trip to Bute would involve a ferry crossing. Every time Craven had boarded a boat of any description, he had thrown up without fail. Hopefully Haig would be caught long before that stage. He flicked back through the atlas to plan Haig's route for him… The quickest way by road would be; M1 – M6 – A74 – M74 – M8 – A8 and then the A78 to catch the ferry at Wemyss Bay.

Craven jotted all this down then smiled as he added a little sketch of Joe in a kilt gleefully clutching a wad of notes.

*

Nick Dodds had parked his little Peugeot discreetly at the top of the cul-de-sac. A light rain persistently settled on his windscreen. Every now and then Nick would flick the wipers but would only permit the blades to complete one sweep up and down. The damn things squeaked like a startled schoolgirl. Twice he'd thought the noise had given him away. He watched DI Craven sitting motionless beneath the interior light of his Lexus, the driver's door slightly ajar. He had to concede it was a nice looking car. Probably cost three times as much as his. It didn't seem fair. He bet Craven's wipers worked in perfect silence. Bastard. What was he doing? Nick strained his neck trying to see what Craven was holding. It looked like a road map. He wondered where the hell this magical mystery tour would lead him next.

He had already followed Craven to London where he ended up waiting for several hours outside BBC Television Centre. To allay the boredom Nick had allowed himself the luxury of a brief stroll before returning to the car to stuff junk food into his face. He turned on the radio while he ate but the drivel the DJ inflicted on him became unbearable. That's when he listened to it again. Cathy's compilation

132

tape. The tape she had been playing in her car shortly before she was murdered.

The ninety minutes caught on the tape's rusty surface represented a floodgate through which countless moments swept through him. Since her death he must have played the cassette a thousand times. He felt he knew every word, every bar, every note contained on each of the nineteen songs by heart. The music fed the malignant growth glowing somewhere deep within his chest cavity. The anger inside had to be carefully nurtured. Nick needed the beast's focus and drive. It gave him the courage he needed to see this through to the bitter end.

Listening to *Breakfast* by the Associates' fuelled the strongest ache of nostalgic melancholy, not only because he knew how much Cathy loved Billy Mackenzie's voice but because this was the very last song Cathy ever heard.

His mind had drifted so much Nick almost failed to notice the barrier rise and Craven pull away from Television Centre. Jolting into action in a bit of a fluster Nick had to let several cars flash by before he could pull out.

He managed to keep the tail lights of the Lexus in sight and following became easy when they hit the M1. They came off at Junction 14 where Nick soon found himself driving through a weird city of seemingly endless roundabouts. He tailed Craven firstly to a hotel where the detective appeared to book himself him and then on to a nearby police station to pick up reinforcements before finally arriving in this nondescript estate.

When he watched Craven and those two local uniforms step out of their respective cars and approach the door of number thirty-two, it occurred to Nick that the game might be over and perhaps the police had discovered where Dumfries was hiding out. For a horrible second, not knowing what to do, he began to feel the twisting panic in his chest. If they whisked Dumfries away Nick's chance was gone. The fucker would be chucked behind bars again and that would be the end of it. It was at that point Nick realised he still did not have a cohesive plan for when the moment of truth came. The moment when he would come face to face with Haig Dumfries.

… Squeak… The windscreen wipers cleared his view of the detective sitting motionless in the Lexus…

There was a hefty kitchen knife tucked in his glove compartment and various tools stored in the boot including; a saw, a claw-hammer, a length of rope, several screwdrivers, a carpentry plane, a hedge trimmer, two power drills and an industrial nail gun. There had been no real logic when it came to compiling that list; they were merely objects with the potential to inflict damage (and therefore potentially useful) which happened to be close at hand when Nick drove out of his garage back home.

He knew he might only get one shot at Dumfries and he knew it might prove necessary to take out a couple of policemen in the process but that didn't matter. His mind was concrete. Steadfast. Life had an order. It had to be lived in an orderly fashion. Dumfries had disturbed that order and Nick's blood surged with need. The need to restore order. The need to see Dumfries tortured. The need to hear him accept and understand why he had to suffer a thousand agonies before he was permitted to die.

And so, when Nick saw Craven and his cohorts exit the house - expecting Dumfries to be dragged out with them - he opened the glove compartment removed the knife and gently eased his door open ready to hurl himself at the bastard but then an idea flashed and changed his plan. What if he just drove the car straight at him – ran the fucker over? Who cares if his escorts get hurt? They would only have themselves to blame for getting in the way. He could reverse back and forth over Dumfries until his worthless body was reduced to an unrecognisable mush.

This method had its drawbacks. It was less hands-on than Nick would like. He wanted to *feel* the warm, screaming, squirming death throes; to hear every last stuttering gasp until the final rattle signalled the end. A knife attack would provide these sensations. Nick made up his mind. He would impale Dumfries. Push the blade firmly into his flesh. It would be interesting to find out if he would actually hear the squelching, scratching, cracking and scraping sounds as the serrated steel split skin, tore muscles, snapped sinews, punctured organs and forced splintering ribs apart.

...Squeak...

Nick had absolute faith in himself. He knew he was capable of pushing every cold inch of the blade home. There was absolutely no doubt about it. He wouldn't chicken out or suffer from squeamishness at the last moment. However, there was a wider element of risk in such an intimate attack. The police would surely overpower him before the job was done. Or the fucker might prise the knife out of Nick's grip somehow and the roles would be reversed. No. In this instance ramming the bastard with the car was the better option. There was even a reasonable chance he could escape afterwards. Yes. He would run over the prick. Nick replaced the knife and was about to twist the key in the ignition when it became clear the police were alone. A massive anti-climactic surge swept through his system. He touched his brow and detected a trace of cold sweat.

Nick had slid down out of sight when the squad car drove past.

...Squeak... Again the wipers cleared his view of the detective still sitting motionless in the Lexus.

Nick yawned.

How long is he going to sit there with his face stuck in that map?

The question was answered instantly. Craven closed his door, powered up the engine and drove off leaving Nick with a slight dilemma... He opted not to follow. Letting his main lead go was a risk but he was ninety-nine percent sure Craven would head back to that Travel Inn for the night.

Nick stared at the house. It didn't take a genius to work out whoever lived in that compact, two up-two down semi, had some very pertinent information.

He stepped stiffly out of his car, jogged across to the door of number thirty-two and rang the bell. A faint burr resonated somewhere inside. He turned up his collar as the drizzle became fully-fledged rain and heard a voice grumbling behind the yellow door. A latch was released, a lock twisted and the door swung open.

'Aye? What is it? Who are you?' the man demanded grumpily in a strong Scottish accent, frowning his displeasure as he looked Nick up and down.

'I saw the police come to talk to you there. Would that have been in connection with the man who escaped from prison the other day? Haig Dumfries?'

'What if it was? What business is it of yours?' the man scowled.

'Er, I just erm, want uh…' Nick stammered losing his nerve. He swallowed hard. 'I just want to know er – what you told them. I'm a journalist. From the Daily Mail?'

'Is that right? Well I've dealt with your kind before and yer a bunch o' scavengin' bastards. Piss off.'

Nick dug into his wallet and waved a bundle of bank-notes at the man before he closed the door

'Wait! There's a few hundred quid here. All you have to do is tell me what you told them. Do you know where this Dumfries is? Where he might be going?' Nick tensed. He felt vulnerable and inadequate, almost ashamed at how badly he was handling the situation. His quest hung in the balance. He was an idiot for letting Craven go. He was an idiot for assuming the detective had visited the hotel to book a room for the night. What if he'd only popped in to ask the receptionist for directions or something?

Nick was ready to run back to his car when the man eyed the cash and nodded.

'Come on in.'

*

The night drives rain into my face. I'm drenched. I'm shivering like a washing machine on full spin. My jaws are sore, working overtime to keep my firmly clenched teeth from chattering. My hair, sculpted flat to my scalp, is channeling little icy rivulets down my back. I adjust my collar, pulling it tighter around my neck. This suit may be expensive

136

but I might as well be wrapped in a net curtain for all the warmth it offers. I think of Jim Flack. I think of that cosy, warm, inviting prison cell. *Don't you dare...!*

It's not just the cold that's making me shiver. I'm still angry. *How could he do that to me?* I left Joe's house in something of a daze, unsure about what I was feeling or even how I should be feeling. Once I eventually found my bearings I headed back towards the train station. I was so self-absorbed I nearly didn't notice the pair of police cars pulling up outside Milton Keynes Central. Clearly rail travel was no longer an option. A bus bound for Newport Pagnell offered an alternative.

Standing on the verge of the M1 north-bound slip road, I am watching, waiting for traffic to leave the motorway services while the battering rain seems determined to wash the whole lot away.

A pair of headlights swing on to the slip road. I squint through the curtain of glistening droplets caught in the halogen beams. I thrust out a marble white hand and do my best to look as unthreatening as I possibly can. If anything the car accelerates all the more and blurs past me.

'Wanker,' I mutter allowing my teeth to clatter like a deranged typewriter before slamming them tight again. I've been standing here for what seems like most of my life now and that was only the sixth vehicle to go past... This can't be doing my heart any good. If I stay out here for much longer I'll be hitching a lift in a hearse... Something catches my eye beyond the summit of the slip road. A flashing blue light reflecting wetly from the entrance side of the main building. I leap over the fence and into the adjacent field. My feet sink into the dark spongy soil. I crouch and moving stealthily, traverse the sloping, slick grass until I reach a discreet vantage point overlooking the complex. The motorway service station lies in the background beyond the car and lorry parks. The police car glides to a halt at the top of the slip road near the petrol station.

I work my way cautiously around the perimeter fence keeping half an eye on the squad car which cruises slowly over to the service station's main entrance. The driver gets out and strolls into the building surveying his surroundings as he goes. I watch him until he disappears from view and carefully climb over the fence. A splinter from the wooden post I'm using for support pierces deep into my palm. I can't see the wound. It's far too dark. I let myself slide gently down the bank to the lorry park. The creaks and groans emanating from the slumbering giants fill the swirling air like heavy metallic snores.

The squalling wind burrows inside my shirt trying to peel the freezing, saturated fabric away from my skin. Keeping to the shadows I creep steadily past a sleeping juggernaut. Its canvas flank billows, spraying me with great globs of water. The huge buckles ribbed along its shuddering side slap and bluster, straining noisily as if trying to alert the police to my presence.

Inside the squad car there is a policeman in the passenger seat talking into a radio. I never noticed him before. I stop, obscuring myself behind one of the truck's huge wheels.

A stocky character in a baseball cap exits the service station, pauses to take in the weather then jogs across the car park, into the lorry park and passes within a few feet of me. Judging by his laboured, grunting breath it's been a fair old while since his body's been subjected to this much exercise. I watch the truck driver haul himself into the cab of a car transporter fully laden with a double layer of gleaming BMW's bound for the showroom. This is my chance. I quickly retrace my steps to the foot of the grass bank, grab a fist-sized stone from the verge and sprint across to the rear of the transporter.

A monstrous growl scares me shitless. The vehicle's engine has roared to life. Heart pounding I jump aboard the end of the transporter's ramp. I feel the whole grumbling mass of metal shuddering against an onslaught of battering gusts. Above my head, in the diluted glow of a streetlamp I can just make out a line of shadowy executive car bellies. I use the stone to smash the passenger window of the car next to me. I feel sure someone must have heard the explosion of glass... No reaction from the front of the truck... No reaction from the squad car…

With a loud brief hiss of air the rumbling transporter eases forward. I use my elbow to remove the remaining mosaic of shattered glass clinging to the window frame… The driver of the police car comes out of the service station in time to see a second squad car pull up behind his. The lorry sways and jolts towards the exit. My arms protest at the burning effort needed to hang on to the lorry's skeletal frame. My numbed fingers grip hard, hanging on for dear life to the chilled steel of the vertical strut. The car transporter veers on to the sloping slip road. I can sense the massive wheel spinning beneath my feet gathering pace on the descent towards the motorway.

I reach out and grab the black saloon's door handle and drag myself in through the window. Instant relief. Warm and dry. I clamber over the pristine leather upholstery leaving a smeared trail of water and mud and slump on to the welcoming comfort of the back seat. I sigh. Probably the heaviest sigh of my life. I can relax at long last – for a while at least. It's so good to finally find a little piece of sanctuary. The front seats shield me from most of the wind and spots of rain blowing in through the gaping window. My nose is filled with that satisfying new car smell.

The lorry's engine snarls with each gear change and I feel the whole thing lurch as we level out to join the M1. I have absolutely no idea where my unfit chauffeur is taking us but I do know we're heading north which is fine by me. The lorry has reached its maximum speed. I remove my soaking shoes and socks. Nothing to do now but settle back and enjoy the ride.

I think about Joe. His words ringing in my ears again. I feel pained. Frustrated. Not so much by his betrayal but by the fact that despite all my protestations my own kith and kin still refuse to listen and still have me pegged down as a murderer. What do I have to do to convince them? I had expected at least one member of my family to believe me. Where are those Christian values and ethics they hold so dear? Why don't they apply that doctrine to me? I shouldn't have put myself in that situation - I've already admitted as much - but I couldn't *possibly* have known what was going to happen. We were both victims of circumstance but I did not kill her and I have never swayed from that unalterable fact. Maybe life would have been easier if I had... *Cut the self-pity for fuck's sake!*

I shouldn't have gone to see Joe. Big mistake. Still, it makes no difference to my ultimate aim. It was simply a pit-stop that went badly wrong. I could have done without the assault on my increasingly brittle self-esteem but I can't allow myself to break down. Not now. I need to remain convinced that none of this is my fault. I need to stay focused. Focused on the truth. The truth is I *know* who the real homicidal maniac is and what's more I know where he lives...

Oh shit!... Shit! Shit!... I reach inside my jacket. It's still there! *Thank fuck*! I pull out the piece of paper; damp, limp and yellowed with age. I unfold it tenderly and hold it up to the motorway illuminations flowing by outside.

The name and address are still legible. I'm not quite sure why I panicked. I have long since committed the information to memory so it wouldn't have mattered if I had lost the note. Then again memory is not always to be trusted and I do feel better knowing that I have the piece of paper as back-up. I lie the paper flat on the back shelf. Hopefully it will dry out there. I have one more detour to make before my final destination...

Shivering uncontrollably I pick up all the mats from each footwell and use them as blankets. Why does this country have to be so fucking wet and so fucking cold all the fucking time? It is summer isn't it? If I were to die now at least I would escape this relentless fucking cold.

...I heard his voice. A normal, everyday voice that remained normal and everyday even after he had done the deed. I remember. I watched on helpless and powerless. There was nothing I could do and that's exactly what I did. There was a lot of blood... I curl myself into a more comfortable position, foetus-like on the backseat. I hear a car overtaking us... I did see his face but I'm having difficulty visualising those unremarkable features. It's her face that haunts me... I listen to the hypnotic drone of the lorry's engine distorted by the pummelling wind…

So much blood…

9: notes

The replica gun felt real enough. A heavy, dark mass pressing into my palm. It certainly looked the part. Did I? I studied the scrawl of graffiti decorating the inside of the door... *'Eat my shit!'* – In blue biro beside a drawing of an ejaculating penis complete with hairy balls. Standard fare for a grotty pub toilet. I shoved the gun back in my pocket pulled back the stiff lock and headed across the piss-puddled floor to the sink.

Trying hard not to breathe in too much of the warm uric stink I washed my clammy hands and peered into the smeared mirror. Did I look the part? The stubble I'd been cultivating since losing my job itched on cue. Five hundred pounds was all I needed. Five hundred quid... The bullet was bitten and out I went...

Seven months had passed and there had been no improvement in her condition but thankfully there had been no deterioration either. The stroke had left Mum wheelchair bound and paralysed down her right side, making it nigh on impossible for her to carry out even the simplest of tasks. A poor diet, her fondness for vodka and in particular the smoking had finally caught up with her and duly handed over the bill. She would certainly never work again. We could not bear to see her in such pain and distress. Try as she might to appear positive her humiliation with the hand that fate had dealt her was clear for all to see. Struggling to cope with the indignity brought on by the loss of bowel and bladder control she wept herself to sleep every night with the sheer frustration of it all. It was as if her very humanity was being stripped away layer by layer.

There were moments when I would catch a glimpse of Mum when she thought she was alone. Her dulled, distant eyes gave the impression that she wanted to end it all but I knew she would relent and chastise herself for entertaining such selfish thoughts and evil temptations. When people came to visit and clumsily ask how she was, they would sit and listen with fixed smiles shielding their embarrassment as they struggled to decipher her strained speech. She always brushed aside their sympathy by telling them there were millions of people worse off than she was. Amazingly it was those unfortunates she would pray for in church, never herself. This notion that she was not the one occupying the bottom rung of the ladder seemed to be the only thing that gave her the strength to carry on. These anonymous victims needed her. She was still of use to someone.

A nurse visited regularly to help with the arse-wiping, bag changing and bathing. Mrs Reynolds was a pleasant, thorough woman but ultimately she was only delaying the inevitable. I had to set aside my principals and admit the NHS was ill equipped to help us. Mum deserved the best care money could buy. There was no point approaching Joe for help. Moral support was all he was prepared to offer. Right from the start he had point-blank refused to help out with any of the 'mucky stuff'. He was 'attending' art school in Glasgow but the photography degree was nothing more than a minor distraction from his main task of pissing his student grant up the wall.

So Maureen and I cobbled together whatever money we could find (after I'd made her promise not to go cap in hand to the Hairy Heathen) and booked Mum in to see a private specialist in Glasgow. When the doctor interpreted the flurry of tests he'd ordered, any hopes we may have harboured were ruthlessly dashed. Rather than make even the slightest recovery, Mum's health would in fact fall into a slow, steady decline. This much we'd learned free of charge from our own GP. Prescribing a batch of anti-depressants and pain killers, he ended the final consultation by presenting me with an invoice. The whole process added over a grand to my burgeoning overdraft, threw Mum deeper into despair and taught me a valuable lesson. I vowed never to abandon my principles again.

Maureen and I couldn't cope for much longer. We had to face up to the truth. Mum would have to go into a care home. Mum of course, loathed the idea. Hours, days, weeks of gentle diplomacy were required to convince her that leaving the Eden Drive house was for her own benefit and eventually even she had to accept the stairs alone were making life a misery. Given time, when we finally convinced her we were not looking to abandon her in a quiet corner somewhere to slowly wilt and die unnoticed, she grew to accept the idea. The problem now was to find somewhere suitable.

…I slipped out of the pub and into the rain. The street was virtually deserted. I was halfway across the road when I realised I'd left my hat and glasses behind. I furiously called myself every name under the sun and headed back inside *The Crooked Bough*. How could I expect to pull this off if I couldn't even remember to bring the disguise?…

'I've run out of cigarettes son.'

Locked in position in front of the blank television screen, Mum, slouched in her wheelchair, looked so pitiful. Like a broken doll.

I winked at her. I had come prepared. I pulled out a fresh pack, tore open the cellophane, pulled one out and lit it. She smiled as I placed the cigarette in the fingers of her good hand and left the rest of the pack on the mantelpiece. Maureen placed an ashtray by her side.

'Hey! Don't give her them! That's what got her intae this state in the first place!' Joe whined, having blessed us with his presence on one of his infrequent weekend visits home.

'Oh for Christ's sake Joe. Let her enjoy one wee pleasure in life will ye?'

'Don't blaspheme Haig.'

'Sorry Mum.'

'Come here a minute Haig. I've got somethin' tae show ye.'

I followed my brother into the kitchen and watched him as he rooted around in his rucksack.

'I was in Edinburgh last week taking photos for my coursework when I came across this clinic. Somewhere off Princes Street it was,' he explained pulling out a glossy brochure. 'This could be the answer to Mum's prayers,' he beamed looking very pleased with himself as he flicked through the shiny pages. 'Listen tae this... "The vastly experienced Dr Ernst Frischbaum..."'

'Dr *Ernst Frischbaum*!' I had to laugh. Even the name had a whiff of *eau de Con-Artiste* about it.

Joe scowled at me, 'Aye, so? Just listen will ye?... "The vastly experienced Dr Ernst Frischbaum has pioneered a miracle operation which can reconstruct the electrical impulse pathways in stroke victims thus restoring control where once there had been paralysis... The venerable surgeon's groundbreaking Seattle clinic boasts an astonishing success rate of eighty-three percent."' He proudly handed me the brochure, 'What d'ye reckon? No' bad uh?'

With every page I turned, fat American faces beamed out in gleaming technicolour next to quotations allegedly attributed to them in which the unrivalled benefits of Frischbaum's unique talents, charm and success were extolled. Old Ernst was a blatant quack. He was even quoted as saying that - '*To delay the operation was to diminish the likelihood of a successful outcome.*'

'And how much does this *'miracle operation'* cost?'

'Seventy-five thousand dollars.'

'*Seventy-five thousand dollars*!'

'What're you laughing at?!'

'You! You're so bloody gullible!'

'What d'you mean?' Joe's face had grown so red I could almost feel the heat.

'It's a con for Christ's sake! Yer Doctor Fishbum's a shyster!'

'How d'you know smart arse?!'

'Even if it's genuine Joe – Where are we supposed tae get that kind of money? D'ye reckon yer student grant will cover it?'

'Ach just piss off! At least I'm looking out for Mum!' Joe vented snatching back the brochure and stuffing it in his bag, 'You on the other hand – you wish she was deid don't ye?'

He stormed off before I could retaliate.

… Faith was all Mum had left and it was that faith which persuaded me not to give in to the flash of common sense urging me to take a cab back to the train station and call the whole thing off. Instead, after leaving *The Crooked Bough* for the second time, I hurried on through the downpour with renewed purpose... *Five hundred pounds...* I was depressed and walking along the dun, decomposing street of a strange town depressed me all the more. The double measures of Dutch courage simmering in my stomach were threatening to make a return visit. I stubbed my foot on one of the many cracked paving stones. I shook my head annoyed by my own clumsiness and checked to see if my trip had been spotted. I expected to find every window occupied by laughing and pointing silhouettes but the residents must have had better things to do…

Two and a half months after I'd moved into my creaking Castle Street flat, life was about to congeal from rank pish to even thicker shite.

'Twelve years loyal service and this is how I'm treated? Normally I'd expect a kiss before I get fucked!'

I was in Mr Armstrong's office furiously waving the redundancy letter I'd received that very morning. I wanted to kill the ginger-haired, four-eyed, perfectly tailored fuckwit.

'Please. Haig. Calm down,' my boss trembled.

'Calm doon! Don't tell me tae calm doon ya smug little shite! I ought to shove this letter right up your arse! How come you're surviving these cut backs eh? You better watch it pal – you're liable tae catch somethin' nasty with the amount of arse-licking you get up tae!'

I stormed out.

Standing on the pavement outside the bank half throttling myself as I angrily yanked off my tie, I wondered what on earth I had to do to pull my life out of its seemingly endless nose-dive. Even looking on the bright side the situation was dire. And all because those faceless, cigar-chomping, number-crunching eejits otherwise known as 'senior management' had (over)reacted to shareholder concerns over a dip in profits by enforcing a second wave of sweeping, company-wide reforms leaving myself along with hundreds of other front-line staff unemployed.

A small road-sweeper truck inched along the Victoria Street kerb towards me. I noticed my name-badge still pinned to my shirt. I pulled the badge off and dropped it on the road allowing the truck's whirling brushes to gather up my good name.

My loyalty to the company was deemed to be worth a paltry five grand pay-off. By the time I'd cleared my mounting overdraft and settled all other debts and bills, I was left with sixty-four pounds and three pence in my account.

I signed on for the first time in my life the following day.

… I crossed the road and paused for a moment taking shelter under the awning of a shuttered butcher's. I could see the target clearly now. Only another hundred yards to go. I listened to the rain pounding into the ink-black tarmac. The noise filling the air sounded like the amplified static of a radio unable to tune into anything specific.

I had a promise to keep…

Mum's mood had perked up considerably since I'd last seen her. I could see it in her twinkling eyes. She had received the spark of hope she had yearned so long for. She eased out a leaflet bookmarking the Bible on her lap.

'Haig. I have a chance. A chance to be cured.'

She watched me take the leaflet from her hand smiling happily. The church was organising a three day pilgrimage to Lourdes.

'Lourdes? Mum please, Lourdes is just a theme park.'

The leaflet briefly listed some of the so-called miracles which had taken place there.

'It's a chance. My last chance. I want my dignity back. All I need is faith.'

I turned to the back page.

'And five hundred pounds!'

'I have the faith but... but I don't have the money. You know I don't like to ask but can you help me Haig. Please. Lourdes. Saint Bernadette. The Virgin Mary spoke through her. Remember? It's the only hope I have.' Mum's damaged voice struggled to keep up with her feverish excitement and the words jammed into one another making it difficult for me to decipher the details. She angled her head closer to mine until I saw the tears of desperation beginning to well in her eyes. 'Please son. I don't know what else to do. Will you help me?'

I placed the leaflet back on her lap then leaned in to kiss her on the cheek. A pilgrimage to a holy shrine would be no more beneficial than a visit to Santa's grotto but if nothing else she needed this trip to escape however briefly, from her lifeless, soul destroying routine. Who was I to deny her that?

'Of course I'll help.'

'Promise?' she gasped, her face shining with joy.

'I promise.'

Neglecting to tell her I was out of a job, I left her there grinning at the leaflet happier than she'd been in years

Five hundred pounds. Five hundred problems to solve. Who could I turn to? Aunt Elaine had recently moved into her new house and with all the expenses that entailed, there was no way I could ask her to stump up five hundred quid and besides, when it came to looking after Mum, she had already helped us way beyond what could reasonably be expected of her. Maureen wasn't an option either because like me, she was still reeling from the Glasgow clinic's costs. The Hairy Heathen overheard me discussing the issue with his wife in their kitchen and could not resist sticking his oar in. Through gritted teeth I listened to him pompously tell Maureen that there was no way he was going to waste a single penny on what he described as 'that ridiculous French folly of the Catholic Church.'

'Only God's will can cure your mother,' he continued, 'And perhaps you need to ask yourself why the Lord has deemed it necessary to leave your mother in such a state. Perhaps her affliction is there to atone for the sins of her youth.'

Maureen threw herself between us just in time to prevent me from removing the zealot's face and beard with a potato peeler.

… I kept pace with the rain-water flowing urgently by the kerbside. The first storm drain I passed was flooded. The next one gurgled in protest at having to do twice the work. I looked at my watch. Twenty to midnight. Saturday. More than twelve hours had passed since I'd left Rothesay…

Maureen asked me to stay the night and I had accepted the offer to annoy her husband as much as anything but I found it impossible to sleep under the same roof as him and gave up trying when I noticed the first splinters of dawn. I couldn't wait to escape that pious house and left before they awoke. On my way out I left a note for Maureen asking her to meet me in the pub at opening time.

I walked along the esplanade while the rest of the town slept. There was no sunrise to warm the bitter, damp chill - no fanfare to herald in the morning. Night drained away to leave a granite sky stained with low slung, monotonous clouds. I sat on a bench and looked out beyond the bay to the dark hills towering over Loch Striven. The Hairy Heathen's thorny proclamations had infected my reason. Maybe he was right. I imagined God poring over the evidence before passing judgement on her but there really didn't seem to be enough to justify such a hefty sentence. There was the long term lie about Dad and the damage she knowingly inflicted on her body through smoking but these were not big enough sins in my book. Perhaps Mum was being punished for allowing her children to drift away from the faith. I smiled a wry smile. I should have known that sooner or later I would somehow twist the blame in my direction.

I was the first customer of the day at Zavaroni's Cafe and sat by the window with butter dripping from a bacon roll and steam rising from a mug of milky coffee. Saturday morning and the sun seemed reluctant to get out of bed. The ferry docked releasing its cargo of day-trippers. A seagull perched on the streetlamp directly across the road from the cafe. I watched its twitching head and stern eyes constantly on the lookout for an easy meal. I bitterly regretted having wasted my

149

redundancy money clearing debts and loans. Five hundred pounds. It didn't seem all that much. I thought about Lourdes and imagined the look on the Hairy Heathen's face if Mum was to return, miracle performed, fitter and healthier than the rest of us combined. If only…

After draining a third coffee I left the cafe and headed up the High Street still trying to figure out a solution to the problem. I considered the possibility of approaching the bank to see if they would do an old colleague a favour (I felt it was the least they could do after the way they'd treated me) but I knew what the answer would be. No job - no loan. I noticed a chalkboard outside the scout hall – *Jumble Sale Today!* In the absence of anything better to do I went inside.

I paid my entrance fee to the scout-master and was surprised at how busy the place was. The strangely soothing smell of musty old books filled the hall. Surrounded by tables supporting all kinds of junk, I ambled absent-mindedly along the aisles, browsing heaps of ugly clothes, tacky brass ornaments, home-made cakes and biscuits, records and tapes, barely functional toys, antiquated cameras and accessories, fishing tackle, a collection of pipes, lighters and cigarette cases. Someone was even trying to palm off a huge stuffed pike complete with glass display case.

I picked up a twenty-year old 'Oor Wullie' annual. Apart from a few creases on the cover the book was in good condition. I remembered having received the same book for Christmas when I was ten but my copy had vanished a long, long time ago. I was sorely tempted to buy it when my eye was taken by an object on the next table and an idea presented itself. Almost hidden beneath a mound of old medals, toy soldiers, helmets, a ceremonial dagger and a host of other military bric-a-brac, the barrel of a replica pistol was pointing at me. The fake gun cost a fiver and the wee Cub Scout manning the stall looked more than a bit disdainful when I handed over the money - I think he had his heart set on it himself.

I left the jumble sale another pound poorer having bought a red woolly hat and a pair of thick-rimmed stage spectacles.

... My pulse quickened and my lungs shrank. The bright petrol station occupied the corner on the far side of the junction. I took refuge in a nearby telephone box. An empty can of Strongbow perched on the shelf provided the booth with a warm air of stagnant cider. Hanging around in telephone boxes was becoming a habit...

Initially the plan was a simple one. Revenge. I spent almost half an hour in the phone box near the Winter Gardens. I even picked up the handset and held it to my ear trying to look inconspicuous to the handful of people queuing up at the taxi rank but drew the line at miming a conversation. On the opposite side of Victoria Street, sunshine bouncing off its security conscious, plate glass façade - The Bank. The very bank that considered me to be surplus to their requirements. The window displays promoting an array of financial services with their happy, solvent faces were practically goading me on. My mind was made up. The time had come to get my own back on the bastards. Time to teach them a lesson.

I had the advantage of inside knowledge. I knew their procedures. I knew exactly where the money was kept. I knew where the CCTV cameras were. I knew where the panic buttons were and so I would know instantly if they were bullshitting me. They would get no sympathy from me. The place was insured to the hilt. Morally, I had convinced myself I was in the right and in order to retain a certain dignity I would demand five hundred pounds exactly. Not a penny more, not a penny less. It wasn't going to be easy. This was one of busiest areas in town.

I watched the latest trickle of ferry passengers disembark. For a second I thought the woman in the long black coat walking purposefully towards the taxis was Elspeth. My heart stopped juddering only when I saw the woman's unfamiliar face as she turned to pull a purse from her neat little shoulder bag.

Last I heard, in stark contrast to mine, Elspeth's life had taken off. Her career with the Beeb was flying. Quite literally. They had her jetting around the globe dispatching reports from various trouble spots.

She was very definitely one of their Bright Young Things. She had returned to Bute only once since I watched her sail out of my life and during that brief holiday we met up for what I had reluctantly forced myself to accept would be the very last time over a nostalgic pint in The Black Bull. Laughing and smiling we relived a host of treasured memories. I was surprised at how much Elspeth remembered and even more surprised at some of the things I'd forgotten. Then I made the mistake of asking about her love life. Her cheeks flushed before she confessed that there was someone. She had been seeing a cameraman for some months. My heart sank. Another chapter well and truly closed.

I changed the subject.

What would Elspeth think of me now?... I had to shake myself from my daydreams and wished with some bitterness that I could put an end to the indulgent, time wasting habit of subjecting myself to the withering melancholy of these memories. Feeling suddenly foolish standing there spying on my old workplace, I left the telephone box and headed for the ferry.

What was it that old wizened philosopher once said? That was it... *Never shit in your own backyard.*

The plan had changed. To raise money for Mum's pilgrimage I had to undertake one of my own.

The idea had a certain satisfying symmetry to it.

Less than an hour later I approached the ticket booth at Wemyss Bay train station

'Return ticket to Brighton please.'

'Brighton! That's a first! That's a helluva journey son!' the chirpy attendant gushed. 'You off on your holidays aye?'

You have to speculate to accumulate. Or so I told myself when I handed over money I could ill afford.

...I glanced at my watch. The petrol station would close in fifteen minutes. It was tempting to wait until the doors were locked. At least then I would have a valid excuse for not doing it. Peering through the streaks of rain drumming against the window I could see the empty forecourt but couldn't tell what was going on inside the shop itself.

I tugged the woolly hat tight over my drenched hair, slipped on the false specs, turned my collar up and zipped up my coat obscuring the lower half of my face. I checked the gun once again to make absolutely sure the thing wasn't real. Sure enough the inside of the barrel remained well and truly filled in. It was time to stop delaying the inevitable... *Five hundred pounds...* I closed my eyes, took a, deep, calming breath and made a conscious effort not to think. Putting the gun back in my pocket I left the telephone box and jogged across the junction.

The building itself was nothing special. Just your average run-of-the-mill petrol station. I moved to study the wall facing the main road. The very wall Dad had been crushed against. I touched the cold, damp bricks and ran a finger along the mortar wondering if it might yet contain minute particles of his blood, skin or bone. I expected to feel something, his presence maybe, but nothing presented itself. The only thing to mark the spot where Dad breathed his last was an air hose and a list of recommended tyre pressures.

A truly banal shrine.

I entered the shop dismayed to find a group of four young lads surrounding the counter. The dismay grew when I caught sight of the harassed assistant. A big shaven headed man roughly my age. He looked more than capable of beating the shit out of me if things went awry. The lads ordered a large quantity of cigarettes, rolling tobacco and king size Rizlas to go with the mountain of crisps and biscuits they'd gathered. I walked over to the newspapers, picked up the last remaining copy of The Mirror and made a mental note of the security camera positioned behind the counter on the wall above the cigarettes.

Suddenly overwhelmed by self-consciousness, I began to stiffen. My face burned and my eyes smarted. They knew. Surely they knew I was about to perform a criminal act? I looked like a trainee robber. The ridiculous hat itching my scalp and the dodgy glasses made it impossible to act natural. A clammy embarrassment made my skin shrivel. I could not have felt more awkward if I'd walked in stark bollock naked. My stomach convulsed and a glob of whisky regurgitated into my mouth. I forced the acerbic cocktail of alcohol and bile back and felt it burn all the way down my gullet.

I moved to the chiller cabinet pretending to take a keen interest in the wide variety of pies and pasties. Glancing back to the counter I saw the last of the four – a Manchester United fan – gather up his goods and receive his change. The lads happily made their way out of the shop after a brief argument about whether or not they had enough booze back home. I fingered the gun in my pocket, pulling nervously at the defunct trigger. I approached the counter and slapped the newspaper down.

'That'll be ffff…' The assistant stopped when he saw the barrel aimed at his face. His eyes widened and his expression melted into one of genuine terror. A reaction I had never seen let alone provoked in anyone before. All that gawkiness left my system in an instant. I had complete control over this man. He looked close to tears. I felt sorry for him but found the power strangely satisfying. When I worked behind the counter at the bank I would sometimes idly hope for an armed raid to take place just to break up the monotony of a dull day. I would then wonder what I would do if someone pointed a gun in my face and would always come to the conclusion that as long as I didn't soil myself or worse – faint – then all other outcomes were acceptable. Having my face blown off seemed preferable to the humiliation offered by the former options.

'Empty the till into a carrier bag or I'll blow yer fuckin' brains oot.' I demanded in a truly ropey Belfast accent. This was one of many lines I'd rehearsed – I'd been tempted to use; '*If you fail to hand over every last penny within the next three seconds death will fall swiftly upon you.*' – but even Olivier would've had difficulty delivering that line. The assistant stood stock still, eyes pinned on the pistol. I was about to repeat my demand when, with lightning speed, he snatched a box and flung its contents at me. A salvo of Mars Bar missiles pelted my face and skidded noisily all over the shop floor. The assistant took his chance and disappeared out the rear. I caught sight of him sprinting across the street outside before he vanished into the damp shadows. I was alone in the shop and the clock was ticking.

I leapt over the counter, put the gun back in my pocket, grabbed a plastic bag, opened the till and frantically transferred the notes into the bag. An accurate count would have to wait but even a rough estimate suggested I had collected at least three hundred quid. Several five pound notes missed the bag and fluttered to the floor but when I knelt down to gather them up I found myself confronted with a dilemma. There was a small safe tucked under the counter. Should I use up valuable time looking for the key? The shop assistant was probably on the phone to the police already. The seconds raced on while I weighed up the pros and cons. Chances were the safe contained the weekend's takings so far. There could be over a grand stashed in its jackpot belly.

I quickly searched the surrounding shelves pushing aside boxes of till rolls, carrier bags and a pricing gun. I opened a small set of drawers to my left and discovered a petty cash box – also locked. I shoved the box into the bag. I could break into it later. The safe proved far heavier than it looked. I had to leave it. No more time to dally I hurried to my feet and got the shock of my life.

A woman stood at the counter. Sleek and pretty she wore a faded green shirt tucked into the slender waist of her black jeans. Tying a band around her long brown hair to form a ponytail, there was a quizzical frown playing across her confident features as she swept aside the chocolate bars scattered at her feet. I reckoned the woman to be in her mid-twenties and wondered if she went for guys in half-arsed disguises. I felt ridiculous, like I'd turned up at a funeral in fancy dress.

'What's happened here?' she asked.

'Och just some kids mucking about. I haven't had a chance to clear them up yet.'

'Oh,' she smiled opening her purse. 'Number four please.'

There was a black Saab on the forecourt. I took the twenty pound note she handed to me and glanced at the till display – Pump Number

4 owed twenty pounds exactly.

'Thanks,' I smiled hoping the transaction was over.

'Can I have a receipt please?'

I hesitated and stared at the till. I'd never figure out how to operate such a complex piece of technology. So many buttons! I pressed one or two and hoped for the best. Nothing. The woman looked at me with a growing mixture of impatience and sympathy as if she were asking herself how anyone could leave such a gormless idiot in charge of the place.

'Er... um, I've run out of till roll. I'll just nip out the back and get some.'

I hurried into the stock room and tugged at the door the attendant had fled through. Locked! The sneaky bastard! Hunting for a key, my attention was drawn to the black and white images playing out on a pair of security monitors perched on a shelf. Next to these screens a twin stack of video recorders were quietly going about their business. There were two cameras in operation. The first covered the young woman waiting at the counter with the shop spread out behind her while the second took in the forecourt. A van pulled into the petrol station. Instead of drawing to a halt beside one of the pumps the van parked up next to the shop entrance. *For Christ's sake! Why has every bastard in town suddenly got the munchies?*

I saw a key hanging from a hook screwed into the lip of the shelf beneath the VCR's. I tried the key in the door. The lock clicked. I'd barely crossed the threshold when I stopped dead. *Idiot! The money!* I'd left the bag on the floor beneath the counter! I couldn't come all this way and put myself through all this stress only to leave empty handed. I stepped back inside the stock room and paused when I heard a loud scuffling commotion coming from the shop.

'MOVE AWAY FROM THERE!... NOW PUT YOUR FUCKIN' FACE FLAT ON THE FLOOR OR DIE! YOUR CHOICE!' a muffled voice screamed.

The CCTV monitor showed the woman drop to the floor while three armed men in crash helmets cautiously spread themselves around the shop.

'SHOP!?... IS THERE ANYBODY LOOKIN' AFTER THIS FUCKIN' PLACE!?' the same voice hollered.

Making sure I kept myself hidden from view I crouched down and crept out of the stock room towards the counter.

'What's your name by the way?!... Okay Cathy tell me – Where are the bloody staff!?... DON'T FUCKIN' PISS ME ABOUT BITCH. DON'T YOU FUCKIN' UNDERSTAND ENGLISH OR WHAT?!! ANSWER ME!!... Right. Good. Now do as you're fuckin' told and press your face against the floor!'

I clasped a hand around the bag but before I could move away, a head encased in a big silver, mirror-visored helmet leaned over the counter. The barrels of a sawn-off shotgun dipped towards me. I rose slowly upright until the whole bizarre piece of theatre revealed itself. Her eyes clamped shut and her face scrunched in fear, the woman remained face down on the floor beside stacks of engine oil and brake fluid. The man standing over her wore a metallic blue crash helmet. He held his shotgun in one hand, the muzzle aimed lazily at her head.

'What's goin' on with all these fuckin' Mars Bars?' he said kicking a few of the offending black, red and gold wrappers. He was the one making all the noise and spoke like he was in charge. The third robber stood on look-out duty by the doors. He had settled for a plain white helmet to offset his tatty blue denim jacket and jeans. Separated only by the width of the counter I couldn't work out why Mirror Face, his shotgun aimed at my chest, made no attempt to force me to move or hand over the bag.

'Hey uncle,' said Denim Man calmly.

'What?!' Blue Head snarled impatiently. Denim Man pointed his firearm in my direction. I looked back at Mirror Face and realised what the problem was. In the man's visor I saw my own hand gripped tightly around my gun. The business end aimed straight at its own reflection. My finger were locked, stiff as iron. In comparison Mirror Face's quivering hands struggled to keep both barrels focused on my sternum.

I am definitely going to die right here, right now - I thought with a distinct and troubling lack of concern.

'What the fuck...' Blue Head raised his visor to look at me with astonished eyes.

Everything froze. Interminable seconds elapsed while we sized each other up. For the first time I noticed there was a radio humming away in the background. I recognised the song but couldn't remember its title. The young woman looked at me briefly. The sight of another gun left her mortified. Muttering fearfully she pressed her eyes shut against the nightmare. Glaring at Mirror Face I adjusted my grip and my stance. The bag of money began to weigh heavily on my arm. I peered down the twin tunnels of black steel and imagined their pellet offspring mangling my flesh. *Would it hurt? Would I suffer? Would it be quick? Would I even notice I was dead?*

In the reflective surface covering my opponents face I watched Blue Head sidle over to join us and saw him sneak a peek at the bank-notes poking out of my bag. He casually slung his shotgun over his shoulder. I kept up my silence and continued to follow the wide-angled reflections playing across the visor opposite.

'Bill? Should I back off?' the stifled voice of Mirror Face asked nervously.

'Keep yer trap shut!' snapped Blue Head. He leaned a little nearer to me.

'Any closer and yer pal's deid,' I warned coolly.

'What makes you think I give a fuck?'

'Eh?' whined Mirror Face.

'Listen,' Blue Head sighed, 'I don't know who you think you are mate but we seem to be standing on each other's toes here. We need to reach some kind of agreement and sharpish because the Old Bill are liable to turn up any fuckin' second… D'you hear what I'm sayin'?'

The bag handle slipped slightly in my sweating palm.

'I think you know you ain't gonna win mate. Use that gun and you're a dead man. Yeah sure, you might take one of us with you but…' he shrugged his shoulders, '…The money will end up with us whatever happens. That's all we're after. Just the money. We don't want to kill anybody. That's not our style. So just put the bag on the counter and step back. I'll even let you keep pointing that thing at my cousin here if it makes you feel any better.'

'Eh?' Mirror Face seemed none too happy with the idea.

'Then we can all go home. Put our feet up. Watch the telly. Carry on with our lives. What d'you say?' He stepped over to the prostrate woman. 'I'm sure the lovely lady on the floor here agrees with that plan. Don't you love?' he asked resting one badly scuffed boot on her backside. He traced the shotgun barrel over the small of her back, between her shoulders and through her hair. Without looking at him she raised her head just enough to give a terrified nod. 'See? Even Cathy agrees. Can't say fairer than that.' He spread his arms open, 'All up to you mate…'

'Tell you what…' I swallowed. '…That's exactly what I'll do. I'll put the bag down on the counter and step back. As long as you leave me and the woman alone you can take the money and piss off… And, seeing as you don't mind, I will keep pointing this at your cousin because as it happens – it does make me feel better. Deal?'

I waited. Possibly for the first time ever, my mind was free and clear of all other considerations. Keeping it pointed to the ceiling Blue Head gently took the gun from Mirror Face. I heard Cathy emit a short, stuttering, sigh. Blue Head gestured to his nephew at the door to lower his gun. The whole place felt ready to implode with the creaking tension. Hours seemed to drip away. The rest of the world ceased to exist. Only the garage shop charged with a perspiring, crushing atmosphere, orbited in space around the sun – And then the door swung open and the outside world barged in upsetting the delicate balance threatening chaos.

A fat balding man entered. Blue Head aimed both shotguns at him. 'Fuck off cunt!'

He did exactly that.

'Some fuckin' look-out you are!' Blue Head raged at Denim Man. 'Fuckin' pay attention will ya for fuck's sake!'

Blue Head turned back to me.

Slowly resting the bag on the counter I backed away, keeping my eyes and the impotent pistol carefully trained on Mirror Face as I did so. I pressed myself against the cigarettes and watched Blue Head pick up the bag. The cousins tentatively edged back towards the door. Blue Head kicked Cathy on his way past, 'You can get up now sweetheart! It's over. Come on. Up you get. Our boy's come to his senses at last.'

Denim Man anxiously searching the street, held the door open as his colleagues approached. Cathy rose shakily to her feet and retreated across the floor.

'It hurts to say goodbye, eh Cathy? I felt we had something special going on between us there. But we all have to let go sometime. You'll get over me eventually darling,' the gang leader laughed.

There were tears rolling down Cathy's cheeks. She picked up a small bottle of coke and flung it at Blue Head. The bottle exploded against the door frame spraying the gang in a fizzy brown shower.

'Think you're such a hard man don't you?!' she seethed. 'Think you're so tough with that gun in your hand. I bet without it you're a sad sorry little wanker! You haven't even got the balls to show your face you cowardly bastard! Come on! Show yourself!' She threw another bottle. It flew harmlessly over their heads and crashed somewhere outside.

A wave of dread shuddered through me. *What the hell was she doing! Shut up woman!*

Blue Head stuck one of the shotguns under his armpit and proceeded to remove his helmet. An unremarkable face was revealed. Black hair, flecked with grey, thick eyebrows, thin, colourless lips and an ill-defined chin. His grey eyes fixed malevolently on Cathy.

'Here's my face Cathy. Is there anything else you'd like to look at?' he asked with a twisted smile. Cathy said nothing. 'I asked you a question Cathy. Is there anything else you'd like me to show you?'

She shook her head.

'You've insulted me Cathy. I think you should say sorry.'

Eyes wide and unrepentant Cathy stood defiantly on the spot and said nothing. I could only watch in paralyzed horror as he levelled the first shotgun. Time slipped to slow motion... Blue Head took a step forward and took aim.

'Say sorry Cathy.'

Cathy came to her senses. She cleared her throat. 'Sorry...'

The explosion made my ears shriek. She was sent hurtling into the glass of the chiller cabinet door. Another shot shattered the glass and dozens of bottles and cartons within the compartments. Cathy slumped to the floor in a lifeless heap, a bloody mess where her stomach and chest had been. He tossed the spent weapon into the pooling blood at her side and drew out the one he'd taken from Mirror Face. The next blast had me ducking beneath the counter under a shower of burst cigarette packs knocking the specs from my face. Another quickly followed ripping lethal splinters from the counter. The till crashed to the floor where it bounced painfully against my hip.

Mirror Face dashed behind the counter, kicked me hard in the ribs and wrenched my useless gun from my hand. He aimed the pistol at my face.

'What the fuck are you doing? We need to go. Now!' Blue Head screamed at him.

'There's a camera up there!' Mirror Face yelled back.

'So fuckin' what?'

'So you took your fuckin' helmet off you twat, that's what!' Mirror Face pocketed my pistol and ran inside the stock room. A few seconds later he reappeared triumphantly waving a pair of videotapes.

'Problem solved!'

Another kick and a shrill pain sang out behind my eyes... A cold breeze swept through – cold in contact with the warm trickle oozing under my chin...

I heard their van rev then squeal from the petrol station. I listened to its engine until my straining ears lost the fading signal completely. In its place came the sound of distant sirens. I stood up slipping on the debris covering the floor and made my way over to the woman.

The glare of the shop's lights intensified every gory detail. Her entire torso glistened a bright wet red. A splintered rib protruded from the chewed up pulp of flesh and fabric. Cathy's eyes flickered desperately then stared sharply into mine.

I knelt down in the expanding puddle of blood and milk and took her hand. Her face contorted. Her eyes closed tightly. I watched them flit spasmodically under the lids. Her slick red fingers tightened around mine until a broken nail punctured my skin. A soft guttural choke emanated from the base of her blood spotted neck. Her grip relaxed. Eyes became still. A last feeble curl of smoke slithered from the shotgun and a new song started on the radio.

I was dragged semi-conscious into the police station, hands cuffed painfully behind my back and my left eye closing under the weight of the swelling. The arresting officers yanked me towards the desk.

'Name?' the custody sergeant mumbled wearily.

'Haig Dumfries.'

I could taste blood on my tongue... Armed police had barged into the petrol station to find me sitting silently beside Cathy's body... along with the shotgun...

'Address?'

... I offered no resistance whatsoever but that didn't stop the first macho bastard on scene pistol-whipping me just for the hell of it. One of the perks of their job I supposed...

'Date of birth?'

I looked at the clock on the wall behind the sergeant. Twelve thirty-two a.m. Then it finally dawned on me - *Ah yes, of course. How could I possibly have forgotten?*

I answered his question with a resigned sigh.

He double checked the date then looked at me highly amused.

'Happy birthday Mister Dumfries. Many happy returns! Do you always treat yourself to a murder on your birthday?' he sneered.

I crouched there in that grimy, graffiti scrawled and piss coloured police cell; too sore to move, too numb to weep. Thirty years old. I considered what that meant long and hard. My thirtieth birthday... This was the twentieth anniversary of Danny's death and therefore the tenth anniversary of Dad's death. Sitting there with a hollow ache at the centre of my imploded universe, I wanted nothing more than to join them.

*   *   *

Four years later I was still alive and on a relatively even keel mentally having settled into the routine of prison life. I had all but accepted my lot.

Then a bolt from the blue...

'I have someone here who wants to meet you.'

I knew the Governor was talking to me even though he deemed it unnecessary to actually face me. I watched the back of his head as he strode authoritatively down the corridor so fast that both myself and the guard escorting me had trouble keeping pace.

'A journalist. BBC. Pain in the arse. Researching a documentary about the state of the prison service apparently. As if anyone cares. Now she wants an inmate's perspective. For some reason she specifically asked to see you.'

We stopped outside a meeting room. Wrapping a hand around the handle the Governor saw fit to fix me with a no-nonsense glare.

'You've never given me any reason for complaint Dumfries. Let's keep it that way shall we?' He said pointedly.

The door opened and I was motioned inside.

The door clicked behind me. I heard the Governor pound back off down the corridor. The guard took his position on the other side of the door's window.

The room was small, bright, clean and contained nothing more than a table and two chairs, apart of course, from the woman standing with her back to me gazing out of the only other window. She turned to face me.

'Hello Haig,' Elspeth smiled.

My pulse rate doubled, my chest tightened and for some peculiar reason I began to feel anxious. Standing there with my mouth gaping I must have looked like a recently lobotomised lab monkey. I couldn't help it. Fourteen years had elapsed since the curtain came down on our time as lovers. Ten years since I last laid eyes on her inside The Black Bull when we drank to remember. And yet, she was exactly as I remembered. Only more beautiful. The tiniest of creases lacing the corners of her eyes were all that betrayed the passage of time. Her figure, despite being dressed for business in a black suit, possessed the same awesome allure of old. I had to sit down before my knees gave way.

'Elspeth,' I muttered trying to regain some semblance of composure.

Watching Elspeth settle into her chair, I became acutely aware of just how far I'd fallen. At one stage in our lives we were on equal terms but now, when our eyes engaged, I was served a cruel reminder of all that might have been. No matter how hard I tried I could not shift the humiliation I felt when she looked at me through those crystalline eyes. It felt as though I was about to endure another trial. My past had entered the room to judge my present.

Elspeth dropped her eyes to the voice recorder she'd placed at the centre of the table. The machine's little red LED light blinked expectantly.

'This... is difficult,' she admitted running a hand through her long dark hair. Not a trace of unnatural colour I noticed. No rebellious streaks.

'You want to know about the state of the prison service uh? Ask me whatever you want. I don't mind blowing the lid on this place,' I smiled trying to lighten the tension. 'I only hope you brought enough tape with you.'

Elspeth leaned over and switched the recorder off. 'To be honest Haig,' she said with a sigh, 'There is no documentary,' She glanced up at the guard stationed outside the door, 'That was just some bullshit I used in order to come and see you... properly.'

Our eyes locked once again. I felt my trembling arms tighten and my skin prickle.

'You're even more beautiful than I remember.' Without permission, my thoughts had decided to make themselves known. Thank God she'd stopped recording. My cheeks burned and I wanted to strangle every crass syllable before they reached her ears. Too late. Instead, I flashed a jovial smile in an insipid attempt to disguise my embarrassment and made a mental note to remove my vocal cords with one of Jim Flack's scalpel-sharp toenail pickings. 'Christ that sounded shite,' I groaned holding up my hands by way of an apology.

'Sounds like they're not putting enough bromide in your tea,' she laughed.

An awkward silence followed and while the strip light hummed over our heads Elspeth leaned forward, put her elbows on the table, rested her chin in her hands and without so much as a blink, stared straight into me. The hum intensified as her eyes seemed to scrutinize my very soul.

'I don't know Haig. Why can't anything be straightforward anymore? I mean I go away for a few years covering that chronic weeping sore otherwise known as the Middle East. And when I come back? – I find out that my first love has been jailed for murder. Typical.' She sighed. Her voice still carried that same sensuous lilt I could never resist.

'Aye, well. Sorry about that.'

'But you didn't kill anyone did you?' she said in a near whisper. It was more of a statement than a question - like it had been her turn to vocalise a thought. Nevertheless I felt compelled to respond to those soul-searching eyes and shook my head.

'No... thought not,' she confirmed after another lengthy pause. 'You're trial was a farce Haig. I've read the transcripts. I had to pull strings, ruffle feathers but I managed to get hold of a copy. Unbelievable! You might as well have been defended by a blind chimpanzee in a space-suit for all the good that useless eejit was to you. Jeez! He somehow managed to allow virtually every critical point in the prosecution's case to pass unchallenged. Talk about inept! It was painful to read. It really was.'

I had to take her word for it. I was in too much of a daze to realise the significance of what was happening at the time. The only elements of the trial I could clearly recollect were the enlarged, vivid photographs of Catherine's shredded corpse put on display for the jury's benefit and the nullifying dejection that set in when it became clear the police were determined to use whatever means necessary to bed the whole mess down with me. I dimly recalled the picture painted by my prosecutors.

Their version of events had me charging into the garage in a drunken fury terrifying the shop assistant who had been fortunate to escape with his life, after which my first action was to remove the CCTV tapes from the video recorders and give the all clear for the rest of my gang to storm in. Unfortunately for Catherine Dodds I had failed to notice her arrival in the shop and when the others entered, a row broke out over what to do with the poor woman. I lost control and callously blasted her apart. The others were so shocked by my actions they left me to continue my wrecking spree while they made good their escape with several hundred pounds in cash and, no doubt, a pair of incriminating videotapes. When the police arrived they found me cowering over the body in a confused and incoherent state with her blood on my hands and an empty shotgun by my side. There was no sign of a fake pistol.

The story proved convincing enough to galvanise the jury into returning their unanimous verdict in record time. I couldn't blame them. When I'd taken the stand even I could hardly believe the bizarre tale flowing from my own lips.

Elspeth had to repeat the questions she was asking about the CCTV equipment I encountered in the back room. What angles did they cover? Was I sure the machines were recording? Would the tapes have proved conclusively that someone else murdered Catherine? I answered as best I could while she scribbled a few indecipherable squiggles of shorthand into a notebook.

'You shouldn't be in here Haig.'

I looked up to see the look of concern in Elspeth's eyes. It was an astonishing sight. A priceless revelation which instantly extinguished all those discordant misgivings I'd nursed for many a year. I had often wondered if she thought about me as much as I thought about her and always arrived at the same pessimistic conclusion that she would have erased me from her memory banks long ago. But her presence across the table coupled with *that* look provided conclusive proof that I had meant something to her after all.

'And yet – here I am.'

'I want to help you.'

I rested my palms flat on the table hoping the move would stop my hands from shivering. 'I can't see how you can.'

'I have some serious clout in this business Haig believe me. I have a lot of contacts and people who owe me favours. So let me put all that to good use.'

I wanted to show my gratitude, to say thank you but I couldn't. A twisted doubt warned me not to. I would be in her debt and I didn't want to owe anyone anything. She had far too strong a hold over me as it was.

'I'm sure you've got more important stuff to work on. There's really no need to waste your time on me,' I found myself muttering.

'And here's me thinking you'd be pleased to have someone working on your side. Besides, it wouldn't be an entirely selfless act on my part. Exposing a miscarriage of justice can do wonders for a journo's career you know.'

I could tell by her smile she was only teasing about the career advancement part but I went along with the game anyway.

'Well, when you put it like that - Who am I to stand in the way of a rising star?' I said offering a tired smile of my own.

Elspeth opened her mouth as if to say something but kept silent and leaned forward to place a hand on mine instead. Her fingertips fired a shudder of energy through my entire body when they touched my skin.

I wanted her. I wanted to fuck her on the table, fuck her on the floor and fuck her against the wall. I tried to picture all the times we'd made love. I felt ashamed and angry with myself for violating our mutual past when it deserved better. I made a conscious effort to absorb all I could of the woman now holding my hand. Every minuscule detail of each elegant feature. Every subtle nuance of her voice. Everything…

My heart collapsed when I saw the ring. A plain, demure gold band. The sight of it emphatically scrubbed out any last lingering hope that maybe, just maybe we would re-unite someday.

'Congratulations.'

Elspeth looked puzzled. I gently tapped the glinting gold encircling her finger. She removed her hand and sighed.

'Oh that? Just another in a long line of mistakes I'm afraid.' She rubbed the wedding ring as if wishing it would disappear.

The hum from overhead took up the heavy silence for a few moments before Elspeth glanced at her watch.

'I ought to get going. I'm flying back to Tel Aviv tomorrow but I promise I'm going to do all I can to help you,' she said rising to her feet. The notebook and recorder were consigned to her bag. 'You mustn't get your hopes up too high though.'

'I won't.'

We embraced for old-time's sake. The embrace melted into a kiss. A far more enthusiastic kiss than I'd dared expect but the moment could never last as long as I wanted it to and Elspeth pulled away first. She smiled ruefully.

'Elspeth?'

'Yes?'

I wanted to ask what her response would have been if I'd had the guts to propose to her all those years ago. This time thankfully, I managed to hold my thoughts in check.

'Thanks.'

'No problem. Listen, is there anything I can get you. Anything you need?'

I sat back down and tried to collect my thoughts. 'Books,' I replied finally, unable to think of anything else. 'You can never have too many books in this place.'

'Books. Hmm,' she nodded reaching for the door handle. Then she smiled, 'The next time I see you Haig you'll be buying me a drink in The Black Bull.'

'Are you sure it's my round?'

'Fraid so.'

And then she was gone. Sitting alone I looked up at the humming light and wondered if I would ever see her again.

The very next morning a book arrived in the post. Perching my backside on the edge of a bench in the exercise yard, I looked at the cover with a smile. Elspeth had sent me *Remembrance Of Things Past*. The heaviest of the heavyweights. Perfect.

… I stroked the inscription on the flyleaf. It read; '*The stone circle, Ettrick Bay and* that *sunset – I hope you remember. I will never forget – E.*'

'Are you Haig Dumfries?' a very close voiced asked, startling me. I didn't recognise the fidgety inmate invading my space. I frowned and nodded. 'Course you are!' he grinned. 'I thought it was you. I saw you in the queue at breakfast this morning but I wasn't sure y'know?' He was talking to me as if he'd rediscovered a long lost pal. 'I was only brought in here yesterday myself so I've not had much chance to meet anybody. Still, I've got plenty of time to put that right eh? Plenty of time. I nearly didn't recognise you without your woolly hat and glasses by the way,' he laughed. 'Bet you can't guess who I am, can you?' he leaned in even closer to whisper his question. His manky breath was enough to make me gag.

I looked the sorry individual up and down. He was thin and short with receding red hair. His middle-aged, crater-pocked face, criss-crossed with burst capillaries, gave the impression of a dog-eared road map showing only the A roads. A row of withering, nicotine-tarnished teeth furnished his malodorous grin.

'I haven't got a clue pal,' I confessed.

Stretching his right arm towards me, the man slowly uncurled his fist to form the shape of a gun. 'Once upon a time – there was this petrol station, not so very far away from here…' His smile split yet wider and now looked like a bad omelette with fragments of eggshell carelessly left in the mix.

I shook my head in disbelief. Countless times I'd tried to imagine and even dreamt about the face that lay behind the mirrored visor but somehow I'd always pictured a visage far more brutal than this malnourished collection of blemishes. I wanted to kill the scrawny wee bastard on the spot. Instead I grabbed a fistful of bollocks and squeezed. His peaky eyes bulged and the shooting pain forced him to exhale a rapid series of short, stuttering breaths.

'No-no-ow-no!' he begged, 'Ah, ah, ah, I've got somethin' for you… J… J… Just let me explain. Please mate. It'll be worth your… ah… Ah!… ooyah…while. I promise ya.'

I let him go.

'Ohhhhh…Th, th, thanks… ahhhh…' he stammered sitting down on the bench to massage his aching groin. He cleared his throat and swallowed hard. '… ooowaaah. I know what really happened don't forget… shhhhhooooit… I know it wasn't you that blasted that girl…' He braved a weak smile, 'I remember seein' you on the news when they jailed you. You're one unlucky bastard aren't you, eh?'

I had to agree. 'Either tell me somethin' I don't know or fuck off and leave me in peace will ye?'

'Billy Gardiner. That's your man. That's the trigger happy shit that killed her.' He shook his head. 'Killin' helpless women?! – That wasn't part of the plan. Nobody was s'posed to get hurt. I'm tellin' ya I was as fuckin' shocked as you when Billy shot her… ah-oooohhhyafffffuck…' His face crumpled as another agonising jolt speared through him. He rubbed his balls all the more. 'That psychotic wanker of a cousin of mine raised the stakes way beyond where I wanted to go.'

'Just as a matter of interest – What did you spend the money on?'

'Eh? Hold on. What was it…?' He shut his eyes and concentrated hard trying to access the information. 'Well it was a lot fuckin' less than we thought it would be. Barely scratched four hundred quid! We reckoned there'd be at least a grand or two built up over the weekend y'know? We were gonna take the fags an all but... Fuck sake – What did I spend it on...? Nah, I can't remember mate... No hold on! Yep. That's it. I was that fuckin' wired after what happened I blew my share on booze... that's right. I went straight down the offy an' bought a few bottles. Don't get much for a hundred and twenty quid or whatever it was I'm tellin' ya.' He looked at me shaking his head. 'It was enough though. I was fuckin' bladdered. Never been so fuckin' hammered in all my life. I bought myself some puff as well. Booze and blow that's all I need. But fuckin' Billy? Mad bastard tries everything! Likes to experiment with the hard stuff - oh yes! But that was it for me, y'know? I wasn't gonna work with that prick again... '

'Ffffuck sake,' I sighed to myself. Catherine Dodds had died and I'd managed to screw up my life to finance a fucking drinking binge and this pathetic prick had the fucking cheek to whinge about how little he'd got for his money.

'... And I told him that to his fuckin' face. Told him I was going solo. D'you know what he did then?! Cunt stitched me right up that's what! My own fuckin' *cousin!* Wanker! Fuckin' grassed me up to the Old Bill when I was off on another job. Want my advice? Don't trust any cunt I'm fuckin' tellin' ya,' he moaned quivering with the injustice of it all. After a lengthy silence he looked at me with a glint in his eye, 'I bet you'd like to kick the livin' shit out of Billy eh? I know I fuckin' would.'

Again I had to agree. 'Well you'll be getting out of here long before me, so if you do see him – give him a batterin' from me, okay?' I said trying to return to my book.

'Look at me!' he laughed. 'Do I look capable of sortin' Billy out! For fuck sake! I wouldn't have a cat in hell's chance! Look, if you're not interested, fair enough. I just thought you'd like to know the name of the man that fucked up your life...'

With one hand cupped to his tender testes he stood up carefully and began to shuffle away, '... and his address.'

I grabbed his arm. The offer was too good to refuse.

'Right. Stop pissin' about. Just give me it,' I demanded impatiently.

'Certainly sir…' He slipped a hand into his grubby pocket and removed a stubby wee pencil. 'Have you got a piece of paper?'

I vainly checked my pockets then handed him the book making it clear that he was to write on the reverse of Elspeth's message. With his tongue sticking from the corner of his mouth and making sure no-one was watching, he brought the book up to within a few inches of his eyes, wrote down the address and handed it back to me. It took a while to decipher his spidery, childlike hieroglyphics as English. The address itself came as a surprise.

'Glasgow! What's he doin' there?'

'Billy has mates up in Jockland. He's got fuck all down 'ere. It's not just me he's pissed off mate – know what I'm sayin? There's some seriously deranged fuckers out there who'd love to push the cunt feet first through a bacon slicer. No more than the fucker deserves. You never know,' he added with a nod to the book, 'Maybe you're just the man for the job. Maybe you'll break out someday. Or maybe, if you behave yourself, they'll let you out early. And if they do, maybe you'd like to pay Billy a little visit. If and when you do see him, tell him Barry was asking after him – before you slaughter the fucker.'

He turned to leave then paused and said to me almost as an afterthought; 'By the way. If I'd known that gun of yours was a dud I'd've blown your fuckin' brains all over the fuckin' place.' Barry grinned and left me in peace.

10: rocks

For this you will need a large, sharp knife.

STEP ONE: Place knife just behind the pectoral fins and cut off the head allowing the guts to spill out of the cavity.
STEP TWO: Slice off tail just in front of the anus.
STEP THREE: Slit open belly from top to bottom.
STEP FOUR: Wash away excess blood and entrails under a cold tap.
STEP FIVE: To remove backbone – Lay fish, skin side up, on a flat surface. Press thumb down hard along the length of the spine.
STEP SIX: Turn fish over and using forefinger and thumb, gently tease the backbone away from flesh.

NB: Should you discover any parasitic worms in the offal or fillet, it is advisable not to devour the fish.

… At least, this is how I was taught…

*

He would experience pain such as no human had ever experienced before. He would scream louder than any terrified creature had ever screamed… But this would not make me stop. Red, blue, black, yellow – all the colours of torture. I would choose something apt. A suitable method. Cut his belly open with a scalpel and place a starving rat inside. He had been so eager to hide his face beneath that blue helmet. Maybe I should remove it for him – with a cheese grater perhaps? He had cost me my freedom, maybe I should bury him alive – show him how it felt… That money was for Mum's trip to St Bernadette's miracle theme park ride… Perhaps a small incision in his backbone –

sever the spinal cord, see how he copes with life in a wheelchair…
Maybe I should drive a steam-roller over him (in memory of Danny),
feet first of course… he would beg for a swift end to his life just to
escape the agony.

Right now he's probably laughing at me. At her. Happy with his
work. Not for very much longer…

*

Daydreaming again. Dark thoughts indeed…

I yawn. Voices…

The car transporter has stopped. I've been drifting in and out of
sleep all night. It's much brighter in here now. The new car smell has
been overtaken by the stale flavour of damp socks, shoes and clothes.

I hear the odd car slide past. Dawn has been and gone but it still
feels early. I peer at the clock on the dashboard. Seven fifty-eight a.m.
becomes seven fifty-nine a.m. I wish the BMW was as eager to tell me
where I am.

Voices… Annoyed.

'Aw, bollocks! Look at that! Bloody vandals!'

Is that a Yorkshire accent? Maybe Lancashire? I can't tell the
difference to be honest.

'Shit! When did that 'appen?! Fackin' 'ell,' whines a very
disgruntled London accent. Stuffing my moist socks into my pocket I
quickly slip on my shoes. 'Better check to see if the tossers've nicked
anyfin'.' Footsteps approach. I unlock the back door on the driver's
side. I feel the lorry tilt with the weight of the person stepping on
board. I instantly recognise the truck driver's sizeable head as it looms
in through the broken window. His face almost bursts when his eyes
lock on to me. 'Oi! You little shit!'

'Morning,' I reply sitting up. We've arrived outside a showroom. I
see a diminutive suited sales rep' peering over the trucker's shoulder.
'Morning,' I smile at him.

'Cheeky little fuck! You've 'ad it mate. Get aht!' the trucker rasps plunging his pudgy hands inside, trying to grab me. I feel the car bob and sway as he shifts his bulk attempting to squeeze further inside. I open my door and nip out.

Forgetting the car is actually several feet above the tarmac I expected at my feet I have to improvise a jump to avoid falling flat on my face. Hitting the road, my knees buckle and give way. My hands splay against the road with a gritty slap. The splinter in my palm throbs.

Once again I am running through strange streets. Too much running. This can't be good for my heart.

*

Floating, drifting, gliding in space. Weightless. The colours seem more distant now. Jade, gold, azure, ruby, amber – brilliant jewels and gemstones of sparkling light.

Like a million microscopic suns caught by stellar winds and glued to a boundless black cloth… Even further off, I see entire galaxies revolve in liquid space… trying to hypnotise me. Nebulous clouds of incandescent dust swirl above, beneath, beyond and behind. I watch a comet flash by. Then another and another. Now there are thousands of them latticing the blackness, interconnecting. Colliding. Their tails tear, cut open and scar the dark. Intense lightning sparks between them as they pass information to each other forming neural pathways… and I am caught at the epicentre of this immense firework display… The gaseous clouds converge, flare and glow, producing flickering images… seemingly familiar…

*   *   *

'This is Kennedy Launch Control. The countdown is still proceeding very satisfactorily at this time. The weather is certainly go. It's a beautiful morning for a launch…'

Danny was enthralled. As was I. They were sending three men to the moon. We sat together on the floor leaning back against the sofa where my parents sat at opposite ends. Mum's legs were curled up behind me while Dad's stretched out beside Danny. Four pairs of eyes fixed on the black and white portable Dad had bought especially.

'...*T minus ten minutes and counting. T minus ten. We're aiming for our planned lift off at thirty-two minutes past the hour...*' the bland, monotonous voice from the television continued. Tuned into his strange, exotic accent, I hung on his every word.

'Twenty-three *billion* dollars this is costing the Yanks – Did ye know that? That's one hell of an expensive firework.' Dad said, addressing no-one in particular. The figure meant nothing to me. As far as I was concerned the situation was exciting enough. There was no need for Dad to embellish the proceedings with interesting facts. The television set itself was amazing. We'd never had one before. I understood some rich folk had colour tellies and there was one in the window of the electrical goods shop which I would stand and watch for a minute or two whenever I passed by. Gran and Aunt Elaine each had a television both of which were ordinary black and white sets but good enough to keep me entertained on my frequent visits. This odd little thing however, with the grainy images shining from the centre of its round white plastic casing, was our very own. It looked pretty much like an astronaut's helmet itself I thought. Much to Mum's annoyance, Dad had spent ages fiddling with the aerial, twisting and tweaking the thin circle of wire protruding from the top like a halo, until he was finally satisfied he could do no more to improve the picture. Eager to show off the new addition to the family I'd asked if Danny could join us. Swayed by the history of the moment, my parents reluctantly agreed.

Clouds of white smoke belched ominously from the side of the stationary rocket. The laid back commentator seemed unperturbed by these emissions. I wasn't so sure. Dad felt certain all three astronauts were about to die in spectacular fashion (which was probably the main reason he bought the box – he didn't want to miss the tragedy he'd predicted unfolding live before his very own I-told-you-so eyes). I began to suspect that Dad was about to be proved correct.

'T minus sixty seconds and counting...Power transfer is complete...' the American voice reassured.

Biting his lower lip Danny opened and closed his fists while I chewed my thumbnail. The space rocket continued to spew steam and smoke.

'It's supposed to be bigger than the Statue Of Liberty that rocket,' said Dad folding his arms but the comparison was wasted on me having obviously never seen either of them in real life.

'We are still go with Apollo Eleven...Thirty seconds and counting...Astronauts report it feels good...'

I tried to picture those men strapped inside. Were they scared? Did they know they were about to die?

'Twelve. Eleven. Ten. Nine...Ignition sequence starts...'

Danny and I leaned forward. I chewed harder on my splitting nail. At the edge of my vision I could see my friend, eyes ablaze, mouthing the rest of the countdown in time with the television.

'...Six. Five. Four. Three. Two. One. Zero. All engines running. Lift off! We have a lift off! Thirty-two minutes past the hour. Lift off on Apollo Eleven!'

The screen flared and bleached with the brilliant glare exploding from the rocket's shuddering engine thrusters. For an agonising second it looked like it wasn't going to move but then, with a Herculean effort the craft began to inch upwards. Danny and I each had fistfuls of carpet, both of us imagining ourselves inside the cockpit willing the rocket to climb. The gargantuan boosters strained and shook, lifting the rocket clear of the support tower. I was so tense my little blanched knuckles almost burst through the taut skin stretching over them. I watched big chunks of what looked like ice fall away from Apollo Eleven. The screen flickered and rolled for a few worrying seconds before settling once more on the USA's proud hope as it muscled ever upwards.

Danny clapped his hands then punched the air. 'Yes!' he cheered with a beaming grin.

We followed the ascent until it became just a burning button in the centre of a dark grey sky.

'*Altitude is two miles...*' a new voice informed us, crackling over a radio alive with a succession of background beeps and hisses.

Joe had not been in the least bit interested. He had an awkward grip on a chunky crayon and was scrawling it across a colouring-in book whilst narrating a story to himself about a lonely dog discovering a giant bone. Mum, struggling with an enormous bulging belly, could have used a couple of booster rockets herself to help her rise from the sofa.

'Aye, very good,' she said. I was disappointed by the manner in which she summed up man's greatest adventure and frowned at her as she headed out of the flat to use the communal loo. In a couple of weeks time I was going to have another brother or, heaven forbid - a sister.

After we had finished watching the launch, Mum complained that we were all getting under her feet so Dad took Danny, Joe and myself for a drive in his rusty old Wolseley. We drove out to Kilchattan Bay where Dad treated us all to an ice cream. The unchallenged July sun melted the cones faster than we could eat them. Joe found it difficult to cope and in the end Dad had to take him to the public toilet to clean the sticky pink mess plastering his face and fingers.

The summer holidays were well underway but Danny and I had the sweet prospect of another full, vast and never ending month to fill before it was time to go back to school. It was the final summer of the decade – a decade that, as Aunt Elaine had pointed out, had been swinging everywhere else except Rothesay.

Dad led the way along the coastal footpath with Joe perched happily on his shoulders. Every time he saw a seabird Joe poked out a bony little index finger and yelled; 'Look!' I had to admire Dad's patience. Somehow he never became annoyed by the wee man's incessant excitement. Danny and I each found ourselves a stick and ran around performing some intricately choreographed sword fights until,

178

succumbing to the busy heat, we were forced to call a temporary truce. Damp with sweat we removed our shirts and tied them round our waists. I held my arm out next to Danny's to compare my paper white skin against his healthy olive tone and noticed a bruise the size and colours of a peach, branded into his shoulder blade.

With Dad reminding us to be careful on the rocks we eventually arrived at the unmanned lighthouse. Neither Danny nor myself had ever been to this part of the island before. The whitewashed lighthouse gleamed so brightly in the sunlight I had to narrow my eyes to make out the detail. Though much smaller than the ones I'd read about in adventure books or seen occasionally on television, it still reminded me of the Apollo rocket. Danny agreed. We wanted to get inside and pretend to be astronauts but the rusty steel door was barred. Pushing at it gave us about an inch of space to peer through but the cool, staid darkness kept its secrets. Pressing our backs against the building's thick coated exterior we skirted around its foundations. The seaward side stood perilously close to the water. Another couple of paces in front of us and the rocks fell away to the gently lapping sea. We couldn't resist standing on the precipice and looking down through the sparkling green surface as though tempting fate. The patches of calmly undulating seaweed were clearly visible on the bottom but the clear water still looked very deep to me. We decided to head back inland and followed Dad onwards to Glencallum Bay.

Another epic sword duel ensued ending in yet another stalemate. Sticks lowered, we crunched across the beach to join Dad and Joe

'What's that?' I asked spying a distant silhouette cruising darkly down the glittering Firth Of Clyde.

Shielding his eyes from the sun Dad looked to where I was pointing. 'It's a submarine,' he answered.

'Is it a Russian submarine Mister Dumfries?' Danny was quite serious and stood there glaring at the sleek black outline with his hands planted on his hips.

Dad laughed, 'Naw. I'm pretty sure it's one of ours.'

'Has it got an atomic bomb on it?' I asked.

Dad grimaced slightly and turned his eyes to Joe who had wandered off to paddle at the water's edge where he was picking up shells and pebbles. 'Probably son.'

Danny looked peeved; 'Aw shite! Does that mean the Russians will blow us up if there's a war?!' Shocked by his own choice of words Danny quickly covered his mouth when he realised, 'Oh sorry Mister Dumfries, I didnae mean tae swear!'

Lighting up a cigarette, Dad smiled, 'I forgive ye Danny. In answer to your question; Aye. If there's a big war, Bute will be blown up along with the rest of the world.'

Danny shook his head tutting loudly, 'That's no' fair…'

'Gonnae show me your army uniform when we get home Dad eh?'

'Yer Mum's put it in the wash wee man. You'll have to wait another day,' Dad said, rubbing his nose.

'Och. I never get tae see it,' I whined.

'Have you ever killed anybody Mister Dumfries?'

Dad released a ponderous sigh, ' 'Fraid so Danny.'

'Enemy soldjers?'

Dad nodded. He now had Danny's full wide-eyed attention.

'Really! How many did ye kill?'

Dad started tallying up the score on his fingers. He reached six then paused and looked to the sky trying to remember. Another finger slowly uncurled. 'Seven men altogether,' he confessed, finally certain.

'Seven! How did ye kill them? Did ye shoot them? Did ye stab 'em wi' a bayonet or did you blow them tae pieces wi' a grenade or did ye use a flame-thrower or…'

'I don't really like tae talk about it,' Dad cut in to Danny's rapid fire interrogation. 'I'm not supposed tae tell anyone anyway. Top secret y'know? And besides it's not somethin' to be proud of. It's just something that had to be done.'

Joe gave a horrified yelp. We all looked to see his horrified face staring at something on the shoreline. My wee brother staggered backwards and fell on his backside with an unceremonious bump. Dad shook his head with a wry smile and we all trudged over the shingle to see what Joe had discovered.

'What is it wee man?' Dad asked the startled boy.

'Look!' The five-year-old pointed to where the surf gently toyed with a glutinous pink mass.

'It's only a jellyfish son,' Dad reassured Joe, lifting him up and patting the sand off his legs and behind.

'Is it deid?' Joe demanded, still staring and pointing at the stricken organism.

'I think so wee man.'

I studied the weird creature which was about the size of a dinner plate. The water seemed to be investigating the thing as well, delicately lifting and replacing a frayed edge. At its glossy, translucent centre there were four rings set in a square formation like four dots on a die. The rings looked like necklaces of tiny pale, interlaced beads and through the jelly I could see the slightly magnified pebbles of the beach underneath. Delivering a final fatal thrust, Danny the swordsman jabbed his stick expertly though the heart of one of the rings.

'It's deid noo.' He leaned down to touch his opponent.

'Careful Danny. It will still sting ye,' warned Dad. Danny retracted his hand instantaneously and rubbed the palm on his trousers as if reacting to a phantom sting. 'And seeing as we're so far away from the hospital do you know what we'll have to do to your hand if you got stung?'

'No. Whit?' frowned Danny continuing to rub his hand.

'One of us will have to wee on it! That's the only cure for a jellyfish sting.'

Danny took a step back, 'Naebody's weein' on me! No way!'

'Then you'll have tae wee on your own hand.'

'That's disgustin'!' Danny shoved both hands in his pockets out of harm's way.

Dad laughed and picked up a flat round stone from the shingle. 'Anybody want a wee game o' skimmers?'

'Aye!'

'Aye,' piped Joe trying to work out what we were getting so excited about but joining in nevertheless.

We each grabbed a stone. Dad went first. His skimmer bounced over the water's surface fifteen times before sinking way out in the middle of the bay. I was never going to beat that but gave it my best shot. My stone managed a disappointing four bounces. I decided my choice had been too light and searched for a heavier one. Danny carefully angled his pebble in line with the horizon and fired. Five times it skimmed over the water, claiming second place. Joe had a go. He threw his lump as high as he could only for it to come down barely a yard out to sea with a single, weighty *sploosh*.

'Look at this one!' Danny had found an interesting stone. Round and pure white. Dad took a closer look.

'That's a moonstone,' he said with a nod.

'A moonstone?' Danny's eyes widened in wonder.

'Aye. That wee stone you're holding in yer hand comes all the way from the moon.'

I wasn't so sure. 'You told me before that stuff is quartz.'

'Aye but what I forgot to tell you is that quartz comes from the moon. That's what the moon's made of. If you don't believe me, next time there's a full moon, hold up that stone next to it and have a look.'

This was good enough for Danny. He slipped the moonstone into his pocket and renewed his search for the ultimate skimmer.

After three more victorious rounds, Dad left us to it and returned to the spot where he'd left his cigarettes. Abandoning Joe to perfect the art of loud splashes, Danny and I opted to explore the rocks bordering the far side of the bay. After promising to obey Dad's insistence not to wander too far and to keep in sight at all times, we set off tracing the high-tide mark near the top of the beach.

The salty thick smell of rotting seaweed baking in the unrelenting sun clung to our nostrils. We made a point of stomping along the bladder-wrack (nature's own bubble-wrap) to see who could pop the loudest. Danny found himself a new improved stick amongst the jetsam and used it to spear the bits of polystyrene littering our path.

We climbed the slope and carefully traversed the rocks prompting oyster-catchers to take flight squealing in alarm. Looking back I could see Dad lying on his side exactly where we'd left him, contentedly smoking a cigarette. He was keeping an eye on Joe who had resumed his exploration of the shoreline. We methodically picked our way over the jagged outcrops until the vitrified lava came to an abrupt end and we found ourselves staring down into a deep, damp, shady crevasse. The opposing wall of rock greeted us several yards away across the fissure. The only way to continue our expedition was to go down.

We had to descend ten precarious feet before we were finally thankful to reach the sandy floor of the natural corridor. Our voices echoed in the cool, ragged confines as we followed the rift inland. It wasn't long before the petrous walls veered to the right and we found ourselves confronted by a sheer rock face. At first, it seemed as though we'd reached a dead end. Even if we had been able to see the summit there was no way we could climb this barrier. Then I saw it. A shadow even darker than the surrounding gloom. The craggy aperture at the base of the rock face was big enough to crawl through. Following a brief discussion to determine who was brave or foolish enough to go first – I entered.

We stood there mouths agape, eyes adjusting to the glinting shaft of sunlight filtering through the hole several metres above our heads. This was the perfect den. Our perfect den. We decided there and then to come back on our own sometime and explore the cave properly. Then we agreed to promise each other the most unbreakable of promises to never tell another soul about our discovery. To make the oath official, Danny searched his pockets, found an old 'I luv Irn Bru' badge, unhooked the rusty pin and jabbed it into his thumb. A drop of blood oozed forth. I did the same and squeezed the surrounding flesh to coax more blood out of the tiny wound. We pressed our punctured thumbs hard together until they blanched and the vow was made between blood brothers.

Our first ever visit to The Buzz Building was cut short when we heard my Dad's far off voice calling for us. We hurried out, retraced our steps and climbed back out of the fissure. Heading in our direction, I saw Dad strolling along the beach shielding his eyes from the sun and scouring the vicinity until he spotted us and waved us over.

'Don't try and tell me it goes all the way down to Australia. I'm no' daft you know,' I said indignantly, peering down the well. This one was not as impressive as the well in the castle's courtyard but it did have a similar iron mesh securing its mouth from the foolhardy.

Dad had led us on what felt like an epic journey over hills and through valleys to the quiet remains of St. Blane's Chapel. In reality the ancient church was only a mile or so from Glencallum Bay but the unforgiving sun certainly made it a testing walk. For someone who spent so much time away from the island I was amazed Dad knew all these places previously hidden to me.

'You're not daft son. Can't fool you anymore eh?' he smiled.

Sheltered in the shade offered by the cliff face towering above, the well laid a few yards to the west of the low boundary wall encircling the chapel and its grounds.

'This is where St Blane used to get his water,' he told me. I looked down again. I couldn't see the bottom of this well either, the light penetrated only a few feet to the twigs and sticks choking its throat. Too scared to look over the edge Joe kept trying to tug Dad away.

The heat refused to slacken its grip even as the shadows stretched all around. Late afternoon folded into an evening radiating a blanket of gold over the landscape. Dad passed the time smoking and relaxing while we kids ran around aimlessly. Once Danny and I had circumnavigated the boundary wall it was time to study the ancient gravestones. Some of the people beneath our feet had died over two hundred years ago. I admired the intricacy of the writing carved into the older stones and tried to imagine what the bodies belonging to those names would look like now.

After catching a horsefly about to bite into my belly I put my shirt back on in readiness for one last sword fight through the chapel's roofless ruins. We cut and parried back and forth under the Norman arch, over crumbling walls, between more headstones and around the broken slabs forming the altar. Another stalemate. The two greatest swordsmen that had ever graced the face of the earth could not be separated. We agreed the terms of a peace treaty and decided to form an alliance prepared to rid the world of all evil. Several tyrannical cowpats felt the cold steel of our blades and a band of particularly evil trees died in that mercilessly one-sided battle.

Then it was time to go. We had a long walk back to the car ahead of us. I threw away my stick only to have it leave a nasty skelf in the palm of my hand.

Calamine lotion… I was made to pay for that afternoon of fun. Not long after we'd dropped Danny off and said our good-byes, I began to shiver and feel oddly chilled. Then my skin felt like it was being boiled in acid. The raging heat reduced me to whimpering tears. When Mum eventually managed to persuade me to remove my shirt, after I'd spent an age screaming my heartfelt intention to kill anyone who came anywhere near, I could tell by her vicarious flinch things did not look good. Dad sucked in a sharp little breath when he saw me. Mum scolded him for letting me get into such a state and led me into her bedroom where she carefully positioned me in front of the full length mirror. My back but especially my shoulders and the backs of my arms were crimson. I cried at the sight of my own reflection. I looked like a giant strawberry jelly baby. I was inconsolable. It looked so bad I didn't think I could ever possibly recover. Mum calmed me down and assured me she had the answer. Calamine lotion…

She shepherded me into the kitchen. I watched on anxiously as she opened the cupboard under the sink. She took out a brown glass bottle and approached me with intent. She spun me round so that I had my back to her. I twisted my head to see what she was up to and blubbed, pleading with her to be gentle. I could taste the sickly sweet smell of the pink gloop as she glugged a glob on to her fingertips. I braced myself for impact. Mum may as well have pressed an ice cube against my blazing skin. The stuff was *freezing*!. I arched my back, emitted a strangled shriek and grimaced hysterically while she set about basting me in the greasy ointment.

'There. That'll teach you,' Mum said admiring her handiwork once she'd finished.

My humiliation was complete. I now looked like a giant strawberry jelly baby that someone had spat out. Mum inspected my hand and after removing the splinter, applied some of the goo to my injured palm. The lid was replaced and I was happy to see the nearly empty bottle placed back into storage. I looked at my hand, at the clean little hole left by the splinter, raised it to my nose and sniffed.

*   *   *

I inspect my palm. Having travelled with me since Newport Pagnell it's time that splinter was removed. Bastard thing stings. I grip the end of it between my teeth and tease it out. I'm *sure* I can detect a faint tinge of calamine lotion in the air. I spit the fragment of wood on the floor. A drop of blood wells up in my hand – a big red inverted comma at the beginning of my stunted lifeline. The lifeline is crossed in three places by fainter, shorter lines dividing it into four roughly equal parts. I suck the blood off and swallow a mouthful of cider to annihilate the taste I've always hated. I'm in a pub in Preston. The place has only just opened for people like me who fancy a pint at eleven in the morning.

I'm the one and only customer in here. The place reeks of stale fags and beer stained furniture. On the plus side it's warm and dry. I settle back in my cosy corner and look out the window. More fucking rain…

Outpacing the overweight lorry driver and the short-arse showroom dealer proved easy enough but it took me ages to find the train station. I bought a single to Glasgow. With time to kill before the train was due I headed back across the road to this establishment… I still have another twenty five minutes to wait. I examine the ticket. I have about ninety quid left which should be more than enough to get me across to Bute.

…The barman plugs in a fruit machine. I watch its gaudy, enticing lights dance and flutter, promising what it will never deliver. Weird burbling sound effects tinkle and chatter from the machine... The barman is back behind the bar stacking glasses on a shelf above his head. He glances at me... There may have been a hint of suspicion in that furtive look. He's a youngish, bulky guy. Looks strong. Rugby type. If he has recognised me and decides to act the public-spirited hero I could be in trouble. May need to employ dirty tactics in order to make my escape. A swift kick to the nuts. Ear biting. Eye gouging...

The rain patters harder at the window. I really don't want to get wet again. I check my shoes and socks which I've perched against the radiator's searing heat. Nearly dry... Another gulp. I watch in close-up the steady salvo of tiny bubbles firing from the bottom of my glass, rising in an unbroken stream through the golden liquid to burst on the fizzing surface... I need to check my pockets. I need to make sure I still have the piece of paper with Gardiner's address... There it is. I Tucked inside my backside pocket. The deteriorating flyleaf is damp at the edges. Elspeth's words are nice and clear. I turn the page over; Barry's pencilled scrawl has all but vanished. I'm getting closer Billy. Getting closer...

11: borders

The detective sneezed. And again. The third sneeze sent the blackcurrant throat lozenge he'd only just placed in his mouth flying back out. The missile, purple and sticky, bounced against the windscreen and fell into the passenger seat. Craven sniffed hard and wiped his streaming eyes. He unwrapped another lozenge. Slouching lazily in his seat he looked outside to the row of new BMW's sparkling in the showroom's forecourt. Lorna wanted a new car but she certainly wouldn't be getting one of these. She could buy a new house at some of those prices.

He yawned, travel weary. Dumfries was doing precisely what his brother had predicted in heading for Scotland but Craven's superiors were getting twitchy, demanding the impossible. He tried assuring them that everything was in hand. The Thames Valley boys back in Milton Keynes were monitoring Joseph Dumfries's 'phone just in case his big brother decided to call. All angles were covered. It was not a question of if - but when. Unfortunately they had baulked at his suggestion to allow Dumfries to reach Bute where it would be particularly easy to pick him up as he stepped off the ferry with minimum fuss. They cited media and political pressures as their reasons for wanting the escapee recaptured ASAP. Craven's throat had been too sore to argue. He had almost lost his voice completely when speaking to the car salesman and the lorry driver who showed him the vehicle Dumfries had chosen to stow himself away in. The only thing Haig left behind in that sleek Beemer was the whiff of smelly socks.

His mobile phone chirped from his inside jacket pocket.

'Hullo?'

'Is that Detective Inspector Craven?' inquired a female voice with a pleasant Scottish accent,

'Yes.'

'At bloody last. Have you *any* idea how long I've been trying to contact you?' she asked sounding slightly cross.

Craven sat up sniffing. 'Who is this please?'

'Elspeth Donnelly. Journalist. BBC. I must have left you half a dozen messages. Have you just been ignoring them?'

He had indeed received several messages from this woman and he had indeed ignored them all, putting her down as another pain-in-the-arse hack. He wondered how she'd finally managed to get hold of this, his personal number but knew any half decent hack could do it eventually.

'No,' he yawned.

'Anyway. Doesn't matter. I have some information in regard to Haig Dumfries that you *will* be interested in…' She paused. Craven could hear her rustling something.

He took up the dead air, 'I'm sure you have Mrs Don…'

'It's Ms not Mrs…' Elspeth corrected. Craven heard a sudden screech of braking tyres from her end of the line followed by a succession of dull bouncing thuds and then the piercing wail of a car horn swiftly mirrored by a more distant horn with a different tone.

'Aye! You know where you can shove that ya useless little prick!' she yelled with muffled fury. A loud scratching noise took over and then he heard Elspeth's engine accelerate… 'Sorry about that. Some idiot boy racer cut me up and made me drop the phone. When can we meet up?'

'I'm really very busy Ms Donnelly and to be honest we're closing in on him as I speak,' - and as he spoke his voice started to crackle again, 'It really won't be long before he's caught, so…' he cleared his sandpapery throat, 'I can guarantee whatever information you think you have will become redundant in the very near future. Now, I'm sorry you've been trying…'

'No, no, no! Hold on!' she broke in urgently. 'This has nothing to do with his escape or whether or not you catch him. This relates to the original robbery and murder he was convicted for.' Elspeth took a deep breath. 'Look. I really don't want to discuss it over the phone. Suffice to say new evidence has come to light. New evidence that makes Haig's conviction look shaky to say the least. Do you understand what I'm saying?'

Craven crunched on the dissolving sugary blackcurrant sliver. He got the picture. She'd been nosing around and found something she shouldn't.

'You win. I'll speak to you. Where are you?'

'Brighton.'

'Well I'm in Preston at the moment but I'm on my way to Glasgow. That's where Dumfries is heading...'

'Not a problem. I'll catch a flight and meet you there this evening. I'll give you a bell as soon as I get there. Okay?'

'Fine,' Craven slurped on the molten sugar swilling around his mouth.

'This is important so please don't try to fob me off.'

'Wouldn't dream of it. You've managed to get hold of my mobile number so I can't avoid you now can I?'

'Just make sure you leave that phone of yours switched on, that's all I'm saying.'

'I'll speak to you in a few hours Ms Donnelly... Bye.' Resisting the urge to switch the unit off he stuffed the mobile back inside his pocket.

Craven started up the Lexus and drove off reflecting on why nothing in life was ever simple.

*

The Cumbrian Fells bore down on each side of the motorway, their peaks devoured by a brooding sky. Little waterfalls were bouncing down the granite slopes to his left. The lower sections of these slopes were smothered by a vast wire net to prevent the crumbling hillsides spilling over the dense traffic. Nick had little confidence in this flimsy defence. It seemed no more than a token gesture designed to put the vulnerable, easily squashed minds of passing drivers at ease. It would take more than a string vest to hold back a determined rock slide.

A hefty gust slammed the Peugeot's flank making the wheel twitch in Nick's grip. As if following Craven wasn't difficult enough, the obese raindrops spattering noisily against his windscreen were

190

seriously hampering his visibility. He flicked the wipers to the fastest setting. Thankfully the grim conditions had forced Craven to ease off a touch. Once they'd rejoined the M1 at Preston, the power difference between the two cars had become all too apparent. Nick's foot had been nailed to the floor almost constantly and even now his inferior engine still protested at being asked to maintain a steady eighty.

His backside had gone numb. He hoped Craven would pull into the next service station. He needed to stretch his legs and the hollow burn in his stomach reminded him he hadn't eaten all day. A quick glance at the petrol gauge revealed an equally urgent need to fill the car's belly.

The radio reception cackled, stuttered and finally capitulated to white noise. Keeping his eyes on Craven's car curving round the hillside half a mile ahead, Nick slotted a tape into the deck. The opening strains of The Blue Nile's '*Let's Go Out Tonight*' sent a shivering wave of melancholy through him. '*Hats*' was the last album Cathy ever bought and this was the track she'd chosen to add to her compilation tape.

Ten years on and the memories continued to persecute him. The cloying guilt would never allow him to relax. The weather at her funeral had been much like it was now. He remembered the procession of Cathy's black clad friends and family, a slow moving queue of sullen crows following the coffin he helped to bear. He remembered Cathy being lowered into the ground and the little puddles forming on the coffin lid while he stood there thinking about being a free agent and who he should be trying to chat up next. He remembered how he'd viciously shaken his head trying to rid those awful, disgusting thoughts from his mind. He remembered the wake where, after he'd consumed a mite too much drink, he'd shamelessly made a pass at Andrea; Cathy's gorgeous cousin. Thankfully she brushed him aside, blaming his behaviour on the wine and his confused emotional state... Nick shuddered at the mere thought of that embarrassing episode...

… Andrea had sat next to him at the trial on a few occasions but much to his relief, she never mentioned that incident at the wake. Nick sat through every torturous second of those proceedings desperately trying to channel all his energies, all his anger and pain straight into Dumfries's soul. He concentrated hard on the murdering bastard's face hoping they'd make eye contact so that Dumfries would be crippled by the sheer hate in Nick's stare. Problem was his concentration levels dropped whenever Andrea was in attendance. He could not resist flicking the odd, surreptitious glance at her smooth black stockinged calves and he longed for those glorious, prick-twitching moments when she shifted in her uncomfortable seat to cross or uncross her legs and so treat him to an eyeful of those luscious thighs. Again he would feel profoundly ashamed and mortified by the notion that he was sullying his wife's memory. Nick had wanted to take a scalpel to that mordant part of his brain that literally wanted to move on to the next woman before the grass could grow over Cathy's grave and slice it away. Perhaps if he'd paid less attention to his base instincts, she might still be alive…

… 'No Nick, I'm sick of it. I've had enough. It's over.' Cathy sounded surprisingly calm. She swiftly circled the living-room snatching up the bits and pieces she needed. 'You're not going to sweet talk your way out of this one. You forget. I know you. I know what a manipulative bastard you really are and in time…' she slipped her cheque book and credit cards into her bag, '… so will she.' She stopped suddenly, glared directly at Nick and threw her arms open. 'Is this *really* not good enough anymore?' she asked, referring to her trim body. 'Bored with it now, is that it?' She shook her indignant head. 'No surprises anymore eh? Well I know for a fact there's plenty of men out there who'd love to get their hands on me!' Cathy yelled, her voice wavering.

She was right of course. On all counts. Nick opened his mouth, ready to respond…

'Save your breath. I'm not interested in listening to any more of your pathetic bullshit. Just how stupid do you think I am for fuck's sake? I'm amazed… I'm amazed that you have the… the *conceit* to believe that I can't tell when you're lying!' She stormed through the hall and into the kitchen. 'Why didn't I do this months ago?'

Nick followed in time to see her grab her car keys from the worktop. 'Don't you fucking dare try and tell me that you're sorry and don't you fucking *dare* try and tell me that you wish it had never happened. It's all bollocks. Don't you think you've insulted me enough? The only thing you regret is being caught!' she raged grabbing her coat.

Again, deep down, Nick had to admit she was right. 'Cath. Please. It's late. At least wait until the morning. We can talk…'

'The next time I communicate with you - will be through a divorce lawyer,' she hissed.

It was all over. There was no point in pretending otherwise. 'Where are you planning to go?' Nick asked sheepishly.

'Who knows? I've got the world to explore now haven't I? Maybe I'll go to Paris…' she glowered, her face just inches from his, '… and fuck all the Frenchmen I can lay my hands on.'

'Look…'

She cut him off once more, clearly not prepared to listen to a single word he had to say, 'It makes me wonder why you fell for me in the first place Nick, it really does. I mean, am I a result of your bad taste or is that something you've developed since we got married?' She started rummaging through drawers and cupboards. 'Bernice!' she sneered. 'What kind of a fucking name is that? Of all the women to have an affair with, you manage to find one called *Bernice*! *"I love you Bernie,"'* Cathy mocked. 'Is that what you whisper in her ear? *Bernie?* As if that wasn't bad enough she's got ginger bloody hair as well! Ginger and a size fourteen at least. And that's me being generous! Just thinking about you two wriggling together makes me want to vomit. Where's my passport?' she demanded.

Nick was crushed. The time had come to let her go. He pointed to the fruit bowl.

'I might call you in a couple of days. Maybe I'll forgive and forget, you never know,' she said dropping the passport into her bag. Cathy strode back through the hall. Nick followed. She opened the front door and turned to face him for the last time; 'Then again, maybe I'll learn to live without you. Shouldn't be too hard.'

The door slammed shut so hard the letterbox rattled. Nick leaned against the wall, closed his eyes and listened to his wife start her car and drive away. He listened to the sound of that familiar engine fade into the distance and continued to listen long after his ears had lost contact. He thought about what he'd done, about Bernice and felt feeble and foolish. She embarrassed him. He would have to put an end to their ridiculous liaison.

… It was only a matter of hours before he saw Cathy again. A formal identification was all that was required of him but it made him feel very peculiar. It was as if everything inside him had broken down, his body no more than a jumbled mess of faulty parts. His heart stammered, his lungs lost their rhythm, his muscles seized up and his brain struggled to weave a coherent sequence of thoughts together. The police had to repeat everything they said to him because even his hearing seemed to shut down. He could barely muster a series of grunts and groans in response. He had already lost Cathy once that night and now he'd lost her again. Nothing made any sense.

His soul chilled at the sight of her face. An alabaster mask. Set… Expressionless… Permanent. He had never felt so inadequate in his life. He outstretched an uneasy hand and gently touched her cold, ashen lips with the tip of his forefinger. The same lips he'd kissed countless times. Dead. A thousand questions flooded his mind demanding immediate answers. When those answers arrived he found himself consumed by an onslaught of rage, guilt and confusion.

Those same emotions returned to torment him at the trial when the events of that hellish night were recounted in gory detail for the benefit of the court. He couldn't believe it when Dumfries confirmed his date of birth. Was Cathy's murder his idea of a birthday present to himself? The sick fucker deserved to die and when Dumfries pleaded not guilty, Nick wanted to leap over the benches, grab the judge's gavel and beat the lying fuck's brains out but fortunately Andrea had managed to restrain him. How could he brazenly stand there and plead *'Not guilty'* when they'd all seen the photographs of Cathy lying on the floor of the garage shop with her guts blown out.

They had all heard the arresting officer's damning testimony. How he'd found Dumfries kneeling beside Cathy with the murder weapon at his side. Dumfries had Cathy's blood on his hands probably as a result of searching through her pockets looking to steal her money. They had all listened to the unfortunate shop assistant recall his terror at having Dumfries aim a gun at his face. The poor man was still clearly traumatized by the ordeal. The mountain of evidence presented against Dumfries by the prosecution had been overwhelming in Nick's view and thankfully the jury didn't fall for his poor little victim-of-circumstance act. They knew he was guilty. The judge issued the maximum sentence and that was that.

He never did make eye contact with Dumfries…

Determined to celebrate Nick hit the town, fell hopelessly drunk and found himself fantasising longingly about Andrea's legs.

… Nick looked at the petrol gauge hovering just above the red. Through the haze of spray thrown out by the lorry in front he caught sight of the road sign…

Welcome To Scotland.

12: goals

The confused screen spun in a sickening, dizzy blur before the image settled. The lens bounced and jerked briefly while Elspeth manipulated the hidden camera in her shoulder bag into position. The camera pointed to a television set standing in the fuzzy orange glow of a lamp in the corner of an otherwise drab, poorly lit room. The skinny silhouette of a man leaned into shot to turn the television on. His face frustratingly obscured by a baseball cap he reached underneath the television to slot a tape into the VCR.

'The whole thing runs for twenty minutes near enough but I'm just going to show you the good bit.' The mystery man spoke in a hard London twang roughened by a lifetime of smoking. He dropped himself into a armchair leaving the camera to focus on the flickering television. After a faint whirring sound the VCR rolled on to play footage captured by another static, clandestine camera. Though coarse, monotone, mute and suffering from drop-outs it was evidently a security camera's point of view of a shop.

'That's Dumfries there behind the counter with his back to us and that's Catherine Dodds on the right of the picture. See? Over by the fridge? Oops. Big mistake. Shouldn't have thrown that bottle Cathy love...'

The television flared momentarily. 'I bet Dumfries wishes that gun of his was real at this point, eh?' There was a smile in the man's voice. The screen flared again. 'She's well and truly dead now... See how all the shots came from that nutter in the doorway? The one that took his helmet off and not from Dumfries? Not really open to debate is it? ... Look there - see? I know the camera's a bit shit but you can still see the twat's face and it ain't our boy.'

Haig Dumfries ducked beneath the counter as two further blasts destroyed the till and caused the CCTV camera itself to tremor violently. The robber nearest the counter saw Haig on the floor and appeared to kick him, snatch his pistol and aim it at his head. After a brief animated exchange with the real murderer Haig's assailant gestures to the CCTV camera before disappearing into the back room. A few moments later the CCTV footage ended abruptly and the television filled with static…

'There was another tape covering the outside, y'know the pumps and stuff, but it didn't have anything interesting. Just everyone turning up then leavin' that's all. You're bloody lucky I've still got this bleedin' tape sweetheart! A few months back I came home one night just in time to stop the missus using it to record Friends or some shit like that. No wait - 'Sex And The City' that's what it was. Sex And The fucking City. She does watch some bollocks my wife, I'm tellin' ya.' The man laughed.

'Ten years. You've been holding on to that tape for ten *years*?' Closer to the hidden camera's in-built microphone, Elspeth's dismayed voice came across louder and clearer than her mystery contact's. 'Is there any particular reason as to why? I mean why have you been happy to let a man you *know* to be innocent rot away in jail all this time?'

As she posed the question Elspeth cautiously manoeuvred her bag until the secret camera covered the man silhouetted in his chair against closed blue curtains. The man sat silently for a moment then reached into a pocket and pulled out a pistol.

'Don't even attempt to lay a guilt trip on me sweetheart,' he said taking aim at Elspeth.

'What? No. Wait… I'm not… You're right. I'm sorry. Just take it easy.' Elspeth's voice tried hard to sound calm and soothing but the microphone picked up the fear in each tremulous breath. 'Please. Put that thing down and we'll talk.'

With a throaty chuckle the man lowered his weapon. 'Don't panic love. It's a fake. Still, it's not very nice having a gun pointed in your face is it?'

'Hold on a minute,' said Elspeth regaining her composure. 'Are you saying that was you on the tape?'

'It was. And this is the gun he shoved in my face, cheeky bastard. I kept as a souvenir. Don't go getting any ideas by the way. If you try

197

calling the police I'll burn that fucking tape. Do you understand?'

'I do. But I don't understand why you were happy to let that madman with the shotgun walk free. Don't you think he deserved to be put away after what he did to that poor woman?' Elspeth asked starting to sound exasperated. 'One anonymous tip-off to the police is all it would've taken. One quick phone call telling them they'd got the wrong man.'

'I might be many things love but I'm not a grass. And I couldn't give a flying sideways fuck about Dumfries. That tosser got exactly what he deserved. I thought the fucker was gonna kill me.' Losing his patience the man shoved the pistol back in his pocket and stood up. 'Can we stop fuckin' about? The bastard's escaped right? So this tape now has a value. All I'm doing is reacting to market forces. So stop pissin' me around. Are you interested in buyin' or not? I've always had a bit of a soft spot for you when I've seen you on the telly. More like a hard spot I should say, catch my drift? But don't think for one second you're the only reporter I've contacted. As things stand ten grand is the highest bid so far. Ball's now in your court darlin'. What have you got…?'

Elspeth switched off the television and turned triumphantly to Craven.

'That's about the gist of it. I know the quality is a bit ropy but you get the idea. And you can take my word for it; the original tape is crystal clear. Haig did not murder Catherine Dodds.'

Sitting on the end of his bed feeling a little flustered Craven sniffed and wished he had never bothered to meet this bolshie journalist even if she was pleasing to the eye.

'And just what do you expect me to do exactly?'

'Get on the phone to your superiors and tell them that you are, in effect, chasing an innocent man.'

'Look Ms Donnelly, don't push your luck with the *innocent* bit okay? I'll accept that what you've shown me puts a whole new perspective on things but nevertheless Dumfries did commit armed robbery.'

'Armed with a *fake* pistol.'

'Even so...'

'Come on Inspector! This *proves* Haig has been telling the truth all along,' Elspeth argued brandishing the videotape she'd just removed from the machine. 'Yes he committed robbery but that's all he was guilty of. Not murder. And you have to admit, ten years is a bit steep for what he *actually* did. And as for escaping? Can you blame him?' Elspeth's eyes followed Craven as he rose from the bed. He looked peevishly around his hotel room for nothing in particular then made for the window.

Easing the curtain aside he peered through the rain trickling down the glass to the puddles glimmering on the pavements of Hill Street four floors below. He smiled. No doubt about it, he had a dose of Hill Street blues. He looked up into the night and tried to follow the progress of a single falling raindrop.

'Where did you meet this character?' he asked switching focus to watch Elspeth's reflection in the double-glazing. She stepped towards him rummaging through her bag.

'He suggested we meet in some dingy Bed and Breakfast in Brighton not far from the Pavilion. I have their card in here somewhere. He said it was good place to conduct business because the owner didn't ask questions. He told me he uses the place whenever he needs a bit of female company. Apparently his wife just doesn't supply the goods anymore. Poor woman. Who can blame her? Ah! There you go. I've written his contact number on the back.' She handed over the business card which Craven pocketed. 'Can't be too many women who have George Clooney's mobile number?'

'George Clooney?'

'That's the name he checked in with. Cheeky sod even asked me to pay his bill as a good will gesture.'

Craven coughed as he watched a man hurrying through the rain carrying what looked like a take-away and watched him clamber into a small Peugeot parked across the narrow street.

'Do you think he's really been offered ten grand for that tape?' he asked.

'I very much doubt it.'

'Have you arranged to meet him again?'

'Not yet. I told him I needed to have a word with my editor first before I could make an offer. He said he'd give me twenty four hours.' Elspeth leaned against the window arms folded and waited until Craven looked at her. 'So what do you think?'

'About what?'

'About the next step? Given that we can safely assume we're not dealing with a Hollywood superstar how do you suggest we play this? Do you want me to arrange a meeting now? Then you can swoop in, arrest him, seize the tape and the pistol?'

'I suppose,' croaked Craven, his warm breath misting on the window. His nose started to run. He angled his face away from her view, took out an already damp hanky and blew hard. He didn't feel well enough to cope with all this. His left temple had started to ache ominously. He watched Elspeth in the glass. She was staring at him with an incredulous expression.

'Don't go overboard with the enthusiasm on my account will you? Jeez, I thought you'd jump at the chance to sort this out. Surely this is the sort of thing promotions are made of? Don't you want to clear up a miscarriage of justice? And don't you want to put those who *were* responsible behind bars? Once you find out Clooney's real name surely that could lead to uncovering the rest of his little gang. Including that bastard with the shotgun.'

Craven sneezed and had to blow his tender red nose again. He stepped away from the window and sat down on the edge of the bed facing Elspeth. 'Barry Sloper.'

'Pardon?'

'Mr Clooney's real name is Barry Sloper.'

Elspeth perched next to Craven. 'How the hell do you know that?'

'I would imagine every police officer in Brighton knows Barry Sloper.'

'But how can you tell? I mean you don't really get a good look at his face on this tape.'

'True but I'd recognise that voice and those mannerisms anywhere. That's our Barry.'

'Who is he?' Elspeth asked.

'Oh, let me see now. He's a thief, drug dealer, robber, burglar, a wife-beating alcoholic… a general all round charmer.'

'Then what are you waiting for? Get on the phone. Get him arrested. We need to pick up that CCTV tape before his wife uses it to record *Celebrity Bowel Movements* or some other piece of high quality programming,' urged Elspeth hoping to inspire a burst of dynamic action from Craven. The detective remained seated, looked up at the ceiling and sighed.

'I don't think there's any great urgency Ms Donnelly. Barry may not be the brightest of buttons but he has managed to keep that tape safe for ten years after all. And trust me, if he thinks that tape is worth ten grand there's no way he's letting it out of his sight. Besides, we can't just wade in to someone's house at the drop of a hat. There's paperwork. There's always paperwork. I'll need to organize a warrant first.'

'How long will that take?'

'A couple of days maybe. But I will need to hang on to that tape of yours though.' Craven gestured to the tape in Elspeth's hands. She seemed reluctant to let it go and eyed him for a moment as though suspicious of the request. 'It will help speed up the process.'

Finally persuaded Elspeth handed over the videotape. 'Do you think this will be enough to see Haig released straight away?'

Craven scratched the stubble irritating his jaw. 'Well, escaping from prison and robbing that Conservative Club hasn't done him any favours that's for sure. But, once we get the original CCTV and a confession from Barry, no doubt there'll be a fresh enquiry. And taking the last ten years into account, Dumfries will probably be out within six to eight weeks. First things first though. We still have to catch the slippery bastard before it's too late.'

201

'Too late?' Elspeth frowned.

'I believe he's on something of a suicide mission right now. If we don't catch up with him before he reaches home and settles whatever score he feels he needs to settle, then...' Craven cleared his raging throat. Suddenly rising from the bed he threw on his coat and headed for the door, 'Christ I need a drink. Do you fancy a drink Ms Donnelly?'

Down in the hotel bar, after Craven had outlined the doctor's misfired practical joke and the subsequent trail that led the detective to Glasgow, Elspeth hung around long enough for a brief exchange of superficial personal histories before she called time on the small talk, made her excuses and left. He managed one last sneaky glance at her exposed bra strap as she collected her things. Black. Very nice. Her breasts were a good size from what he could judge, smaller than Lorna's but no doubt firmer.

He treated himself to one last drink, one last whisky to stare into. For the first time on this demented journey Craven felt a pang of homesickness. Only five days left before the twins turned sixteen. He wondered if Rachael's mood had improved and he longed to rest his throbbing head against his wife's welcoming chest.

A gloom perforated his weary thoughts. The scenario had taken on a whole new form. Elspeth Donnelly expected him to swing into action and put everything right. High expectations indeed. Craven yawned and wished, as he had done many times in the past, that he'd chosen a different career. Something simple. Less messy. He should've taken his mother's advice and followed his old man into abattoir management after all.

*

It's time to go. I can't sit in this grotty bus shelter forever. It might take longer than that for the rain to stop. This is Scotland after all. And there's no need to keep scouring this Glasgow A-Z. It's served its purpose. I know exactly which way I'm headed. Not far. Walking distance. He should be in his bed by now… Using the tatty flyleaf to bookmark the Drumchapel area I close the pocket street guide.

I turn right up Kinfauns Drive then pause at the entrance to Linkwood Drive. I feel the need to double-check the grubby piece of paper with Gardiner's name and address – I don't really know why. I could just as easily close my eyes and picture every scrawling twist of faded graphite it contains. I can't resist another look at Elspeth's inscription on the reverse –

"… *that* sunset…"

I proceed along the empty street, passing an unbroken line of sleeping cars. It seems to go on forever… I arrive at the tenement block I'm looking for. I stop, gazing up at all the individual apartments. It's late. Only three have lights on inside. The rain refuses to let up but I'm long past caring. Being cold and wet has become second nature. My only thought lies with what may be about to happen. I am keen to see his face. I can't remember what he looks like. I didn't really get a good look at him. He took off his helmet and the next thing I remember is blood, chaos and noise.

He needs to suffer. He owes me that much. I need to make sure he understands why he needs to suffer. I want to see his eyes fill with dread. I want him to beg for mercy. But if things go tits up and he turns out to be some kind of black belt ninja bastard then I must, if nothing else, put up a decent fight. I couldn't bear the embarrassment if he stabs me in the heart before I even manage to introduce myself.

His place is on the second floor. I stare at each of the second floor windows in turn. Which one is his? All of them are in darkness… Is he watching me from one of those black rectangles? Ready and all too willing… A car motors by on the wet road behind me… *Stop delaying. This needs to be done…* I step into the building.

The close is well lit and no matter how quietly I try to proceed, the smooth concrete stairs echo warnings to Gardiner with every step… I reach the second floor. The light in the communal hallway flickers spasmodically. I can see the silhouettes of hundreds of dead winged insects trapped in the cracked light casing. A moth flutters pointlessly within, caged by its own folly. I stop outside a solid blue door.

This is it.

The glossy blue paint holds my shadow. The door has been reinforced. There is a spy-hole. The little glass lens looks like the eye of a dead fish … I try to keep my breathing down to a dull roar but I'm sure my stomping heartbeat is destroying all the glassware contained inside the flat… Decision time… If I barge the door I'll probably break my shoulder… I should knock… Will he recognise me…? I smile at the absurd possibility that he might answer the door still wearing that blue crash helmet of his… I have no weapon on me. He could have all sorts in there… I breathe deeply and knock. The knock is enough to push the door ajar.   …?!…

A smell seeps from the inch-wide gap. Unpleasant. Darkness inside. I continue to wait. Expectant. Nothing… Was he watching me standing in the street after all? Am I about to do something even that jittering moth would consider idiotic? I gently ease the door open.

The fitful light behind me pulses a dim glow through the hall. I see objects strewn all over the floor, a minefield of little silhouettes stretching into the total darkness beyond. The smell hits me hard forcing me to hold my nose and breath as I enter. My other hand fumbles for a light switch. I feel something powdery give way beneath my foot. I turn on the light.

The hall carpet is peppered with dog turds at various stages of decomposition. A particularly aged specimen has crumpled chalk-like, under my shoe. Letters and junk mail litter the threshold. I pull my shirt collar over my mouth and nose. There is a sound … a faint, persistent hum coming from behind the closed door at the far end of the hall. I step forward gingerly tip-toeing between the faeces… *Christ,* I can almost *hear* the smell! If the fucker jumps out on me now he's got me because I can hardly breathe in this squalor.

There's an open door to my left. I peer into the gloom. A bedroom. The bed is neatly made. The whole room would appear tidy if it wasn't for the ubiquitous dog shit, a few of which are comfortably curled up on the pillows… assuming it is *dog* shit. Still no sign of Gardiner. I tread carefully on down the hall. A door to my right… I push it but it won't budge more than a few inches. The gap is blocked from floor to ceiling with junk… cardboard boxes and carrier bags stuffed with God only knows… I try again but the wall of trash behind the door refuses to give. I hear something tumble softly inside the unseen room and move on.

Another door to my left. Open… Rain patters on the opaque glass window catching fragments of halogen light from the streetlamp. Stepping in, I feel the string switch dangling from the ceiling nudge my face. I pull it. *How much more of this is there?* The stench somehow manages to slap me even harder and fills my mouth with an acrid taste. I smother my jacket over my face but it's not enough. Nausea burns in the pit of my stomach. I retch dryly… The bathroom is small. More dog mess. I notice the rancid vomit pebble-dashed in and around the toilet bowl. There's more, much more crusting in the sink… I catch sight of my own bewildered eyes in the mirror… Dried blood stains the edges of the bath. An untouched bar of soap sits patiently in its dish between the taps. I turn out the light…

I reach the door at the end of the hall. My sore heart thuds louder and faster. I strain to hear any hint of movement from the other side… Only that barely audible, incessant hum is to be heard. I swallow the sour saliva collecting under my tongue. My breath feels hot and moist against the fabric covering my mouth as I carefully wrap my fingers around the handle. Should I charge in guns blazing or try to creep inside. My hand decides for me. The handle bends slowly downwards. The spring mechanism inside creaks… *He's got to hear that!…* I grit my teeth and push the door open as softly as I can. I feel small objects gathering at the foot of the door and swept aside as I open it further. My fingers probe the wall inside for the switch. I find it… it doesn't work. Surely, if he's here he would've heard that click? But… nothing lunges at me. A panicky surge of adrenaline breaks out the goose-pimples… I check over my shoulder half expecting to see him sneaking up the hall with a fucking great big knife… He's not.

The front door seems like miles away. I'm tempted to run for it... The fear eases and my chest collapses under the weight of anti-climax. *The bastard's not fucking in!* - I'll wait for him to come back if I can find somewhere to wait in this cesspit...

I open the door fully. The stink reaches its zenith. I blink the water clear from my smarting eyes. The illumination from the hall spreads thinly over a section of what must be the living-room. Every morsel of space is coated in an explosion of newspapers, plates, ornaments, plastic bags, clothing, books, videos, CD's, shit... I spot a lamp, its shade caved in on one side, lying on the floor half buried in the indeterminate rubble. I pick it up and test it. It works...

I discover the source of the hum. Flies. Scores of them patrolling the centre of the room in darting, agitated circles. I rest the lamp on a bureau by the kitchen door to my left... Again, the kitchen reveals no sign of life, just the sugary scent of rotting food is added to what's left of the air...

My stomach convulses. I think I'm going to be sick... I hurry to the nearest window unable to take another breath of this fetid air. A brief wrestle with the latch, one hard push against the stiff frame and the window jerks open with a loud crack. A damp, fresh breeze wafts in from the night dislodging a number of the fly corpses sprinkled along the window ledge. A living specimen zips past my ear deserting its comrades to escape into the hazardous rain. I thrust my head outside, tug down the T-shirt and gulp in as much sweet oxygen as my lungs will allow. The nausea subsides but the taste in my mouth is unbearable. I remember my cigarettes... Only one left in the pack. I light up and draw heavily. It helps – a little. I blindly toss the empty packet on to the floor and breathe in more of the crystal pure air... *What was that...?*

I turn and face the room. Listen hard. Nothing but flies... I step towards the middle of the room where a broken light bulb hangs from the nicotine stained ceiling. Below the bulb a squadron of bluebottles buzz in demented spirals. Now and then the insects dive-bomb each other and engage in a mid-air tussle for supremacy.

I'm *sure* I heard something. It's difficult to pick out anything in all this crud… A mound of dubiously stained duvets and cushions with the stuffing ripped out swamp the sofa. The shattered television lies face down on the floor near the gas fireplace. Needles and syringes clutter the glass topped coffee table along with pill bottles, burnt-out candles, spoons and small fragments of scorched tin foil. More needles lie on the floor beside the swaddled sofa…. *There it is again! …* A whimpering sound… I spin round and stare at the sofa's matching armchair by the fireplace.

Beneath a mass of sheets and rugs a pair of big brown eyes stare at me pathetically. It's a dog… I lean over cautiously, half expecting the beast to pounce at my throat. I remove the suffocating layers and uncover a grotesque sight. It could be an Alsatian. Hard to tell. The poor thing really ought to be dead. Its skin, covered in sores, is moulded to its skeleton like shrink-wrap. Flies strike around its backside, damp and matted with its own waste… There's an open wound on the stricken dog's hind leg. Bloated maggots squirm over what little red flesh exists over exposed bone. The dog's rattling chest heaves with each laboured breath. It tries to lift its head but it doesn't have the strength. A collar hangs loosely around its scrawny neck. I take a look at the name tag… *Dixie.*

Those forlorn eyes refuse to let me go. Another whimper strains to be heard. I didn't expect this. I didn't expect to feel pity in this place. That was not on the agenda. I take an old towel from the back of the chair, cover the Alsatian's head, then wrap my hands around its neck and squeeze for all I'm worth. I feel its bones and windpipe collapse but carry on crushing them, determined to make this as quick and as painless as possible.

'That's it. Show the dog mercy.'

The voice was nothing more than a strangled whisper but enough to make me stand and face the sofa in a scared shitless blur. A hideous face pokes out from the base of the textile heap. Sallow skin hugs the skull. Muddy teeth are fixed in a scab encrusted mouth.

'Are you Billy Gardiner?' I ask.

The face contorts with a peculiar, popping laugh. 'As if you didn't know. Come to finish me off at last have you? Has that sick fuck Mullett sent you? Ha...ha, ha, ha. Hee-ee... I am Billy Gardiner. Won't mum be proud! Haa - aa. You'll never get a penny from me. Hey you!' his glassy eyes widen suddenly, 'I saw Satan in here last night I'm fuckin' tellin' ya. He was in here. Eatin' them flies. He knows. He knows I want to eat them but... but he won't let me... Oh at last! That's the way. You kill me, please. Finish me off. Tell Mullett he's made his point and that I'll catch up with him in... in...' his voice runs out of steam.

I pull away the various layers; duvets, sheets, blankets and sleeping bags – I shove them all onto the floor. That voice. I still remember. Cracked and torn now but nevertheless...My heart sinks with bitter disappointment when I finally uncover Gardiner naked but for a pair of badly soiled briefs, festering in his own filth. Lying on his back, his knees drawn up in an arch, hands and feet tied together underneath him he looks like a famine victim, barely heavier than his dog. His marbled skin flaking and riddled with sores slides over his bones like damp tissue paper. *How long has he been in this state?*

He starts to tremble slightly. His head is too heavy for him to move. There's no telling what his shrunken face would look like in normal circumstances and try as I might I can't get it to fit my own fuzzy ten year old memory of him. He's weeping now. I see puncture marks dotted over his arms. A needle has broken off in the fold of his left elbow and an infection has erupted around the metal spike. His left ear is torn at the root leaving the hanging lobe necrotic and black. I see a couple of maggots nuzzling in its recess... *Jesus*! – Is all this a belated hallucination induced by the chemical cocktail I swallowed back in prison? I feel panicky... This is all wrong... I want him to be able to put up a fight. I *need* him to put up a fight...

'I'm hungry. Are you hungry?' gasps Gardiner, 'Let's eat the dog... I tried to eat 'im before. I chewed his leg but the fucker woke up and bit my ear. Little shit hasn't come and sat next to me since...but if we work together y'know...?' His face creases into an expression of abject sorrow, '…I love my dog… Whatsisname…? Oh fuck, I can't remember his name…' his voice falters and Gardiner begins to weep again.

I bend down to face the wretch and look straight into his eyes. Does he remember me? Is he aware of the pain he's caused? Does he care? Has the soul buried behind those pin-prick pupils ever entertained even the tiniest spark of repentance? I somehow doubt it.

'Do you remember me Billy?' I ask searching for a twitch of recognition on the bastard's ravaged face. My mind flashes back to the shotgun blasting into Catherine Dodds' stomach. I slap Gardiner's face; not too hard – I'm scared I might break his neck, 'Look. Carefully. Do you remember me ya murderin' basturt?!'

'Course I know you. You're one of Mullett's boys come to finish me off. So go on mate, kill me for fuck's sake. You win. I can't… I can't see properly anymore. There's not enough light… never enough light…' Gardiner's voice tails away. His decaying teeth clamp together and his sinewy neck stretches until his Adam's apple looks like it's about to pierce the taut skin of his throat. He's in serious pain… He relaxes and laughs his eerie, choking stammer of a laugh. 'Let's eat the dog… No! Let's eat the flies. Go and catch the flies… Is there any bread left?'…

'Listen. Don't fuckin' drift off,' I tap his face. 'Pay attention. You hear me? You killed a woman. Ten years ago. You raided a petrol station in Brighton but I beat you to it. I had the money…. Listen tae me! Remember? Your cousin - Barry is it? Remember Barry pointing his gun at me and me pointing mine at him? Remember, huh? Didn't know mine was fake though did he eh?…'

'Dixxxxxxeeeeeeeee…Ach,' Gardiner coughs. He's pissing me off. He's away with the fairies.

'Shit… Come on concentrate ya wanker. Think. Catherine Dodds. Remember her?' I grab hold of his emaciated jaw, forcing him to look at me, 'You blew her apart. Blew fuckin' great big holes intae her. You must remember that. Her insides were all over the place. You did it. You killed her in cold fuckin' blood. Remember? Eh?'

He thinks long and hard with a deep wrinkly frown, 'Brighton?' he mutters eventually, '...I know a good club there. I've got contacts. Shall we go...? Have we got any bread left? I'm sure I bought some not long ago...' His eyes suddenly widen and stare over my shoulder in terror. 'Fuck! You're back! Eat the flies! Eat them all!' he wheezes and splutters into a coughing fit.

The fear in his eyes turns me cold. Whatever he can see is standing right behind me. Of course there's nothing there. *Of course there's nothing...* But it feels like there is... I have to turn and see what he's looking at...

Nothing but flies...

The feeling of dread fades leaving me standing in the middle of this midden in complete despair. I don't know what to do. The poisonous air is making my lungs ache. I lean back down to his face, frustration twisting into fury.

'You fucked up my life! Ten fuckin' years! Ten useless, wasted fucking years! It should've been you, ya shite! D'you hear me?' I rap my knuckles against his scalp. 'Hullo? Is there any fucker at home? Why do people like you have to exist uh? Tell me! Why?'

He remains silent. This is a pointless exercise. His brain has been reduced to mush.

'Billy Gardiner - you do not know how lucky you are. You should be thankful this Mullett character got to you first because what he's done to you is fucking *nothing* compared to what I had in mind. D'you understand me? *Nothing!'*

No effect. The blank expression remains set.

I return to the window to swallow some clean air before I pass out. Still raining. I let the drops cover my face, cooling me inside and out. A wide yawn takes me by surprise... I'm exhausted. I want to curl up in a clean bed and never have to wake up again. I want to be warm...

'Last time I saw you, you thought you were so fucking tough, so fucking clever. Full of cocky bravado. But we both know how easy it is to be all those things when you've got a shotgun and a bunch of mates to hide behind. Just like Catherine Dodds said, remember?' I turn to focus on his vacant eyes. 'Course you don't. But look at you now Billy. I wanted to see just how fuckin' clever you really are. No weapons. No masks. Just you and me. I wanted to find out if you had the bollocks for a fair fight or if you were the spineless wee coward Catherine suspected you were.' I pause and shake my head unable to resist a wry smile. 'I was gonnae make you weep like a bairn and beg for mercy – which, of course, you'd never have got...'

'Go to the unit by the kitchen door. There's a gun in the top drawer.' Gardiner's tone catches me off guard. His voice sounds unexpectedly lucid. Even his eyes betray some straight thinking taking place in the background. 'Well?' he says, 'Go and get it.'

The room is now crawling with suspicion. What is he up to? Is this a trick? Is that otherwise innocent but ugly looking piece of furniture stuffed with explosives? This situation is weird enough to admit any eventuality.

I pick my way through the debris to the unit and slide open the top drawer... No trip wires. No explosions. Sure enough, lying next to a pair of scissors, I find a handgun. I lift it out. Heavy, cold and... *real*.

'It's loaded. You've all had your fun. Now pull the trigger and blow my fuckin' head off. Please...' his voice degenerates to a throaty creak. His dull stare follows me as I head back to the sofa. I turn his head straight until he faces the ceiling. He squints at me and cackles for a moment. I use the scissors to cut the bonds and free his hands. Too weak to move it himself I take his wasted right arm, rest the gun in his palm and raise it to his mouth. He clenches his loose, rotten grin around the muzzle. A thick blue artery pulses weakly under the tracing paper skin of his neck. I carefully wrap his fingers around the handle, pushing the index finger through the trigger guard.

'Do it yourself,' I tell him coldly. I move away. Gardiner's arm quivers with the effort required to keep the handgun in place. He continues to fix me with that unblinking waxwork gaze. 'Too many enemies, eh Billy?'

Standing outside, I want the rain to cleanse every contaminated pore. I feel filthy and infected as though a million tiny insects are scurrying over my skin and through my hair. I can't get rid of the bilious odour lining my nostrils. I walk to the kerb where a stream of rain water flows quickly towards a storm drain. I step in stamping and scraping my shoes, trying to remove as much dog muck as possible. I rinse my hands in the freezing water. A gunshot rings out from the open window on the second floor... I came here wanting to torture the bastard. I wanted to hear him scream in agony. Instead – I've somehow managed to indulge in a spot of euthanasia. I wonder what Gardiner could possibly have done to piss off this Mullett guy so badly... Curtains are twitching. Time to move on...

*

The stars shift. Realign and cast forth an astral shiver. An influence felt a lifetime away. Fate is tempted. Paths collide and cross. Colours flare then fade. A coincidence is planned and then blamed... It has happened before and in a cosmic blink, will happen again. Even the most fleeting of dreams echo out across the universe to be experienced *everywhere... ...* The points of light are fading...

*

I am in Scotland. I am in Glasgow. I am standing in Parkhead. I am standing in Janefield Street craning my neck skywards in awe of the cathedral that is Celtic Park towering over me. Last time I was here I was nineteen. I watched us brush aside St. Mirren with consummate ease. After Dad's death and subsequently missing out on the club's offer of a trial, I couldn't bear to come here but time, age and curiosity have all combined to soothe away the pain of what might have been... Almost.

The stadium has been completely revamped. I'd heard all about its reconstruction during my time on the inside but standing here in its mighty shadow and wondering what it must be like inside is making me feel light-headed. I realise it's foolish for a forty-year old to feel such childlike wonder but it's been so long… and it's such a good feeling. I am determined to enjoy it.

The rain clouds slip greyly towards the southern horizon having gilded the city with a polished sheen the sickly sun would like to erase. The stiff wind makes me sniff. I wipe the damp tip of my stone-cold nose on the back of my cuff. After spending a numb, uncomfortable night in a shelter at Drumchapel train station, I had intended to make a beeline for Wemyss Bay but couldn't resist making this one final stop before heading home.

I kept falling asleep on the trundling local train that brought me to the East End of the city and each time I woke up I could tell by the disapproving looks on my fellow passengers that I stank. Even I had to turn up my nose at the scent given off by my clothes and shoes. I stepped off at Duke Street station where I did my best to wash away the aftermath of last night in the toilets before heading along Millerston Street to arrive in Gallowgate as the traders were raising their shutters. I treated myself to a fry-up in a greasy café where I sat by the window to watch the rush hour traffic building up outside. Afterwards I gave in to a bout of shopping therapy, bought myself a new pair of cheap shoes and socks, sprayed myself liberally with a can of deodorant and picked up another pack of cigarettes.

I light up my fifth smoke of the day.

'You okay there pal?' a white-haired, old man with a heavily lined but pleasant face asks me.

'Aye. I'm fine,' I reply rousing from my thoughts., 'It's been a while since I was last here. I was just admiring the new stadium, y'know?'

'Aye. The best in Britain. Manchester United can take Old Trafford and shove it up their arse.' The old man grins, stands next to me and looks up, 'When was the last time you were here?'

'Twenty years ago.'

'Twinty year!' he whistles, 'An awfie lots changed in that time. Where've ye been?'

'Um... travelling,' I mutter. Thankfully he doesn't push for further details.

'You a Glesga boy originally, aye?' he asks.

'No. Rothesay. Bute, y'know?'

'Oh aye!' he smiles, 'Rothesay. Used tae go there for ma holidays when I was a wee boy. Aye – lovely wee place. I bet it's changed since those days, eh? Mind you, show me a place that husnae.' The old man looks around slyly, takes hold of my wrist and looks at me deadly serious, as if he's about to divulge a fail-safe plan to assassinate the Prime Minister. 'Listen,' he utters in a low voice, 'I'm no' supposed tae dae this but...' He jerks his head towards a side entrance, 'Follow me.'

'... and bein' the heid groundsman I huv a bit of authority y'know?... And the big boys respect me. They don't mind me takin' the odd wee liberty. As long as I do a good job that's the main thing... but come the end o' next season, that's it for me. Time tae hang up ma pitchfork...'

The old man talks on enthusiastically but I'm only half listening. I'm a quivering wreck. The elderly groundsman has led me inside and *on to the pitch!* I can't believe this! I am *actually* standing in 'Paradise'. I have finally set foot on the soft cushion of its precious turf. I know my mouth is gaping but I'm incapable of closing it. I twist round in a tight circle trying to take in everything at once. The massive green and white stands are awesome. It must be an incredible feeling to play on this pitch when every one of those sixty-thousand seats are occupied... I'm finding it difficult to breathe in the airy silence of this monumental space. I feel dizzy. I can sense well over a century of history welling up under my feet... I watch the flags fluttering above the main stand. I look at the dug-outs and the goals... *If only...*

'The pitch looks fantastic. Pristine,' I tell my guide.

'Thanks very much,' he seems genuinely chuffed with the compliment, 'I take a lot of pride in my work.'

'It shows.'

'Aye well, it's one thing to huv a decent pitch,' he sighs, 'All we need noo is a decent team tae go with it. Looks like the other lot have won the league already eh?'

I smile, 'Let's not talk about that shall we?'

He laughs, 'Quite right... What's yer name by the way son?'

'Haig. Haig Dumfries,' I tell him without thinking... *Shit!*...Feeling a murmur of panic I realise what I've done... I watch him frown; thinking – trying to place the name. I'm going to have to make a hasty exit...

'Sounds familiar... Dumfries?' he repeats, continuing to inspect me beneath questioning wrinkles. Looking up at the VIP boxes I back off a couple of paces ready to sprint back to where I entered this wonderful arena. I really don't want to go. Not yet...

'Haig Dumfries. From Rothesay... Oh aye! I remember noo!' he suddenly shouts clicking his fingers and pointing at me with a broad, beaming smile which I surely wouldn't get if he thought he was face to face with an escaped murderer, 'Ma brother told me aboot you. Twenty years ye say, aye? Aye it must've been,' he rubs his chin, 'Ma brother was Celtic's chief scout. He used tae keep harpin' on aboot this talented lad from Rothesay. Bored us all tae death he did. – "Could be the best Scottish striker since Dennis Law" – he kept sayin'... "Haig Dumfries! Celtic huv got tae sign him!" – he kept sayin'... Christ. And here ye are!' the groundsman exclaims offering his hand. I shake it. His grip is hard and eager, 'My name's Alec. Alec McIntyre.'

'Your brother must be Tom then.'

Memories hit me like a tidal wave.

'Aye. Tom was ma big brother... Passed away twelve years ago noo, bless his soul.'

'I'm sorry to hear that.'

Alec smiles, dismissing my awkward condolences with a small wave of his hand, 'You were offered a trial were you no'? How come ye never took it?'

I clear my throat, 'Well, my dad died the week before. I had to support the family. Couldn't take the risk and quit my job,' I sigh

215

heavily, feeling depressed. I stare into the players' tunnel... *If only...* My eyes start to burn...

'Aye, I heard aboot that,' he nods sympathetically, then looks puzzled, '... But Tom told me he'd had a word with the boss at the time. He recommended the club should offer your family financial support until you were ready tae sign on the dotted line. That's how confident he was in ye.'

Something splinters darkly at the back of my mind. I'm not sure I want to know this...

'... I'm sure that's what happened... Aye that's right it's comin' back tae me noo... I remember Tom tryin' to contact you for ages. Ye see, because they trusted ma brother's judgement so much he got the go ahead. Celtic were prepared tae give you and your family all the tender lovin' care ye needed, just tae get ye on the books. How could ye turn an offer like that doon?'

'I never knew about it,' I mumble.

Alec looks perplexed, 'Never knew?! But Tom went on and on aboot it. He even showed me the letter you sent rejecting the offer. He was gutted. Couldnae believe it. I think he suspected Rangers had got their claws intae ye.'

The massive walls of green and white begin to melt before my eyes, 'I never... I didn't er... I never wrote that... letter.' It hurts when I swallow.

'Och away, I saw it masel. What're ye tryin' tae say? - Someb'dy wrote it for ye?... You okay son?' Alec sounds concerned.

Of course... It makes sense now. Things are slotting into place... I have to clear my head. I blink fast and press my palms against my eyes to suppress the tears.

'Aye. I'm fine,' I lie, suddenly feeling the cold again, 'I must've been mad to turn down a chance like that eh?' I try to feign a smile, 'I was just... Och, I dunno – I was daft. Young and daft. I shouldnae have done it.' I rub my hands together. Alec is not convinced and seems to be on the verge of saying something consoling but I cut him short. 'Listen Alec. This has been magic. Seriously. I'll never forget this,' I shake his hand again. 'Very, very kind of you to do this. It's been a pleasure to meet you but I've got to make a move before I start greetin' an' wishin' I could turn back the clock, y'know?'

This much is true but the main reason I have to go is you… Joe.

13: blades

I forced the rickety sash window upwards as far as it would go, pulled up my one and only chair, placed my coffee on the sill and settled back to enjoy the show. Not that Castle Street ever really put on much of a show. From my third storey vantage point I watched the rain teem down from a ceiling of leaden clouds to drench the parked cars and the occasional pedestrian hurrying by. It was mid-morning but the murky weather made it feel more like dusk. I had an hour to kill before The Black Bull opened for business. An hour to gather my thoughts and forge some kind of master plan before meeting up with Maureen.

There was a little fleck of black paint adhered to the otherwise bare grey wood of the decaying window sill and for some reason its presence began to annoy me. I picked at it with the nail of my index finger but it wouldn't budge. At first its refusal to shift fooled me into thinking that the blemish was in fact a tiny hole in the timber. I tested the idea by seeing if my nail would sink inside. It didn't.

A fat raindrop scored a direct hit into the coffee. I took a sip. Lukewarm. I still had the three mugfuls I'd downed at Zavaroni's swilling around in my stomach so there was no need for a tepid fourth. I held the mug out of the window and tipped the contents out on to the pavement below. A car swished past, its tyres slicing through puddles before swinging left to disappear down Bishop Street. A gull watched the comings and goings from a lamppost on the corner. I pulled my recently acquired gun from my pocket, aimed at the bird and pulled the dead trigger. Unperturbed, the gull twitched its rear end and let loose a white blob of shit which missed a scuttling, rainproofed granny by inches.

I replaced the gun with a yawn - a yawn cut short when the back of my neck suddenly tingled. It felt like a soft cold breath on the skin. Then came the creeping sensation that I was not alone. Something else was in the room. Something intangible. Something was watching me. Panic rising I turned quickly to confront whoever or whatever had invaded the shadowy gloom of my drab bed-sit.

218

Nothing... and yet I found it impossible to shift the vague impression I was sharing the space with an uninvited guest. I shivered while my eyes worked overtime investigating every last detail.

The tiny flat had a pervasive mouldy odour thanks to the blotches of persistent mildew occupying each high corner. The wallpaper, carpets and fittings – faded, brown and worn; were all refugees from the fifties. I hated the place but it was the only one I could afford. I had spent only eleven weeks in the miserable hole and already I was desperate to move out. I looked at the large cardboard box by the foot of the bed. All I would need to transport my belongings. The sum total of my life would fit comfortably inside that solitary box.

I glanced at the letter lying on the floor by the musty wardrobe. The single sheet of A4 topped with the bank's solid, dependable letterhead had been lying there for several days... Then my chest tightened and the blood stalled in my veins. From the corner of my eye I saw someone in the wardrobe mirror. A small boy. Standing still. Faceless... I had to force myself to look at the figure full on...

My imagination gave way to the truth. I breathed again. There was no ghost. The mirror was simply reflecting my coat and the red woolly jumble sale hat hanging from the door on the other side of the room.

I removed the hat and coat from the door and threw them on the bed.

I'd been stalling long enough. I found it difficult to look at their faces. There was never going to be a suitable moment. I knew it wasn't my fault but I couldn't help feeling ashamed and helpless.

I told them I'd been made redundant.

'Whit?! Yer kiddin'! But why?!'

Joe was far more upset then Maureen.

We were gathered round my favourite corner table in The Black Bull. Maureen had found my note and, as requested, had not brought her aggravating husband. Instead, she brought Joe after spotting him heading up to visit Mum. Despite being the first to arrive I still hadn't been able to formulate a convincing plan of action. With no cards to lay on the table I placed another round of drinks there instead.

'I mean what're we s'posed to do about Mum now eh?' my brother demanded. He was gearing himself up for his finals, maybe this was why he was uptight. Or maybe it had something to do with the cluster of empty pint glasses on the table. He was averaging a pint every fifteen minutes so he had time to demolish a fourth before the clock hit midday.

'Please let me talk to Alan. I'm sure I can persuade…'

I had to cut in. There was no way I was going to give the Hairy Heathen the satisfaction. 'After what he said last night? Are you joking?' I knew he would be revelling in my misfortune. And I knew a big gloating smile would split that bristling foliage the instant he learned I was out of a job. He'd meant what he said about Mum getting what she deserved and he wasn't the type to go back on his word. Maureen would ask him to help us and he would say "No" - He would *relish* saying "No"…

'Oh you shouldn't pay any attention to that. You two just wind each other up the wrong way sometimes,' Maureen said assuming a motherly air.

'What did he say last night?' Joe asked sniffing controversy.

'No offence Maureen but don't you dare ask that husband of yours for help. I don't want to owe him or his God anything.'

'I bet they sacked you didn't they? I bet you fucked up someone's account. I wouldn't put it past you to do somethin' like that,' Joe grumbled sipping the head off his new pint.

'What is your fuckin' problem?'

'Keep your voices down you two. And stop swearing. There's no point arguing now is there?' Maureen said calmly.

'Unless you've got somethin' useful to say just shut it okay Joe?' I fumed, voice lowered. 'I mean you haven't exactly contributed much to Mum's upkeep have ye? And showin' her that Seattle crap – Doctor Fishbum's clinic? What were you *playing* at? You build up her hopes then bugger off and leave it up tae us tae tell her that the whole thing's a con!'

220

'It wasnae a con. It would've worked,' Joe bleated.

'I thought it was photography you were studyin'?'

'Aye. So?'

'Well seein' as your clearly such an expert on the subject I was beginning to think you'd taken up neurosurgery.'

Maureen shook her head wearily while I continued to lay into our brother.

'When are you gonnae start pulling your weight eh? When are you gonnae pull yer thumb oot yer fat lazy arse and actually dae somethin' useful tae help mum?'

'Just you wait and see,' Joe sneered dipping into a pack of cigarettes – a cheap brand I'd never seen before. 'When I get my Degree I'll get a decent job – unlike you – and I'll earn more money than you ever will. Guaran-fuckin-teed!'

I had stuffed all my jumble sale purchases deep into my coat pocket. My finger squeezed the useless trigger.

'Cheeky wee basturt! Have you forgotten who's been sendin' you the money tae get ye through yer fuckin' Degree eh? You ungrateful…

'Have they offered you any redundancy money?' asked Maureen trying to cool things down.

'Five grand but it's…'

'Is that it? After all the years you've given them? That's an insult. Stingy bastards.'

'I need a grand to get me through my last term,' Joe's suddenly cheerful eyes glittered.

'What? A grand! Are you mad? After all the crap I've had tae put up with, you expect me tae give you a grand just so you can smoke and piss it up the wall! You've got a brass neck so ye huv. Besides it's all...'

'C'mon Haig. Don't you want your wee brother to achieve his ambitions?' Joe grinned cheekily.

'Aye, like I'm sure you wanted me to achieve mine.'

'Och c'mon give us a break Haig will ye? That was fuckin' years ago man. I admit it. I was jealous. I shouldnae huv ripped up they letters but I was jealous and I was only fifteen don't forget. Christ it was ten years ago - Time tae forgive and forget, naw?... I only want the money tae help pay my rent and buy all the books n' stuff I need tae revise. I'm no' gonnae waste it, honest,' he rambled, speech slurred.

'What're you on about rippin' up letters?' I asked puzzled.

Joe focused his inebriated gaze on me. My expression must have triggered alarm bells behind those bloodshot orbs because he seemed to make a determined effort to compose himself, thinking long and hard about what he'd said.

'Nothin,' he mumbled eventually, 'Junk mail n' stuff – that's all we ever got.' He sprang out of his chair instantly switching back to angry mode, 'Look! If you don't want tae gie me the money, fine! I was only asking. Don't really need it! Just don't get on yer fuckin' high horse eh?' he yelled for all to hear.

'I huvnae got any money left for fuck sake! It's all gone!'

'What d'ye mean it's all gone?! On what?' Joe's face flared as red as his eyes.

'I used it tae clear my overdraft, pay off debts, pay my rent and bills and Mum's bills and your bloody course...'

'You mean you wasted it a' on yerself ya selfish bastard! What aboot yer family?!' he sputtered.

'Joe! Shhh...!' Maureen grabbed his arm. He yanked it free.

'Well listen tae him. Thinks he's so bloody clever. Thinks we owe him everythin'. Look at him playin' the martyr. Thinks he's such a big man for lookin efter us. You think ye shite gold bricks don't ye? Well ye don't! Yer a sanctimonious wanker and I'm sick of all yer self-righteous bollocks.' Joe bent down to rant into Maureen's face, 'As soon as Dad died he thought that gave him the right tae treat me like shite and act like some fuckin' Mafia don or somethin'.' He snatched his jacket from the back of his chair and wrestled it on.

Joe's histrionics had attracted a sizeable audience causing Maureen to flush with embarrassment.

'Joe, calm down...'

I was aware that Davey the barman was less than happy.

'Bollocks tae ye Haig. I don't need yer help and as far as I'm concerned you've got some fuckin' nerve havin' a go at me for building up Mum's hopes. Fuckin' *Lourdes*! Talk about a fuckin' con! That's a' she ever goes on aboot noo-adays – "Haig's gonnae pay for me to go to Lourdes!" - She's expecting a miracle Haig but she's no' gonnae get her miracle is she? Because yer no' gonnae pay for her tae go, are ye? Because ye don't huv the fuckin' money dae ye?! It's time we all just accepted it – Mum's no' gonnae get any better and you shouldnae make promises ye cannae keep. Lourdes...' he shook his head, 'She's *expectin'* tae be cured. Christ, yer takin' advantage of her faith Haig and that's just plain fuckin' cruel!'

Joe downed the rest of his pint and banged the glass on the table as Davey stepped over to make his feelings known.

'Don't worry pal,' he scowled at Davey, 'I'm off.'

True to his word, Joe disappeared through the Albert Place doors.

I sank back in my chair shaking my bewildered head, mouth open; stunned. Joe had left me reeling. We had never really seen eye to eye since Dad died but Joe had never spoken to me like that. Maureen tried to make excuses for him but there was more to it than a bellyful of beer and a quick temper. Much more. But what? What had I done to provoke him?

I watched Bute fold into the mist from the upper deck of the *Jupiter*. Joe's words continued to rattle inside my head throughout the crossing. Cruel and wounding though they were I needed to hear them again and again. There was a certain vague pleasure to be had in reliving each vitriolic syllable, like picking at a tiny flap of dead skin at the base of a fingernail and pulling it until it tears deeper into the flesh and starts to bleed. My mood demanded that I concentrated hard on making those words ring true. It made things easier to accept if I could convince myself that Joe had been right. It made it easier to strengthen my resolve and resign myself to what had to be done in order to make amends.

I felt queasy which was unusual for me and for some reason, despite the wintry conditions, the urge to experience the journey in the open air rather than from the warmth within came from an abstract call to watch the island fade into the grey curtain completely. With the drizzle slashing at my face and the squall tearing at my hair and numbing my ears, I leaned over the side to see the ferry's hull slice into the coal black water and listened to the birth of the wake. White spray sloshing and fizzing.

The rough sea inspired me, as it always did whenever I made this crossing, to imagine what would happen if we started to sink. To the best of my knowledge no vessel had ever sank sailing this route but there was always a first time. I pictured myself jumping into the sea – deeper, wider and colder than anything. *'Would the ferry be able to turn quickly enough in these conditions in time to save me? Would they bother?'* I asked myself.

I curled my right hand around the replica gun tucked safely out of sight deep in my pocket. Joe and Maureen hadn't even mentioned my imminent thirtieth birthday. Everything had either fallen or was in the process of falling apart. The Dumfries family had ruptured; Joe was a selfish no-hoper doing his utmost to squander whatever talent he had, Mum was an invalid in search of a miracle, Maureen had married an undeserving nutter and I was jobless, broke and pining for a relationship that had long since been relegated to nostalgia.

And as if all that wasn't bad enough, eleven years after coming to power the Milk Snatcher was *still* in charge, stealthily selling off the country to the lowest bidder. Even worse, it looked like Rangers were about to win the league again.

*   *   *

I hear a weird clicking noise followed by a faint whirr.

'Joe?'

'Hallo? Who is it?'

'Don't you recognise your own brother's voice?' I ask trying to remain calm.

'Hold on a minute Haig will ye? You've just got me oot ma bed.' Joe sounds flustered. I hear his phone clatter and bump along with some creaking and scratching. I peer out of the telephone box through the rain towards Glasgow Central station. There is a train to Wemyss Bay in fifteen minutes.

Joe comes back on the line, out of breath, 'Haig? What d'ye want?'

'I want you to cast your mind back little brother to just a week or two after Dad died. I know it's been twenty years but I'm sure you can remember. A letter came through the post didn't it?' I wait... Silence on the other end. 'Okay. To be more specific - you opened a letter addressed to me from Celtic Football Club, didn't you?' I grind my teeth trying to keep my anger in check.

'What the fuck are you on about Haig?' he says slowly.

'Joe don't fuckin' bore me! The letter. The one from Celtic offering to help us out if I signed for them. I know you fuckin' remember so don't come it wi' me! You turned them down. You fuckin' wrote a reply, signed it in my name and fuckin' turned them down! Admit it!'

My temper's cracking. *I want to kill him.*

Silence...

Warning pips. The phone's eaten all the money. I shove another pound coin down its throat.

'C'mon!' I yell, losing patience. 'You virtually said as much that time in The Black Bull remember? – The last time I saw you before I was jailed? When I told you I'd been made redundant and you had the fuckin' nerve to ask me for a grand?!... What was it you said? – *"Don't you want yer wee brother to achieve his ambitions?"* – Fuckin' slimy wee hypocrite! Then you apologised for tearing up some letters of mine because you were jealous! But like a prick I never cottoned on to what you were on about! I just thought you were talking shite because you were pissed. And that's what that slanging match was all about wasn't it? Shoutin' and bawlin' in front of everybody in the pub?! You were just makin' sure I didnae get a chance tae ask ye any awkward questions, eh?! Oh aye, it's all clear as fuckin' crystal now

Joe! - All I need tae know is why? Why do it?! What the fuck had I done to deserve that?!' I have to draw breath. My voice hurts.

'Honestly. Haig. I don't...'

'Aw please, *fuck* off! I spoke tae someone at Celtic this mornin'. He told me! D'you understand?! He told me they got my letter rejecting the offer! *My* letter! But we both know I didnae send any fuckin' letter because I'd have tae be some kind've world champion masochist to turn down a chance like that! So who the fuck could it've been? I know Mum can be devious at times but she's never malicious! And Maureen was only ten at the time and besides, she hasn't got a vindictive cell in her body. So who does that leave? Eh? Don't fuckin' insult me anymore! Just admit it... That's all I want to hear from you.'

I press my eyes shut, chew the inside of my cheeks and inhale a deep, purging breath. Why isn't he saying anything?... More odd noises. I'm sure I hear the faintest of whispers in the background... Of course... Of course there's someone else there but right now I could not care less.

'Aye,' Joe says softly, 'I did rip up those letters. There was three of them altogether,' he sighs, 'The guy even came tae the hoose once. I told you'd gone tae Edinburgh tae stay wi' a pal. I... I told him I'd make sure you contacted him. So I wrote him a letter saying you weren't interested and copied your signature... Satisfied?' he asks coldly.

No. I'm not. 'What about the letter I did get? The one from Mr McIntyre telling me they'd found other strikers and wouldn't be needing...'

'I wrote that one as well.' He sounds almost pleased with himself, 'I went for a day out in Glasgow, found a printer's and got them to do me a copy of the Celtic letterhead... Easy. Cost more than I thought it would mind,' I hear him swallow, 'I'm no' proud o' myself Haig. And yer right, of course I was jealous – really fuckin' jealous. I wouldnae huv been able tae handle it if you'd gone off and been really successful. I would've felt like a right dildo, y'know? I couldnae allow it... Christ. I'm sorry. I shouldnae huv done it – There, is that what you wanted tae hear? Doesnae make ye feel any better though does it? And don't forget, I was just a boy at the time… Haig…?'

Maybe I would have done the same to him. Maybe it's in all of us. A natural instinct to push a sibling out the nest, destroy the nearest rival, claim his territory and ensure the survival of your own peculiar, particular line…

'Haig? You still there…?'

The admission has drained me completely. Nothing remains except an empty, rusting vessel echoing to the disembodied voice of a stranger I will never understand.

'Haig…?'

I hear movement in the background.

'You were fifteen. Old enough to know the damage you were doin' to me.' I've been reduced to a whisper. All the shout has gone.

Cain and Abel…

'C'mon. It was just immature rivalry. I told ye. I was jealous… I made a mistake.'

I should have disabled him with a cane when I had the chance…

'What're you laughin' at?' he asks sounding a touch put out. I stop laughing.

'If only you learned from your mistakes eh? Instead I catch you trying to fuck me over again…' I catch sight of some activity in the street…

Silence.

Warning pips.

'Make sure you keep stacking those shelves. D'you hear me?'

A squad car slides to a halt immediately outside the telephone box.

I place the receiver back in the cradle and step out of the booth in time to see a powerful, red Lexus squeal up behind the squad car. I raise my hands over my head. I'm not going to put up a fight.

Two of Strathclyde's finest rise from the squad car and head towards me. A second police car screeches into position, blocking off the busy street.

Time slows. A bloated raindrop settles on my lashes distorting the view momentarily before dripping away with a blink.

I take a few, steady paces backwards across the pavement until my back is pressed against the building behind. The sign fastened to the wall above says 'Union Street.'

A face I recognise steps out of the Lexus. It's the guy I saw on Joe's television set appealing for my whereabouts... *What's his name?...*

The two strapping police officers are only a couple of metres away. In perfect unison they both suddenly look to their right. I follow their startled eyes. A small white car is hammering up the pavement aiming straight towards us. The car brakes to a shockwave of shrieking and skidding rubber. The first policeman leaps back into the road with inches to spare. The car slides into the second knocking him sprawling backwards into the phone box, shattering the glass into a myriad of fragments.

The car stops right beside me. The driver door flies open banging against my hip. The driver has his arm around the back of his seat and is pushing himself as far forward as he can to expose the inviting space behind him. He stares at me with panic in his stern eyes.

'Get in!'

I leap in to the back seat. The door slams shut and the car screams off again.

Looking through the rear window I see police frantically scurrying in all directions. The Lexus is the only vehicle on the move, working hard to back out of the confusion. This is all I see before being hurled against the back of the driver's seat and on to the floor as my unexpected getaway hares round a corner. I try to free my shoulder from under his seat. The floor is smothered in a layer of empty crisp packets, cartons, newspapers, half eaten apples and junk food.

'Get out the way you dozy prick!' he yells pummelling the horn.

Looking up I see imposing sandstone buildings zip past. We're still speeding along pavements. He presses on the horn continuously for several seconds. Outside the noise wails, changing tone with each of the various surfaces it bounces off. The engine roars with every rapid shift in gear. My spine whacks into the floor as we fly off the pavement to rejoin the road with a horrible, metallic crunch. I hear a woman's scream flit by. The car spins like a dodgem and makes off down another street. I feel it weave past slower obstacles, wheels squealing in protest. Another vicious right turn whacks my head against the ashtray set beneath the side window. Bloody thing flicks open spilling its contents into my face. I splutter, brushing the dusty mess from my face and hair. The brakes slam on hard. The G Force thumps me flat into the front seats. My backbone wails, I feel my brain wobble inside my skull while my stomach tries to force its way out through my throat.

'For fuck's sake woman! Look where you're going!'

The revs rasp into the red and we lurch into action again. This time I somehow gather myself on the back seat and hang on. We're hurtling over the Clyde. The driver pays no attention to me. I finally notice the music contributing to the overall din. Frantic and surreal, the windscreen wipers are flicking back and forth in time with the drums like twin metronomes… Don't recognise this song… I look behind me. I can see flashing blue lights struggling way back in the distant traffic. No sign of the Lexus.

The car pitches up a slip road and we blend on to the M8. I look at the driver's freckly frowning eyes in the rearview mirror; they remain firmly focused on the road ahead. We're accelerating towards even darker clouds.

'D'you want to climb in the front?' he asks. He has an English accent. Again he wraps an arm behind his seat pushing it forward to create a gap for me to pass through. I squeeze into the space catching my foot under the handbrake and have to fight it free with my hands before slumping into the passenger seat. The driver… he seems vaguely familiar. Roughly my age. Shorter and slightly heavier. His receding brown hair crowns a face beginning to puff with middle age… Definitely something there… He looks a wee bit like Donald Sutherland – but that's not it… All I'm offered is a profile facing rigidly forward with eyes fixed on the road. He flicks a glance to the rearview mirror. I peer over my shoulder to check the following traffic... No immediate danger.

'You've got a cigarette butt in your hair,' he tells me.

I ruffle my head and sure enough there it is accompanied by a shower of ash. I acknowledge the craving and search my pockets.

'D'you mind if I smoke?'

'Only if I can scrounge one off you,' he answers facing me full on... No – I still can't place him.

'By the way, um...but... er - Why?' I venture handing over a cigarette.

'Can't stand the police,' he says flatly while pushing in the dashboard cigarette lighter, 'Useless bastard's the lot of them.' He yawns and turns back to the motorway. 'You're that Dumfries guy aren't you? The one that's escaped from jail?'

'Fraid so...' I shuffle uncomfortably in my seat. What's he up to? *Who is he?*... 'Don't get me wrong. I'm grateful and all that but – this is a big risk you're takin' to help me out here. I mean they're bound to have got your...'

'Number plate?' he finishes for me. 'Couldn't give a monkey's. Is this a menthol by the way?'

I nod.

'Menthols are scientifically proven to make you sterile. Did you know that? Personally I'd make that the main selling point,' he says filling his lungs. 'The car's stolen. Plates are false. I was looking for somewhere to dump it when I saw you in a spot of bother back there... It's important that people like us stick together, don't you think?'

Is this numpty a 'care-in-the-community' experiment or what? This is all just a wee bit too convenient for my liking, though I've long since given up trying to decide what should or shouldn't be the natural course of things. And anyway; at least I'm heading in the right direction.

This car smells. It's a sugary, muggy smell. Sweet wrappers, crushed coke cans and fast food boxes carpet the footwell under my shoes. The dashboard shelf is overflowing with rubbish. The tight, warm space reminds me of a miniature, mobile version of Billy Gardiner's flat but thankfully, minus the dog shite.

'Yeah, I'm sorry about the mess but this is how I found it. Some people eh?'

The M8 becomes the A8.

I feel heat close to my cheek. I turn and almost burn my nose on the car's cigarette lighter the driver is offering.

'Sorry,' he mutters with a puff.

I take the lighter and press the glowing orange filaments to my cigarette.

'What's your name?' I ask slotting the lighter back in its hole.

'Nick.' He looks at me, 'What's your first name again?'

I find his detached, unblinking eye contact unsettling.

'Haig.'

He offers his hand. I shake it. His grip is half-hearted. Nick shifts in his seat. Placing his hand back on the wheel he returns his attention to the road and moves us out into the fast lane to overtake a caravan.

'Where are you heading Haig?'

'Wemyss Bay.'

'Really? I'm heading that way myself. I'll drop you off,' he smiles thinly.

I open my window a couple of inches to allow the smoke to escape into the rain. I gaze out over the firth. The tide is out. The river is no more than a thin ribbon in an expanse of sand. It gives the impression that I could easily walk to Dumbarton Castle on the other side. Perched impressively on its own granite crag poking out into the Clyde, the castle drifts by across the sandbanks. From this angle the outcrop looks like a separate little island…

'You catching the ferry to Rothesay, yeah?'

I nod.

'Off to see your wife?'

'No. I'm not married. I've got family over there. Thought I'd pay them a visit.'

Nick falls silent.

He turns the radio off. 'I can't listen to any more of this mindless crap. D'you mind if I put some decent music on?'

'No, go ahead.'

Nick slips a cassette into the deck. The music swells. Lush strings. Pained vocals. A moody ballad. I vaguely remember this song... The words are having a noticeable effect on him. He swallows hard and shivers slightly.

'This is my wife's tape. She loves this sort of stuff. Sentimental type y'know?'

Nick adjusts his seat with a glance in the rearview mirror. He's becoming increasingly agitated.

I watch increasingly familiar landmarks roll by... The Firth Of Clyde dips out of sight as we turn into Greenock.

The A8 becomes the A78.

Catching a glimpse of Gateside Prison I remember my old cell-mate Jim Flack locked up in another jail hundreds of miles away. I feel sorry for the next unfortunate sod who has to put up with his flaky feet and manky habits.

We pass the sprawling IBM facility to our left...

I check my side mirror. Way back in the gloom there is a car, moving at speed, headlights rising and falling with each dip in the road.

'They're back again,' Nick states stoically with a squeeze on the accelerator.

The Firth opens up once more to our right revealing the massive grey chimney tower hogging the Inverkip shoreline. A thick curtain of rain and cloud obscures Bute but I know it's just over there. So close... I'm starting to feel anxious. I must try to keep a clear head. To have come all this way only to fail now would be a catastrophe. The rail bridge looms hard and fast. The road sign by the tunnel entrance shows a speed limit of thirty. We enter the mouth, passing beneath the tracks at seventy. The tunnel's moist black walls bounce the engine noise loud and close to my ears. We exit and the sound cuts back to the swish of tyres tearing over wet asphalt.

'Drop me off anywhere along here. That's fine,' I suggest trying not to sound worried even though we've arrived in Wemyss Bay and don't appear to be slowing down.

'I think I'll catch the ferry with you. See if I can lose the police,' he says pressing the brake firmly. Wrestling with the wheel he slides the car around the train station and into the car park by the pier.

Gently lolling in the swell, the familiar black and white hulk of the Caledonian MacBrayne ferry greets me like an old friend. The *Saturn* is ready to sail. Deck-hands are preparing to raise the ramp at the ship's stern. Coasting the car down the slip Nick sounds the horn. With an impatient grimace we are waved on board.

Another deck-hand guides us into a parking space while loud clangs and rumbles reverberate all around. The ramp is raised.

Nick turns off the engine with a sigh, 'Close call uh?'

I nod. My fraught nerves are warning me to retreat. I still can't place this man but I know it wasn't coincidence that put him here... I need to open the door before something weird happens.

'Thanks very much Nick. You're a life-saver,' I smile offering my hand, hoping that this will be our final interaction. My foot tramples on something – a newspaper; *The Brighton & Hove Advertiser*...

'No probs. Maybe I'll catch you upstairs in a minute yeah? Could use a coffee myself,' he grins shaking my hand, much harder this time.

I step out into the swirling rain and shut the door almost slipping on the slick car deck. I hurry inside where I am hit with a wall of hot air infused with a mix of diesel, beer and fags... Exactly as I remembered. Everything is exactly as I remembered. Ten years...

The ferry sways and lurches with a groan. The engines churn up deep and loud. Through a porthole crawling with rain I see the pier struts and supports, like the bars of a giant cage, slowly ebb away. We're moving. I have touched the mainland for the last time. A surge of overwhelming relief takes me by surprise and I nearly burst into tears. Instead, I laugh quietly to myself. I find the ferry very comforting. Protected here in its belly it's good to know that no matter what happens to me or anyone else, she will continue to undertake her constant, banal routine - yo-yoing back and forth, half an hour each way across this peril-less stretch of sea (weather permitting of course).

I must not allow myself to become complacent. There's still a long way to go. The police will be ready and waiting when I reach the other side but I'll deal with that problem as and when. I have so many things to do, so much that needs to be settled... The hardest part is yet to come.

Time to pay the ferryman. I fumble around in my pockets searching for money. I pull out the last note - a grubby twenty - and pay the yawning cashier in the ticket office. He passes over my change and I'm about to take issue with the man and his glinting fillings when I remember that one pound notes are something else that haven't been replaced around here.

I need a piss urgently. I head into the gents glad to find the place vacant - *Why is it I can never pee when someone's standing next to me?* I empty my tanks aiming high and sweeping back and forth along the steel trough experiencing a different kind of relief and release – *Why the hell did I bother buying a ticket? I'm probably going to have to make a run for it as soon as we arrive anyway... Bloody Catholic upbringing...* I stagger back in mid-flow when the vessel rolls unexpectedly causing me to add more mess on the already dubiously puddled floor. I laugh out loud, remembering when this happened to me as a boy and I'd pretended I was a drunken old man like the one I'd seen pissing on the outside wall of the public toilets by the pier.

Leaving the lower deck I take the steep, narrow stairs up to the next level needing both hand rails to counterbalance myself against the swaying ferry. I arrive in the passenger lounge finding it sprinkled with no more than a dozen or so people.

A couple of kids are happily slamming the buttons on an arcade machine even though there's no credit in the thing. I drop a few coins in for them.

'Cheers mister!' the older boy beams before they both set about squabbling over the controls.

'Me first!'

'Naw, me first!'

The smell of fresh coffee and scones is too tempting. I weave down the gangway towards the snack bar. A youngish woman in faded denims, her face framed with lank black hair, heads towards me concentrating intently on the two coffees she's holding out before her. We catch each other's eye and smile as we wobble past each other, all too aware of how ridiculous we must look thanks to the pitching ship.

I use up two of my one pound notes on a scalding coffee and a hard, crusty scone - the fresh smell was a piece of false advertising. I am forced to perform a weird waltz over to the table bearing the milk and sugar. Pushing the lid securely over the Styrofoam cup I bite into the scone and head outside.

I lean against the rail overlooking the car deck. Things have been happening so fast I didn't even notice the daylight draining away. Peering over the stern I see the lights of Wemyss Bay shrinking with the distance. There is a single car parked on the slipway by the pier, its headlights struggling to pierce the downpour. Standing motionless between those lights a man is watching the ferry. Perhaps he's watching me.

*

Craven sneezed, coughed hard and, once he was sure no-one was looking, spat the yellowy green lump onto the tarmac where it was instantly diluted by the rain. Leaning against the front of his car he stuck another disgusting Fisherman's Friend into his mouth and watched the ferry fading into the darkness. A nearby timetable confirmed he'd missed the last crossing of the day. He was actually quite pleased because the way the boat was listing from side to side, Craven knew he would have been inspecting the inside of a toilet bowl for the duration. Nevertheless, he had to make the trip over to Bute sometime and with the weather looking as mean as ever, that bilious date with destiny was inevitable.

He shook his head annoyed at not having caught Dumfries before

235

now. The local boys would be waiting for Haig as soon as he stepped off the boat but it would have been nice to have been there at the death after having chased the slippery swine the length of the country... And who *was* that twat who scooped him up back in Glasgow? Bloody maniac...

Craven continued to watch the shrinking ferry. His mobile rang. He slipped back into the dark warmth of his car to take the call. The wife. And she sounded less than pleased.

'You've got some explaining to do. When are you coming home?'

'Pardon?'

'When are you coming home?' she repeated, losing patience.

'Tomorrow hopefully. Or maybe the day after. Depends. What d'you mean I've got some explaining to do?' Craven wiped away the water trickling down his face from his matted hair.

'I've found out why Rachael's been in such a foul mood. And I can't say I blame her.'

The line hissed silently for a moment, irritating Craven.

'Are you going to let me in on this big secret because my mind reading skills aren't what they once were?'

'It happened when she was looking for a blank disk to store her revision notes on. You do remember the twins have their exams coming up, don't you? As if she hasn't got enough on her plate. Anyway she was looking through your computer desk and found some disks in a drawer mixed in with your tapes and CDs...'

'How many times have I told those kids not to go poking around my stuff without asking me first?' Craven was on the defensive. Rachael had found them. The nightmare scenario had come true...

'And now we all know why don't we, Julian? She had a look at what was on those disks and had the shock of her life when she found them full of your disgusting pornography!' Lorna railed no longer able to control her fury. 'What on earth were you playing at? Oh don't bother answering that. It doesn't bear thinking about. Can you imagine how she felt seeing all that? Thinking her dad's a filthy pervert? Those are the very words she used - "Dad's a filthy pervert!" - If you insist

236

on downloading that, that *muck* - you could at least make a half-decent effort to hide it, Julian!'

Craven sat in stunned silence. He thought he *had* hidden the disks properly. Rachael must have done some pretty serious rummaging to have uncovered them. He felt like he did that time when as a spotty adolescent his mother entered his bedroom unannounced and caught him masturbating. A cheap, insipid shame. *Why are women so adept at finding things they're not supposed to?*

'Look Lorna. That stuff. It's to do with work. I've been trying to track down the bastard responsible for producing that stuff. Those disks are evidence...'

He stopped talking when he heard his wife laughing in disbelief at the other end. Craven knew how feeble his awkward excuse must have sounded to her.

'Oh *please*...' she added indignantly before the line went dead.

Craven recalled the images - mostly lesbian threesomes - with a demoralised sigh. *They weren't that bad were they?* He punched the steering wheel furious with himself.

'Fuckin' bollocks...!'

*

Looking down to the car deck. Only a handful of vehicles occupy the space. The white Peugeot is parked directly below me. Nick is not in it as far as I can tell. I need to find a less public spot and hopefully avoid him. Stuffing the last of the stodgy dough into my mouth I climb the stairs to the upper deck.

A wild gust coupled with a hefty roll to starboard almost sends me flying straight back down the stairs. Using the central handrail I lever myself on to the top step and lean into the gale. My hair is instantly stripped horizontal, flapping at the back of my head. Not surprisingly I'm the only one up here. I struggle on through the whipping vortex, passing the lifeboats and pilot-house to reach the starboard bow. I slump on to a wet bench and settle back under the deck light. At least

237

this spot provides a little shelter from the wind. I try to ignore the rain and the dampness seeping through from the bench. I think I've forgotten what it's like to be completely dry just as my blanched hands and face have no recollection of warmth.

Removing the lid from my coffee cup I try to place it in the bin but the wind snatches it from my numbed fingers and skies it into the stratosphere. Absolutely no point in trying to light a cigarette. The coffee is still steaming and helps strip away some of the scone mush cemented to the roof of my mouth. With every breath the bitter saline air is clearing my head and calming the restless bile in my stomach. The best way to prevent sea-sickness according to Dad, is to stare at the horizon - good advice provided you can actually *see* the horizon. I'm more inclined to blame the nausea on the whiff of diesel rather than the sea.

A murky dark mass, darker than the sky is taking shape through the rain. Tiny pinpricks of light.

Approaching Bute.

'So you've never been married then?'

Startled half to death I nearly choke on my coffee. Nick has appeared ghost-like beside me on the bench. Dipping a tea-bag in and out of a plastic cup, staining the hot water, he's now wearing a heavy green wax-jacket and a black baseball cap.

'How come?'

I stare straight ahead, muzzy thoughts desperately trying to formulate a plan of defence or attack... I mustn't give anything away. I must at least *appear* composed. Answer him...

'Just wasn't meant to be I s'pose,' I sigh shrugging my shoulders and thinking of Elspeth without meaning to.

'Never been in love, no?'

'Not for a while.' I'm finding it difficult to picture her face... but her voice, shape, hair, mannerisms...

'I can imagine being stuck in prison isn't exactly ideal for developing a healthy, loving relationship,' Nick nods thoughtfully.

I'm so wound up I can hear the blood pulsing into my head. I fix my gaze to the Pavilion on Argyll Street. Rothesay Academy is on the hill above and behind it. *This bastard is ruining my moment* - a moment I've been rehearsing in my head for years... usually imagined with sunny weather...

'What were you inside for?'

I can feel his eyes burning into the side of my face.

'Armed robbery.' - That's all he's getting.

Nick snorts, stifling a laugh. 'What was it? The crime of the century you were trying to pull off eh?'

'Something like that.'

Drawing parallel with Skeoch Wood... *Get ready...*

'I've never been to Rothesay before. I always preferred to take my wife to more exotic places for our holidays y'know? More upmarket places...' Nick sounds smug. 'She deserved the very best.' He sighs, 'Yes, I always gave her the very best. Right up until our marriage ended. Ten years ago now it was.'

I look at him.

'Shame really. We had just bought a nice place just outside Brighton. Georgian. Detached. Four bedrooms. Huge garden. Plenty of space for kids. But we never had any in the end,' he smiles regretfully then interlocking the fingers, looks down at his clammy hands. 'No doubt about it though,' he sighs again, a bit too melodramatically for my liking. 'I loved that woman. My wife. Catherine... Cathy...'

Closing in on the pier now. My head can't deal with this. Alarms crunch within me. Time to react... but I'm distracted... The pier terminal has been rebuilt since I was last here... My nerves are strung out like bow-strings. Muscles, cold, stiff, sore... There are two police cars on the pier. Waiting...

'You would've liked her...,' Nick raises his voice over the squall.

That's right. Milk it for all it's worth pal.

I glance at my coffee.

'Oh I forgot! Of course! You did meet her didn't you?' he proclaims with a mocking smile, his hands fidgeting deep in his jacket. 'Catherine Dodds. Remember her Haig?'

Enough. I spring to my feet hurling the coffee towards his face but the fucking wind is so strong it just blows the liquid harmlessly away from him as if he were protected by a force-field. He dives at me. We slip, fall and slide across the deck...

A surge in the ferry's engine noise. The vessel banks, turning and slowing on its final approach... I am underneath him. My head poking through the rails, exposed to the churning sea twenty-feet directly below... I struggle to see him, raindrops pounding around my eyes. His face leers through the barrier, separated from mine by a white crossbar.

'Remember me now don't you? Murderin' bastard! Did you honestly believe I'd let them pick you up and drop you back in your nice comfortable cell, eh? Not this time! This time you're gonna get what you fucking deserve!'

I can't think of anything to say. No point. Survive... My hands are stinging. Something warm quickly runs very cold down my wrists...

'Give you a thrill murdering my helpless Cathy did it? Give you a fucking hard-on? Is that what you think of whenever you have a wank uh? My wife begging you for mercy? You sick fuck!' The wind tugs at the spittle trailing from his furious mouth. 'Ten years I've waited to get my hands on you! That was my *wife*! You took a shotgun to my wife! You're a fucking coward! I'm going to skin you alive!'

My whole body trembles with the strain of pushing back his opposing force. I see my hands... *Oh shit...* I'm grabbing his knife by the blade, my palms right up to the hilt as he tries to press it down towards my chest.

'I was there at the trial. For every miserable second. You never looked at me did you? Not once! Well I fucking looked long and hard at you!' His voice wavers higher in pitch, becoming hysterical. 'I saw what you did? I saw the pictures! Cathy's blood! Her insides! They were all over that fucking floor! Well now I want to see what your insides look like! I'm going to gut you like a fucking fish!' he rasps yanking the knife out of my grip. My palms sear... Something is said over the tannoy...

The ferry judders and rolls with the swell sliding us back over the deck. I bang into the bench with Nick gripping my neck. I squirm as he brings the knife down. I feel it jar against the point of my hip bone and slip off. I kick out, frenetic. My feet land a blow to his stomach. He loosens his grasp. I have time to get upright and struggle to the handrail. The winds sucks the air from my lungs... I hear shouts from the pier...

Nick comes at me again. I twist snatching his wrist. The knife tears through my jacket but not me. A wet, hard thud against my nose... He punches me again. My eyes stream... Everything is blurred. His hand wielding the knife is caught up in my jacket, tugging and pulling. I lean as heavily as I can against it, feeling the bone bending against the guard-rail. He yells with the pain... I press harder... A scream as his forearm snaps. Cold slippery fingers try to clutch my throat again... A gust splays open my jacket, something in the inside pocket chinks against the metal barrier... Conservative Club... I let him squeeze my throat, let him think he's winning... Got it...

Nick's eyes bulge. He tries to scream but can only manage a horrible choking gargle. The corkscrew has plunged deep into his neck where chin meets throat. I thrust upwards, hard as I can pushing deeper. I feel the tip of the corkscrew jab in to the roof of Nick's mouth. I feel the back of his head crack against the top of his spine. His blood smothers my clenched hand... He won't let go of my neck... He leans against me pushing... I try to force him over the edge... Cloth tears... I lose my balance... He pulls me over the barrier with him... Freezing air roars past my ears. The ferry expands ever upwards while the pier spreads dark, black and smudged. I brace myself... slam into the angry sea splitting the crest of a wave and we are separated...

Sinking... water engulfs everything, cutting the image of the ferry's towering hull from my eyes - a liquid door slapping shut... Sinking. Ears flood... The brutal grumbling, low pitched grinding and swooshing of engines and propellers aches through the crazed, filthy water. I feel the heat being sucked from every pore... Something's clawing at my leg. An unseen predator. Panic. I lash out. My foot

241

connects with an object and whatever it is falls away... It feels like I'm caught between the opposing poles of two magnets. Everything is pulling, pushing, pulsing, swirling...

I open my eyes - they sting instantly and reveal nothing. My withering lungs are screaming... The ceaseless racket of the turbid chopping rhythm swills louder. I can feel a current working on me. I kick out with everything I have left and can only hope I'm moving away from the propellers... I bump into something solid. A rough, warty surface. I feel out - my arms don't quite wrap fully around its circumference. A pier support. I haul myself along the massive timber. Fifty-fifty chance I'm moving upwards. If I'm not...

I break the surface. Inhale deep and sore. Almost pitch black.

A wave slaps over my head... I resurface. Coughing, choking... The thick wall of sound changes pitch. I cling grimly to the pier support shivering, barnacles cutting into my already shredded hands like fragments of glass. I feel nothing, too numb for pain. The ferry is a curtain of black, its hull obscuring all else. Here I am directly beneath the pier deck having somehow managed to swim through the first row of supports. Deep within the structure I look up. Between the enormous wooden beams of the deck slits of light flicker orange and blue... A horrible grating sound carries through the water as the propellers stutter... Running footsteps and frantic shouts filter down... My body is running out of time. I work out my position relative to the shore and swim towards the next black pillar.

14: boxes

I ring the doorbell. My luck's held out this far. I realise I'm continuing to push it but... *Come on! Be in!*

I made it. After swimming under the pier and across the harbour I hauled myself aboard a shabby fishing boat moored against the wall where I collapsed on the greasy deck an exhausted, spent force.

As I lay there listening to the commotion coming from the main pier with the rain harassing my shuddering body I realised my options were limited. Find shelter or die of hypothermia. I gathered myself together, climbed ashore, trudged across the road and headed up the hill beside the Kettle Drum cafe. I only saw two other souls braving the elements neither of whom bothered to look out from under their umbrellas.

I ring again. The door opens immediately. The tall elderly lady looks at me suspiciously, studying me from head to toe. Sensing danger she closes the door back until only her head is visible.

'Yes?' she says sternly.

'A-a-auntie El-El-Elaine. It's m-me. Haig. Your neph-nephew!' I shiver, exasperated she hasn't recognised me.

Her eyes narrow to make an even more detailed investigation of my pleading face. A sudden smile illuminates her heavily made up features. The door swings wide open.

'Haig! Come in son! How did you manage to get in such a state?'

Aunt Elaine's house is big, warm and plush underfoot. I'm embarrassed to be dripping all over it.

'Don't you worry about that son,' she insists, 'We need to get you sorted out, get you out of those clothes. I'll run you a bath... Have you been in a fight Haig?'

I look at the torn jacket and the hole in the hip of my trousers. I open my palms wide. The deep crimson slits gape like mouths. I feel queasy thinking about what they might have to say. Only now are they beginning to hurt though thankfully they're not bleeding as much as I'd expected. The freezing sea water must have cut off the circulation.

I clench them into tight fists squeezing the pain.

'I've not had a very good day I can tell you that much,' I mutter but she has vanished and already I can hear a torrent of bath water running upstairs. I move wearily and painfully up the steps.

'I heard about you escaping from prison! It was on the news! Very exciting I must say! Have you visited your mother yet?' she shouts.

I enter the bathroom relishing the warm fragrant steam wafting up my nostrils. Looking at the suds crowding the rim I think she must have added half a gallon of bubble bath.

'No. Not yet. Maybe tomorrow.' My throat is becoming hoarse. I gingerly remove my jacket trying not to stretch my throbbing palms.

'Well I'd be careful if I were you,' Aunt Elaine pulls a concerned face to match her voice. 'The police have been bothering her these last few days.'

'How is Mum, is she okay?'

The question leaves Elaine looking pained. 'Some days are better than others. She gets depressed bless her. Not being able to talk or walk properly. But her mind's still sharp that's for sure.' She turns off the taps then gathers up my discarded clothes.

'Oh and she had another visitor today so Mrs Armstrong was telling me. It was that old girlfriend of yours. Elspeth? That's right - Elspeth. She's on the telly did ye know that? Don't know what she was saying to your mum. I'll find out tomorrow no doubt. She's a fine lookin' lassie that one. You two should never have split up. That's where you went wrong my boy.'

My chest tightens and my stomach flutters - *She's here!* The mere mention of her name provokes a desperate desire to see her but I know I can't. It would make what I have to do virtually impossible. I'd definitely lose my resolve.

'Frankly Haig, these clothes reek. Where *have* you been for heaven's sake? No don't tell me. I'd rather not know... Oh!' she frowns, spotting the wound on my hip as I ease my battered bones into the soothing bath. 'That's nasty. That will need a couple of stitches... Oh my God look at your hands!' she exclaims with a sharp intake of breath finally noticing the blood trickling from my fists. 'Let me see.' She inspects the wounds with medical precision, 'Those will definitely need stitched. You need to go to the hospital.'

'No Elaine. I can't go to the hospital. That's not an option.'

'But you have to get these cuts seen to.'

'Please Elaine. You have to trust me. If I go to the hospital, that's it, it will be all over for me. I can't go. I just can't.'

Elaine looks me in the eyes and considers for a moment. 'All right. I won't argue. As long as you let me clean, stitch and dress those wounds myself.'

'It's a deal.'

'Right. I'll leave you to it then. But as soon as you're out that bath we're going to fix those hands of yours.'

I watch her gather up a stray sock from the floor and add it to the pile of my clothes in her arms.

'Elaine? Promise me you won't call the police. Please. I need you to promise.' I feel compelled to ask this because I haven't a shred of energy left and therefore if she did pick up the phone there would be absolutely nothing I could do about it. I would have to surrender without a whimper. This has been the longest day of my life and my knackered body has postponed all further fight or flight responses until further notice.

Elaine seems genuinely bemused by the request. 'What on earth would I do that for? Of course I won't phone the police. But I imagine it'll only be a matter of time before they come knocking at my door. And if they do - you let me deal with them. So stop worrying yourself and enjoy your bath.'

She hurries off with a sigh. I know she'll keep her word. I put a hand to my chest trying to feel my heart. I locate the beat. A moment later I detect the irregularity. I'm amazed the damned thing didn't haemorrhage in the sea. I slip deeper into the bath allowing the hot water to rise up to my chin. I close my eyes and listen to the washing machine thrum somewhere downstairs.

'Oh Jesus... Oh sweet Jesus take me now,' Craven moaned leaning over the side of the rickety fishing boat for the fifth time.

His stomach had long since bailed out what ballast it contained and all he had left to offer the angry sea were a few glistening gossamer trails of bile. Craven had never *ever* felt worse in his life. Numb with cold, his head felt like it was under attack from a wrecking ball, his throat burned with every breath, the muscles seem to have evaporated from his leaden limbs somewhere along the way and his frenzied guts continued to spasm. A quick painless death would be a blessing but the wind freezing his temples, the stink of diesel and the sea spray biting into his face as the boat lurched and bounced kept demanding more from what was left of the detective. Feeling his organs rushing for the nearest exit Craven winced. This was it. He was definitely going to puke himself inside out.

From the comparative shelter of the pilot-house the fisherman chuckled to himself as he had each time Craven had made a dash for the side. He looked at his passenger with a sly, self-satisfied grin. Craven wanted to punch the fat bastard's lights out but appreciated he needed the man's skills. In another life he might even have admired the man's ability to navigate through the pitch black, the battering waves and the relentlessly vile weather in a boat clearly designed to sink at the first puff of a slight breeze. To his eternal relief Craven spotted the approaching lights of Rothesay Pier through the thick veil of rain.

The sound of the vessel's engine droned into Craven's skull swilling up questions and answers from his scrambled brain. *Why had he persuaded Captain Birdseye to take him over in the first place? Why couldn't he have waited until morning and caught the first ferry?* Because he wanted to be there at the end. He wanted to smash Haig Dumfries' face in. Dumfries was solely responsible for the mess Craven now found himself in. Dumfries had ruined his life and he'd never even met the bastard. If it hadn't been for Dumfries he wouldn't be here now feeding his intestines to the fish. He would be in his centrally heated home sleeping snugly in his bed and with the help of Lorna's healing hands, making a speedy recovery from his miserable cold. If it hadn't been for Dumfries there would be no family crisis. Craven would have been there to stop Rachael using his computer. And even if he'd failed he certainly would have handled Lorna better. He would have been in a far sharper frame of mind and therefore would have made a far more convincing job of explaining away his sordid secret. In fact he would have blamed his son.

Perfect! Craven would have pretended to be as shocked as Lorna and Rachael when the stash of porn was discovered. He would have played the part of a furious father to perfection on confronting Nick with the sullied disks. Obviously Nick would have (justifiably) denied all knowledge but Craven would simply have accused the boy of being a shamefaced liar. And that would have been that. In the end it would have all blown over and the whole episode dismissed as nothing more than the result of a teenage boy's hormone addled mind and things would have returned to normal.

But all this was fantasy.

What about the reality? What did Lorna have planned for his return? Would she even be there or would he find a note on the table saying she'd taken her stuff and left? What if she'd started divorce proceedings already? If so there was no way he was going to bother fighting a custody battle. She could have the twins... *fuck them.* They were nothing more than money sucking leeches anyway. Lorna would not be getting the house though. No way. The house was his.

Haig Dumfries had a lot to answer for.

At long, long last the boat pulled up by the pier. Craven handed over the promised fifty pounds. Again the fisherman grinned at his passenger's blanched, miserable features before helping him on to the access ladder. Craven's fingers had trouble gripping the slippery cold metal rungs and he hardly had strength left to haul himself up but the promise of a solid stationary surface on which to plant his feet spurred him on.

Stepping on to the pier deck Craven made a beeline for the nearest bollard and sat down clutching his mangled insides. An archaic smear of chewing gum welded to the puddled floor near his feet provided his grateful eyes with a fixed point to latch on to while the numbing rain rinsed the cold sweat from his face. He heard the fishing boat chugging away and praised the Lord with a protracted groan. His innards twitched again but thankfully this proved to be an empty gesture. Craven sneezed then belched. The belch deposited a packet of bile at the top of his throat which he forced back down with a grimace. The detective stuck a lozenge into his mouth and sucked quickly to remove the coating of vomit from his teeth and tongue.

'I take it you're DI Craven?'

Craven raised his fragile head to the local police sergeant bearing down on him and gave a half-hearted nod.

'Rough crossin' eh?'

Craven gingerly took to his feet. 'Just... fill me in would you.'

'This way,' the sergeant nodded towards the ferry moored at the other end of the pier.

Massaging his bruised and sore belly Craven followed his guide.

Along the way they passed a pier-hand graphically using his hands to illustrate what he saw to a shivering, wet and thoroughly miserable looking constable. The sergeant acknowledged his colleague with a nod before pressing on towards an ominous looking mound covered by a grey wool blanket lying by the edge of the pier. Taking hold of the saturated cloth the sergeant pulled the blanket back.

'Man versus propeller. Propeller wins,' the sergeant said introducing Craven to the mangled remains of an adult male. The man's body had been cleaved almost in two just below the sternum. The top of his skull had been sliced off and his right leg remained attached by nothing more than a thin strip of skin and sinew. The nausea swept back through Craven's delicate equilibrium.

'For Christ's sake cover it up!' The sergeant replaced the blanket over the gore. Composing himself Craven took a deep breath and swallowed hard. 'So what the hell happened?'

'Two men were seen fighting on the upper deck of the ferry as it was pulling in. Quite vicious by all accounts. Both men fell overboard and that was that. Neither of them were seen to resurface.' The sergeant looked down at the sodden blanket. 'The divers found this mess about half an hour ago. There's enough of his face left for us to be pretty sure it's not Dumfries. Besides, we know Dumfries was wearing a black suit.'

Craven peered over the edge of the pier to watch a pair of divers sitting in a dinghy preparing for another plunge. He hoped this time they'd find a man in a black suit.

'So who is this poor sod then?'

'Don't know yet. No ID on the body. There is one car left on the ferry. Could well be his. It's being checked out as we speak.'

The glare of headlights trailed over the wet ground. Craven turned to see a car pull up by the ticket office. A silver Focus. The lights died, the door opened and out stepped Elspeth.

'Oh for fuck sake. This is all I need,' Craven muttered under his breath, the journalist's arrival only serving to fuel his darkening mood.

'Has the videotape been picked up yet?' Elspeth asked walking briskly towards him.

'Stay behind the cordon Ms Donnelly.'

She ducked under the police tape without breaking stride.

'Has Barry Sloper been arrested?'

'It's all in hand. Now you have to step away please.' Craven took her by the elbow and tried to lead her back through the cordon.

'It's all in hand? What does that mean exactly? Have you got the tape or not?' Elspeth persisted, stubbornly holding her ground.

'Paperwork Ms Donnelly. Proper procedure. As I told you before, these things take a little time.'

In truth Craven hadn't even started the ball rolling with regard to Sloper and his CCTV tape. Less than twenty-four hours had passed since Elspeth revealed the tape's existence. Not long in the great scheme of things but time enough for his life to implode and right now Craven could not have cared less about that tape or its implications for

249

Dumfries. Again he tried to lead her away and again Elspeth refused to budge.

'Surely you can speed things up? This is important. For Haig's sake we need to get hold of that tape ASAP.'

'I don't have time for this right now!' Craven snapped losing his patience. 'As you can see we're a little busy here! What gives with you and Dumfries anyway? Why do you give a shit? Personally I'm sick to death of running around after that prick and I'm sick to death of being harassed by people like you. So please, do me a favour, stop bothering me and fuck off.'

'Everything okay here sir?' the sergeant asked feeling the need to intervene.

'Yes. Everything is just dandy,' Craven replied keeping his eyes fixed on Elspeth's. She glared at him making it clear she was in no mood to yield,

'I'm sorry if you feel I'm harassing you but I made a promise to Haig and I intend to keep that promise.'

'If I were you *Miss* Donnelly I'd think twice about the kind of people I make promises to. Let me show you something.' Craven led her to the wet grey heap and threw back the blanket. 'Take a good hard look. Why would you want to keep a promise to someone capable of doing this?'

He knew it was cruel but Craven couldn't help derive a certain pleasure from Elspeth's reaction. The colour drained from her face as she stared mortified at the shredded remains. She raised a trembling hand to cover her open mouth. She deserved this. It was high time someone put in her place and forced her to understand just who exactly held the balance of power here. Craven took a step towards her and waited for Elspeth's eyes to move from the corpse to meet his.

'You can be sure of one thing. When I catch up with him he won't be getting any sympathy from me. Do I make myself clear?'

Satisfied that the message had been received and understood Craven walked away from the pier and headed for the nearest hotel.

Somewhat disturbed by the DI's behaviour, the sergeant replaced the blanket over the body. He placed a comforting hand on Elspeth's shoulder and guided her back to her car.

*

I told her not to worry too much about the sewing kit not being sterile, then put the wooden spoon she'd suggested as a bite-guard between my teeth. One by one the sutures pierced in, under and out of my flesh. The creaking noise of enamel crushing wood grew so loud inside my skull it seemed either my teeth or the spoon were about to splinter and give way. I yearned to scream and somehow managed to suppress the overwhelming urge to clout my auntie. Left hand took four stitches. Right hand, much worse, required ten. The hip wound needed only three by which time, having come close to passing out several times, I'd become almost blasé towards the torture. I hardly noticed the stinging antiseptic she liberally applied to the bite wound on my ankle.

Afterwards in the lounge, I sat on the sofa wearing one of her dead husband's dressing gowns and nothing else which made me feel a wee bit self conscious, naked and vulnerable. Elaine fussed over me as if I were a toddler, plying me with food, hot toddies and tea. When she finally sat down she brought me up to speed on ten years of Rothesay gossip of which Elaine was a true specialist. During that time she had married only to lose her husband four years later to bowel cancer but at least poor Ross had been financially astute enough to have taken out an excellent life-insurance policy, allowing Elaine to retire and pay off the mortgage - 'I bet you thought I'd turn out to be a lonely old spinster didn't you? Well you were wrong. I've turned out to be a lonely old widow instead!'

We talked about my old friends. Some had left the island seeking greener grass. Others were still around; marrying, divorcing, impregnating... She reeled out a list of people who had died over the decade most of whom I knew but only vaguely. Then we talked about the fabric of the town itself. About the new buildings that had sprung up and the old ones that had been razed; including my childhood High

251

Street home. The most exciting thing to have happened recently was the discovery of a cannon under Rothesay pier. The ancient weapon was found by workmen dredging the area during the pier's repair and had since taken up pride of place inside the castle.

'How's Maureen?'

'She's doing fine now the custody battle is over.'

'Custody battle?'

'Aye. For wee Shona. Maureen won I'm pleased to say. I can't understand why Alan contested it in the first place - big useless eejit that he is. No wonder she divorced him... Did you not know any of this?'

I shook my head and wondered how many more lies Joe had spun.

'When did they split up?'

'Two years ago now. He'd been behaving like a moron demanding that they all move to Russia.'

'Russia?'

'Aye. He wanted to set up a church over there. The man's a mental case. Nobody up in Brora was prepared to listen to his ridiculous sermons so he reckoned Russia would be a more fertile ground for him. After the Soviet Union collapsed he reckoned the peasants would be crying out for God's guiding hand and he wanted to get in there quick before any of the "Black Faiths" dug their claws in.' She shook her bewildered head. 'Can you believe that? "Black Faiths" - that's what he calls them. The man needs his head examined.'

'How old is Shona?'

'Five.'

Five! I should've kicked the shit out of Joe when I had the chance.

'Maureen wants to move back to Rothesay as soon as possible. It'll be nice to have her round the place again and Shona's a cute wee thing so she is. You must try and see them. Maureen really misses you.'

'Does she?'

'Of course she does! We all do. Your mum especially. She could never understand why you didn't want her to visit. None of us could for that matter.'

'What? I was desperate for you lot to visit but Joe made it crystal clear that none of you wanted anything to do with me – ever!'

Elaine sank back in her chair clearly shocked.

'The wee bastard! He said it was you that wanted nothing to do with *us*!' She furrowed her brow trying hard to understand. 'Poor Maureen. She was forever asking Joe to convince you to let her visit but he would just tell her to forget about you. *The rows they had!* No wonder they don't speak to each other anymore. And *Alan*... Christ, he threw a dizzy fit every time she mentioned you. She only gave up after Joe told us you'd threatened to kill yourself if any of us tried to visit. He was so convincing! The lying toe-rag!'

Elaine drifted away for a few seconds silently absorbing the full extent of Joe's deceit then asked with disappointment in her voice, 'Did he pass on our letters like he promised he would?'

'No... I never received any letters.'

I really, *really* should have sorted my brother out when I had the chance.

'What?! Not even your mother's?'

'No.'

'But he even helped her to write some of them. You know how difficult it was for her to use her hands after the stroke. Why?' Elaine asked angrily. 'Why would he do that to his own family? What was he playing at? I'll throttle the wee shitebag next time I see him so I will.' She stood up suddenly as if ready to do battle then looked at me with sorrowful eyes. 'God – how did you cope? Thinking your own family had abandoned you?'

'It was probably no more than I deserved anyway...'

'Don't be daft. You didn't deserve *that!*'

We looked at each in silence for a while until, no longer able to deal with her soul-searching gaze, I looked down at my bandaged hands.

'You have to believe me Elaine – I didn't... I didn't kill that woman,' I whispered hoarsely feeling a lump at the back of my throat.

Elaine sat back down and looked up at the photographs lining the mantelpiece above the steady blue flames of the gas fire. 'I remember what you did for your Mum and Joe and wee Maureen after your Dad died. The sacrifices you made. I *know* you're not capable of killing anyone.' Her eyes returned to mine. 'You're capable of being an eejit, a truly spectacular ccjit, you've proved that much – but that's all.'

I had to smile.

Ending with a heavily censored account of my journey I went on to present Elaine with my side of the story steering well clear of all details concerning my heart. There was no way I could face another *"you're going to hospital"* argument - especially when I knew there would be no chance of her backing down this time even if I did offer to let her perform the operation herself.

She listened intently 'oohing' and tutting in the appropriate places. Joe's life expectancy took a further tumble when she learned about his new career as a police informant.

Elaine noticed that the washing machine had fallen silent. She tumble-dried and ironed then turned her darning skills from flesh to fabric. It took me an age to persuade Elaine to go to her bed but after I'd thanked and reassured her for the umpteenth time that I was more than comfortable, she complied. I wondered if she offered the same overpowering diligence to all her visitors.

Before she left, she admitted to feeling lonely sometimes in this big house and told me ruefully of how life had changed. With the graveyard filling up with friends and relatives and her sister slowly fading away in a hospice, the old town seemed to contain more and more strangers. The local kids were more interested in vandalism nowadays than exploring the beaches, fields and woods. To her credit Elaine refused to feel sorry for herself and found a sense of purpose in her voluntary work at the hospital. Work which she found rewarding and, as an added bonus, provided a rich seam of gossip.

It's easy to feel alone here. Cut off. Stranded. I stand in the darkness. The spare room is spacious and uncluttered. I stuff the letter, all fifteen pages of it inside the envelope I've marked *Maureen*, seal the flap and leave it on the bedside table.

Elaine has placed my clothes in a neat pile at the foot of the bed. My hands sting, my spine aches and my hip is sore but I feel relaxed in here. Safe. I'm still adjusting to the weird experience of being warm and dry. I didn't realise just how many bruises I had collected on my travels. My skin resembles a palette belonging to an artist with a fondness for blues and purples with a touch of red and a hint of yellow. I sit in the seat by the bay window looking down to Rothesay Bay laid out before me. The esplanade is ringed with lights. The weather has settled. Calm.

It is well past one in the morning but there is still activity surrounding the pier. The ferry's lights are ablaze. Like flies circling a corpse, several little motorboats flit around the vessel, torches prodding the sea. The police cars parked on the pier have been joined by an ambulance, its blue lights flashing lazily... Too dark and distant to pick out more detail...

$$*\qquad*\qquad*$$

Closing in. Closing down. Catching up now. No more rainbows. Only an intermittent, stuttering flash. The journey is ending. Running low on fuel... Flash... pulse... almost over...

$$*\qquad*\qquad*$$

Green polluted water rouses me. I'm lying in the recovery position at the water's edge, my face half-buried in bone-dry, chalky clay. A sulphurous wave licks my feet. Bitterly cold. Another wave. Scalding. Another wave. Freezing... scalding... freezing. I stand. Look down. My body has left a perfect imprint in the ground. A surge of water leaps forward and snatches the outline away. Sun roasts from above. Look around. Is this a quarry? I can't go back. The toxic water will not allow me to. A steep, crumbling bank veers up. A white cliff overexposed in the sunlight. I must climb up but it doesn't look possible.

An arm's length above my head something burrows out of the bank sending a little flurry of dust cascading to my feet. A hand protrudes from the chalk. A few feet higher and another hand burrows out. A few feet above that and another appears. All the way to the cliff's summit, a line of hands appear contributing to the mini avalanche of dust raining to the base. The first hand clicks its fingers, beckoning me. I take hold of the first rung of the ladder-of-hands and start my ascent. Each hand holds me firm. I know I won't fall.

I reach the top. Pause for breath. It's dark here. A crescent moon smiles. A path flanked by thick, impenetrable hedges leads directly to a tunnel entrance which stares at me black as a pupil. I approach the tunnel. Stop. A body lies prostrate on the path. Huddled over the body a cloaked creature tears fiercely at the victim's clothes. Its claws rip through the flesh to scratch against the bones. I see blood surging from the wounds. Face obscured by a black veil, the creature looks at me. Terrified I run past the monster and its prey. The demonic angel hisses at me, wings quivering in anger. When I look back it tears off a piece of clothing and throws it at me. I am rooted to the spot. Unable to move. The rag catches fire mid-flight and disappears inches from my face. The creature returns to the carcass. I feel a wrenching within. My breathing stops. Fear engulfs every cell. The face on the carcass is mine.

Frozen with apprehension I enter the tunnel. I must pass through to the pinpoint of bright blue light at the distant exit. I continue, unable to see the surface I'm walking on or the roof above. My steps make no sound. I'm aware of liquid dripping thickly somewhere in the tunnel. The point of light has doubled in size. A noise. A nerve-shredding noise rumbles louder and louder. Unbearable. A train passing on the surface? The tumult rattles my soul. My ears are bleeding. Dread seeps from every pore. The noise ceases. An abrupt, empty silence.

Drip...

The darkness trembles like oil and a shadow blacker than the background issues forth. The shadow wears a featureless mask.

'Which way do you want to go?' I am asked in a barely audible whisper. Too scared to speak I tentatively point a trembling finger towards the light. A breath oozes over the back of my neck. I spin round expecting to die. The same masked shadow confronts me. 'Which way,' the same voice asks. I point to the light. I am struck with vicious power. I never saw the blow coming. The force fires me bullet-like through the tunnel. Everything bleaches blue and grows colder.

The blue dissolves back to night. I have landed at the foot of a tree. Silver leaves shimmer under the now full moon's tallow aura. I struggle painfully to my feet, gather myself together and brush myself down. The tree is very odd. Its branches creak under the weight of its over-ripe fruit but this tree bears no ordinary fruit. Innumerable clocks of all shapes and sizes are dropping all around me. Demented clock faces also appear to be growing fungus-like from the bark of the trunk. None of the clocks have any hands. Seconds, minutes and hours are scattered in the leaf-litter and dragged away by eager insects. I look at my watch. It too is pointless.

Beyond the Clock Tree stands a line of five others like soldiers awaiting inspection. Each of these trees is laden with fruit - a plethora of boxes dangling in the foliage. Some are no bigger than my thumbnail, others look big enough to contain a man. I walk across to the first box-tree.

The boxes are indeed a living, organic part of the tree. All the boxes are closed. The one nearest to me, head height and head-sized, starts to vibrate. The lid eases open releasing a torturous, heart crushing screech. I grit my teeth and cover my ears against this infernal assault. Now fully open, rich, fertile earth pours out of the box. The soil turns to water in mid-air. The instant the water hits the ground it bursts into flames. The process stops. The screech ends. The flames settle. I look inside the box. An umbilical cord trickling blood lies curled around a decomposing placenta. The sticky looking flesh looks as though it should stink to high heaven but I can't smell anything. Another box flips open spewing millions of seeds.

Scrabbling through the carpet of germinating seeds I discover birthday cards I'd long since discarded and faded family photographs including one of myself as a smiling baby. Before I have the chance to complete my harvest, a third box springs open releasing dozens of long forgotten toys. I see my favourites. A threadbare teddy and a die-cast toy car, paint chipped and battered. When I try to look inside this box a water pistol squirts me in the face.

A box blooms high in the canopy. An object tumbles out glinting in a moon-beam. I catch it. The pain is merciless. A shard of mirror is embedded in my palm. I pull it free. It leaves no scar or blood. Looking in the mirror fragment I see The Buzz Building. The tide is in. A desperate hand thrusts from the charcoal water. Danny's hand. A cold wind, sick with sadness sways the trees.

The second tree is taller. Broader. Several weeping sores infect the trunk. I open the largest box. Elspeth pushes her head and shoulders through to kiss me gently on the cheek. She smiles at me. I try to speak. Her features fade away. I try to bring them back, try to remember them but I can't. Elspeth is vanishing. Only an indistinct outline remains which quickly turns to drifting smoke. A breath of wind dissipates the smoke into nothing... Indistinct in the shadows, something rushes through the bushes.

The third tree frustrates me. These boxes are the most intriguing. Perfectly formed. The tree itself the strongest, healthiest example. Bright flowers with tempting scents spread their petals but clamp shut when I try to touch. I try to force open some of the boxes. All in vain. I move on.

A single solitary box hangs from the fourth tree, starting to decay. I dip my hand inside feeling my way through soil, dead leaves, twigs and beetles. I pull out a palm leaf crucifix. I hold it up trying to view it in the weak light. The crucifix turns to grey ash and applies itself to my forehead.

The boxes on the final tree are all empty. I can't even find a clue to determine what they may once have contained. The ground surrounding this tree is barren. No decaying plant debris. No insects. Nothing but cold, unyielding stone. I step forward to the smallest box and carefully place the shard of mirror inside. I retreat a few paces and wait with no idea what I'm waiting for. The lid on the box slams shut with an unearthly chime. Every single box on every single tree comes crashing to the ground... Dust... confusion... The moon tears apart wrenching the sky in two... A distant voice...

*   *   *

... My eyes blink stickily. Light seeps in. I push my face deeper into the pillow. My eyes flicker to a close...

*   *   *

... The man was walking along the street ignoring the shop windows with all their false promises when he spotted a razor blade twinkling by the kerb. Holding the blade between forefinger and thumb he slit his wrist.

As he lay there in the gutter dying, with people strolling by pretending not to notice or dismissing it as some piece of bizarre street theatre, the man remembered something. He had forgotten to set the video recorder to record tonight's film.

The last drops of the man's blood drip down the storm drain to mingle with the effluent of the city's inhabitants. A river of blood, shit, piss, spunk and paper...

... Five billion years later the sun in its death throes expands to become a red giant and, not wishing to die alone, destroys everything in its murderous path. The Earth too is engulfed, exploding in a final contagious act of surrender. Every simple, single little particle that ever existed on the planet is cast by the solar winds to sail the universe - including those that once formed the man's blood.

Time passes. Gravity pulls. And the particles re-converge in the formation of a new sun... Matter... Does it...?

A voice...

*

I open my eyes and slowly adjust to the room's brightness. The dream retreats into the ether. I clutch at the fading images. Something about a razor blade? ... It's Elaine's voice. Breakfast is ready.

*

The weatherman warned of further storms to come as borne out by the darkening clouds. I take shelter under a haggard, archaic tree whose roots are doing their best to rupture the dry stone wall I lean against. The cold grey half-light perfectly suits my mood as I look over the graveyard. The drizzle slowly adds a sheen to the headstones. No one here but me and the dead. A breeze flicks into my watering eyes. Another long day is drawing to a close but there's still so much to do...

15: the buzz building

'I'm not even going to ask where you're going so keep it to yourself. I don't know how I'd cope under police interrogation. But if you do visit your mum, be careful. Do you hear me? They'll be waiting for you there,' warned Elaine as she fussed with my collar.

I smiled and felt like a lad heading off for his first job interview.

'Could you give this to Maureen when you see her.'

Elaine took the letter. 'Of course I will.'

'Thanks Elaine. You're an angel.' I kissed her on the cheek.

'Och wheesht! Stop being daft!' she blushed, 'And don't leave it so long before your next visit,' she teased.

I'd spent all morning recuperating in front of the television, my body feeling as though it had been pummelled relentlessly with a meat tenderiser. Elaine kept herself busy cleaning and redressing my wounds in between bombarding me with tea and food, all very gratefully received.

When the regional news came on, we froze hanging tensely on every word regarding the incident at Rothesay pier last night. A body had been found torn apart by the ferry's propellers. Identifying the mess was proving to be a problem. Witnesses popped up on camera describing a fight between two men that ended in the water. No sign as yet of the other body. I recognised DI Craven standing at the quayside, surprised to see him here on the island still doggedly on my tail. He looked a little weary and fielded the questions posed by the assembled journalists with more than a hint of contempt. He refused to confirm or deny that the decapitated remains belonged to me or that I was the other (not necessarily dead) body they were searching for.

Elaine pointed out the editor of *The Buteman* defending his spot at the front of the thronging hacks. I couldn't resist a wee smile. I imagined he must be both overjoyed and as nervous as hell at having a national news story land on his patch for possibly the first time in living memory...

Panicked by a knock at the front door Elaine switched the television off. She took a deep breath, calmed herself and strode off to confront whoever it was.

Alone in the room, I went to the window and looked down across the bay. The ferry had been allowed to resume its service leaving the police divers free to bob around in the waves surrounding the pier. A handful of dinghies patrolled the structure. More police manpower scoured the shoreline, poking and prodding every crevice and rock pool. Overhead, a helicopter patrolled the bay. Elaine returned. The gas man had arrived to read the meter.

*

Sitting on one of the benches under the long shelter by the taxi rank, Elspeth watched the mêlée of reporters and photographers jostling around DI Craven on the pier nearby. Elspeth couldn't hear a word he was saying above the general din of quick-fire questions but it was plain by the look on the detective's face he was sorely pissed off with the whole situation. She herself had been squeezed inside enough of these press scrums in her time to know exactly what was going on. The same tired ritual; uninspired questions volleyed back by the standard evasive responses.

On this occasion however it felt very odd. Looking behind her through the window of the shelter she saw the picture postcard Winter Gardens with its pristine flower-beds and putting greens. Looking back; the Esplanade Hotel, the amusement arcade and then a bus pulling up by Guildford Square to pick up a teenage girl in a Rothesay Academy uniform... Elspeth's frantic cut-throat professional world had collided head on with the safe, closeted world of her youth. This kind of nonsense did not belong here.

Then her eyes fell on the Black Bull. She smiled. Maybe Haig was in there right now casually downing a pint. Elspeth used to enjoy their drunken attempts to put the world to rights at their favourite corner table. Her smile gave way to a sigh. What went wrong? Why had she allowed and even encouraged their relationship to wither and die? Her mother had warned her on a number of occasions she was too young to get bogged down in a heavy relationship at that age. But when had she ever taken her mother's advice? Every man Elspeth had been involved with since eventually revealed his true colours and always demanded far more than she was willing to give. None of them came close to claiming her heart the way Haig had. It seemed that old chestnut about first love was a truism after all. Why else would she exert all this time and energy in trying to help him?

The mischievous devil-hack within offered other reasons. Reasons not tainted by dewy-eyed nostalgia. She knew the tabloids would happily cough up a few quid if she were to sell them the *'Escaped Killer Was My Lover!'* exclusive. Elspeth smiled as she imagined the lurid centre page spread. They would probably want her to pose topless as well.

Elspeth was at the heart of a big story. A simple but classic miscarriage of justice tale had snowballed into something with far more potential since Haig's break out. What would those idiots buzzing around Craven give to know what she knew? If only she could catch up with Haig. She tried to imagine his thankful face when she would tell him his problems were finally over. She would then take him under her protective journalistic wing, persuade him to write the book with her, secure the rights and negotiate a decent serialization deal into the bargain... Elspeth cursed herself for thinking such nonsense. All she really wanted to do was find Haig and tell him he was safe.

She looked across to the pier and shivered when she remembered the body under the grey blanket. Without that CCTV tape Haig would never be safe. Surely she could have outwitted a dullard like Barry Sloper and secured the tape without getting the police involved? What in God's name possessed her to trust Craven? He seemed reasonable when she first met him but after last night's run-in she knew she was in trouble. She had to get her hands on that tape. Until she did, Craven had Haig at his mercy.

Elspeth stood up on seeing Craven push through the throng of reporters. She stepped over to Craven's car, leaned against the bonnet folded her arms and put on a smile for the approaching Inspector. As soon as he saw her Craven reacted as expected with a roll of his eyes and a heavy sigh.

'Listen Miss Donnelly... I've got a blinding headache...'

'Any news for me Inspector? Has Sloper been arrested yet? Have you got hold of the CCTV tape?'

'Ah yes, funny you should ask. I had the tape sent to me by overnight courier. Hold on. Let me get it for you.' Having geared herself up for a battle Craven's weary response took Elspeth by surprise. Craven opened the boot of his car. 'Here it is,' he said after rummaging inside for a few seconds. He took out a tape and offered it to Elspeth but as she reached for it he snatched it back. 'Say thank you first.'

'Seriously? Are you kidding me?' she asked exasperated.

'A little courtesy is all I'm asking for Miss Donnelly, that's all. But why should I expect that from you or from anyone else for that matter. I mean, I don't know why I bother. So... Fuck it.' Craven hurled the tape over his car and into the harbour.

Horrified Elspeth ran to the railings and scanned the water below. The tape had landed on a raft of seaweed floating near the harbour wall. She turned furiously to Craven.

'You idiot!'

Flashing a malicious smile the detective started his engine and sped off.

Driving up High Street towards the island's police station, Craven took the empty video cover from his pocket and chucked it on the passenger seat. *Sleepy Hollow.* It was supposed to have been Rachael's birthday present. She had a thing for Johnny Depp. But it had been worth destroying the cassette just to see the look on that aggravating bitch's face. Besides he could always buy Rachael another copy.

*

264

Setting off through town I tried to make myself as invisible as possible, nipping in and out of closes and doorways and crossing streets when the need arose. The police were mainly concentrated along the sea-front but I still had to be ultra cautious. I couldn't afford to drop my guard for a millisecond. The place still felt like home. Natural and familiar. The same roads and buildings. The same colours, smells and sounds. The same light... The same persistent rain. But the rain kept the streets clear allowing me to screen myself with the umbrella Elaine thrust into my hand before we said our goodbyes.

Turning into High Street, I saw the castle with a scattering of seagulls taking shelter in the ruins and raided my memories to picture the inside. I walked past the police station head bowed, umbrella angled to cover my face, poised to sprint off on the first note of a raised voice. I dared to stop for a moment on the section of pavement that once lay below our windows. Despite what Elaine had told me during her potted history of the last decade on Rothesay, I fully expected to see it nevertheless. But my aunt hadn't been joking and she hadn't been mistaken. It wasn't there. The old tenement building had vanished. It hadn't mattered to me as a kid. I'd taken it for granted. It was where I lived, nothing more. For some reason however, standing there on the cracked pavement, it mattered more than anything.

I focused on the open-air, on the first floor space that had, for so many years, been occupied by my earliest childhood home. It was raining inside my bedroom. And all the other rooms for that matter. I tried to picture them, the decor and the young family. I tried to hear the conversations. I wanted it back.

I moved to the spot where the little sweet shop used to be. I remembered the old man standing over his till, counting the ha'penny chews I spread on the counter. I remembered other times, grumpily ordering the cigarettes Mum had nagged me to get for her. All gone. Only the ground itself remained but even that had been pilfered. The overgrown jungle at the back had been hacked away and flattened.

Most of the area had been cordoned off with a rope to stop people walking over the recent discovery. Regular lines of bulky stones forming shin-high walls angled across the damp earth on either side of a wide, cobbled surface.

An information board had been hammered into the ground, roughly on the spot where the sweet shop man used to stand. I read about the uncovering of the four hundred-year-old street and studied the little line drawing of what the unimpressed artist imagined the street might have looked like all those centuries ago. Those homes had been knocked down to make way for others and now mine had been cleared away to provide a future focal point for someone else's childhood memories. Next to the archaeological essay was a Council Notice outlining plans for a new development of flats to be built on those long forgotten foundations.

St. Andrew's Primary is still perched on the hill, bleak and empty. I spent a few moments at the school railings, eyes open but ignoring the cold, empty present - concentrating instead on old reflections playing out on the puddles scattered over the deserted playground. I recalled a thousand fleeting episodes starring Danny, myself and the wonderful Mister Mac. Some of which made me laugh again under the pattering umbrella. Why *did* Mister Mac always sing *Arrivederci Roma* whenever he was in a good mood? I wondered what lay in store for the current population of future lapsed Catholics and their teachers. Did they still have to cover their text books with wallpaper dust-jackets?

I wanted to visit St. Andrew's church but found the great oak doors firmly shut. I decided to indulge in a cigarette outside those pious red sandstone walls and waited for the rain to ease. *Bless me Father, for I have sinned. It has been twenty-four years since my last confession...*

I backtracked and walked the half mile or so westward to visit Dad... I stood in the centre of a field of marble and granite markers and concentrated hard, thinking back twenty years to when we'd all gathered around that hole. Eleven years had elapsed since I'd last followed Mum on our annual pilgrimage on the anniversary of his death... *But I couldn't remember...!* Becoming increasingly anxious I paced along row after row of graves, glancing at name after unfamiliar name. Even the stones began to irritate me, annoyed that even in this place the class system was alive and well. There were some ludicrously over-sized monuments casting patronising shadows over simple, basic stones. I don't know how long I patrolled the graveyard before finally giving up the ghost but I felt sure I'd covered the entire area. I had to accept the fact that I simply could not remember where my own father was buried.

Maybe some bastard has exhumed him. Maybe the bastard isn't dead. Maybe he's been pretending all along and the funeral was another carefully stage-managed lie and Dad is actually fighting fit and keeping bees on the Sussex Downs... Heavy with shame and I admit, a wee bit embarrassed, I gave up.

... Shit! How long have I been daydreaming? Daylight's gone and I'm still sitting under this bloody tree like an eejit. The rain is picking up again. I push myself to my feet angry and annoyed...

Inside a Russell Street tenement block I arrive on the third floor communal landing, led more by instinct than anything else. I feel uneasy. Pangs of guilt about my failure to locate Dad's grave grate against the bitter recollections of this place. This door. I'm trying to locate another dad. Someone else's. *Surely he can't still be living here thirty years on?...* Silence... No gruff shouts from inside. The nameplate on the door - *that name* - remains the same.

A. CRARAE...

My chest thuds. I go to knock but draw my hand back and turn for the stairs. I stop. Confused. I don't know what to do. I feel as pathetic and impotent now as I did when I was a boy shuffling on this very spot, terrified by the violence I could hear screaming out from behind that barrier. Back then I was no match for the monster within.

I knock. Wait. Listen... My ears strain suddenly hyper-sensitive, amplifying static. Footsteps approach. The latch is uncoupled. The door opens sweeping over thick pile. Mrs Crarae, Danny's mum, is still recognisable, though the years have not been kind. Crowned with thinning white hair, her face is scored all over with more than mere wrinkles, these are deep, thick worry lines. She freezes. A spark of fear ignites in her eyes, recognising danger.

'Mrs Crarae,' I swallow, unsure of how to phrase my introduction, 'You probably don't remember me. I used tae play wi' yer son Danny when...'

'I know who you are,' her wavering voice cuts me short, 'Haig Dumfries. Your face is all over the place right now. What do you want? What are you doing on my doorstep?' she asks shaking with nerves.

'I'd like a quick word with your husband if possible. Just want tae ask a couple of questions then I'll be on my way. Can I come in please?' I try to sound as reasonable and as pleasant as I can because she's clearly becoming more and more fraught by the second.

'Don't... don't hu-hurt me pl-please,' she stammers letting me through, 'I, I'm too old to fight back and... and... and we've no money. Don't... don't hurt us, please,' her voice collapses into a pleading whisper.

Jeez, she really believes I'm going to do something horrific to her! Poor woman is petrified. I raise my hands in the air and try even harder to sound unthreatening. Not the best of moves. She cowers at the sight of the blood stained bandages around my palms.

'Please. Mrs Crarae. Believe me. I swear on all I hold dear I am not going to lay a finger on you or your husband. I'm not here to steal anything or hurt you in any way whatsoevers. Believe me Mrs Crarae. Please... try and calm yourself. A wee word with Mister Crarae - that's all I'm after.' I speak slowly and clearly like I'm reciting a children's story. She listens carefully, an anxious frown folding even deeper creases into her brow. She nods slowly and leads me into the lounge. She has developed a pronounced stoop and her waddling gait propels a pair of fluffy pink pig novelty slippers.

268

'Take a seat Haig,' she offers nervously plumping a cushion and ushering me to the settee. The dark brown vinyl couch creaks alarmingly as I sink down far more than expected until my knees are almost level with my face. I try to sit up. More creaking and squeaking.

'We have a visitor Duncan,' she says, her voice still tinged with nerves. 'Haig. Haig Dumfries? Remember? Danny's wee friend?'

Mister Crarae is sitting in a matching armchair by the fireplace on the opposite side of the coffee table from me. He is rocking incessantly, his head bobbing back and forth, his hands gripping the arm rests, fingernails digging in to the plastic. Mrs Crarae leans forward to wipe away a glistening trail of drool from the corner of his gaping mouth. His yellow glazed eyes do not blink and remain fixed on a certain indeterminate patch of the orange and brown paisley patterned carpet.

This once brutishly powerful man is now a slavering wreck. Lost and beyond repair. There are stains dotted down his shirt. Any semblance of a jawline has been smothered by drooping jowls. Everything about his face seems to be sliding downwards. He looks like a melting candle. Tufts of grey hair are sprouting from the waxy recesses of his big puffy ears. Only a few stubborn, insolent strands remain attached to his flaky, piebald scalp.

'Would you like a cup of tea?' asks Mrs Crarae.

'Yes please, that would be grand,' I smile politely, 'White, one sugar please.'

She disappears into the kitchen. I hear cupboard doors opening and china being withdrawn. With a fair degree of difficulty I wrestle myself free from my groaning seat and step across to the grotesque old man. I lean in towards his repulsive ear. There is a peculiar, sour odour wisping from him.

'What happened to you Mister Crarae eh?' I whisper tersely. 'What happened to that big hard bastard who used to punch and kick his wee boy black and blue? Did it make you proud Mister Crarae, knowin' you could beat the shit out of a child? Did it make you feel brave? Did it make you feel like a proper man? I've never forgotten what you did and I never will. I remember the cuts and the blood Danny used tae show me. And I remember how he wished he was strong enough to kick lumps out of you, to smash ycr brains in and make you scream the way you made him scream. But of course he couldn't could he?'

I need to swallow a breath. My tear-ducts ache. The image of Danny's grasping hand breaking the surface of the water flashes inside my head.

'I saw him... I watched him die. I was there. I saw him drown and I wasn't strong enough to pull him out... He jumped in on purpose. He *wanted* to kill himself. Barely ten years old and he *wanted* to end his own life! Because of you. You made his life a miserable, joyless hell, so I can't blame him for what he did. I blame you.'

My chest trembles with the pain of remembering. There is a companion set by the coal fire. A poker, brush, tongs and a little shovel. I pick up the poker feeling its heavy iron weight. I raise it over his head and imagine it bursting his skull. Mister Crarae continues to rock monotonously. His eyes locked. The eyes of a dead fish. Oblivious. I can't do it. If anything I would be doing him a favour. I put the poker back.

'You'll never know how much I wanted you to suffer. Looks like nature has done me a favour... I only hope that somewhere, deep inside that fucked up brain of yours, you can understand what I'm saying... I hope you're sufferin' badly in there. You'll be dead soon Mister Crarae and you know what? Danny will be waiting for you.' I hear cups being stirred and take that as a cue to return to my seat.

I watch the old man. Relentlessly swaying. The liver-spotted stump of his mutilated finger twitches. First Billy Gardiner and now Mister Crarae. Has God has been paying attention after all? Then why does He have to have such a sick sense of humour and timing? Crarae's mouth starts to open and close, rapidly blowing meaningless kisses to no-one in particular. From melting candle to demented goldfish. Retribution for a father's sins? Perhaps. But it doesn't seem enough. Mister Crarae had already reached a decent age before the onset of whatever condition is currently devouring his mind. His son was allocated a mere ten tormented years, enough for Danny to decide he didn't want to experience any more.

Mister Crarae's eyes suddenly widen and his mouth flutters rapidly. He's staring into the corner apparently terrified but there's nothing there. I shiver with a horrible morbid depression. I can't stay here another moment. I apologise to Mrs Crarae, make my excuses and before I leave, knowing full well she'll pick up the phone the instant I'm gone, tell her I'm heading to the hospital to have my hands seen to. She is patently relieved to see the back of me. I can't help but feel sorry for the woman. To have wasted her life suffering at the hands of that prick only to feel obliged to look after the unworthy animal now is a tragedy in itself.

Stepping back into Russell Street a flash of lightning jars the night. The heavens have truly opened... And I've left my umbrella back at the Craraes. No point going back for it. I hurry headlong into the wind still curious to know why I'm being denied the opportunity to mete out some justice of my own.

Passing the leisure centre, I cross the road to stand at the perimeter wall encircling the castle. A sturdy iron railing grows from the top of the waist-high wall and ends a foot above my head in a line of serious looking points. I grab the rails and climb on to the wall to peer over the spikes curving around the broken silhouettes of the ruins. The freezing cold metal stings the tips of my fingers and every bruise and cut hidden under the bandages throbs with the effort.

Gently resting my chin on one of the points I stare into that lonely, trapped piece of history. Caged. A memory in broken stone that we daren't let escape. The moat looks like an oil slick in the darkness... Lightning... For an instant the well in the courtyard is revealed... No sign of the cannon... I hear a police car hurling up the High Street. I let go of the railings.

*　　　　　*　　　　　*

'One... two... three... Go!'

My legs seized up as they always did whenever I was involved in a race. A pair of lead weights, they simply wouldn't respond. I couldn't help the stuttering, panicky laugh coming from my flushed face. I dug my heels deep into the snow and pushed hard against the frozen ground beneath. It seemed to take forever but eventually my piece of linoleum began to gather speed. I was only a couple of feet off Danny's lead. His section of cut-off lino' was slightly longer than mine but he was heavier and taller after all.

'YEEE-HAA! HA, HA, HA!!' hollered Danny laughing as we slid towards the ridge beyond which the incline would separate the men from the boys. 'See ye at the bottom Haig!'

I grinned, gripped the curling front edge of my make-do sledge tighter in my gloved hands, pulled my feet on board and braced myself. I was tempted to chicken out there and then but once I'd traversed the ridge there was no going back. The wide open expanse of the hill flanked by woods on either side, stretched out before me veering straight down. The thrill shot through me as it did every time without fail. There was traffic dotted all over the slope. If they were unlucky enough to get in my way – too bad. Kitchen flooring was hard enough to steer at the best of times. Accelerating at the same rate, almost neck and neck with Danny I caught sight of him skimming over an impressive bump.

'OOHYA! My arse!'

I burst out laughing again even though the bumps were playing havoc with my own bony posterior. The icy air rushing into my face made my eyes water and numbed my clenched teeth. The speed was frightening. The glossy linoleum fairly zipped over the snow like a magic carpet. I zoomed past an older boy riding a proper sledge. Two girls trudging back up the hill together were forced to take evasive action when they saw us hurtling straight towards them giggling inanely. A snowball flashed past me. I didn't see where it came from. Faster and faster I went clinging on for dear life, loving every exhilarating moment. I wished the hill went on forever but the base reared up fast. A line of evergreen bushes signalled the end. We'd both crashed into them on our previous run and come away unscathed thanks to our bulbous padding.

The instant I considered putting my feet out as brakes I hit an obstacle submerged in the snow. The sound of my ride slicing over the white course ceased... to be replaced with the rush of night sky. Everything was smudged, tumbling in slow mid-air motion. I landed unceremoniously face down in an extra deep drift. I struggled to an upright position dazed but unhurt. I saw four kids sharing the same huge piece of linoleum shoot past me almost at eye level. I laughed again breathing hard and fast. This was what life was about. I let myself fall softly backwards, sinking into the snow filled bunker.

I looked up to the sky. The moon was full and the stars were out in force. The snow glittered blue under their influence. I reached out a hand and watched snowflakes settle on my itchy-wool glove. Two weeks since Hogmanay and the snow had been around for both of them. The best sledging conditions were to be found at Rothesay Golf Club, particularly on the steep first hole of the course. I knew there were bunkers around but this especially well camouflaged trap had caught me out. It seemed to me like we'd been here for hours though in fact this was only our third run.

Danny had joined us for dinner. After we'd demolished the mince and totties I sat back with a snug, warm and full stomach and asked Mum if we could go sledging. She was in a good mood and told us to make the most of it as the forecast was for rain tomorrow. To make sure we would have fun she told us to forget the carrier bags we were planning to use and supplied us instead with linoleum from an unused roll she found under the kitchen sink. So, after tugging a tight balaclava over my skull which she'd knitted herself from the itchiest wool taken from the scraggiest sheep, she sent us on our way looking like a pair of recalcitrant mini SAS men off on some arctic mission.

'Haig!' I heard Danny shout.

I pulled myself up and poked my head over the lip of the bunker. A few yards further downhill Danny plodded up the slope scanning the snow for me while dragging both sections of lino' behind him. He looked comical, his duffel coat ballooning out with all the layers beneath. I waved. Danny spotted me and laughed.

'Did ye reach the bushes?' I asked.

'Aye. Nearly ended up in the car park. I found yer sledge just behind me. Is that a bunker yer in?'

'Aye. I went flyin'. Did ye no' see me?'

'Naw. I was too busy tryin' no' tae crash myself.' Danny smiled and plunged into the deep snow beside me sinking out of sight. He resurfaced laughing and spluttering snow from his mouth. We started to brush the snow off each other's coats before realising just how futile that was and gave up. We let ourselves fall back into the bunker where we lay on our backs looking up to the sky, giggling hysterically until our sides couldn't take any more.

'This is pure gallus i'n't it?'

'Aye. Too right,' I confirmed.

And it was. We remained there catching our breath and gathering our thoughts while kids slid, slipped, sledged, climbed and threw snowballs up and down the hill. The night echoed with laughter and excited whoops and yelps. A small lad on a big tea-tray almost joined us in the bunker but somehow he managed to clear the jump and sailed over our heads to rejoin the course.

I really didn't want it to rain tomorrow.

Danny took out his precious piece of quartz and held it up to the sky, lining it up next to the moon. 'Ye see. Yer dad was right. Quartz does come from the moon. Look.'

I angled my head until I could follow Danny's line of sight comparing the moon and the stone.

'Same colour an' everythin'. It's even got those wee grey bits in it. Just like the moon.' Danny sounded pleased with himself, knowing he was right.

'D'ye still want to be an astronaut when ye grow up?'

'Oh aye. I'm gonnae go tae the moon. Find the hole where ma

moonstone fell oot and put it back. What aboot you? What're you gonnae dae?'

'I don't know. I want tae play for Celtic... Did ye know Archie wants tae be a butcher like his dad? He told me that they eat pig and coo hearts for tea in their hoose.'

Danny screwed up his face, 'That's disgustin'.'

'Aye. And no' just hearts either. They even eat lungs. Archie was saying that, when ye bite intae a lung it makes yer cheeks puff oot with all the air in them.'

I puffed out my cheeks, miming the act of chewing on an inflated lung. Danny laughed. 'Shall we go again?' I asked picking myself up and grabbing my magic carpet.

Danny jumped to his feet with a huge grin, and crunched up the hill as fast as he could. I wasted no time in catching up.

*   *   *

Tina Moffat loves Billy Simmons... This is what the graffiti assures me. Should I care? Well, good luck to the both of them anyway...

Out on the esplanade at Craigmore, I listen to the rain battering down on the shelter's roof. I'm finding it difficult to stay awake. Shivering. My chest judders... *Don't burst now for Christ's sake...* Soaked again. I'm so tired and sore I just want to sleep. The sea is a short distance behind me in the blackness but I'm watching the old folks home across the road. An ornate stone arch tops the gateway to the grounds. The name *Sea View* bends round the arch. Very original. The gates are open enabling me to see all the way up the long winding gravel driveway to where a pair of squad cars and a familiar red Lexus are parked outside the front entrance. The building itself is a spacious, Georgian pile. Looks impressive... Under the bright portico lights a bored looking constable leans against one of the modest columns. His yawn is interrupted, he turns to look inside and nods to an unseen colleague before disappearing through the door.

I run across the road, slip under the archway and edge along the tall bushes. Crouching into the shadows, I creep closer to the building. Mum must be in one of those ground floor rooms, she's too infirm to use stairs. I check to make sure the coast is clear, then make a dash for the south wing of the home.

I peer over the window-ledge into the first room. An old man standing naked at the foot of his bed, lifts a roll of flesh from his belly then lets it flop back into place. He carefully twists and bends to study other sections of his swollen, sagging corpulence before poking a finger deep into his belly button. He removes the finger and sniffs it. I move to the next window...

Complete darkness inside. This could be hers. I might have to come back to this one...

The third window again, reveals nothing - a pair of heavy floral curtains block everything. Another possibility... I follow the wall around to the rear of the building.

Filtered and dissipated by the rain the windows cast an orange haze that barely touches the manicured rose garden. I cautiously approach the nearest window. The curtains are open and the room is lit by a lamp in the corner but no-one's there. I am beginning to feel faintly ridiculous prowling around the gardens of a hospice. What if she's on one of the upper floors? I wouldn't stand a chance even if I did manage to sneak inside.

The next window is partially veiled by a net curtain... *There she is!* Fast asleep under the dim glow of a bedside table lamp her head sunk into her pillow facing me. The rest of the room is in darkness but I can make out the folded wheelchair propped against the end of the bed. She looks so... old. Would she recognise me? If she were to wake up now she'd probably scream the place down at the sight of this dripping madman staring into her bedroom.

A flicker of lightning and a hefty thump of thunder scares the shit out of me. I think my heart's stopped... I glance at the sky then look across the grounds expecting police officers to be closing in from all angles. Instead it seems that I remain the only one stupid enough to be outside in this downpour. I look back into the room. Mum remains untroubled by the storm. *She is alive isn't she?* I assume so but I can't see any sign of the bedclothes rising and falling with her breathing. I try the window. It lifts open easily. I climb inside.

Apart from the hiss of rain spilling in through the window the room and its shadows remain still and quiet. I approach the bed and look closely at Mum. She's breathing. Softly and slowly. I wonder if I should wake her. I want to talk to her. I need to explain things. But she looks so peaceful. There are a pair of framed photographs on the bedside table. The first one is of me as a kid holding baby Maureen awkwardly in my arms. Beside us, five-year-old Joe stands smiling. The other picture is of me alone. I must be about nineteen. I'm sitting in '*The Black Bull*' at a table cluttered with glasses. Some full, some empty, some in-between. I'm smiling and looking at someone out of shot. I can't remember who took this picture or when. It doesn't matter. The pictures are proof that Mum hasn't tried to erase me from her memory despite what Joe said. I wonder what these last ten years have been like for her. A twinge of guilt and suddenly I want to tell her I'm sorry...

Let her sleep.

I undo the Celtic cross from my neck and carefully drape it over the lamp. I lean in and gently kiss her on the forehead. Now she'll know I've been. I step away from the bed and move towards the window...

Haig crashed to the floor. Stunned he looked up to see DI Craven step from the shadows rubbing his right fist. The detective was smiling, fully satisfied with his expertly thrown punch. He blew his nose and closed the window.

'You have to admit you deserved that,' Craven smirked making no attempt to hush his voice. Haig glanced to the old woman. Still sleeping. 'Oh don't worry. Your mother's out for the count so the nurse tells me. With all those pills they pour down her throat I'm surprised she doesn't rattle when she walks. You're a real pain in the arse do you know that? Don't you think I've got better things to do than run up and down the fucking country chasing a waste of space like you?'

Pushing himself against the wall by the door Haig dabbed his split lip on the back of his hand covering it in smears of blood.

'Apparently you don't.'

'No. You're right. I don't. Not anymore,' Craven conceded unable to resist an ironic smile. He grabbed a chair and sat before the battered individual. 'You'll have to excuse my foul mood Haig. You see I'm not feeling too good and it looks like my wife is leaving me.'

'My heart bleeds,' Haig muttered with all the sarcasm he could muster prompting a snort from Craven.

'So I hear. Dr Brooks told me about your condition. All this excitement must be putting a hell of a strain on that dodgy ticker of yours. I'm surprised it's held out this long. Still, every day's a bonus eh?'

Briefly lit by lightning the room reverberated to a distant growl of thunder. Craven sneezed.

'Poxy weather.'

'So what happens now?' Haig asked wearily. Tired, sore and trapped he was ready to admit the journey was over and accept defeat.

'Good question. Well, as it happens, you're in luck.'

Haig stifled a laugh. 'Please. I don't know how much more good fortune I can handle.'

Craven leaned forward in his chair. 'I've been waiting here for hours thinking about what to do with you. To be honest I want to kill you. Because this is all your fault. All of this shit is your fault. If it wasn't for you I wouldn't be here. I'd be at home and everything would be normal and dull just the way I like it. And I wouldn't be so ill. I'd be tucked up in a warm bed being nursed back to health by my loving wife. Instead I find myself caught up in this endless fucking rain and having to eat all these fucking disgusting cough sweets. But thanks to you, my family life seems to have imploded. That's why I want to kill you. However, luckily for you, I've managed to persuade myself you're not worth the effort and I should be altogether more...

278

professional.'

'Tell you what,' said Haig bending forward to offer a hand for Craven to shake. 'I feel so bad about the trouble I've caused why don't you let me buy you a drink or two? Then we can call it quits. There's a nice wee pub just round the corner. What d'ye say?'

Craven smiled and waited until Haig dropped his bandaged hand. 'Very funny. Elspeth told me you were a bit of a comedian.'

'Elspeth? How d'you know Elspeth?'

Craven relished the troubled look on Haig's face. 'Long story. She's like a dog with a bone that one. A deeply fucking irritating dog with a bone. Suffice to say she approached me with some good news Haig. She's found evidence that proves you didn't kill Catherine Dodds.'

'What?' Haig gasped. He was having difficulty taking this in. Elspeth had kept her promise. An unusual feeling invaded him. Hope was something he'd learned to live without. 'What has she found?'

'That doesn't matter because the bad news is I'm going to make sure you're put away for the murder of that poor lump of mince we found down by the pier.'

'Whoa! Wait a minute! That was self defence! The bastard was trying slice me in half. You can't do this!'

Craven sprang from his chair and shoved Haig's head hard against the wall.

'I can do what I bloody well like! It's your word against mine.'

Haig stared defiantly into his persecutor's eyes only inches from his own. 'Why are you doing this? What the fuck are you playing at?'

Craven smiled at the confused scowl creasing Haig's face. The detective was having way too much fun to pull back now. Winding Dumfries up and watching him squirm was so satisfying.

'I can't tell you how much fun I had the last time I used these,' he said producing a set of handcuffs from his pocket. 'I'll say one thing for Elspeth, she's a demon in bed isn't she? She nearly killed me the other night. I'm getting too old for some of those positions. Know what I'm saying?'

'I know you're full of shite. There's no way she'd go with the likes of you.'

'You think so? You should have seen her wriggling when I slapped these around her wrists. She's up for anything that girl,' Craven leered.

'Can I make a suggestion?' asked Haig watching the cuffs move towards his own wrists.

'By all means.'

Haig smashed a headbutt squarely into Craven nose. 'You have to admit you deserved that.'

Eyes streaming and nose dripping blood the detective punched Haig hard in the ribs. Hauling him to his feet Craven balled his fist ready to plant it into Haig's face. The door burst open just as he was about to let fly. A bulky nurse rushed inside collided with Craven and knocked him clean away from Haig. Her startled eyes latched on to the detective's.

'What's going on?' the nurse demanded.

Craven glanced to the bed where the light spilling in from the open door fell on Mrs Dumfries. She was sitting up with her finger on the alarm button. Craven followed her eyes towards the open window. He could hear Haig's running footsteps fading into the darkness beyond.

I run, feet loudly churning up the gravel as I skid across the path, turn the corner, sprint past the windows I looked in earlier and head back towards the front of the building. I slide to a halt. Panic... The policeman I saw guarding the entrance is opening the door of a squad car. He turns and sees me rooted to the ground like a startled rabbit dazzled by headlights. A car turns into the gateway and proceeds up the drive towards us. Bending down I grab a handful of gravel in both damaged fists. I run at the policeman hurling the stones. He shields his face as the missiles shower around him, pinging and clattering into his car. I punch him hard in the stomach.

Pain jolts from palm to elbow.

He crumples to the ground winded trying weakly to grasp me while I snatch his keys. I push him aside. Craven races out through the front door swiftly followed by another officer and sprints towards me. I thrust myself into the police car, slam the door and start the engine. Blood is blotting across the dressings on both hands. Ignoring the pain I thump both door locks into place and not a moment too soon. Craven pounds at my window, yanking the door handle. I rev the engine drowning out whatever it is he's shouting and reverse almost slamming into the car pulling in... Ram the gear-stick back into first and wheel-spin forward passing Craven now hurrying into his car. Turning hard. I lock the wheel. There's a woman stepping out of the newly arrived silver Ford I almost wrecked. *Elspeth...* Heart stutters and stalls. So does the car. I coast alongside her. She looks bemused by the commotion. Elspeth peers inside. She recognises me.

Glance in the rearview mirror.

Craven's headlights flare into life. The other squad car is now occupied... Frantic. Restart the car. Elspeth knocks urgently at the window. She wants me to wind it down. Wind and rain whisks hair across her beautifully concerned face. Can't think straight. I desperately want to speak to her. So much I want to say. To ask. *Did she really fuck Craven?* But instinct takes over and all I can offer her is a forlorn shrug.

Glance at my pursuers.

I pull away. Elspeth runs alongside. Signalling. A hand frantically taps her chest then wags a frenzied finger at me. *What is she trying to say?...* She yells. Can't hear a word. *Is she telling me not to run? To give up? That Craven is a liar?* The Lexus begins to overtake and tries to nip in front of me. Foot to the floor. Squeeze on to the grass picking up speed down the slope and rejoin the driveway near the gates. Check my wing mirror. The jerky, water-streaked reflection shows the Lexus and the second squad car right behind me. I think I can see Elspeth jumping back into the distant Ford.

Turning right out of the driveway and on to the coastal road. I accelerate hard. The car lurches. The engine whines in protest. I almost lose control and threaten to veer into an oncoming van. The van flashes its lights and howls its horn braking hard. I haven't been behind the wheel for over ten years and this thing is far more powerful than any vehicle I've ever driven. I fight with the gears, wincing with each amplified rasp. Grating and crunching I push harder on the clutch... Everything slips into place and I finally speed away like a good car thief should. More problems. I can hardly see where I'm going. I fumble with the levers and switches projecting from the steering column and dashboard. The car bounces against the kerb prompting another fight with the wheel. I continue to fiddle, twisting and pressing controls until the wipers finally flick into life and the headlights point me in the right direction.

The siren is wailing. I have no idea how I did that.

No traffic in front of me but three sets of speeding lights are chasing. The third seems to be falling behind. Blue lights are flashing furiously on the roof of the second therefore that must be the Lexus tailgating me. Craven swings his car out and tries to overtake. My right foot squeezes the pedal, blocking him off and gaining some precious distance. Seventy miles per hour... Ascog comes and goes on my right... Now racing towards Kerrycroy.

The Firth Of Clyde lies lost in the night somewhere to my left. Over on the mainland, distorted by the weather, a line of distant lights represent Largs. A sheet of lightning flickering through a layer of thick blue-black clouds reveals the dark contours of the two Cumbrae islands... My stomach leaps as the car plunges into a dip. Flood water slams against the underside launching walls of white spray on either side of me. Tearing noisily through the water I feel the car aquaplane. I have another battle with the wheel... Rejoining the tarmac the grip returns.

Craven has fallen back, still bouncing through the water-logged dip. The other pursuers have yet to round the corner... Indistinct voices suddenly hiss from the crackling radio. The car thuds over a pothole sending an agonising shockwave of pain along the length of my right arm. I have to pull my hand away from the steering wheel. A sound like Sellotape being ripped from its roll. I look at my palm. The dressing has come loose exposing the burst stitches and the smeared blood.

Kerrcroy... Slow down. Turn sharply inland rising and falling with the hills. Passing the grounds of Mount Stuart - the Marquess' gothic residence, hidden somewhere behind the blurred rows of shadowy pines... Craven's lights continue to bounce in my mirrors. I'm shivering and sniffing. The warm air rushing from the vents is having no effect. My eyes are watering but my throat has dried up. I feel a dull echo chill through my core... I break hard to avoid overshooting the left turn at the Kingarth Hotel. I don't know these roads as well as I thought. The car spins, the tyres screech and I'm pointing at the fast approaching Lexus. Craven has to practice an emergency stop. I twist the wheel, full lock and power away. Craven continues to skid and misses the turning. He reverses hard, too hard and hits the squad car. My mistake seems to have bought me a little time...

Flash... Kilchattan Bay shows itself for an instant... My followers are closing in again. The lights of the third car are now just behind the other two. Nudging eighty again. Won't take long to travel through the village at this speed. Only one person braving the elements walking a barking dog. The person stops, mouth wide open, watching me roar past.

The road comes to an end, turning into a rough rubble track forcing me to ease off the gas. The wheel flicks and jolts in my grip. Joints and bones complain about the juddering ride. Overhanging branches slap the windscreen and scrape the roof... A gate appears ahead. I push harder on the accelerator... *BANG!* An almighty crack and crunch - wood snaps and splinters. The gate is annihilated. A piece flips over the bonnet and whacks against the windscreen. The glass shatters into an intricate, silvery mosaic. I punch away the fragments. Unchallenged, the storm gusts violently into the car making it even harder to see where I'm heading. I try to recall the landscape from memory filling in the blanks missed by the headlights shuddering across muddy puddles and wild overgrown shrubs...

The engine screams. The car is airborne. Leaping over a burn. Something gives way big time when the car slams back to the marshy earth. The steering wheel cracks into my ribs. I yell out in agony. I see it. Coming up fast. Too late... I brace myself. The car hurtles headlong into the ditch. The impact makes my ears sing...

I open my eyes. Water splashes up from the flooded ditch cushioning the landing. More water cascades through the ruptured windscreen. The engine has died. The downpour is all I can hear. The glove compartment is hanging open, its little interior light pointing out various papers, notebooks, sweets... and a torch. I hear the other cars closing in. I take the torch and scramble out through the windscreen...

I won't use the torch just yet. I won't make it easy for them. I feel my way along the slippery coastal footpath. Unseen waves crash against massive boulders to my left and I remember. I remember running along this very path thirty years ago with Danny. I remember trying to keep up with him and looking at the horrific bruises staining his neck and arms. I recall the feeling of utter inadequacy, of being unable to help him in any way. Unable even, to break his silence as we fled...

Lightning pulls me back to the present but that gnawing helplessness remains. I hear raised voices way behind me easily swept up by a grumble of thunder. Reaching the highest point along the route, I pause. Catch my breath. I look back. It's difficult to define anything in this busy darkness and sheeting rain.

Two torches. No. Three points of light are jerkily progressing beyond the headlights of three stationary cars. *Flash...* Moving past the ditched car, the three figures gripping those torches are snapped in a celestial photograph. The wind shoves at the back of my head telling me to get a move on.

And there it is... The lighthouse. Its beam skirting defiantly through the turbulence, goading the lightning. The swinging glow helps me negotiate the sharp rocks. I wait for each passing sweep, gradually picking my way towards safer ground... Pushing on across the beach at Glencallum Bay, memories of skimmers, sword-fighting and stranded jellyfish threaten to overcome the surrounding tumult but only for a moment. The lighthouse throws its light over the shingle. Looking back to the rocks. The torches are gingerly following in my footsteps. The beam swoops and picks out Craven and the policeman... and Elspeth. Not far from the beach now. The light moves over me. They've seen me. The gale makes it impossible to hear whatever it is they're yelling at me.

I reach the far side of the bay. Impossible to attempt these rocks without the torch. Jittering uncontrollably, my numbed fingers fumble for the switch. I aim the light into the glistening jaws of stone and try to remember the route. I push on through a maze of ankle-shredding crevices and freezing rock pools, forced to descend and ascend with the clawing rock. I reach the apex of a familiar outcrop. Across the divide my torch picks out the corresponding wall opposite. I aim the light into the seething gully separating the two talons of land finding it pulsing and rising with storm-frothed water. I climb down into the sea, knee-deep. All those years ago it would have reached my waist and maybe even higher. I point the torch to where the channel bends. The current is trying to persuade me to wade faster.

I can see the entrance - just. The sea is only inches below the top of the aperture. I swallow a lump of air and dive. It's a struggle to stay under. My hands clutch at the jagged sides of the entrance taking hold. It's a tight squeeze. Panicked by the thought of getting stuck in this hole, I pull harder. I can sense the tide pushing and flowing through the gaps on either side of me. I'm wedged between the top and the sandy floor. I try shovelling away at the sand. Now or never... I bang my elbow and feel my sides scraping against the rock. Sensing the open space beyond I heave myself through, bubbles rushing from my mouth and nose.

I surface... The cacophonous buzzing hits me instantly. The noise agitates the very core of my being. I'd forgotten just how loud and unsettling this sound was. I stand up and try to get my bearings. The sea slides around my thighs. The noise reverberates, searching out every niche, making my wounds itch. Shining the torch against the side of The Buzz Building I scramble up to the ledge and sit back, exhausted, quivering and colder than anything I have ever experienced.

A flash of lightning reveals the hole near the cave ceiling, like a blinking white eye. Spatters of rain bounce inside scattering beads of water into the shadows. My hand touches something behind me. A white plastic bag. Discoloured, timeworn and stuffed into a crack in the cave wall. I tug it out. Point the torch inside. I find a couple of candles and several boxes of matches. I remove a box, slide it open and study one of the matches between forefinger and thumb utterly astonished. I try to strike it but the pink match-head crumbles damply away leaving only the bare wood.

I breathe faster. Exciting possibilities are opening up. Ignoring all the discomfort I set about exploring the cave, shining the torch into every half-forgotten recess. Nothing has changed. Not a thing... Why should I be surprised by this? Candles are dotted all around, inside crannies and glued to jutting edges. I wish I could wish them alight...

A coke can now rusted almost beyond recognition rests exactly where I left it three decades earlier... The buzz is hitting its peak. There it is... Our altar. The seahorse, perfectly intact, standing proudly. I reach out. Touch it. I feel a charge. A jolt of electricity fires through me. My febrile mind is racing... It's as though I've stepped into a time machine. I turn, half expecting to see two ten-year-old boys from another age lighting a fire in the depression just over there... I walk over to our fireplace and pick up a lump of charred wood. It's almost a surprise to find it cold.

Sweeping the torch I pick out the host of other items we used to decorate the Buzz Building... Everything is as it should be. Everything is in its place. Starfish, urchins, crab shells, fragments of sea-worn glass... I can remember when and where each object was found.

I sit down. Exhausted but exhilarated. Even after all this time no-one... *no-one* has discovered our den. A secret safely harboured. The world outside has undergone so much startling, frightening, irreversible change. My own life has stuttered and spluttered from minor pleasures to major crises in a manner way beyond my control. I can accept that now... But the Buzz Building has remained loyal. Waiting. Expecting. Existing only to provide shelter for this waxing and waning water and taking no notice of what happens beyond... Perhaps it doesn't seem as big as it did back then but as it's proved, it can still put me in my place...

I make no attempt to halt the tears. Flowing for all the things I know I'll never do or see, say, learn, taste, touch or admire... As for Elspeth. Time to bury that last lingering fantasy of the two of us getting back together in a whirlwind of love and fabulous sex, laughter, forgetting and forgiving...

The torch lying at my feet is pointing at a deflated leather football. The white paint has deteriorated into a filigree of cracks. I push the ball with my foot and uncover a rotting brown paper bag. Something glows inside the bag. I pick it up and let it settle in the palm of my hand. A beautiful piece of quartz. Pure and unblemished. I close my bleeding fist around the moonstone. I shut my eyes.

Opening my eyes... I'm shot through with a spasm of fear. I retreat against the wall... A face in the water... The face disappears into the creeping black liquid sending waves rippling to all corners. *It looked like Danny!* Yes... *I'm sure that was Danny's face!*... No! How could it have been? I stand, frantically scanning the surface... The tide has swollen to its fullest and the buzz is fading... There it is again!... A seal... My flurrying pulse eases down... Only a seal. Its head bobbing in the middle of the pool staring at me. The retinas at the back of those curious eyes gleam jade green in the torch-light. We study each other. A moment which feels like a stopped clock. The seal disappears.

I am safe in here... Thunder and lightning, both feebled by distance, are absorbed by the Buzz Building. I can hear urgent, far away voices filtering in through the hole. Raised and questioning. I recognise her voice but can't make out the words... The voices fade.

I wedge the torch into the rock and stand over the edge to watch my shivering reflection on the black mirror. Made it. Safely... almost. Soundly. Our secret will remain just that... There is a certain, satisfying symmetry wrapped up in this moment... I fall into the sea...

Sinking... I open my mouth and inhale... Lungs, chest, everything within - floods. The surroundings invade. The overwhelming cold and the pitch black... A flashing panic. Natural and instinctive. I have to concentrate. To suppress the primal urge to survive. This is my choice. My decision. I am in control... At last...

So very cold... Are my eyes open? So very dark. Intense... calm. Surrounded. Pulled by the undertow. There is nothing to fear... The tide will turn soon enough. And here they come... Images, memories, colours... And there they go... The here and the now departs with them. I experience nothing. No heat or cold. Sound or vision. No external or internal sensation... No time... Apart from this last flickering thought... Darkness...

'Why are you doing this?'

... absolute...

'Haig?'

... darkness...

'Open your eyes.'

Who...?

'Open your eyes.'

Eyes open.

'Why are you doing this?'

Everything is *so* bright. So bright it cushions my fall. The glaring sand; soft, dry and warm under my splayed palms. Where is the water?... Everything is *so* bright. I sit up shielding my eyes.

'Haig?'

He is sitting in front of me. In his school uniform, cuffs tugged over his hands. He has the football in the hollow of his crossed legs. The ball looks brand new... *so* bright... I look behind and above him. Our secret den. Perfect in every detail. Candles burning, the fire good and strong, our treasures glimmer.

'Why are you doing this?' he asks again. I am so confused.

'Where has the sea gone? It was here just a minute ago. It was supposed to take me.'

'The sea can wait.' His voice envelops me, swirling softly all around as if it were the whisper of the cave itself. His wide eyes contain not a trace of white. Instead I am fixed in place by a pair of glistening black gemstones. 'D'ye really want it tae end like this?'

'Are you a ghost?'

Danny smiles. 'I'm yer best pal remember? We're blood brothers.' I look at my thumb. A drop of blood oozes from a tiny puncture wound. 'See? But I need tae know why yer here. What yer trying tae dae doesnae make any sense.'

'It makes perfect sense.'

'Why?'

'Because I'm taking control Danny. Don't you understand? I *have* to do this! I've had enough...' A sudden pain to the middle of my chest. A hard push over the heart... sore... then another... 'I just want it to end Danny.' The pressure comes and goes... comes and goes. 'I want it to stop.'

Danny stares at me silently for a moment... Comes and goes...

'But Haig, it *has* stopped. The tide has turned.'

Pushing... pushing... The Buzz Building rumbles. The ragged walls tremble. I look at Danny and I remember everything at once. Every smile, every laugh, every game, every prank... every cut and every bruise. A lifetime of regret and guilt and a mountain of 'If onlys...' collapse over me.

'If only I could've saved you. If only I'd tried harder. But I did try so hard, believe me. I just wasn't strong enough. If only I was stronger but I was only wee. Just a wee boy. If only I could've stopped the bruises. If only...'

Danny's smile broadens in sympathy. 'Yer as daft as ever d'ye know that. Look...' he tugs down the neck of his jumper showing off his throat and shoulders. 'The bruises have gone. I made them go. There was nothing you could dae. Nothing. I did what I did because I had nae choice. But you Haig, you dae have a choice.' He laughs. 'And here you are making the wrong one. Daft as ever! And look at you! So big! Is it good being a grown-up?'

I don't know what to say. The short, sharp shoves to my chest are becoming unbearable. Danny leans forward to place a hand next to mine. It is such a small hand. Were mine ever really that size?

'See?' he grins. 'Yer too big for the Buzz Buildin' noo. There's only room for me.'

'I can't leave you on your own again Danny.'

'Och, I'm fine,' he insists. 'I'm safe in here. It's oor secret remember? Nobody knows. You kept yer promise. I knew I could trust you. You've never let me doon.' He sighs a sad sigh. 'But you've got tae trust me now. You cannae stay here. You have tae go. Here...' Danny takes something from his pocket. 'Take this.' The moonstone sparkles as I take it. 'It doesnae come from the moon after all. But that doesnae matter. It's still a nice stone. Worth keeping. Worth holding on tae.' He stands and pulls me to my feet. 'Understand?'

I think so. He pushes at my chest, encouraging me towards the hole.

'Danny, wait...'

'No. You've waited long enough.'

'Will I see you again?'

'That's no' up tae me.' Pressure... pushing... pushing... pushing... Into the scorching brightness. 'Bye Haig.'

He forces me through. Outside, I hear The Buzz Building's familiar call. Gentle at first, then louder and louder. Louder than ever before. The ground beneath me quakes. Through the entrance I see Danny walk away. A rock tumbles from above and blasts into the sand sealing the entrance tight. The secret is secure. Permanently.

Pushing... pushing... pushing... Excruciating pain. *Please stop...* Closing my eyes I clutch at whatever is trying to crush me and try to scream.

'Haig!'

The sea burns my choking throat and fizzes from my mouth... Air. Cold and sharp. It rushes inside to claim my aching, thankful lungs. I feel rain against my face hurled by a furious squall and rock pressing into my back. I open my eyes to see hands on my chest.

'Haig!'

There's a torch lying at my side, shining on Elspeth. *So* bright...

Her hair is drenched and she looks so cold. I see the overwhelming relief in her eyes as she takes her hands from my chest and cradles me to her. She whispers something. Lightning fractures the night above her. I see the stone in my hand. The black sea beyond. The curious seal watches us for a moment then vanishes under the waves.

'You're safe now...'

*   *   *

Lightning Source UK Ltd.
Milton Keynes UK
UKOW03f2223240414

230569UK00001B/80/P